THE TYRANNY OF GHOSTS

TOM DAVIES

First published 2006 by The Berwyn Mountain Press

The Berwyn Mountain Press,
PO BOX 29,
Corwen,
LL21 1AJ

A catalogue record for this book is available from the British Library

ISBN-13 978 0 9553539 0 1
ISBN-10 0 9553539 0 4

Designed by Brian Thomas
Printed and bound in Dubai by Oriental Press

The author would like to thank Mary Parkes, Don Dale-Jones and Kate Jones who all helped him when he had lost his way but this book is dedicated to his wife Liz — so glad we made it.

THE TYRANNY
OF GHOSTS

PART ONE

1980-1981

A Plague On All Your Houses

'It's not just what we inherit from our mothers and fathers that haunts us. It's all kinds of old defunct theories, all sorts of old defunct beliefs, and things like that. It's not that they actually live on in us; they are simply lodged there and we cannot get rid of them. I've only to pick up a newspaper and I seem to see ghosts gliding between the lines.'

HENRIK IBSEN: GHOSTS

'Oh she doth teach the torches to burn bright.'

WILLIAM SHAKESPEARE: ROMEO AND JULIET

ONE

Towering black clouds canopied the roof of London as the last of the day's sunlight held the Post Office Tower in a glory of raindrops and Lisa Moran drove into a flooding Bedford Square.

Unable to find somewhere legal to park she just abandoned her Mini on an empty corner before grabbing her handbag and bounding over the road into the hallway of 74B where lots of others with wet hair and feet were hanging up their coats. Downstairs was the gathering hullabaloo of Rosemary Ward's literary launch party.

'Oh Lisa how wonderful to see you again. Come and meet Jack.'

'Lisa, darling, you won't remember me but it's been years and years since ...'

Lisa's hands clenched and unclenched as faces gathered all around her and she tried to make her way in, faces calling out for her attention, faces smiling false *bonhomie*, faces alive with mistaken recognition. Hands were thrust out for her to shake too but she couldn't be doing with all this fuss: the ones she always liked were the ones who always ignored her. They were her sort. Why didn't *they* ever speak to her?

But the real problem with all these faces, in a manner of speaking, was Lisa's own face because there was nothing quite like it, all angular bones, long fidgety lips and cloudy blue Bette Davis eyes. Perhaps it was her high cheekbones which were her most striking feature and when she smiled, she could look like a hamster who had just had a good meal and was examining its fillings proudly in a mirror. Her nose was all right until you got down to its tip which shot upwards like an Alpine ski-jump. Her make-up had been put on quickly and carelessly but, with a face like that, you simply didn't need any further embellishment or delineation. It was, well, a face in a million so other faces reacted to it even when they were not, at first, sure to whom it belonged. They had seen it somewhere before and, even if they hadn't, they should have. Almost as soon as they looked at it they wanted to look at it again.

Dear Rosemary Ward, the theatre critic, had been a friend of Lisa's from way back, largely because she had never gone in for any destructive criticism like so many of the other embittered practitioners of her trade. So Lisa had simply come to the launch of her collected reviews and essays, hardly the literary event of this or any other year, out of loyalty: thanks were thanks after all. Loyalty and thanks were always big items in Lisa's book; she was famous in theatrical circles for her outpourings of thanks, usually on undeserving heads, but that was the way she was.

'I always remember the time when we were travelling back from Manchester with Larry and you socked that guard. Did you have to go to court over that?'

She picked up a glass of red wine, cheap by the smell of it, with one hand and one of those cheese and oniony things on a toothpick with the other, ducking away from the faces and keeping to the side of the room as she tried to work out who was and who was not there. Well at least some of the old stage dames had come out to play, she was relieved to see. That was Judi over there and that had to be Maggie trying to hide behind that chiffon rag and, oh good, Ava had finally managed to prise herself out of her Chelsea flat where she had become a virtual recluse. A loud and drunken dinner at Langan's already looked on the cards. Oh boy did they shriek when the golden girls got together and the stories were the filthiest ever.

Lisa and Ava had got on well since the American actress had come to live in London, sharing many a quip about such things as the use of the proscenium arch which Lisa reckoned was only ever good to be sick behind. Yet the one thing they didn't have in common was their attitude to their, ah, 'advancing years'. Ava had told Lisa again and again that she should learn to treasure every single wrinkle. 'Lisa, babe, you've worked your butt off for all those wrinkles. Adore them like they were your own kids. Let's face it, none of us are going to get out of this alive.'

But Lisa remained appalled at the appearance of every new wrinkle. She would have given anything to have her salad days back and fuck the wrinkles.

It wasn't long before yet more faces crowded around her small frame although she was, even if she said it herself, looking particularly sparky tonight in her indigo Azzedine Alaia dress which perfectly complimented her tiny waist and apple-cheek buttocks. She also wore a thin silver choker, high heels and matt-black stockings which did wonders for her greyhound legs.

A bout of air kissing broke out all around her – *mwah, mwah, mwah* – and she told herself to keep moving to avoid being trapped by bores. This was why all such gatherings kept breaking up and reforming into new groups like some relentlessly energetic amoeba. No sooner had one group settled than some big bore managed to poke his nose into it, whereupon the whole group broke up and the scattered fragments started re-forming in some distant part of the room until a completely new bore made a flank attack and the whole process started again. Yes, you had to keep on your toes in parties like this. One false move and you were done for. Or, heaven forfend, the air kissing stopped and some creep actually managed to land a full wet kiss on your disgusted lips.

She escaped behind the stocky bulk of Clive James, who was talking to a woman with earrings the size and shape of bicycle clips. 'The trouble with the new Updike is the same as all the other Updikes,' Miss Bicycle Clips was telling him. 'There's a brilliant lacquer of words but nothing by way of real meaning.'

Lisa caught the tail end of what sounded an extremely promising situation – 'You know Maggie has never been the same since she had her arse bronzed' – which was giving her a good chuckle when her eyes fell on a tall young man with a slight hunch in his shoulders working his way along the food table, not actually eating anything but putting sausage rolls in one jacket pocket, cheese and pickled onions in another and cigarettes in a wine glass straight into an inside pocket. He had a vast, tangled bush of curly hair, a nose that could only be described as senatorial and rather lashy eyelashes. And if he was odd his tailor was far odder: his suit was clearly Brideshead on a bad day with huge turn-ups on trousers which may have been fashionable in the early Thirties. His buttondown shirt hadn't seen an iron in a long time and was held together by a tightly knotted white and black tie.

She was about to say something to him when a huge woman, dressed in black taffeta, loomed over her like a noose on the gallows and asked her what she was working in at the moment. 'A few projects on the drawing board,' Lisa said, her face assuming a bright, interested smile to conceal her rapidly clogging gloom. 'But it's probably best not to say too much about them at the moment. You know how things can go wrong.'

'Now I know a man – a writer – who's got a play which might be just up your street and …'

'Darling, I simply have to go,' Lisa muttered before diving out of the conversation sideways. 'Ring my agent. Agents know all about scripts. I can't read anything any more you know. It's the eyes. They're completely buggered.'

She sidled up to the young man with the hair and the nose. 'If you don't put those cigarettes back I'm going to call the police,' she said quietly. 'You'll probably get six years in the jug for that.'

He looked down at her briefly but that did not stop him. That nose of his was even bigger than she had at first thought but there was a quality of jazz about his face: it was a face with a long history of sin and, when she stepped back a bit, to get a better focus on his eyes, she found them so enormous and blue she felt quite faint.

'Well, well, it's Miss Lisa Moran,' he said agreeably, seizing the last of the

11

cigarettes. 'I'm Daniel Jenkins, the freelance you wouldn't speak to the other week because you were *too busy*.'

'Oh yes, I remember. You were from *The Sunday Times* weren't you? Don't they pay you on *The Times*? Or do you always go around stealing other people's food and cigarettes?'

'I'm not really a journalist. I just do the odd freelance job to pay the bills. If you'd have agreed to see me it wouldn't have come to this. I haven't eaten since you cut off my money supply.'

'I just didn't want to be interviewed. That's all there was to it. I simply wasn't in the mood.'

'Moods are funny creatures aren't they?' He smiled at her with those big, blue eyes and she was embarrassed to find her pelvis jutting out provocatively. Sometimes her sluttishness depressed her. This man works for newspapers, she had to remind herself. *He's one of them!*

'I've been in a good mood all day,' he went on. 'Can't understand why. I got drunk last night. Nothing unusual about that. I hope to get drunk again tonight. The thing is, when I was in the middle of the blackest black-out, a phantom gobbler had her way with my body.' He studied the air just above Lisa's head as if he had just found something interesting in it. 'This woman – I'm hoping it was a woman – took me unawares and left me with this vast hole of pleasure which I only ever get after good sex. I don't know where she came from but she had her way with me and vanished like a ghost chasing after the last bus. Have you ever had anything like that happen to you, Miss Moran?'

'You'd better be more careful where you get drunk.' Had he lost his marbles? Were there several screws loose? She liked to work out these important matters as early as possible.

'I was in my own bed, I think. I live on my own and it was in my own bed. I don't know how she did it. Even took my trousers off and I've been in the most brilliant mood all day.'

'And you don't remember anything about her?'

'Nothing. Nothing whatsoever.'

Other guests were crowding around them so thickly she had to keep turning him until they ended up in a huddle in the corner with their faces close to the wall like a couple of terrorists muttering behind their hands about where to fling the bomb. She knew it would be fatal to look around: if you wanted to keep a private conversation going in a public party like this, you had to hang on to it for grim death. Show one tiny opening and every bore in the room would charge straight through it.

He took out a cigarette from his inside pocket for her and another for himself, found a stray match in his sausage roll pocket and lit it on the skirting board.

'Let's go over this from the beginning,' she said vaguely, waving her cigarette about as the smoke stung her eyes. 'Take it very slowly because I am very dim and want to know all about this phantom gobbler. It's a new one on me.'

Men only ever got to Lisa Moran through her ears. Some women liked their men to look good or throw their money around or engulf them with flowers. She had no objection to any of that but it was only ever a man's words which moved her. Eloquence hooked her immediately; a few poetic phrases and her heart was lost.

She was also always intrigued by unusual facts. 'Do you know that in La Paz, Bolivia, the air is so thin the flies have to run before they take off' was one of her favourites. A few of them and she could be putty in any man's hands. But if there was an element of the amusingly perverted in his talk she was his for the asking and, whether he knew it or not, this hack with the hair had struck the mother lode. She was his and, if her pelvis jutted out any further, she was going to need a zimmer frame to get around the room.

He continued talking about his midnight blow-job and she continued trying to work it out. She usually had the strongest forensic ability when it came to men but she couldn't read this one. Apart from his unruly hair and dirty mind, he gave off the most confusing signals. That suit of his might have been fashionable in some Sally Bowles dive in pre-Nazi Berlin but those brogue shoes could have been fashionable at any time this century. His creased shirt and frayed collar looked like something Noël Coward might have cast off but, rarity of rarities in men, he did seem to have a larky sense of humour.

Ah well, if she had got it all wrong, she could always assume a migraine and escape in her Mini.

But he was not disappointing her just yet, moving sunnily and easily through his adventures in various parts of town the night before an alcohol-induced blackout overtook him and he could remember no more. The identity of the phantom gobbler still vexed him and he was hoping she was female, not too ugly and had managed to get home safely since there was every possibility that she had been as drunk as him.

'You can still perform when you are drunk can you?' she asked with the *faux* politeness of someone asking the time of the next train.

'I should say. Never suffered from brewer's droop in my life.'

'Foof! That's what they all say. Men always think they are great in bed when they're drunk. Usually they're hopeless.'

'Listen, I've never had any complaints about my performance, Miss Moran. It's always been gold, gold, gold. They never forget going to bed with me. Never. That phantom gobbler has got to be the happiest ghost in London.'

She laughed aloud again, completely happy as always when she found someone who amused her, particularly with a comic bit of filth. Already she felt as if she had known him for a long time, felt something familiar and yet long forgotten moving inside her. This hadn't happened for years and she was most surprised to feel it again: a dart of something fresh and alive breaking through her various levels of decrepitude.

So he was well on his way into her interested affection when he abruptly danced straight into the very aching heart of it by telling her that he was a serious writer who was madly and hopelessly in love with London and trying to write a sort of Cockney *Ulysses*. She'd always had an absurd veneration for writers and had often referred to herself as a writers' moll. 'What is it, exactly, you're trying to write then?'

'I suppose you'd call it a novel but it's really a Valentine to London. I'm trying to pull everything together, pub, park, hospital, river, attempting to find a unifying energy in them all, trying to understand the life that makes a city.'

'Sounds very vague.'

It was vague and it was long, in the same way that life in the city is vague and long. But he wanted to write a novel as big as the city, with the Thames running through it like a great artery. The river was the key to it all, the heart of the metropolis, but this week he was working on a section which mingled descriptions of overgrown parts of Highgate Cemetery with births in the maternity ward of the Royal Free Hospital. Sometimes he lived rough with the dossers in the streets of the West End and he also wanted to explore the city sewers when he could work out how to do it. So the novel was going to be a giant, multi-layered prose poem in which the whole city groaned, lived and breathed.

If his big speech had been designed to impress her it did. She had never heard of a book like it. The ambition was Napoleonic. The ideas astonished her with their grandeur. Had he asked her for her hand in marriage she would have run away with him to Gretna Green right there and then.

But she still couldn't quite work out if he was simply mad.

TWO

Later that night, in the centre of St James's Park, directly between Buckingham Palace and the milky, majestic towers of floodlit Whitehall, they stood on the bridge in the middle of the lake, drinking a bottle of wine from two glasses purloined from the party. He kept pulling sausage rolls, cubes of cheese and onions from his pockets and arranged them prettily along the parapet 'in case you're feeling peckish'.

The rain clouds had long passed over the city and ducks lay on the banks all around. Stellar bursts of yellow light and the shadows of trees lay across the glittering surface of the lake and all that could be heard, above the incessant hum of distant traffic, was Lisa's laughter as Daniel, glass in one hand and bottle in the other, lectured her on the secret life of a London park.

'Thousands walk through this park every day but they haven't a clue what's going on. If the Queen knew half of it she'd pack her bags and move straight to Windsor. Right there, in those bushes, is a terrible story of murder, cannibalism, madness, mob riots. Don't laugh. It's all true. A truly terrible true story.'

He moved from one side of the bridge to the other, full of animation. Even when she wasn't laughing aloud, her lips were full of chipmunk smiles. His voice was rich and his flies unbuttoned.

'Those pelicans might be sweet to look at but they eat the pigeons. Swallow them whole. It's the most awful sight you'll ever see. Almost any lunchtime you can sit here and watch the kestrels polish off the sparrows. There's a pair of crows nesting in that tree over there who will attack anything and the swans are always bullying the other birds and, if one falls dead, the rest flock in to push and pull the body about. And there's a duck living over there who thinks he's a dog and follows the park keeper around all day, wagging its tail.'

'All very interesting, I'm sure, but how does it all fit into your novel?'

He began poking the air with the wine bottle. 'It's hidden detail. It's there but hidden from normal view. I spend most of my time digging out the secret facts of London so I can seed them through my novel. The problem is to make everything fresh and new, to come up with new angles on the city that have never been seen or heard before. In the fullness of the novel then we will see the city in a new way; it will make us all love it a little bit more.'

Just then a man with a peaked cap emerged from the warm, damp darkness.

'Sorry, you two, but this is a Royal park and it's closed for the night,' he began. 'Oh and drinking too,' he went on, flashing his torch at their glasses and the food on the parapet. 'And eating as well. That's *definitely* not allowed.'

'We're not doing any harm,' Lisa pointed out.

'I'm not saying you're doing any harm, madam. All I'm doing is enforcing the rules of the park. Now please leave and, if that's your Mini parked on The Mall, drive it away now or it'll get towed away.'

Lisa's benevolent mood turned to irritation with the tectonic plates beginning to rumble quietly if ominously. She had never been known for turning her back on a quarrel or a fight. 'Just what possible harm are we doing here? We're standing on this bridge talking about the park, interfering with no one and you've come out of nowhere ...'

'Madam, my job is to keep the park clear at night ...'

'And I am out here with a man who is telling me all about your park,' she continued with her plates warming up quite fast and a few bits of lava about to spit any minute, when two police officers appeared from behind some bushes, one of them waving a torch whose light revealed the distinctive structure of her celebrated face.

'A bit late for you isn't it, Miss Moran?' one asked matily.

His friendliness calmed her down a bit; she stopped pacing and lowered her voice. 'We weren't doing anything, officer, nothing at all,' she said shielding her eyes from the inquisitive torchlight with her right hand. 'My friend here was telling me about a duck who thinks he's a dog and old Mussolini here came up and told us to get out of his park.'

'He's only doing his job, Miss Moran. Royal parks have to be kept clear at night. It's the law, I'm afraid.'

'Well, the law's an ass,' she grumped. 'Where's the harm in going out in the middle of the night with a friend?'

'No harm, Miss Moran, but why don't you and your friend get on your way quietly? I'm not trying to be funny either but, before you get in that car – I'm assuming that's your Mini over there – I suggest you go to that van at the top of the park and get yourself half a dozen black coffees, if you get my drift.'

'I'm not sure why people can't talk in a park in the middle of the night,' Daniel chimed in, muddying a situation which had just cleared. 'We're hardly going to wake the Queen after all.'

'Now look, sir, I am ...'

Lisa, not at all keen on a looming night in a cell, which had happened once or twice before, broke in with 'I've got an idea …' which was about as far as she got before they were all interrupted by a woman in a wedding dress clattering unsteadily towards them on high heels. She was holding up her dress with both hands and her wedding garter was clearly visible on one fleshy thigh like a deep wound.

'Beep, beep, beep,' she kept going like a car horn desperate to get somewhere fast. 'Beep, beep, beep.'

Everyone stood out of her way and, as the beeping bride disappeared into the darkness on the other side of the park, a man in a wedding suit with a top hat in one hand, came panting in her wake. 'Have you seen my wife?' he puffed.

Lisa pointed in the direction of the vanishing cloud of white tulle and the bridegroom took off after her, closely pursued by the two policemen anxious to know more.

There didn't seem much to say after that so Daniel brushed the sausage rolls off the parapet for the ducks and gathered up the glasses. 'Come on, Miss Moran, let's try the coffee.'

She linked her arm in Daniel's and they nodded good night to the park keeper before walking towards Whitehall, careful to drop their bottle and glasses in the bin since he kept watching them. 'So what odds do you give that marriage working?' she asked him.

'Mmm. Very slim indeed I'd say. She's probably running for her divorce lawyer as we speak. Stay here while I get the coffee.'

He walked towards the van and, although it was past two in the morning, the area was so lively it could have been the middle of the day. Five old drunks in flat caps were playing leapfrog along the pavement and another was haranguing a tea-drinking group near the van counter. 'There will never be a republic in this country because the country will do exactly as I say.'

A bag lady swayed past clutching her belongings in a plastic carrier. 'Get on a diet of fried spiders if you want to lose weight,' she told Lisa. 'But don't, whatever you do, eat the cobwebs.'

Daniel had just returned with two steaming cups of coffee when a smelly tramp's face loomed close to Lisa's. Most of his nose was missing and one of his eyes was a criss-crossed quilt of skin. His lips dribbled as he muttered blessings and curses and held out his hand.

'Poor, poor man,' she sighed, digging her hand into her bra and bringing out a fat wedge of notes. There was clearly nothing wrong with his only eye because he snatched them off her with the speed of a striking cobra.

'Do you keep much else down there?' Daniel asked peering curiously down her cleavage.

'Just my mad money. And my tits of course,' she replied cheerfully, taking one of the coffees from him. 'You'll usually find a few pounds down there but don't go getting any ideas.' She kissed him lightly on the cheek. 'And let's understand one thing now, Mr Daniel Jenkins. You are never, *ever*, to write about me in any newspaper. Just promise me that, will you? Good. Perhaps we can become real friends. Come on, finish that coffee. I'll drive you home.'

'So are you going to sleep with me tonight?' he asked as he opened the unlocked passenger door of the Mini, still parked in The Mall.

She looked at him over the roof of the car, beginning to feel strangely anxious. 'I haven't decided yet.'

'I'm dynamite in bed, you know. A sex machine on wheels, that's me.'

'And modest with it!'

'You won't be sorry,' he went on. 'No girl has ever regretted going to bed with me – or forgotten it. Ever. Only be warned that all you're ever sure to get out of it, in the end, is a broken heart. But it will be great fun while it lasts. It will be simply terrific while it lasts.'

She put both her hands on the roof of the car, smoothing them around as if feeling for cracks in the paintwork. She had always liked – even approved of – cockiness in her men but this one was far too cocky for his own good. *And* there was the age difference. She usually didn't worry about that but there could have been at least twenty years in it. 'You don't believe in underselling yourself do you? But, actually, if you must know, these days I often feel so lost and empty so I don't know … perhaps another broken heart might make me feel alive again … so … yes … maybe … oh, I'm talking rubbish now. I do talk a lot of rubbish you know.'

'I'll make you feel alive again all right. Your body will be singing hymns for weeks by the time I've finished with it.'

There he was, at it again and worrying her to death at the same time. She had long regarded love as a vague memory and wasn't at all sure that she could cope with all that again. She couldn't even remember her last decent fuck although there had been quite a lot of drunken fumbles. All the men she met just fumbled drunkenly and fell asleep. There wasn't a good fuck among the lot of them.

Yet his confidence was not without its charm and she still liked the look of his blue eyes and enormous nose and even began warming to his ratty suit. 'Yes, well, I might. I said I *might* but I haven't decided yet. Normally I would have decided by now. I'm not worried about losing my virginity after all. So stop bragging about the size of your dick and I might get there in my own time.'

'I haven't been bragging about the size of my dick.'

'Yes you have. Men are all the same. They're always going on about what whoppers they've got.'

'I never did.'

After a few false turns Lisa managed to find her way down into Hackney where they parked near the Voodoo Parlour in Dalston Lane and Daniel absolutely insisted she locked her car. He put his arm around her and led her up three flights of dimly lit rickety stairs, with flaking wallpaper and rubbish scattered on every landing, until they came to the top where he unlocked a door with a key hidden above the door frame and, with a mock bow, invited her inside.

The light clicked on and he excused himself for a pee while she toured the garret. In one corner was a pile of yellowing newspapers and in another an armchair with a seat which had long since collapsed. Empty beer cans were stacked in a wastepaper basket and, standing forlornly next to it, half a bottle of Californian red. Next to the wine were three pairs of underpants, long past their wash-by dates and, in what she took as the seating area, a Formica table holding up a few food-spattered tinfoil trays of Chinese takeaway. Dirty dishes were piled up in the sink and, along the window ledge were no fewer than nine full milk bottles, all with their silver tops still on and in various stages of going sour. Oh my God, what a mess!

Daniel showed no sign of returning and her ears picked up the sound of long, whinnying retches amplified by the echoing emptiness of the lavatory pan. She bit the corner of her mouth. She knew all about throwing up but he wasn't going to last much longer the way he was going.

Her eyes swept the flat again and she was charmed when she spotted the alcove where he wrote, books piled up on either side of it and everything as neat and clean as a shrine to a little-known saint. With its single spotlight and Olivetti portable it almost gave off an aura of holiness. Neat piles of paper were at the centre of this particular altar and she wouldn't have dared touch them let alone try and read them. Manuscripts were sacred; even bad writers were saints, in her view.

Yet as she stood there a fresh terror hit her when she asked herself what, exactly, was going to happen when Daniel finished whatever he was doing in his toilet. Well, clearly, he was going to be interested in some sex, she supposed, something along the lines of what the phantom gobbler had done the previous night. He had also been bragging about how good he was at it so that's what he was going to be after all right.

She grabbed her handbag and peered into it anxiously, finding a few pills which she swallowed with a wildly butterflying hand. They didn't seem to calm her down so she threw down a few more of a different type. Her problem, she knew, was that although she often thought about it vaguely, she hadn't had any decent sex for years – or certainly nothing she might want to write home about – and she wasn't totally convinced that she would still know what to do. She guessed it was a bit like swimming or riding a bicycle: that it all just came back to you given the right circumstances. But she wasn't sure and certainly didn't want to make a fool of herself in her old age. Down went a few more pills but all that was happening was that she was getting more and more worked up.

He *still* hadn't come out so she decided to do the washing up, clearing the sink and filling it up with hot water before locating some washing-up liquid and starting on a pile of dishes which had probably been there for weeks.

'There's no need for you to do that,' he said amiably when he *did* return, standing so close to her she could smell the toothpaste on his breath. So he *was* after her body; men only ever cleaned their teeth at night if they were after your body.

'I don't mind. Washing up relaxes me. But tell me why do you keep all those disgusting milk bottles?'

'Oh, I don't know. I like to watch them grow, I guess. See how they clear in the middle and curdle into a brownish cheese at the bottom. Then the top expands like a cauliflower with a tin hat on. See?'

So what was he going to do now, she wondered, as she washed another dish carefully, since he was almost certainly going to do *something*. Perhaps he would have her straight up against the sink, hitch up the bottom of her beautiful and expensive dress and take her from the rear. The dishes were crashing from sink to draining board and back again so loudly and pointlessly nothing was getting cleaned.

A long silence followed and she just couldn't look around. Perhaps he was getting the bed ready, pulling out some silk scarves for a bit of bondage with the bedhead. But not a bit of it: he was clearly about to do nothing at all because when she took a quick look around she saw that he had sat down by his Formica table and fallen asleep among the takeaway tinfoil. She couldn't believe it. There she was in a dress which cost at least six hundred pounds, shaking from head to foot with worry about some impending rape or similar sexual outrage and there he was fast asleep *while she was washing his fucking dirty dishes*.

Well at least she felt a lot calmer now, and cleared the rubbish from the table top. Then, with a sort of smile, she sat down next to him, mussing his curls lightly. He'll come with a crown of vine leaves, burning and unashamed, she thought, looking down on him and recalling one of the lines from *Hedda Gabler*. Hedda had always applauded when she met anyone prepared to do beautiful and courageous things and this young man certainly had a lot of that in him. She had never even heard of — let alone met — anyone who wanted to tackle the complexity of the *whole* of London. John O never wanted to tackle anything more complex than opening a bottle of champagne and often that was too much for him.

Hedda, trapped in a loveless marriage, had longed for real love herself, was desperate for it in fact but never quite made it. But that hadn't stopped her looking and Lisa wondered what that suburban Lady Macbeth would have made of young Daniel here. She would have applauded him surely and planned to make him her own.

Lisa often found herself thinking in terms of the roles she had played from the young Juliet to the scheming Regina Giddens. She had inhabited all her roles and made them her own, sometimes finding them come alive inside her, shaping her thoughts and motivating her behaviour. To understand Lisa you had to first understand the body of her work.

She put her own head down on the Formica table and with her various pills clouding her brain, she too fell asleep and there they both stayed, stretched out like two passengers in an airport lounge who had got too drunk to catch the plane.

Lisa only ever took short naps and was awake within a few hours. Dawn was filtering in through the curtains and Hackney pigeons burbled on distant ledges. Ah well, if he needed to sleep he needed to sleep. Real sleep was for late mornings or early afternoons in her profession and, feeling surprisingly relaxed and energetic, she took another tour of his flat, noticing that pictures seemed to have been recently taken off the walls, parts of the bookshelves were empty but not too dusty and there were piles of records but no record player. All this pointed to a woman who had deserted him and a bad patch on the bottle.

She knew all about such plights and understood completely what it was like being a writer, particularly when you were as unsuccessful as he was. That's why writers learned to drink so much so early; why they saw so many dawns through a glass darkly. Drink was the only way a writer came to terms with his inherent failure. Even success often arrived dressed up as failure in the writing game and failures turned out in the end to be even bigger failures than they had at first appeared. She knew every line of the script on writers; she'd hung around enough of them and found it amazing that anyone ever bothered to write a word.

He was still sitting at his table snoring into his hands. A strange one sure enough, Welsh she guessed by his accent. She didn't usually get on with the Welsh and had actively hated Richard Burton, who had always tried to have her as another notch on his belt, although dear old Rachel Roberts had been one of her best pals.

Well, if Daniel couldn't do anything for her at the moment she could do something for him so, with an enthusiasm which she found most depressing, she began cleaning up the flat, finding a black bin bag and throwing all the debris into it – the bottles, the underpants, the mouldy loaves – everything went into the bag and, when she had filled it, she found another and filled that too.

It wasn't likely he would have any furniture polish so she washed every surface with a damp cloth, breaking into a sweat which she wiped off her forehead with the insides of her arms, before clearing the fag-ends out of the firegrate. She had cleaners to do all this in Cheyne Walk but she had wanted to do something for him and this was all she could think of in the circumstances. But, oh, she always liked to impress with her difference too; she was always careful to arrange herself differently to everyone else in the landscape. What she feared more than most was that someone might perceive her as being the same as everyone else.

She took her lipstick out of her handbag and wrote her telephone number on his living room mirror, adding that her bill for the cleaning would be in the post. She then left the flat quietly, carrying two enormous bags bulging with rubbish and clinking bottles, which she arranged around a lamp-post in the street before jumping into her Mini.

She felt oddly warmed as she drove past the Stock Exchange, racing through the sleepy, pigeon-fluttered streets of the City, jumping one red light after another. There was a fair bit of promise about Daniel and she did hope he'd ring her. She hadn't cleaned anyone's flat since she'd left RADA or even way before that. You certainly wouldn't have ever caught Hedda cleaning up after some man. Oh the stupid things girls do to impress boys. A couple of tears fell down her famous cheekbones as she decided she might have gone and fallen in love again. The sheer improbability of love always took her by surprise. Always made her cry too. Without fail.

THREE

'Lisa, honey, I just don't know what it is but I do know it's really bad. I've been to the doctors two or three times now and they say I've got a bad chill or some virus. There's nothing to worry about, they say. But I know my body's in some sort of trouble.'

She was sitting in her old chum Harry Kirby's flat on the Old Brompton Road trying to allay his fears about his health but, the harder she tried, the more upset he got.

'Look, Lisa. What's this black spot here behind my knee? I ask you. Does that look like something that's a bad chill or some sort of virus? Have you ever seen anything like that because I haven't?'

He cocked his leg up beneath his silk dressing gown and she bent over to peer at where he was pointing but couldn't see anything that close without her spectacles. You would have thought he'd lost a leg or something, not just acquired some silly black spot.

'So doesn't the doctor have any idea at all what it is?' she asked, after a fair bit of squinting.

'He's an Indian. Doesn't know a thing.' He gave the top of his balding head a nervous, exasperated wipe with his palm and his big, brown eyes began brimming with tears. She had always loved the bigness of his eyes but they always seemed to be full of tears these days. His thick eyebrows were attractive and slightly comic, almost as if they had been stuck on his bald head as an afterthought. 'I ask you. All those national insurance stamps I've paid all my life and all I get is an Indian doctor who can't tell the difference between a black spot and a madras curry. All he does is keep doing an impression of Peter Sellers by telling me not to worry. "Do not worry, my friend. Worry kills far more people than black spots."'

'Maybe it is just a black spot, Harry. End of story. Harry, I'm always finding spots. You wouldn't believe what I find on my skin some days. I've even given up counting them.' She didn't want to spend all afternoon discussing some mysterious black spot. He looked all right, that was the main thing – gays like him always needed something to worry about. They were always full of guilt about their sexuality; almost all of them believed that something truly appalling was going to happen to them at any moment.

His flat was a tribute to a life long past. Hockney prints, full of sparkling swimming pools and Californian sunshine, hung on the white walls. Seagrass mats were strewn over the white tiled floor. Silver Indian bowls sat on the low white coffee table and near the door was a birdcage shaped like the Taj Mahal with two lovebirds in residence.

'I'm not making myself clear, Lisa.' His voice was getting shrill again. 'I just know there's something very, very wrong with me. It's not a medical fact as such, it's just something I know to be true. If you listen to your body you always know when there's something wrong. My body is afraid. I can't tell you how afraid it's become.'

'Well, if you feel like that Harry, go and get a proper check-up at BUPA. I'll pay. I can pay. They'll know if there's something wrong with you; they love finding things wrong with you so that you can pay fortunes to put it right. Then you'll have nothing to worry about, Harry. Nothing at all. Right.' She clapped her hands like a school mistress calling class to attention. 'How's your love life been lately? You haven't told me anything about that and I like to know about these things.'

'Oh, what love life? I couldn't start thinking about sex while I'm this tense. You've got be relaxed for sex and I couldn't take anything let alone get it up. And who would I do it with anyway? I've always hated cottaging and all I ever do is pick up rent boys who rob me blind.'

'You had that nice boy from San Francisco. You were talking about going out there to see him.'

'Ach, he turned out to be the same as all the rest. Another kid turning a quick trick. He took some money too.'

'Harry. How *much?*'

'How much? Well the bitch took the lot if you really want to know. Got hold of my cheque book and bank card and swiped the lot. As true as I'm sitting here, Lisa. The first I knew about it was when the bank started bouncing my cheques.'

'Oh Harry, this is terrible. Didn't you go to the police?'

'What do they care? As far as they're concerned faggots deserve everything that's coming to them.' He threw his be-ringed fingers up in the air and those brown eyes pooled with sorrow again. 'They're only ever interested in my money, Lisa. I'm just an old queen now. No one wants this shrivelled body any more. No one.'

Lisa began feeling sick herself since his self-pitying complaints had aroused one of her oldest and most enduring fears: that everything about her would get so wrinkled and withered that no man would ever want to touch her body again. Old age had hung over her body like Damocles' sword since she was eighteen. Doughty, slash'n'burn characters like her friend Ava managed to cope well with the ageing process but Lisa's fears just kept growing. She could barely look at herself in the mirror in the mornings any more, worried what she might find, and the gossip columns were always going on about how she was 'unattached and living on her own' in Cheyne Walk. And she was pretty certain she would end up permanently unattached and living on her own if she stopped trying to make herself as youthfully attractive as possible.

Not that she was going to admit such anxieties to Harry. Her role here today was to reassure him: try and make him feel good about himself. 'Oh don't be so silly,' she snapped. 'Harry, you've got a wonderful body. There's no flab on it anywhere. That's the main thing. And your arms are looking so strong too. Any man would love to be hugged by arms like that. You're in wonderful shape. Wonderful.'

She was pleased to note his back stiffen and a smile brighten his lips, even if his eyes remained sorrowful. Well, we're all suckers for flattery aren't we? Every one of us needs buttering up now and then.

'You're not just saying that are you, Lisa darling? I do try so hard to keep myself in good shape, you know. I've never fancied anyone fat. Fat is horrible. Uuuuurgh! Horrible. Fat is ugly. Anyway enough of me. How's *your* love life doing?'

'Well, let's just say it's interesting. The Tory twat got the heave-ho and The Bouncing Codpiece keeps saying he's coming over from New York soon but, if he does, all I know is I'm going to have a simply thrilling time sitting waiting for him to see some muscle specialist or other.'

'Is he dancing now? I haven't read anything about him in the papers lately.'

'Is he dancing? Poor Andrei Barapov can't even splash around in the bath. There's something wrong with every single joint in his body, the way he tells it. Every ligament is arse backwards or upside down and there's more pills in him than Jack Nicholson in *One Flew Over the Cuckoo's Nest*. He goes everywhere on crutches and even needs help to get on to a barstool. But the odd thing is, if he thinks anyone is watching him, he can walk as well as you and me and, as soon as he puts on a pair of tights and hears the sound of applause, he's zooming through the air like a swallow.'

'Does he still want to marry you?'

'Who knows? Sometimes he does and sometimes he doesn't. But he's not going to have much money left the way he's carrying on in Manhattan. He now tells me that some other woman is claiming he's got her pregnant. He's already got three little bastards over there and they're all costing him a mint. They just put in a claim and he pays up.'

'Haven't you told him about condoms?'

'He's not interested. He's just a Russian peasant and, if a girl moves, she gets fucked and that's it. Money doesn't matter, he says, and anyway he likes the thought of lots of little ballet dancers leaping around America. He's a stupid twat really; I'm not at all sure why I bother with him.'

'And what happened to that mad writer in Hackney? You haven't said much about him lately.'

Ah yes, dopey Daniel of Hackney. Her eyes went quite misty at the thought. They had seen one another a few more times since they'd first met and she was amused to find herself continually and girlishly fretting about him, ringing him at inappropriate moments and sending him mad little love notes.

'Well, we've been seeing quite a lot of one another over the past few weeks and I really like him. He can keep me laughing for hours but, truth to tell, we haven't had it away yet.'

'You *what?*'

'Harry, nothing's happened. We're, like, *courting*. He comes over to Cheyne Walk with some flowers he's just stolen from the park, takes me to the pictures or for a meal or a drink in the Kings Road, then we do a bit of necking in some shop doorway and he catches a bus home to Hackney. Ah. Home to Hackney. Sounds so romantic doesn't it?'

'Something's happening to my ears. *A bit of necking?*' He made it sound the vilest act he'd ever heard about. 'Is there something wrong with him? He's not one of us is he?'

'Not a bit of it. I can feel a real truncheon down there when we're necking but he doesn't seem to want to put it inside me. I'm not encouraging it much either. Well, maybe a little bit. Harry, I *like* this courtship lark. I like sending him little love notes. It's making me feel young and girly again.'

'Mmm. Lucky old you.'

'But there's a lot of problems with him, Harry. He just can't seem to get on with Percy for one. Seems to think it's an affront to his manhood if he so much as looks at him. I'm always telling him to give the dog a pat or something and he says, "I gave the mutt a pat last Thursday. How many pats does he want?" So the next thing we're arguing about how many times you should pat a dog and he's in a huff and off on his bus home to Hackney.'

She threw back her head and laughed as she so often did when she talked about him. Daniel could make her laugh for no reason at all, out of sheer, sudden joy and he might barely have arrived home than she was on the phone telling him how much she missed him and wished he could stay longer. 'The thing is, although he doesn't know it, he seems to have got total charge of the relationship. I'm doing almost everything he says.'

'Well that won't last much longer, that's for sure.'

'Then there's another thing about him. He's cocky when he's drunk but he can get very quiet and shy when he's sober. There's no aggression in him when there's no drink around and he gets as delicate as a lily. But I quite like that. I quite like a bit of delicacy now and then. But he does drink a lot. Like a fucking fish. That's another problem.'

She let out the longest sigh and looked down at her dirty fingernails.

'I don't know what to make of it really. I can't see any future for us – he's much too young for a start – but there again there's nothing about him that's boring *and* he's a writer which always helps with me. I'm very confused really. Oh look, Harry, I'm being wishy washy now and I hate being wishy washy. I long for some work. *Work*. I've been asked to do any amount of rubbish and turned it all down. They offered me a fortune to do a commercial for some fucking soap or other but I flatly refused. It's not that I'm worried about my image, you know, it's just that you need a brash and phoney exuberance to do commercials and I just can't do it. If only I could land a decent role, a little light comedy in an Oscar or a Noël or something … ah if only. I could stop worrying about my men then and start concentrating on some proper work.'

'We all need some of that Lisa darling. I've been out of work for so long I've clean forgotten what a stage looks like.'

'Me and you both. Oh, while I think about it, I won't be here next week because I'm going to Paris for a few days with Daniel. He's got a job for a magazine out there about the wrap of some film and I'm meeting him there when it's all over. Paris in the autumn, Harry. And with Daniel. I'm so excited.'

'Mmmm. Lucky old you. But I do hope you manage to get up to something more than necking in Paris. That city was built with fucking in mind.'

At eleven o'clock Lisa emerged through passport control, flush with free champagne and glamorous as a tropical sunset, wearing a full length Russian lynx coat which fell open to reveal one of the flimsiest 'it's time for a good fuck' numbers. One look from the right man and it would float away into the ether, like a magic carpet, this dress said. Not a fastener or safety pin in it anywhere. A trail of her favourite Opium stretched out behind her, together with three businessmen she had acquired on the flight, each carrying one of her Louis Vuitton bags.

They closed around her like bodyguards with an American president as she stood on the thrumming concourse, her eyes seeking out the huge mop of hair of the new love she had travelled so far to be with. She had always loved to travel long distances for trysts; nothing was ever too much trouble when it came to matters of the heart. Yet there was no sign of the big, useless shit who had not only *not* bought her flowers but had not even bothered to turn up.

27

It was all too much. The champagne-euphoria of her flight was seeping away when her eyes caught two words on the sign: AEROPORT ORLY.

A smile flickered briefly before dying on her lips. 'This is Orly airport isn't it?' she asked loudly, certainly not prepared to admit to her bodyguards that she didn't know where she was. They confirmed that this was indeed Orly airport and her eyes narrowed as her mouth dried up. She had thought all along that she was flying into Charles de Gaulle and her beloved Daniel had been informed by phone and telegram – not once but three times – that she was flying into Charles de Gaulle and, if he was sitting over there with a bunch of flowers, he was going to have a long wait before she met up with him again. She needed to cover up her gaffe. 'Right, boys, my lover is clearly not coming so why don't I buy you all lunch?'

She knew for certain she was off her head when, after lunch for the four of them in Maxim's – only the second most expensive restaurant in Paris – she dropped her American Express card on top of the folded bill which she hadn't even bothered to examine. She didn't look at the credit card slip when she signed that either although she did catch a glimpse of what might have been hundreds of noughts – they had all been putting away plenty of that fizzy white stuff again. But what the hell? It had been a most enjoyable lunch – full of loud laughter and tall stories – and she had acquired three new lifelong fans who had now not only forgotten whatever business they had come to Paris to transact but were planning to hit the drinking clubs of Pigalle and determined that Lisa was going to join them as their guest-of-honour. 'And this time *we* pay.'

Lisa was always game for a larky adventure – especially in the drinking clubs of Pigalle – but she was already quite sloshed and felt she had better get to the Sheraton in Montparnasse where she would doubtless bung Daniel some excuse about getting lost in fog over Manchester. But she did agree to share one last bottle of champagne with her boys at a little nearby drinking club, where one of them just happened to be a member, and one bottle progressed ever more raucously and effortlessly to four and, full of hiccups and happiness, all three were giving her a good grope in the semi-darkness until she abruptly stood to attention, shook off their wandering hands and announced she really had to get to the Sheraton since she feared she had a migraine coming on.

They absolutely insisted on coming with her and, by the time their taxi pulled up outside the hotel, they *all* had a migraine coming on and it was only by some miracle of bodily manipulation that she managed to get out of the taxi at all while one of her bodyguards was throwing up one of the most expensive lunches she had ever paid for over his briefcase in the back seat. This, as might be well imagined, filled the taxi driver with pure delight, and he began screaming to be compensated with big piles of francs.

She felt completely stupid as she stood at the reception desk, baggage arranged all around her feet, too drunk to remember the name of the man she had come to meet. And, even if she could remember his fucking name, she daren't see him in this state. Her eyelids were bouncing up and down like slow-motion trampolines and the receptionist must have been surrounded by mirrors because she kept breaking into two or three persons before coming back together into one again. Oh fuck me high and low just *what* was the stupid Welsh sod's name? At least she remembered his nationality. Oh well, at least she remembered that bit.

The row outside with the taxi driver had escalated into threats, gesticulations and angrily waved briefcases. In the distance a police siren sounded.

'Avez-vous un chamber with a bed ce soir?' Lisa finally asked one of the revolving receptionists, pronouncing every word with pedantic 'O' level care. 'Je veux a bed in a room.' More trampolining of the eyelashes and a bit of thoughtful sniffing. 'With a pillow and a lavatory, s'il vous plaît?'

'Yes, madam. Would you like a single or a double?'

Oh fuck what would she like? 'I would like a double.' A brief window appeared in the champagne fog and she lifted a revelatory finger and pointed it at the receptionist. 'Now there is a young man here from *The Sunday Times*. Yes, that's it. I want to leave him a note but I do not want him to receive it before six o'clock in the morning because I very badly need a very long sleep to recover. From my flight. You do understand do you? What I am trying to tell you.'

'Certainly madam. I think the name of this man of whom you speak is Mr Daniel Jenkins.'

'That's him. Daniel Jenkins. That's the one.' She picked up a Biro, gestured for some paper and, sighing and squinting a lot, wrote: 'Dear Daniel Jenkins, sorry darling but got lost in a fog over Manchester. I'm in room 105. Lots of love. The Old Bat.'

She tottered to the escalator following her luggage while outside one of her stumbling bodyguards was being pushed into a police van.

'How the hell can a plane from London to Paris get lost in a fog over Manchester?' Daniel wanted to know after he had knocked on her door early the next morning. 'I was there at de Gaulle at twelve. I was there.'

She lay supine on the bed, still fully dressed and wanly holding her forehead between thumb and forefinger, doing her Ophelia in a deep funk number. 'Don't want to talk about that now. All that's history.'

'I waited for both flights from London.'

'I'm here. That's all that matters doesn't it?' She raised her head, her voice stiffening with hungover anger. 'What happened at mid-day is history. Can't we just forget it? Take a drink out of that cabinet thing if you want one. Perhaps we can have a walk. I can usually get rid of a migraine with a good walk.'

'Do you want a drink yourself?'

'Pour me something. *Anything.*'

He opened a small bottle of champagne and gave her a fizzing glass. She sat up, frowned at the noisily exploding bubbles, held out her hand to take it, and waved it away. He shrugged and sat down in the armchair to drink it himself but she jumped up off the bed and grabbed his wrist before he could put the glass to his lips.

'I'd better have it after all,' she said. 'You drink too much anyway. I've got a few headache pills in my handbag. Pass it over to me will you darling?'

'I'll have a few of them too if I may.'

She drank half the glass and crunched on a few pills, then closed her eyes for a few seconds before opening them to smile at him and hand him the rest of her drink. 'Let's just have a pull on a pipe of peace or something, shall we?'

He raised the glass in the form of a toast. 'Well, here's to a pleasant few days in Paris.

'Yes, darling,' she agreed, smiling generously and forgiving him, as if it had been his fault all along that she'd got lost in that fog over Manchester. Then, casually, 'So, now we're in Paris, are you going to fuck me now or what?'

He finished the drink and wiped his mouth with the back of his hand. Had she ever seen such a nose on any man? Such a condor's nest of hair? 'I suppose we're going to have to do it one day and Paris is the best place to do it but let's do it later. Let's go out and walk for a while. Let's let Paris put us in the right mood.'

'You're the boss,' she said conceding gracefully. Indeed she was getting a bit worried about how much she was conceding to him, particularly as she wanted him in such a craven, wanton way. But she was still prepared to put some time into this relationship. She so wanted this one to work out well for a change.

FOUR

Her skirmishing tensions drained out of her within minutes, so happy was she to be back in her favourite city, surrendering to the autumnal air, the distant rumbling of the Metro or, her favourite sensation, standing on the grilles and feeling that lovely, warm air swarming all around her knickers as if trying to pull them down.

Yet, even here, she was not exactly incognito and the eyes of the men in particular often fastened on to her strange, compelling face. They might not have seen one of her performances but they saw something remarkable in that face which meant they probably should have. Some even stopped and stared at her in a form of mesmerised wonder. One man began applauding her.

Wine-addled *clochards* kept stumbling out of the darkness to put the arm on her for a few francs and, when she ran out of cash and mad money, she told Daniel to see to them. Every beggar struck gold with her. 'For God's sake stay away from Cairo or you'll end up as broke as they are,' Daniel said.

They stopped and leaned over the iron parapet of Alexander Bridge while the Seine, turbulent with fresh rain, surged in silence beneath their feet. He pointed at some giant sunflowers growing on the roof of a moored houseboat. 'They watch your every movement,' he said. 'Their eyes follow you when you go past.'

She laughed and brought her face close to his. He slipped his arm inside her coat and they kissed, lingeringly, in a splash of pale yellow lamplight.

'Your nose is freezing,' he said. 'You need a couple of brandies to warm you up.'

'I was wondering when you were going to get on to the subject of a drink. You've got to watch that alcoholism of yours. My father had a lifelong affair with a bottle of gin and what happened to him shouldn't happen to you.'

'What happened to him?'

'He just died, and when he did die no one was too sure that he had ever lived. Least of all my mother.'

They walked down to Notre Dame Cathedral which towered, big and black, over them. It was open and they were gazing into the cavernous nave when Lisa decided to light a candle for her mother. 'Just a few seconds, Daniel darling.'

She smiled and bowed her head slightly as she approached the glimmering bank of votive candles, all a-tremble with incandescent prayer. She could see her mother's face in them; those severe features she had so loved. Her mother, a genuine eccentric, had given birth to Lisa while clutching her favourite greyhound for comfort and her love had never faltered or failed, even when Lisa was thrown out of all those girls' schools for seducing the prefects. She was about the only one who could handle Lisa's famous volatility, always telling her daughter not to take it out on her men but, if she really felt the need, to come home and take it out on her.

'Hello Mummy dearest,' she said, setting a candle among the others. 'Still watching over me, I hope.'

She found Daniel standing in front of the altar where Napoleon had once been crowned. 'I always feel so calm in a church,' she whispered to him. 'Are you a believer, Daniel?'

'I'm a believer all right. Can't help it really. God keeps trying to talk to me all the time. Sometimes I get totally fed up listening to him.'

'Really?' It didn't cross her mind that he might not be telling the truth and she was genuinely awestruck. 'What does he talk to you about then?'

'Never words as such but a lot of mental commotion, flashes, sudden visions. They're all extremely difficult to explain. Most of the time I think he's just trying to share his anxiety about the way things are going in his world. But he can't come out with it straight and sometimes it drives me mad. You don't think I'm mad do you?'

She shook her head and was about to kiss him again when she remembered where she was. 'No, I don't think you're mad. Just a little crazy maybe. A little crazy like me.'

With the last of the autumn leaves slithering under their feet they followed the bank of the Seine and chanced on a park of modern sculpture, a strange assembly of alienated shapes. They circled these making disapproving noises, agreeing they weren't art. 'Daniel, we must get to the Louvre one day,' she cried all at once, as if the Louvre was on the other side of the world instead of the other side of the river. 'I hate all this modernism. There are paintings in the Louvre so beautiful they'll make you cry.'

'The Louvre. Ah yes. We can decide what the Mona Lisa's smiling about. Lawrence Durrell reckoned it was the smile of a woman who had just eaten her husband. I say it's the pained grimace of a woman who has just failed Part Two of her accountancy exams.'

It was getting dark and they drank a little *kir* in St Germain des Prés, sitting outside *Les Deux Magots* as the night-people surged past or gathered in groups to watch the street theatre. There were fire-eaters spouting huge tongues of fire, men lying on beds of nails, unicyclists skipping up and down with ropes and kaftanned blacks selling anything from African curios to yo-yos, single roses and Rubik's fiendish cube.

'You never had any children then?' he asked her.

'Not for want of trying. Almost went the distance a couple of times and must have had hundreds of miscarriages. They seemed to just drop out of me after two or three months like other women have periods. I once miscarried right in the middle of the balcony scene in *Romeo and Juliet*. Fortunately the balcony hid the blood and, of course, being an old trouper, I finished the scene didn't I? The Press would have loved that one. With Juliet supposed to be a virgin and all. I must have been a virgin once but I can't remember anything about it now. Did *you* ever want children?'

'No, never.'

She had become so relaxed by *kir* and Paris she even managed to talk about her marriage with the playwright John Orland who was not exactly one of her favourite subjects. It had got so bitter in their final days together, she said, that as soon as they decided on a separation she had leapt on a plane and gone straight to Zurich to take their money out of the Swiss bank account. But the manager, all tender concern and bows, had taken her into his office, poured her a glass of calming champagne and revealed that John had been there an hour earlier. This 'new and angry voice of the disenfranchised and dispossessed' as that *Observer* critic had laughingly called him — had drawn all the money out and made off with the lot.

Buoyed up by laughter and *kir* they walked off into the night again and perhaps it was the old City of Love up to her tricks again but Lisa could feel herself becoming almost terminally sloppy about Daniel as he talked about his writing. John O used to talk in manic bursts when they first met, full of unbridled enthusiasm for his ideas and work, as Daniel was now. But John O had soon lost his passion and pride so it was good to hear it again. Not that they had anything else in common. John O only saw visions after drinking too much, whereas Daniel had mystical qualities which she found attractive and his book about London sounded truly original. Could such a huge project work? Could Daniel actually write? He had never offered her anything of his to read, alas. She would have been honoured by that but he had simply ignored all the hints she had dropped. Well maybe he could and maybe he couldn't. She would wait.

But she was still worrying about his connection with the Press. He had assured her often enough that journalism was just meaningless verbiage for filling empty spaces in a newspaper. If he could make money from literary fiction he would soon give up his journalistic fiction. He simply had to eat. But she mustn't worry. She was safe with him; he would never let her down.

She doubted that. All men let you down sooner or later.

Her body stretched out and stiffened slightly before relaxing and tensing again, feeling his hands holding her tightly around the small of her back, almost as if somehow, and she was not at all sure how, he was holding her high up in the air and about to eat her in full, not just a part of her, but the whole lot and, final and absolute though this meal might be, particularly for her, she felt she really didn't mind it at all, quite welcomed it in fact. She found herself stiffening again, not at all sure where this was going but loving every minute of it anyway as she twisted her torso around again with a smile breaking out between her legs while his hands took a new, stronger hold on her. She felt like a butterfly, just pinned there to a board, skewered by her own mounting and collapsing pleasure.

He loosened his hold on her and she moved over him on the bed, holding him around his head as weeping broke out in the fires inside her and his tongue worked along the inside of her hidden flesh, making her stiffen and think about the end of her life again as her heart began straining on its guy ropes, wanting to break out of her chest and run free, just dance over the cluttered rooftops and into the Parisian night to get lost forever.

'Give me my Romeo,' she said, reaching out to touch his cheek with her fingertips 'and, when he shall die, take him and cut him out in little stars and he will make the face of heaven so fine that all the world will be in love with night and pay no worship to the garish sun.'

Dawn was beginning to turn the edges of the night silver when they walked into the Jardin des Tuileries, the dark oblongs and ovals of the flower beds stretching away in studious symmetry. As they crossed the pigeon-fluttered Place de l'Opèra a man bicycled past with an aspidistra in a pot on his wobbling handlebars. Chairs were piled up outside the shuttered cafés and fresh water streams came gurgling down the cobbled slopes, helping the street cleaners, already up and about in green overalls and with brooms which looked as if they had just been borrowed from the local coven. Daniel dropped Lisa's hand to dodge a drunk busy throwing up over the pavement.

They stopped only to look into a shop window or kiss. Lots of kisses were enjoyed in that awakening Parisian dawn; it seemed the right thing to do.

Hardly noticing their aching legs they hauled themselves up the steep slope to the Sacre Coeur, slipping often on the thick layers of damp leaves on the pavements. A caped gendarme watched them and, just as they reached the top and were looking out over the slate roofs and studio windows of Montmartre, Daniel let out a soft moan and clamped his right hand across his forehead. He threw both hands up into the air, as if in astonishment, and fell backwards. She just managed to catch him before he hit the ground and knelt down, cradling him in her arms and looking into wide open eyes of golden fire.

The fire died but he stayed in seizure for a full minute, his mouth open, his face rigid until he began blinking a lot, as if emerging from a *grand mal*.

'Daniel, what happened to you?'

'One of those visions again I'm afraid. The whole city seemed to burst into fire and undergo so strange a resurrection.' He sat up and swallowed hard. 'Do you think we can have a drink of something strong? That's what I really need now.'

'What you really need is a doctor. That's what you really need. Not a drink.'

'These things stop if I have a drink. Drink relaxes me and helps me deal with these things. That's why I drink so much.'

They found a small café behind the basilica and she sat him down, bringing the café-cognac herself from the counter. Daniel soon became completely coherent again and no more than usually dishevelled.

'Tell me about it again,' she said. 'Tell me what happened.'

'Almost impossible to describe really. Everything sort of moves around and, this time, there were thin rivers of gold running through the city. Then these thin rivers of gold turned into towering skeletons of fire.'

'Meaning what?'

'These visions always seem to be saying the same sort of things. They keep telling me about cities heading to destruction. Not always by fire: I've seen rainbows explode and black rain pour out of clear blue skies.' He shook his head, still distressed. 'But I'll tell you something. I don't think I could take it if it all started again. Feel my brain. Here. See it keeps throbbing and I get these headaches. The only thing that really helps is a lot of drink.'

His brain was indeed still pounding feverishly, as she found by putting her palm on the top of his head. 'You mustn't worry about this too much darling. There'll be a reason. You *will* be given a reason.'

'But I don't want a reason. What I want is to be left alone. I'm not well you know. I'm always throwing up. I can't take all this excitement and anxiety. I just don't want any more messages but, just when I begin feeling all right, it starts all over again. Nothing's happened for about a year now and I *do not* want it to start all over again.'

She folded her arms around him and kissed the side of his neck. His hands were shaking as they moved indecisively around his cup, almost as if he didn't know how to pick it up. She placed her hands over his, squeezing them tight as he began to cry. 'You'll be all right,' she crooned. 'I'll look after you and you won't have to worry about a thing.'

'The real problem is I know one day I'll have to go into the Church. There's no point in my trying to become a writer; I've just got to end up in the Church.

I'm pretty sure God will stop beating me up if I go into the Church. There's nowhere to run on this one.'

'Oh shush. Let God do the worrying. He'll get you into the church if he wants you in there, so there's nothing to worry about is there?'

He sniffed a lot into his coffee, his drying tears staining his cheeks, then adopted a slightly portentous tone: 'Can you explain one thing to me I've been worrying about for ages.'

'Ye-e-e-e-r-s.' Her every muscle tensed; this was sounding really ominous and she did so hope he wasn't about to start any trouble between them.

'Why are your fingernails always so dirty? No matter how smartly you're turned out you've always got dirty fingernails.'

She laughed out loud, mostly with relief at the trivial innocence of the question. 'Ah now, dirty fingernails are always the sign of a great actress. Ken Tynan once wrote that in a review about one of my plays. Great actresses always – but always – have loads of muck under their fingernails, he wrote.'

He lifted his arm over her on the bed, almost as if he was swimming before his other hand clamped her bony hip hard and she too, dizzy with several emotions, none of them clear, held him and, for a few long moments, they didn't seem to be breathing at all, just holding one another as they waited for their bodies to tell them what to do next.

But waiting to go wherever they were going next, she felt him go quite limp and fall asleep. She gathered him up in her arms and kissed his forehead tenderly as she might have done with an ailing baby. Poor Daniel. Such an innocent and he seemed to have such a lot to cope with. Those visions sounded horrifying and she couldn't imagine how she would have reacted if she had seen one herself. The first flicker of any vision and she would have screamed out for a big bag of pills and a strait-jacket before signing herself into the nearest loony-bin.

Every part of her body ached for sleep but, although she had lain her head down on the pillow and closed her eyes, feeling his breath warm on her face, she still couldn't nod off. Her mind was too alive with what he had told her. Did God really talk to him? Why was God so anxious about the world? What else kept God awake at night? And why was he so keen to talk to Daniel, of all people?

She opened her eyes, smiled, and kissed the side of his big nose again, making him splutter. It had been a long time since a man had made her lie awake thinking about him rather than herself. She was tired of thinking about herself all the time and here, at last, was someone who could fill her thoughts. What a mystery he was, impossibly vague about his background. He had been brought up by his mother in a small Welsh mining town where he had spent most of his youth worrying about its smallness, he had told her. He had worried about the smallness of the houses and terraces all huddled together in the pit of the high volcano walls that surrounded them. He had never liked the smallness or mean-ness of the gossip either and always yearned for something bigger where he could be himself and lose himself.

Almost from the first day he had set foot in London he had regarded the city as his home. He could breathe there, he said, and let his dreams of identity grow wild.

Yes, it really did feel to Lisa as if she had lost her heart again and found her hero at last. Harry Kirby had always said she was looking for a hero. Dear Harry. So useless when he was left on his own. She mustn't forget to ring him soon.

'Beloved, let our sleep be sound,' she told Daniel, recalling those lines from WB Yeats. 'That have found it where you fed/What was the world's alarms/To mighty Paris, when he found/sleep on a golden bed/ That first dawn in Helen's arms.'

Ah yes, to mighty Paris in Helen's arms. Mighty beautiful for sure.

FIVE

They did manage, eventually, to drag themselves out of their rumpled, stained sheets to feed one another slices of pepper steak and down a bottle of *vin* in Le Coupole before bearding the city again. They wandered past the cafés and brasseries of the rue Notre-Dame-de-Lorette, where Zola's Nana once plied her trade; enjoyed the rich comings and goings along the rue Saint Sébastien; listened to hot jazz licks in the place des Vosges; stopped for a quiet *kir* or three, which made their kidneys chime, near the Folies Bergère; decided against the Eiffel Tower but were unable to resist going to the Louvre to goggle at the Mona Lisa, wonder at the perfect shape of the Venus de Milo and, Daniel's favourite, the painting of that woman holding her left nipple firmly between thumb and forefinger.

Then back on the streets, following their noses until they stumbled across Montmartre cemetery where they wandered hand in hand along the avenues of glooming Gothic tombs, not saying much as they looked around the encroaching weeds and hovering stone angels. Occasionally they stopped to watch the wild cats which gave birth inside the tombs and hissed threateningly if intrusive gazers came too close. In some of the larger tombs they saw wood-wormed coffins stacked on crumbling shelves like suitcases in a derelict left luggage office. Death and decay were underlined by the smell of rotting leaves piled in slimy brown drifts against the lop-sided gravestones.

'Darling, your book about London sounds wonderful but what puzzles me is this. If God keeps talking to you in those visions of yours, why don't you write about *them*?'

'I couldn't do that,' he replied, shaking his head decisively.

'But why not? This is the age of mediocrity and loss of faith. There must be millions of people who would love to know what God is thinking about. If only you'd explain that God is worried about the future of our cities that would be something of a first.'

'I can't do it. You don't understand. I don't want to encourage him. Every time he talks to me he tears my brain apart. He doesn't seem to know how loud and upsetting his voice can be and anyway I don't want him to get the idea that I am prepared to deliver any messages. He's got the Archbishop of Canterbury. He's got the Pope. Why doesn't he pick on them? It would all sound fine coming from the Pope but who would listen to me? That's another reason I drink so much. Even God finds it almost impossible to talk to me if I'm drunk so, if I stay drunk, there's almost half a chance he might pick on some other delivery boy.'

'Daniel, you are just not one of us. The roof's off and all the rain is coming in. And I don't suppose there's any decent dirty bits in this London book of yours is there?'

'Are you meaning sex?' he asked mock-snootily. 'Certainly not. I don't want to write about anything like that.'

They stopped to watch a veiled woman in black tending to a huge, bright eruption of flowers in a far corner of the cemetery. Racked by grief, she was arranging and re-arranging the vivid colours of the blooms on the grave which stood in direct contrast to the dull greys and thin browns of this autumnal afternoon.

Lisa put her arm around Daniel's waist and rested her head on his shoulder. Despite the sadness of the veiled woman she just couldn't suppress strange feelings of mirth that kept breaking out inside her. Such a marvellous feeling to be overtaken by love again; nothing remotely like it in the whole wide world. Their few days in Paris together had soared like a perfectly ascending crescendo of notes with barely a discord anywhere which was most unusual, particularly when she was around.

Yet these new raptures also owed something to the spirit of this French capital, she supposed, where the very streets seemed to glorify passion. Lots of other couples were forever kissing and canoodling in doorways; there were the glittering shops with their windows festooned with frothy lace underwear and the worship of the naked form as evinced by the classical sculptures of nudes in the parks. Rodin had caught a certain purity of passion in his marble while Abélard and Héloïse had burned one another here with the heat of theirs. 'Do you believe in love?' she asked.

'No, never.'

'What do you mean? *Never?*' She almost became breathless with disappointment. What kind of man was this? 'You don't believe in love at all? Is that what you're saying?'

'Oh I believe in love in the general sense like loving your neighbour or marrying your best friend because you like being with them. But not romantic love. No. On the subject of love I'm an Indian. If you've got to marry do it for money or position as they did in Jane Austen. I believe in arranged marriages. They work.'

'What rot. They only work because you can't get out of them. You're such an oddball you know. Here I was half thinking I might be falling in love with you and now I suppose you're saying you're only interested in my money.'

'I wasn't saying anything of the sort. And I don't recollect asking you to marry me. But I do love being with you and do you know what? You're a really good kisser.'

She laughed at this unexpected, if dubious, tribute. 'Yes. You're a really good kisser too.'

The unmistakeable figure of the Irish playwright Samuel Beckett came walking down the rue Richer, his silvery hair sticking up like a great-crested grebe as he carried a bag bulging with shopping. Yet it was not his hair, nor his drawn, cancerous features which were so attention-grabbing but his brilliant eyes, blue with a steely malevolence.

'Samuel Beckett,' Daniel whooped, his arms windmilling. 'I'm going after him.'

'No you're not,' Lisa said, grabbing a revolving arm. 'You're not going anywhere. He's a private person. You should never intrude on a man's privacy.'

'Come on Lisa. Help me out here. I'm not going to hit him. He never gives interviews and I just want a few words and then I'll leave him alone. He'd make a great piece for Atticus and I haven't paid my rent for two months.'

'No, no. You can't.' She hung on to his struggling arm ever more firmly.

'Lisa, James Joyce's daughter fell in love with Samuel Beckett before she went mad.'

'What's that got to do with anything?'

'Sam Beckett knew James Joyce. Sam worked for the greatest writer of the century, the godfather of us all. Please, please, Lisa help me out. I have *got* to talk to him.'

'No, no, no.' She was going to thump him if he carried on like this. Not only was she not letting him talk to the reclusive writer, she was determined to push him in the opposite direction. 'You don't understand how awful it is to have your privacy intruded on by strangers, particularly in the street. It's horrible, horrible and I am *not* going to let you do it.'

He did manage to wrench his arm out of her grip but, by now, the great miserabilist had long disappeared down a side street. 'He's gone, gone, gone,' Daniel moaned with a Lear-like anguish. 'I've wanted to talk to Samuel Beckett all my life and now you've gone and mucked it up.'

'Good, I'm glad. What do you want to talk to him about anyway. He doesn't believe in God you know. God doesn't talk to him. Sam's universe is a hostile journey from nothing to nothing.'

'I could have explained to him that God was very disappointed with his attitude. I could have told him that God wanted him to pull himself together and brighten up his ideas.'

'And a fat lot of fucking use that would be, wouldn't it? I can just see Beckett rushing straight to Notre Dame and getting down on his knees because some loony from the Welsh valleys has just had a word with him in the street.'

'Lisa. All my life I have wanted to talk to Sam Beckett. All my life. He lived with James Joyce. He was Joyce's secretary. Joyce's daughter *loved* him.'

'Daniel, I do hope you are not going to be whining about this all day.' Those tectonic plates began rumbling ominously with tongues of magma running up against one another. 'How many times do I have to explain it to you? You cannot intrude on people's lives just because you recognise them in the street. Apart from anything else it's simply bad mannered.'

'People intrude on everyone all the time. *You* get it all day long and anyway I do work for a newspaper and I've got bills to pay like everyone else.'

'What bollocks!' The two words exploded so loudly out of her lips a man in a passing taxi dropped the book he was reading. Earthquake time.

'That's pure fucking bollocks! I thought you were different but you're just the same as all the rest of them. *I do occasionally work for a newspaper.* Another bloody Fleet Street pimp. Another fucking Indian pimp who doesn't believe in love. So what you've been saying all along is that you're not an interesting writer trying to say interesting things but some fucking old hack who does what he's paid for.'

He opened his mouth to try some form of defence but her hand gestured him to shut up. She was only warming up, the old Fleet Street demons of misquotes and wounding reviews flaming through her consciousness as she erupted into a furious, spitting tirade.

'Sam Beckett doesn't talk to the Press because he's a real artist. No one who's a real artist talks to the Press because you – and brain-dead twats like you – are creatures that have just crawled out of the fucking slime to tell lies and make people's lives a misery.

'You're just another Thatcherite cunt aren't you, tearing people's lives apart for money? You lot from the Press are a total shower of shit, every single fucking one of you.'

'Lisa, I only wanted a few words with Sam Beckett.'

'There's no privacy for anyone any more is there? Even walking down the street we're fair game to be solicited, badgered, buggered, interfered with, lied about … well, you are not going to do that with *me*.' Her flashing eyes swivelled to her swelling audience of Parisians, who had gathered to listen to her roaring soliloquy, and, with eruptions of magma still leaping around like an undiscovered level in hell, she started on them. 'What do you want, you bunch of frog wankers. Eh? What do you want? Go on. Fuck off or I'll call the police. You understand? The fucking gendarmes will get here and it'll be the fucking lockup for the lot of you. You got that, four-eyes? All of you, straight to the fucking Bastille.'

They burst into laughter and applause, rolling their eyes comically at the mere mention of the Bastille. Hadn't anyone ever told this English turmagant anything about the Bastille? Turning back to Daniel she saw that he, too, had joined in the general merriment. 'You appalling little shit,' she yelled at him in her best Bette Davis, her lips curling pugnaciously as she packed each word with pure venom. 'You piece of pure fucking Welsh shit. To think I travelled all the way to Paris to see *you*. Well, we all make mistakes. I'm going back to ...'

The abuse dried up in her spitting lips and she choked, seeing herself, in a blinding flash of self-revelation, as her audience must have seen her, shrieking and wild. Oh this was hopeless, hopeless, and she saw herself spinning across the stage, totally out of control with the audience looking on, slack-jawed and embarrassed, as she was unable to hold herself properly let alone speak any of her lines.

Just what was the matter with her? Here she was abusing her new love like a scorned fishwife and all he'd wanted to do was to talk to his lifelong hero. She would have quite liked to talk to him too.

Well she knew what this was all about well enough. She knew there were too many ghosts brawling inside her – her mother, her past loves, her humiliations, her triumphs, the Press, her botched roles – and one did get out as now – and it was always the ugly, rogue one, always spoiling for a fight.

But how could she explain all this to Daniel? How could she explain it to *anyone*? Oh please Mr Jenkins don't take any notice of a word I say because it's really all down to a bunch of old ghosts who keep fighting inside me.

Yet, perhaps sensing her difficulty, Daniel didn't run away but became quite sweet, lighting a cigarette and handing it to her. 'Have a quiet pull on this and we'll walk back to the hotel slowly. Look, let's sit on that bench for a while.'

'I'm sorry, Daniel,' she said simply. 'I am so very sorry.'

Sometimes she couldn't get over how sweet he could be. John O could be quite sweet, for about five minutes, when the mood took him, but Daniel was sweet all the time.

She did feel relieved when they sat together in front of a fountain, looking out at the passing traffic. The gawping Parisians had long gone but she said no more, just smoked her cigarette shakily. Yet she did have a feeling that some great and invisible barrier had somehow been lifted between them and she did allow herself a little hope that, following many clashes, she and Daniel might yet touch that blessed state of mystical union that DH Lawrence was always going on about.

It happened between them very quietly and gently that night as their bodies rocked together feeding one another with warmth and reassurance. She had known times when she had practically re-staged the world boxing championship with her lovers in bed, fighting them and wounding them even, making them bleed as she fought to hold her ground in some bloody row about nothing at all but it was different this time; oh it was different all right.

Most of all it was thoughtful and what she really wanted out of it, she guessed, was some sort of healing, some way in which he could drive out all her mad old ghosts or even make them nicer and pleasanter while also making *her* nicer and pleasanter in the process.

They were also, she hoped, smoothing over those old, angry words too: those reckless, wounding tirades which had cost her so much, so often and for so long. She had lost almost all her men because of those furious tirades; even the tougher ones could last only so long: her tongue had driven them all out in the end. But there were ways in which bodies could cope and talk to one another without words, she had always believed; bodies could have extended conversations about love without words and that was the real brilliance of love.

He moved her somewhere between a soft dream and a hard place and, when she had settled there, she waited and listened to his body, ready to answer its calls when, not so long ago, she always *took* her needs simply because she wanted them so badly, oh yes, played the game for a while perhaps but then grabbed those needs greedily, stuffing them into her handbag and making off with them almost regardless of how the man felt: *indifferent* to it, if the truth be known.

But now here she was shivering with gratitude that a mere man had managed to make her feel like this again. Like what exactly? Oh, she didn't know. Somehow he had managed to show her a truth – a healing truth – for the very first time, not only for her but for everyone else in the world. This just had to be the very first time *any* woman had been shown this and that's why she was positively throbbing with gratitude and not a little unpeeled tenderness too. She was showing everything about herself to him and, far from plundering it and trying to run off with it, he was showing her everything about himself too and they were helping one another to get well. For the first time. Ever.

A foolish smile had also opened up between her legs and she could almost feel those mad old ghosts escaping through the hatch of that smile. And not just escaping but not being allowed back in again either. A little love and a little hope and a little grace. That's all she wanted and needed just now.

SIX

Winter bit hard into the neck of London, covering everything with a patina of greyness which drifted down from the sky like drizzling rain, gathered thickly in the clogged gutters, blurred the trees and seeped out of the high buildings, until everyone and everything shared a gloomy monochrome which spoke of funeral parlours and great parties to which you had not been invited, hosted by people who you had always thought were your friends.

Everything was damp: statues and iron railway bridges gleamed dully with it. The cold chilled the marrow and life became difficult for the animals that foraged in the underbelly of the city. By night a fox began using the subway at Hyde Park Corner to get to the rubbish bins in the park and by day the ducks and geese got so hungry they would follow visitors along the paths, making the children cry as they pecked boldly at their elbows to be fed. Kestrels javelined out of the grey city sky to pick off sparrows and one man came so regularly to feed the wood pigeons in St James's Park they flew straight at him as soon as he appeared and followed him around until he caught the tube back to Forest Hill.

Christmas had already begun to threaten the city. Christmas trees were being put up in the squares and shop windows were piled high with mountains of twinkling rubbish.

Lisa clenched her fists and stretched out her fingers slowly as she strode the length of her drawing room in Cheyne Walk, followed by her Pekingese. When she turned so did the dog; they were like a pair of synchronised swimmers in the Olympics. Back to the french windows they went, where she paused to look out over the Thames and the giant birthday cake of Battersea Power Station, her nostrils flaring with a huffy hauteur. She was wearing a white silk blouse and a long navy skirt which skimmed tightly over her taut figure. A silver art deco bangle curled around her left wrist.

The mantelpiece was lined with white stiffies for Christmas parties and the walls chequered with bright paintings by Francis Bacon, Lucien Freud and one of her long-standing chums Patrick Proctor. The Proctor was actually of her, caught in a moment of despair when she was outside the court in the process of divorcing John O. There were also framed photographs of herself smiling her huge, gappy smile together with other smiling stars of her vague vintage – Bette, Rachel, Peggy and Ava – and posters of her theatrical successes.

She had done all the big ones, the posters testified: Juliet and Ophelia at the Oxford Playhouse, Blanche duBois, Regina Giddens and Hedda Gabler at The Royal Court, a role to which she had brought her 'quivering sense of insecurity disguised by an invincible aggression' and which had made her one of the greatest Heddas ever, according to Kenneth Tynan.

But now there was nothing in the offing except a stupid, brainless movie in Israel and half a chance of Mrs Borkman on tour with the Royal Shakespeare Company. She didn't want the tour but was concluding dismally she would have to take it. The play wasn't the problem – though it was a complex, difficult piece of writing in which timing and pace were everything *and* dear Ralphie had said he might do Mr Borkman – nor was the company, even if she had never exactly hit it off with Trevor. What bothered her were all the associated horrors of touring like struggling to have a pee in a hand washbasin in the middle of the night or sliding around on nylon sheets in camphor bedrooms in damp, provincial towns. You never get a decent hotel, not even with the RSC on tour, and she'd had enough of all that. God alone knew she had paid her dues on that front.

So, of late, her calls to her agent had become more frequent and peremptory: there must be a decent role for her somewhere in the world but she had noticed her agent, the great Karen Duffy, was taking longer and longer to respond to her calls, forever in some mysterious meeting or other. A mysterious meeting with a glass of something strong no doubt. If her Percy ever took a bite out of Dipso Duffy they'd have to treat the poor pooch for a hangover.

Her main difficulty, of course, was because the West End stage was in its normal state of darkness with rows of empty seats and sobbing impresarios. But oh how she longed for a big one again; how she longed to see her name up there in the bright lights in a role which would bring *le tout* London to its knees. She wanted to show them all she could still do it. That's all. She wanted to be up and about in the public eye again. The stage was in her blood and the closest she got to heaven was in a rehearsal room. The nearest she got to a family of her own were the casts she mothered incessantly. They all brought their problems to her but not today they wouldn't, not now; they were all on the dole and doubtless suffering the same unemployed gloom as her.

Her salad days were but a dim glimmer in a black night, she was out of fashion, on the far edge of everything, a redundant cog in a vast obsolete machine, a duster with no dusty surfaces to dust, a spanner without a nut. Who could endure a life of such complex pointlessness? She had no better answer to that question than her dog.

The telephone rang. Her agent had actually finished her mysterious meeting with a bottle and was answering her call, billing and cooing with oily affection but surprise, surprise, hadn't found anything suitable and, to make matters worse, added that Dame Peggy Ashcroft had contracted to do Mrs Borkman.

'Peggy! What's the matter with her? Can't she put her feet up for a change? She's *far* older than me as well.'

'Oh you know what Peggy's like. She thinks a morning in bed is a waste of a lifetime. She's a woman who has always got to be doing something – a man if she can't get a play.'

'I need to be doing something too Karen. Me. Lisa Moran. Remember me because no one else does?'

'But Lisa, darling, there's still that film. I know it's not *Easy Rider* but it is somewhere in the sun. I'm sure we can improve on the money they're offering and they're mad to get you. They're simply mad for you, darling.'

'Why don't you ask them if I can take my name off the credits? I really don't want to be associated with that kind of stuff.'

'Fine. We can always ask. We can always ask for anything you want. We'll try for a lot more money too. I'll get back to you soonest.'

Even with Christmas also menacing her mental well-being – Christmas had always driven her crazy particularly as husbands would go home to their wives at Christmas – her love life was still in reasonably good shape. She had been seeing Daniel regularly since their Parisian sojourn and, apart from a few skirmishes which barely registered on the Richter scale, it was going well.

There might be a problem over the next few days however, since her Russian ballet star was turning up for a round of muscle and bone specialists which she had booked for him. They were both going to be quite busy getting to the various appointments – she half-carried him if his injuries had got too bad – but, fortunately, he had agreed to stay at Blake's, his favourite hotel in London, so there was every prospect she could keep him away from Daniel until he flew back to New York. The Russian peasant would have gone totally mad if he suspected that someone else was giving his Juliet a seeing-to. He really did appear to believe that she sat around Cheyne Walk like Miss Havisham, draped in cobwebs and weeds, waiting for his return.

The front door bell rang at 11.15am and she smiled to herself. Daniel Jenkins had a lot of strange habits but being late wasn't one of them. If he said he would be there at 11.15am that was when he arrived, not a minute before and not a minute later. To ensure such punctuality she was sure he hid away until the appointed hour, probably sitting on a garden wall in nearby Flood Street so he could get there right on the dot.

'Hello, Daniel darling,' she said putting her hands on his shoulders and kissing him with a smile. His flies were unbuttoned as usual, she was relieved to note, and he'd clearly been stealing flowers out of the local Physic Garden again. 'So nice to see you looking so well.' Just as he was punctual with her she was always good manners itself with him and they were almost courtly with one another. Today they were going to have lunch at Le Caprice, walk through the parks for a while afterwards and then a few hours in bed before she packed him off back to Hackney. It had become a little ritual of theirs and, being a theatrical, often away from home for long periods, she always approved of little rituals which enabled you to do things without having to think or make decisions.

But first a little glass of fizz to get themselves in the mood for the lunch and afternoon ahead.

'I've been dying to tell you all morning but Kennington's have asked me to come in and see them about my London book,' he said after taking his first sip and lighting a fag for her. Another of their little rituals.

'Oh, darling that's wonderful,' she replied, feeling wonderful herself and it wasn't just the first hit of the champagne in her bloodstream. She loved it when he told her anything about his work, if only because it was such a rare event. She would have preferred to mother a writer than any number of brattish kids. Only writers had ever really touched her heart: she had married one artist in her three marriages but that had barely lasted five minutes before, bored senseless, she had made off elsewhere. The other two had been writers who wrote words that would sing forever.

'I sent them a chunk of my work and they want me to come in and talk about it.'

'What does that mean, do you think?'

'Only that they want me to meet me and talk about it. We'll probably have a good lunch, of course, publishers are famous for their good lunches.'

'Listen. I don't want you stumbling around here trying to get your hands on my body after this good lunch.'

'Oh aye, playing hard to get are we?'

'Yes we are. When is this lunch anyway?'

The front door bell rang like the start of a police raid and her eyes shot around in alarm. She always liked to know exactly when the front door bell was going to ring and who, precisely, was ringing it. She had no further appointments that day: she cancelled everything when Daniel came over. So who was this?

She went to the french windows and looked down to see a huge Daimler with tinted windows and a man in chauffeur's livery standing on her doorstep. He rang the bell again before returning to the Daimler, first opening the passenger door and then the boot from which he began taking out the biggest bunch of yellow roses Lisa had ever seen and which had certainly not been nicked from the Physic Garden.

Oh fuck, she knew who this was all right. Her Russian cynosure had got his times and dates mixed up yet again and, from the luggage that was already being stacked up on the pavement, she could see that he clearly believed he was going to spend the week with her, here in Cheyne Walk. Oh fuck, shit, bollocks, fuck. And what was she going to tell Daniel here? He knew they were friends but she had never actually explained he often stayed with her and, oh shit, actually shared her bed.

Still standing there, champagne now fizzing mockingly in her glass, she couldn't think what to do and was pretty much frozen to the spot when Andrei Barapov proceeded, in a tangle of legs and walking sticks, to get out of the car. You've got too many legs, she thought. The hands gripping the walking sticks were small and strong, as was the tight body in the immaculate Armani suit. A white silk scarf was knotted around his neck and he wore black and white leather lace-up shoes. His face was youthful – almost boyish – but there was nothing youthful about the tragedian's jaw and intense blue eyes which spoke of a century of Russian suffering.

She glanced back at Daniel who was unconcernedly flicking through a magazine and down at Andrei who was standing poised on the pavement, trying to sort out his balance from his walking sticks and looking as fit as you might expect someone with a wonky sternum, a rotating cuff which wouldn't rotate, torn tendons, innumerable hammered toes and just about everything else that happens to a man who bounces around a stage for hours on end every day. The Press were always going on about how this man walked a delicate tightrope between light and gravity but she knew better than anyone that this man was a mess. Exotic he might be but, of all the stray puppies that had ever wandered into her life, this one had to be the most broken-down.

But what was she going to do now? Had she thought of it in time she could have merely taken two steps backwards and pretended she wasn't in. Just not answered the door. But she didn't and Andrei looked up at her and waved his walking sticks around in greeting.

She couldn't even think of a decent lie to tell Daniel about why a world-famous Russian ballet star was piling up his luggage outside her front door and waving walking sticks around so she just went down the stairs and opened her front door yelling out his name.

'Lisa, my beautiful angel of the heavens,' the gesticulating walking sticks caused the chauffeur, almost invisible in his bower of roses, to shuffle hurriedly aside before taking the flowers into the hallway and then proceeding to carry the luggage up the stairs – five monogrammed suitcases in all, three cases of vintage champagne, his portable practice *barre* and weighing scales. 'Lisa, the beat of my heart! Oh Lisa I think my heart is so vild with delight it is goink to leap out of my body. I zinc I am goink to faint clean away.'

They made no move to embrace since there were a few more formalities to be gone through yet. He made a profound, florid bow, almost falling flat on his face before projecting his voice into: 'Lady, by yonder blessed moon I svear/Zat tips with silver all zose fruit-tree tops ...'

She threw back her head. Raised a warning finger: 'Oh! Swear not by the moon, the inconstant moon, that monthly changes in her circled orb/lest that thy love prove likewise variable.'

'What shall I svear by?'

'Do not swear at all;/or, if thou wilt, swear by thy gracious self,/which is the god of my idolatry.'

Romeo and Juliet had always been their play. She had acted Juliet often enough and, when he had come to dance it, he had, with her help, found an interpretation which had delighted critics and audiences the world over. It was simple enough, she told him. All he had to remember was that here were two lovers itching to fuck one another to death and, out of that insight, an astonishing dance had been born with a consistent turn-out of genitalia and all significant movement coming from below the hips. It had become one of the sexiest dances ever to grace the boards and balletomanes complained they couldn't wait to get home from the theatre – one couple reportedly got straight down to it in the back of a taxi from Sadler's Wells.

The chauffeur returned to pick up some more luggage and Lisa was vaguely horrified to see that he had evidently dragooned Daniel to help him. She simply couldn't read the look on Daniel's face as he walked past her carrying Andrei's weighing scales and her mind remained a blank as she helped her ailing star up the stairs and parked him on the chaise longue. With nothing still coming to her she offered to make some tea. Daniel was happy to remain with the champagne but Andrei said he would love some tea which, at least, gave her the opportunity to withdraw to the kitchen where she could consider her position while waiting for the kettle to boil.

She was normally an expert liar but nothing came to her and she was intrigued to hear them chatting happily to one another even if she couldn't quite make out the words. Andrei never chatted happily if something was upsetting him so Daniel must be doing all right. When she returned with the tea tray Daniel said that it was nice to talk with someone who also liked windows. Windows? Windows!

'I was telling him how I've come to measure up your windows which have gone rotten in places, probably because of the damp coming up out of the Thames.'

Oh have you now?

'But we've found a new way of seasoning the wood so they'll last years instead of months. Anyway I'll send you a quote in the post, Miss Moran, but it won't be for some time because I'm going away for Christmas. Mr Barapov says he's going to be here for some time.'

'Six, seven days maybe. Depends on specialist. Depends on what they get vorking in this body. This vreckage. My legs back to front, you know. My head up my arse. Back cannot take veight. Arms cannot carry sack of feathers. No funny. I am old carthorse. Old fucking carthorse.'

She looked at Daniel and back at Andrei, wanting to cry. Sweet Daniel was giving her a way out of this mess but she was already worried by that line of his: *It won't be for a time because I'm going away for Christmas.* She didn't want him to go away for Christmas; she wanted to spend it with him.

Daniel nodded at her primly and left the room, closely followed by her, waving her arms around behind him as they descended the stairs with her like some schoolgirl who had been caught doing something very naughty and wanting to explain it all. 'I didn't know he was coming here,' she whispered urgently. 'He said he was going to Blake's. I fucking booked him into Blake's myself so I just don't know how he got the idea he was staying here.'

'It doesn't matter.'

'But it does matter. It matters a lot. And where are you going to when you say you're going away for Christmas? I don't want you to go away for Christmas. You were supposed to stay here with me.'

'And him? I don't want to spend Christmas wheeling *him* around.'

'You won't have to wheel him anywhere. He's not even supposed to be here. He's supposed to be in fucking Blake's. Anyway he *is* flying back on Christmas Eve. And he *will* be flying back then if I have to pilot the plane myself. Look, ring me tonight will you? No, I'll ring you. I'll sort this out Daniel. I'll ring you tonight.' She was becoming a little frantic, she knew, and it didn't help when she noticed that Daniel's lower lip was quivering. He'd been hurt.

'I'll see you soon,' he said and, after the front door closed behind him, she put her forehead to the hallway wall and just spluttered a meaningless stream of obscene words.

SEVEN

She decided not to waste the booking at Le Caprice so they both went there for lunch and were given the usual warm welcome by Christopher before being seated at her favourite table near the window. They certainly made a glamorous couple with Barapov, in particular, causing near panic in the kitchen with many male heads appearing from everywhere to catch a glimpse of the Russian star who never seemed to notice the ripples of startled recognition he always caused all around him, particularly now as he sipped the champagne which appeared immediately on their table, and chatted away happily.

'Lisa, I am going to buy you new house,' he said as he studied the menu. 'This house will be in basement. Every-sing in future in basement. I cannot climb stairs anymore. Stairs not good for me. You vill receive keys to this new home in basement soon. Vill be good for my legs.'

She wondered if this latest extravagant promise would be kept. He had said often enough he was going to give her a Daimler with her own chauffeur but there was no sign of that – she was still rattling around London in her old Mini.

He finished his glass of champagne and called for another. Everyone but everyone loved him in Manhattan and LA, he said; Paris also beckoned and there was a strong possibility he would be allowed back into Moscow to dance there. 'The Bolshoi, Lisa. Fucking Bolshoi say I maybe goink to dance on their old planks soon. Is marvellous.'

The prospect of seeing his aged mother again in Moscow left him cold but he nearly pissed himself with excitement at the thought of seeing his dog again. He rang home to Moscow once a week to listen to it bark. But Lisa never really asked any difficult questions about his chaotic life. Ever since he had made the giant leap into the amazed arms of immigration officials in Hawaii he had run into problem after problem. Why hadn't he stayed in Russia where, he said, he had always been happy? From the moment he had applied for American citizenship, everything had gone wrong. No fairy he: three starlets were now running around Manhattan claiming he had fathered their babies and Lisa had tried more than once to explain to him that the freedom of the West didn't have to involve buffaloing every starlet in the galaxy and there was always that great invention of Colonel Condom. But he hadn't taken any notice and so he was now doing pointe three nights a week just to pay the maintenance.

Lisa was pretty sure he kept running back to her because she mothered him and had a good working knowledge of all the muscle and bone specialists in London. There was also no chance of her getting a bun in the oven at her age so that was a bonus for him too. And there was undoubtedly the age-old attraction of the peasant to the aristocrat at work here: she turned all her upper class airs to their finest pitch when he was around. It was all first nights, royal friendships and foul language with her Andrei and he loved every glamorous second of it.

Yes, she loved his fame, success and glamour but not really him, alas and alack: he was far too silly to fill her ears with magical words like her other great lovers and, if the truth be known, he wasn't particularly good in bed either, all angularity and jazzy acrobatics, satisfying for the Bolshoi no doubt but most disappointing for her. Another reason why she welcomed him into her grand home was that he liked to put on a pinafore and potter around the house polishing furniture and fixing faults. His idea of heaven was to have a screwdriver in his hand replacing electric plugs or nailing up collapsed blinds. She sometimes liked cleaning and fixing things but always put her feet up when he was around. Once a peasant always a peasant, she guessed.

She wolfed her food down as usual but he no more than played with the bleeding steak which he had as a main course before fretting about his body again. That was the other snag with him. He was always going on about his body and usually for good reason. He had fallen over his crutches the first time they had met and the real mystery was that, as soon as the curtain went up, something magical happened and his spirit seemed to transform his broken body as he investigated the very length and texture of the air in those long, thrilling flights. And she had watched his bourrées, arabesques and jetés as he did his morning prayers at his barre in her own bedroom often enough to know that there was very little wrong with his body that a good smack wouldn't put right. But he was a world-class artist. He had a perfect right to worry about his body if that's what he wanted to do. Artists could worry about whatever they wanted to worry about. Real artists had the right to do anything at all — even murder, she believed.

He also worried incessantly about his weight, jumping on his weighing scales almost three times a day and checking any unwelcome variations. The loss or gain of a few ounces was bad; the loss or gain of a pound or two was a good excuse for a new war in the Balkans. He would clutch his breaking heart or sulk in the lavatory for hours on end, sighing windily and grumbling dark Russian oaths about his impending demise.

Yet she did find his sense of melancholy deeply and overwhelmingly attractive and she came into her own then, soothing and reassuring him with a quiet force which suggested she would really have been the greatest matriarch since Regina Giddens if all her babies hadn't fallen out of her before their time.

So this relationship was far from what it might have been and, as she laughed at his little jokes and gave little claps of glee at his various news items, what she was really worrying about was her relationship with Daniel. She needed to talk to him and explain exactly what was going on between her and Andrei but, albeit unwittingly, she had hurt him and she did so want to get to him before the wound turned septic. No matter how famous you were you had to nurse all your relationships, she knew, and she had a positively Chekhovian attitude to her relationships; she always wanted to keep them all on the boil even long after they appeared to have gone cold. She certainly wanted to keep it going with Daniel; almost alone he seemed to know how to placate the ghosts which tormented her.

They returned to Cheyne Walk, giggly with champagne laughter and twice Lisa left Andrei stretched out on the chaise longue while she went into the spare room to telephone Daniel, but twice she got no reply. This was hopeless and she became really worried when she returned to her living room to find Andrei messing about suspiciously with a mirror, a twenty-dollar bill and some white powder. 'Andrei, darling, just *what* are you doing?'

'I have found a little some-sing new in Manhattan, Lisa. Is great help to me and my body. Zis is my new secret weapon. Is fucking good too.'

'Andrei, *what* is it?'

'Zis is cocaine, Lisa.' He took a small silver snuff box out of an Armani pocket and opened it showing a small mound of snowy white crystals. 'Zis is Andrei's new helper and today Andrei is going to take you by the hand and we do a *pas de deux* in heaven. Zo. Ve have small mirror. We have razor here. I have special dollar bill. Roll up dollar bill like zo. Now, two lines along here. Ve chop, chop like zo. Zis one line for me. Now, zis line here for you. Zo.'

Lisa, shivering with delicious illegality, took the rolled-up banknote and stuffed it up her left nostril. The drug was relatively new in theatrical circles and she had never got her hands on it before but, somehow, she knew exactly what to do. She had no reservations about taking it. The old can afford the reckless risks of youth if only because the old have nothing to lose.

'Andrei, you've learned some disgusting habits in Manhattan,' she said, hoovering up half a line and feeling the cocaine chill her nostril and bring tears to her eyes. 'I bet they never got up to this when you were in the Bolshoi.' She snorted what was left of the line up her right nostril.

He mopped up his line quickly and expertly and sucked the tip of his forefinger before sweeping the last few grains off the mirror, rubbing it around the outside of his gums and inviting her to do the same with the couple of grains he'd left. 'Do this in the Bolshoi?' he asked, about half an hour later. 'You do snow in Bolshoi and the secret police would clean off your balls. Phut! Clean off.'

She studied his beautiful face as an unfathomably deep silence swirled around them. 'Andrei darling, do you think,' she asked finally. 'Do you really think you could dance the way you do ... Do you really think you could dance like ... oh, I don't know ... like an angel newly released from hell, if the secret police cleaned off your balls?'

He smiled patiently at her question. For about an hour. Maybe a bit longer. As if thinking through the problem of how to dance without any balls from the beginning. His mouth opened. He let out a belch like a ship's siren.

She clamped her hands on her ears as the fat, long, snoring sound droned into the fog. 'Andrei, I am being very serious now,' she said. 'Do you honestly think you could dance the way you do if the secret police sent your precious balls to the Siberian salt mines? You could dance without them could you?'

'Dance without my balls?' Distant laughter started softly like a lone tinkling cymbal only to build up in power until it was a whole packed football stadium helpless with mirth. 'I dance without balls? Sure. Andrei Barapov can dance without balls. It's only his walking sticks he can't dance without.'

They were both in the football stadium, laughing helplessly before moving again into the unfathomable and eternal silence, broken only by the sound of the traffic along Cheyne Walk. Big Ben chimed – ONE-TWO-THREE... had it ever sounded so loud? FOUR-FIVE-SIX... Had they turned the amplification up for Christmas? *They* were always doing stupid things like that, always in some new conspiracy, usually directed at her.

Yet apart from a numb nose and a few silly sniffs she felt quite happy and really didn't have a care in the world and merely mumbled contentedly as she watched him dice up a few more lines with his razor.

'Ve also call this blow as in blow up my ass. Zo vhat you say, Lisa? You blow up my ass and Andrei blow up your nose. Is fun. Is nice. Here.'

'Andrei, just what are you talking about?'

She snorted another line and moved her lower body around, feeling powerfully and almost overwhelmingly randy when her attention was caught by a huge damp patch forming in the corner of her ceiling like some great disgusting stain left after a couple of giants had been making love up there. A murderous itch was also itching like mad under her bra strap. She would have scratched it if she had been able to find a finger. Find a finger! Hah, hah. That was a good joke. Find a finger! Hah, hah, hah.

Her feet had also gone missing. What had happened to them? Andrei looked at her quizzically as she leaned between her knees looking for her feet before she sat up again and began laughing like a drain, her splayed-out fingers clamped over her bosom to stop her breasts shattering into many shards.

Andrei then stood up and walked out of the room and it was only long after he'd gone that she realised he'd done so without the aid of his walking sticks. Foof! This cocaine stuff was clearly good for him but, funny thing, it hadn't any effect on her at all and she couldn't see what all the fuss was about.

Some time later he returned completely naked and she stared hard at his chemically erect old boy with her chemically enlarged eyeballs. What had he got there? And more to the point what was about to happen now? Well she soon found out because half a dozen hands – of which two might have been her own – stripped her of everything but her ear-rings and, the next thing, they were conjoined and he had gathered her buttocks up into his outstretched palms and was swirling her around her living room.

She quite enjoyed this as he whirled her up and down as if they were on the Bolshoi stage, lifting her up in a sort of high jeté, twirling her around and then sending her dipping towards the floor again, a plummeting Spitfire about to crash-land on her own Balouche carpet before pulling out at the very last second as yet another lift sent her soaring towards the ceiling, a dove released.

The whole ballet could have been choreographed by Twyla Tharp but then, rather oddly, she lost interest in the proceedings and began looking around her room, at the view of the Thames, at all her expensive paintings and the theatrical posters telling of her past successes. Yet even as she gazed at the emblems of her life all around her she had to admit that she felt no real connection with them, suspecting she had amassed so much because she always felt terminally insecure and that, in some ways, she always clung to little Andrei here, not because she loved him in any serious way but rather because he was yet another expensive and exotic possession. There were certainly no deep feelings she knew of which connected her to him, certainly nothing like the profusion of healing breezes that Daniel turned loose inside her. Now *he* didn't seem to need any possessions: he didn't seem to want to own *anything* and in that one endeavour at least he had been fantastically successful. She had even given him presents which, he later admitted, he had given to the landlord of his local pub on the way home.

Oh God, she had messed it all up with him hadn't she? And at Christmas too. What was there about Christmas that fucked everything up? And there she was: the spoiled child who always went and broke her favourite toy at Christmas. Just what was the matter with her?

'Are you all right then Andrei?' she asked as he landed her on the keys of the grand piano in a jumble of excited discords. 'Is this how you do it with all those actresses in New York?'

'Coke is very good no,' he replied, completely missing the point of her jibe. Anything remotely ironical always passed straight over his head. 'I bring you some more soon. Coke is great for fucking don't you zink?'

She let out a theatrical whoop as he hoisted her into the air again, striking a series of poses as if she were Dame Margot Fonteyn being held aloft for the audience to admire and applaud. He hadn't been much good at love-making before but this cocaine had made him completely hopeless. She would have to get out of this before she went mad.

He lay her down on her back again and was continuing to dig away between her legs, like some famished dog frantically trying to locate his favourite bone, and it had all become like watching a really poor B film and not being at all interested in it but sitting there anyway because it was raining outside and you had a few hours to kill before an appointment.

But she really had to do *something* about that damp patch. Should she get a ladder and go up to look at it herself? But this peasant would probably love to do something about it, if he ever finished looking for that bone. He could probably sort it out with Polyfilla or something if ... God ... he was going to be after that bone for another week at least. Whatever it was that she had ever wanted out of sex it wasn't this.

She thought about that Israeli film she was in danger of doing. Just a cursory look at the script had confirmed it was a crock and, even worse, it involved spending a few months in Israel in the early spring. She had been to Israel and had no desire whatsoever to return. But there was a big pile of shekels on offer – which might get bigger after Karen Duffy had finished with them – and, in her present state, she couldn't afford to get sniffy about cash in any currency.

And he was *still* at it. Stifling a yawn, she started to worry about Daniel again and saw, in a ballooning panic, her mad Welsh scribe prostrate in his flat, dying of something nasty, his mind imprisoned by some appalling vision and calling out her name. She saw his coffin being carried through a cemetery, a single rose in a whisky bottle on top of it, followed by just one mourner – her! *Her!* She was throwing earth onto the coffin lid. *Thump, thump, thump.* Oh Daniel, my baby. Daniel!

She gave Andrei a sharp slap on his pistoning bum, grasped his bobbing head and shouted into his ear: 'Andrei, darling, this is all beautiful, just beautiful, but I've got to go out for an hour. If I don't see that producer I'm going to lose a role I've been after for three years. It's all to do with winter, Andrei. Damp in the ceiling and the beginning of Christmas. April's the cruellest month too. Bye.'

EIGHT

She flung on her clothes, almost knocking herself out on her coffee table as she tried to get two legs into the same knicker hole. In a few seconds she was in her Mini, accelerating down Cheyne Walk at eighty miles an hour, before screeching to a halt behind a corporation Bulkmaster somewhere in Pimlico, with four dustmen hurling black bags into it. Aggressive honking wouldn't budge them so, tyres screaming, she reversed and came out around Hyde Park Corner, which she circled three times on two wheels, before tearing down in front of Buckingham Palace, hanging a right and a few lefts, then braking again ... directly behind that same corporation Bulkmaster in that same Pimlico street. Something wrong here.

The baffling City loomed over her again as she clattered down the middle of Fleet Street. This was more like the right direction. No more cocaine for her. Windows flashed the neon news about another hateful Christmas. Onward Christian soldiers! How she had always loathed Christmas. Carol singers who didn't know the words to any carols knocking on your door. Tinsel over everything. Drunks puking over your shoes. Had she been Queen she would have abolished the whole fucking mess. Right now. Calm down Lisa. Cool head. Concentrate on the road to Hackney. This was going to be the very last time she tried that stuff. She wished her brain would stop whizzing around. It whizzed around enough when she was drinking nothing stronger than a cup of tea but now, after snorting all that stuff, her brain was threatening to spin off straight up into the air.

She knew she had reached Hackney when she spotted the sign that always made her laugh: 'Welcome to Hackney – A Nuclear-Free Zone'. Hackney streets were always overflowing with rubbish and there were so many houses boarded up or derelict it looked as if the Russians had already nuked this borough as an offence to world socialism.

The Moran Mini accelerated past a string of travellers' caravans guarded by ferocious dogs on the ends of long bits of rope and turned past the Empire, empty for years, where she had once done a Christmas panto which she preferred to forget. She honked at a drunk in a flat cap wobbling on the edge of the pavement, turned her head to stare at a group of melancholy blacks standing together in a reggae-loud snooker hall doorway, then swerved up Dalston Lane and stopped outside the Voodoo Parlour. There she sat, fiddling with her steering wheel and worrying whether she dared knock on Daniel's door. She should have rung to say she was coming. He might be in bed with the phantom gobbler: knowing him, he might be in bed with almost anyone. Or anything. It would be *something* if only she could stop sniffing all the time. Oh shit! Shit! Shit! Shit!

So it was a fearful Lisa Moran, as sick as first night nerves, who felt her way along the balustrade in the darkened, rubbish-strewn hallway. Her cautious steps creaked on the ancient stairs with exaggerated loudness and her timid knockings drew no response. She took the key from the top of the door and let herself in, gave the room one huge sniff but found no sign of Daniel, dead or alive.

She sighed and chewed on her lower lip. This was the home of a man who was not going to last long. There were lots of empty brown bottles in evidence, ashtrays overflowing with butt-ends – a few with lipstick on them! – and she could not even start to guess the origin of the darker stains on those sheets; one was so vast he might have been having it off with an elephant. The phantom gobbler?

Oh well if he needed to write in this state, that was how it had to be. Not for her to interfere. Well, a little bit maybe.

And here it was again, the holy of holies, the altar of creativity, with the spotlight illuminating the grail of his typewriter. She stood in front of the desk, hands clasped together as if in prayer and studied the notes pinned to the wall.

She smiled when she read the Elizabethan watchman's goodnight admonition – 'Now say your prayers and take your rest with conscience clear and sins confess'd' and her heart leaped right into her throat when she spotted one of her own mad notes pinned up there. 'I'll wear that fur coat next time if you'll put on the other one,' it said.

A noise from behind her, and she turned sharply to find a large West Indian standing in the doorway. 'Y-e-e-e-e-rs. Can I be of any help to you?' she asked.

'Ah now you're Lisa Moran ain't you? Daniel tole me a lot about you.'

'Y-e-e-e-ers,' she said again, holding her best Lady Macbeth pose.

'Boyce. Winston Churchill Maxwell Boyce. I live downstairs. Fought you might be 'im back early. Daniel 'as gone walkabout. Won't be back 'til after Christmas 'e said.'

'Gone walkabout? Where?'

'Got a few problems 'as Daniel. You know. Up 'ere.'

'*What* are you talking about?'

'Daniel. Not in the 'uman race is 'e? A few mental problems if you ask me. But it's 'ard to say where 'e's gone really.'

She frowned. Had Daniel gone into outer space or something? Emboldened by the West Indian's friendliness, she took a step towards him, cooling the aristocratic bit. 'Mr Boyce, would you please *try* telling me where he's gone?'

'Would you fancy a cup of tea? Me gaff's in a better state than this tip. I 'eard you did a bit of cleaning though.'

'No thank you, Mr Boyce. Well, not for the moment anyway. Please, just tell me where he's gone.'

'Well, 'e came down 'ere this afternoon and said you'd given him the elbow.'

'I did no such thing.'

'Well that's what 'e said. 'E said some ballet dancer had come to town and you'd given 'im the elbow. 'E's really cut up about it too and I even told 'im to go over to the Voodoo Parlour an' send the ballet dancer a coffin.'

'A coffin?'

'Yeah. You know a voodoo coffin to fix him good.'

'Works does it? I'll be sending a few voodoo coffins this Christmas then. But please tell me Mr Boyce. *Where* has Daniel gone?'

'Daniel 'as always said 'ow much he hates Christmas so he's gone off for a week with Ironing Board Dave.'

She swallowed once, opened her mouth in disbelief, swallowed again. 'Ironing Board Dave?'

'Yeah. Well I tole you that 'e's as mad as ten hatters and Ironing Board Dave is a tramp that Daniel met in the West End years ago. There's this crowd of them wot lives on the streets an' Daniel goes to live with them when 'e feels like an 'oliday.'

'Doesn't sound like much of a holiday to me.'

'Well, it's not exactly the bloody Costa Brava is it? All they ever do is roll around the gutters as pissed as parrots. 'E says it's somefink to do with the book he's writing on London. You sure you don't want a cup of tea?'

'No, Mr Boyce, thank you very much all the same.' A migraine began gathering and her eyesight was going funny with a blind spot in the centre of her vision. Could she, Lisa Moran, winner of the *Evening Standard* best actress of the year award (twice), really have gone and fallen for a man whose idea of a fun Christmas was to lie drunk in the gutter with a gang of pissed-up tramps?

'What about *The Sunday Times*? Are they aware he takes his holidays lying pissed in some gutter?'

'Why should they care? Wasn't 'is real job anyway. You know Dan. 'E only ever worked if 'e 'ad a few bills to pay. Lives for 'is book 'e does. In some ways 'e *is* his book.'

'And what's all this going to do for his health?' she shrieked as if Boyce had personally ordered her lover out into the cold. 'He's a sick man. He's got trouble enough with ulcers as it is.'

'Can't 'elp you there but writers is all fruitcakes ain't they?'

The tectonic plates ground furiously and pointlessly. The lava bubbled, flamed and spat. Big red sparks flashed through her gathering migraine. God how she had always hated writers. Those bastards were the scum of the earth. Every single one of them should have been nipped in the bud. 'I really don't think I can cope with any more of this,' she sighed. 'I really don't. But tell me one thing, Mr Boyce. How much do they charge for one of those voodoo coffins?'

NINE

Lisa, wearing an old coat and no make-up or jewellery, moved quickly through the Christmas crowds. She wanted to be anonymous as she threaded through the shoppers or turned up side alleys, checking on tramps huddled on warm grilles or behind dustbins. Daniel was out here somewhere and she was going to find him and take him for Christmas lunch at the The Ritz whether he was hungry or not.

The West End streets trumpeted with an incandescent happiness. Shop windows were festooned with multi-coloured lights and the sad sound of carols from the dark yards around St James's Palace floated over the heads of people struggling with ribboned packages and carrier bags stuffed with gifts. Christmas trees glittered in office windows; taxis pulled up at gentlemen's clubs, disgorging befuddled colonels with waxed moustaches and angry eyes. Fortnum and Mason's was jammed with the black silhouettes of people buying out its famous Food Hall.

She checked on the old and young denizens of Piccadilly Circus, the bearded and the fresh-faced, the lost and the mad, for that familiar nose or tousled hair. But that much-loved nose was nowhere to be seen among these desperate people clutching their precious bottles, their warm breath pluming in the cold night air.

By divesting herself of every jewel and ornament she had become one of them. Dolled up she got harassed for money but, plain as a clothes peg, she was as broke and lowly as they, just another piece of flotsam that the tides of bad luck had washed up on the uncaring shores of the city. She mimicked that cowed, haunted look she had spotted in the elderly street women, even adopted their demented mannerisms as she drifted past the huddled shapes, checking on the features of each in turn.

Yet this search excited her strangely. She was the moth flickering at the edge of the candle flame, drawn ever closer to the gutter wherein she always believed that she would one day destroy herself. Here the thin line between her and the gutter had disappeared and she enjoyed the smell of danger.

In an odd sort of way her search brought her closer to Daniel, almost helped her understand him a little more, this strange Welshman who didn't seem to want what most people wanted: light, security, a family. He just appeared to want to embrace empty darkness, to lose himself and be apart from everyone and everything, to hide away from God himself, as if God didn't always know where he was. She wouldn't have minded a bit of all that either – as long as he was there by her side.

She walked the length of Jermyn Street, passing Turnbull and Asser where she had ordered some specially tailored shirts for John O the first Christmas after their break-up and sent them with a note saying that she wouldn't mind getting the contents back some time. It was a bit of a joke and he didn't even thank her which got her so riled she got someone to telephone Nigel Dempster about the shirts, just to stir it up a bit. The day after the diary item appeared the shirts came back. She also passed the entrance to Tramp, the club where, one drunken night, they had all applauded as Ryan O'Neal had it away with Bianca Jagger. One of Bianca's more expensive mistakes, as it turned out, when rock'n'roller Mick duly served the divorce papers.

A few street people were shuffling into a dark alleyway and she followed them into a cramped, cobbled courtyard with a single hissing gas lamp which could easily have done service in a Dickens novel. About a dozen people were waiting, with barely concealed patience, by a closed door and she spotted six or seven more hanging back in the shadows as watchful as footpads awaiting the next gentleman passer-by.

A man began talking in the softest monotone directly into her left ear: 'They promised to go next week – promised, they did. The police came and took him away to a psychiatrist and that was the last the football club ever heard from him. Honest to God. Didn't even send his own brother a postcard. His own brother! *Nothing.* I'm going to die all right. We're all going to die Thursday week. None of us are going to get out of this alive. We're all going to get our cards Thursday week.'

She twitched her head sharply, snatched at her coat sleeves, grumbling a few incoherent words. Even in this alien place she could stand her ground without flinching. No woman had ever had her balls. The tougher the situation, the bigger her balls. Lisa Moran had been sticking up for herself against men decades before the feminists had charged into the sex war and, largely because of this, feminist claims had always been pretty much meaningless to her. The sisterhood had never told her anything new.

A door opened and a young man in the white tunic of a commis waiter stepped out into the courtyard, carrying two trestles. Another waiter set out a long board on the trestles and a third flung a white tablecloth over the lot. Then came platters piled high with oblongs of corned beef, fat slices of white turkey breast, chunky chicken legs, saucers of pickled onions, veal and ham pie and small pyramids of neatly cut sandwiches decorated with crisps and cress. A few dozen glasses followed, each filled with red wine.

The waiters, having set their fare down, stood behind the table as immobile and unblinking as Vatican guards while the gathered sweaty nightcaps swarmed around the food and drink, waiting for the door to be closed again: the signal that they could get stuck in.

There were not six or seven people hanging back in the shadows, as Lisa had first guessed, but perhaps twenty of them, all now stretching out their grubby hands and grabbing what they could. The most surprising feature of this back-door feast was that they tackled the food in almost complete silence. The only sounds were chomping lips or the occasional slurp. Even in the gaslight she could see that the food was of the finest quality, as was the wine which sang sweet hymns inside her when she tried a few sips herself.

The expressionless waiters only came to life to restrain anyone who tried to stow away sandwiches in coat pockets or grab more than one glass of wine at a time. Many poured the wine down their throats without troubling their adam's apples and were then free to take one of the plentiful refills.

A few latecomers drifted in. Taking another glass, she moved back into the darkness and scrutinised their faces without finding the one she was looking for. A lot of them weren't the rough and ready lot you might expect to find living on the streets. There was an air of distressed city folk about many of them: two were wearing battered homburgs and another looked extremely smart with his camel-hair coat and immaculately coiffed, oiled hair. But Camel Hair had no conversation: he turned his back on anyone who tried to say anything to him. A woman in black, apparently known to all as The Black Tarantula, ate her sandwiches with her smiling head cocked and her little finger stuck out daintily. Most of them squeezed the sandwiches, testing them for freshness, before picking them up.

'We were all getting ready to throw them to the wolves but they weren't having any. Anyone will tell you there's a price to be paid for death but who wants to pay it these days? That's how selfish people have got. The price is always too high. Anyone will tell you that.' Monotone was having a go in her left ear again and, when she moved away, he followed her. She turned to face him. 'Ironing Board Dave,' she said finally. 'I need to find Ironing Board Dave.'

He was so startled by her request he slunk away, leaving her face-to-face with The Black Tarantula. 'Ironing Board Dave,' Lisa growled with a few facial twitches. 'Where is Ironing Board Dave?'

The Black Tarantula laughed and offered her half-eaten sandwich. Lisa took a firm pace forward to let her know she wasn't intimidated. 'I need to find a man called Ironing Board Dave.'

The jaunty sound of a harmonica joined the swelling hubbub. The wine must be warming everyone up. All at once everything was silenced by a roar from the darkness of an adjoining alley and everyone turned to behold the awesome face of the one-eyed man she had given money to in the park on the first night she had met Daniel.

'Weeeeeeel aaaaaaaaall beeeeee gooooooooing to fooooooocking Glaaasgow,' he bawled, stalactites of green snot hanging from his nostrils and his shrieking mouth dribbling copiously. 'Weeeeeell aaaaaaall ...'

'That's fucked it,' a man near her exclaimed. 'They always said any fuss an' the meal's over. Trust One-Eyed Jack. That cunt would fuck up a hangover.'

The meal *was* over too. At the first syllable of One-Eyed Jack's mad shout the door opened and the waiters started carrying away the dishes. The table-cloths were shaken and the trestles disappeared too. The Beggars' Banquet had ended as quickly as it had begun.

A desk drawer landed with a splintering crash on the fire which burned with a vivid and angry fury under the arches at Victoria Station. People circled the fire, peeling off when they were properly warmed up, to be replaced by others for a while. They all looked as if they were suffering from the same illness, their heads bowed and shoulders hunched, their overcoats belted with rope and their legs so thick they might have been wearing four or five pairs of trousers. Fragments of stale food hung in the men's beards and some of the women wore greasy caps or balaclavas.

Hell might look or feel like this, Lisa thought as she joined the circle, bowing her head and shuffling along with them. They had strong, Hogarthian faces, often of spectacular ugliness. There were hare-lips and broken noses, eyes which were not level with one another, lobotomy scars, crooked mouths. Many, perhaps conscious of their ugliness, were unwilling to look anyone in the eye. No one paid her any regard; she wasn't a star out here.

She had noticed subtle hints, however, of an abiding need for love, no matter how fallen the state. Two men had dogs; a kitten's head poked up out of a woman's overcoat. Crucifixes hung around many necks, the sight of which always disturbed her. Unlike Daniel she had almost no relationship with God but, rather like Daniel, she was afraid of him.

Another line of stooping figures was filing through the bluish glow of the railway station in the distance. Some pushed supermarket trolleys loaded with rubbish, all carried bulging carrier bags. She shuffled along in their wake for a while but soon saw that none of their faces was *his* face. She asked a few if they knew Ironing Board Dave but they all looked at her as if she was mad.

Perhaps she was.

This wandering was becoming pointless. She'd a better chance of landing a decent part in a decent play than finding Daniel out here. Yet she was surprised at how at ease she felt with these street people and how much she had learned about their blighted lives in such a short time. Life out here wasn't nearly as hard as she had feared. She could survive out here easily. Perhaps she belonged out here after all. Her *heart* was at home out here or perhaps it was that Daniel was out here. Somewhere.

TEN

'So good of you to come over on Christmas Eve, Lisa. And you must have so many things to do, shopping and all, but I simply had to talk to someone or I'm going to explode.'

Lisa, back straight, palms resting on her handbag, looked Harry Kirby directly in the eyes. She knew his news was going to be bad. Any news at Christmas was always bad and this edition was going to be especially dire. His face had gone skeletal gaunt, his skin dry and flaky. So many dark rings had formed under his eyes she wondered if he had been overdoing the slap again. Even the lovebirds in the Taj Mahal were unusually quiet, as if they too had run out of something to sing about.

'Are you going somewhere for Christmas, or is it going to be a quiet one at home?' he asked.

She shook her head and continued to stare at him coldly. That wasn't slap under his eyes, that was the real thing and his prison pallor suggested something serious was afoot. Lots of scratch marks had cut into his arms, some running into odd, ugly sores.

'I've had a few invitations to go to the country but I think I'll stay here,' Harry went on. 'It's good to spend Christmas Day on your own sometimes. It takes the pressure off when you don't have to worry about other people. I don't even bother to cook myself anything and just settle down here with a good book and a bottle of wine.' He stifled a small cough with the side of his fist. 'Is the ballet dancer still in town?'

'No. Andrei went back home. There was a misunderstanding and he went home.'

The truth was rather more colourful. After she had left him fucking fresh air on her drawing room floor and taken that coked-up drive to Hackney looking for Daniel she had returned to Cheyne Walk to find him in one of his foulest

Russian moods. Among many other wild accusations he told her that she had enticed him across the Atlantic to waste time with all these muscle and bone specialists when there was nothing remotely wrong with his muscles and bones. All she wanted to do – was it not correct? – was spread alarm and despondency about him around the ballet world when – was it not correct? – his physical condition was far better than 'a new tractor on the collective.' She was jealous – yes, madly jealous – of the emotional security he had been enjoying in Manhattan with all his women and children.

She had frowned and wondered if he'd been hitting that cocaine again, doubting that she had ever heard him speak quite such arrant nonsense.

Zo, why didn't she let him be happy for a change? Whenever he managed to put a little happiness together she broke it into many pieces. Even Andrei Barapov was entitled to a little happiness. Andrei Barapov had suffered enough at the hands of the KGB. All his life he had suffered from the KGB, watching him all the time, even when he was having a nice crap. Zo he wanted to be free now, free to do what he wanted, to crap in private, without being watched.

She had listened to this wandering tirade with goggling eyes and twitching eyebrows wondering what she had ever seen in this daft Russian twat. But, although it had happened often enough in the past, this time she did not lose her rag and start flinging things at him. All this paranoia had merely depressed her even more and, calm as a morning sea in high summer, she asked him to leave. She was sorry, she was really, really sorry he felt like that but she was tired and simply wanted to go to bed. 'Use the phone to see if your room is still available at Blake's, if you want. Do anything you like but I'm going to bed. I need a long, long sleep.'

What she had really wanted was a long, long cry about Daniel but, in the event, merely lay on her bed listening to the indistinct noises of Andrei barking orders on the telephone. Later that night the chauffeur returned to take his luggage – and the champagne – to Blake's. She hadn't even got out of bed to bid him goodbye but stretched across the bed to part the curtain slightly to watch the Daimler pulling away along the Embankment. So, where she had once had two pleasant relationships with two unusual men, she now had none. She had pursued these strategies before and still wondered why she came up with much the same results.

The pile of yellow roses which arrived the next morning, by way of apology, made her feel worse and she burst into tears as she opened the front door to behold their expensive profusion. Andrei always believed everything was *his* fault, when he sat down to think about it – even when it was plainly hers – and here he was saying sorry again. 'You can't throw love out of the window like a sack of turnips,' he had written on the card, his favourite saying. She didn't understand why she didn't value him more.

When she'd finished her cry she decided she was going to try a little harder and rang him at Blake's. But he'd cancelled all his appointments, she learned from the receptionist there, and booked himself on the next Concorde to New York. She rang Heathrow but, typically, couldn't get through to the Concorde lounge and, when she did get through, she was told the flight had left. Damn and blast. Here was Christmas with its cold hands on her throat and she was all alone and unloved except for good old Harry here who was also going to spill some bad news straight into her lap at any second now.

'So how's it going with that writer over in Hackney?' Harry asked.

'Harry, if I knew where he was I would tell you. I *think* he's out living rough in the streets of the West End for Christmas.'

'Really? Is there something wrong with him do you think?'

'Well, there's certainly something wrong with me because I've been out there night after night looking for him.'

'What's it like out there in those streets then? I've always wondered what it's like sleeping rough like that.'

'Harry, will you please stop pissing about. What is it you want to tell me?'

'Oh, I don't know Lisa. There's something awfully wrong. I'm rotting away, literally. The doctors say that my immune system has broken down. Apart from that they know nothing, *nothing*.'

She leaned forward and waved her hand around her ear vaguely a few times. 'I don't understand. What did you say was the matter? I'm going deaf as well as daft.'

'Lisa, *I do not know*. My immune system is shot and they say I am going to die soon.'

She swallowed hard and looked down at her upturned hands then over at the silent lovebirds and the dazzlingly clean colours of the David Hockneys assembled here in some twisted mockery of human frailty. Tears puddled her eyes. She had never liked Hockney. All that Californian swimming pool stuff was too shallow and stupidly joyful. Life wasn't like that.

'You're not going to die, Harry,' she heard herself say. 'Take any treatment that's available. I'll pay whatever it takes.'

'You don't seem to understand. They don't think there *is* a cure. They don't have a clue what's going on but they do say I am going to die soon.'

She blinked a lot into her tears and the flutter of her eyelashes made them flow ever faster. She wasn't sure what was going on but she knew, without a shadow of doubt, that nothing would ever be the same again. From this day forth everything would be different – for him, for her, for everyone.

'Harry, there's a reason for everything and there's a cure for everything. You have got to believe that. There is no point to life if you don't believe that. Life without hope is no life at all; it's only hope that keeps us going. You must *not* give in. The doctors *will* find a cure, all they need is a little time.'

'Lisa, darling, you are simply not understanding what I am telling you. Time is the one thing I don't have.'

'Believe me. Listen to me now. They *will* find a cure.' She lifted her hands, flapping them around helplessly as if she didn't quite know where to put them. 'Look, I've got a couple of tickets for the Royal Ballet tonight. Let's dress up in our gladrags and go. *And* Michael Caine is having his Christmas Party at Langan's. I know you don't like Peter Langan – neither do I – but everyone will be there and we can have a good knees-up and forget all this ... this ...'

'Lisa, you haven't been listening. *I am going to die soon.* There is no cure for what I've got. There is nothing that can help you when your immune system breaks down – not even the Royal Ballet or a party at Langan's. I am going to die.'

'I forgot to tell you who called me last night, Billy Gibb, the frockmaker. You always liked Billy didn't you? He said *he* was going to Langan's tonight. I promise you, Harry, it is going to be a simply fabulous party.'

'Lisa, I am going to die soon.'

'Billy promised to send me over a new party frock too. Jean makes most of my stuff but Billy says it's time to try one of his. I've always liked the cut of Billy's stuff. He's a great designer – and an even greater cutter.'

'Lisa, I am going to die soon.'

'I'm hearing you Harry. I'm hearing you loud and clear but I'm gabbling on because I don't know what to say. What is there to say, Harry? Tell me and I'll say it. Just what is there to say when you keep telling me that you are going to die soon?' A lot more swallowing and the tears returned. 'Perhaps *you* ought to help *me* here. It's got that I'm not too good at understanding things any more and it's those ghosts that actually live with us; they are simply lodged in there and we can't get rid of them ...' She paused as she realised she had lost control of her poise, her lines, the script, the lot and that another character was speaking through her, taking over her mind and orchestrating her distress. She tried to take control of herself.

'Every man I care about has gone away or is living rough in the streets or is d... Look, Harry, just look at what I've brought you for Christmas. Open it now, if you like. It's ever such a lovely present and I'm sure you're going to adore it. Don't just sit there, Harry. Say something to me Harry.'

'Lisa, I am going to die soon.'

'Not that,' she screamed straight into his face, spit flecking his wasted features. 'Don't shove all that on me again.' She shook her head back and forth, crying more than ever. 'Talk to me about love, Harry. Tell me about love, a spirit all compact of fire. Tell me of love not gross to sink, but light and will aspire.'

'Lisa, darling, just *what* are you talking about?'

'I don't know, Harry. I don't have the smallest clue. I'm so upset I think I'm going mad. Something's broken inside me and I'm just shouting out words – any words. There's all these people inside me and they keep on shouting out their words too and I don't know what to do, Harry. What shall I ever do Harry? What shall I ever do?'

All afternoon she stood, marooned on an island of pain, crying into a sodden handkerchief under the traffic lights on the corner of Old Brompton Road and Warwick Road. Sometimes she turned the handkerchief around and around, looking for a dry patch. The afternoon light was soon breaking down and, when a packed London bus pulled to a halt at the red light, a few of the seated passengers noticed this small woman in a blue coat weeping alone on the pavement in the red spotlight. One or two did stare hard at her, half recognising those famous features in the shifting lights of the murky afternoon but no sooner had they begun asking themselves if that really could be *the* Lisa Moran, crying on the corner of Old Brompton Road and Warwick Road on Christmas Eve, than the spotlight changed to amber then to green and they were carried away into the city on the traffic's flowing tide.

ELEVEN

She knew she wasn't going to enjoy it; she wasn't in the mood for it and she would hate everyone she met at it, but she went to Michael Caine's party at Langan's anyway if only because she would get plain suicidal if she stayed in on her own.

Her eyeballs felt as if they had been peeled from so much crying lately but she had always been good at disguising her real feelings and did not even get too upset when she bumped straight into the unspeakable Victor Lownes of *Playboy* who yet again asked her to go out for a weekend to Stocks. She declined, politely, and thereafter moved slowly through the chattering, air-kissing mob, a drink in hand, stopping to talk to the occasional face, moving on again. What was the point of all this? Just *what* was the point?

Her radar kept sweeping the room but neither Maggie nor Judi nor even Joanie was there and Joanie went to everything. Glenda wasn't there either, one of the few working in the West End that winter and how Lisa could have done with some of Ava's Yankee cynicism on a night like this, but she'd gone missing too. These were the Division Two liggers of the season, they actually *enjoyed* being impaled in the tabloid gossip columns.

Michael Caine was such a pleasant, amusing man she couldn't even start to think where he'd dredged up this lot. A woman wearing cocktail gloves said she had been working on a farm and simply couldn't get rid of the smell of the pigs, hence her long gloves. Another was talking about the dreadful price of bananas in Knightsbridge. 'When I complained the shopkeeper said there was no such thing as cheap bananas in Knightsbridge.' Taped carols screeched in the background like musical migraines. The pop of champagne corks mingled with expensive perfume and cloying aftershave. Cameras flashed like summer lightning – this was a party with publicity in mind.

Jewelled taffeta cocktail dresses tied at the shoulder were the fashion that season. So were metallic sheaths, ruched from cleavage to crotch. The women still fancied being Marilyn Monroe but there were a few tight busts above black puff-ball skirts and strappy Manolo Blahnik shoes.

Lisa began chatting with someone whose name she couldn't remember about someone else whose name both had forgotten. It was hard to put up with these smooth women who wanted to be Marilyn Monroe and their oily men who wanted to be Bryan Ferry, their eyes constantly swivelling around to see who was and who was not there. That's what she always loved about Daniel; he sort of hovered over her and fixed her with a smile and a blue-eyed stare which remained fixed no matter who was around. He sort of held her in the arms of his eyes and oh Daniel where are you now? Always so real, always so ready to admit to disgusting things like how he had been sick three times before breakfast that morning. He couldn't keep a secret or tell a lie, another reason, she supposed, why she had found him so attractive. She was always boiling over with secrets and lies and did so wish she could simply dump them all somewhere and just be herself. Be like him.

So here we were again, on yet another hopeless Christmas Eve, sitting on the pity pot with this man *still* talking about someone whose name they both still couldn't remember. 'Oh you know, the one who made an absolute mint out of the rag trade in the Sixties.'

A waitress offered to refill her glass but she covered it with her free hand. She could feel her chest tightening and it was becoming difficult to breathe. Her eyes looked around in desperation but only recognised Lady Falkender, Lord Longford and one of Princess Margaret's Ladies-in-Waiting, Lady Davinia Thingy-Thingy. Viscount Weymouth's fingers, one of them covered in a jewel-encrusted sheath, were toying with his pigtail. Money was completely wasted on some.

'Lisa, my deah, how perfectly wonderful to see you. It must have been in Cannes we last met. On the terrace of the Carlton wasn't it? After the premier of that hospital film you did with Lindsay.'

She was turning to face yet another bore when a snorting, bull-necked drunk with gimlet eyes lumbered up shouting: 'Lisa, you old cow' and whipped his hand straight up her skirt, almost grabbing her startled fanny. Peter Langan, the proprietor, was being his charming Irish best as usual. Not so long ago she would have punched him in the eye but she was too upset to even consider such an extravagant response and turned away from the vulgar bastard, worried she was about to faint. Another smiling face hoved into her failing sight.

This just couldn't go on. She had to get out of all this and into a real world somewhere; live in a mining village in Yorkshire perhaps where men were men who wouldn't dream of whipping their fat hands up your skirt. In public anyway. All this artifice and affectation was no use to her: she wanted to be in a place with real people who acted in a real way. DH Lawrence had always been her novelist and she wanted to be in his world, full of hard driving sex, genuine emotions and people who thought with their blood. Yes, that's exactly where she wanted to be. Certainly not here with all these precious tarts and their ponces. Oh Daniel!

Langan looked as if he might be about to grab her again and for one moment she did feel her body swooning and her eyes closing as the taped carol singers burbled: 'God rest you merry gentlemen ...'. There was always a rush of suicides at Christmas, she had been told, and she now understood why. They had all been to a party at Langan's. This new face's perfume wasn't helping either and, with a sort of muted yelp, which could have meant anything, she put her glass down on the table and ran – *ran!* – for the cloakroom, her coat and the front door.

The cold edge of the night in Stratton Street revived her a little and she was already feeling less anxious as she strolled near Green Park wondering if she might try one of the quieter drinking clubs in the West End. Yet she was still furious with Langan who was managing to get more and more gross by the hour.

Piccadilly Circus was in its usual seasonal uproar of drunken celebrants falling into gutters. She continued to Leicester Square with its gaudy neon cinema hoardings, where she had seen her own name more than a few times. But she had never had any success with her films: all of them turkeys, made for the money and thoroughly deserving the critical pastings they had received.

The one form she had always enjoyed was radio, where there were no parts you couldn't play because you didn't look right. Radio is drama at its purest, she had always thought, using as it did only the voice of the actor and the imagination of the audience. The great pity was that there had never been any money in radio.

But her one great and abiding love, of course, was for the stage although there had been even less money in that. There had barely been a theatre in the West End she hadn't graced at some time or other; the stage was almost her private domain and she had ruled it ruthlessly. If anyone ever tried to steal a scene from her, she always stole it straight back with interest. She knew how to steal another actor's applause, and little tricks like how to win back the affection of the audience when it had strayed too far elsewhere.

She stood outside the neo-classical columns of the Haymarket, scene of a few successes and more than a few disasters. Just now Susan Hampshire was doing *Crucifix of Blood* in there which, she'd heard, was not quite as dreadful as it sounded but nearly so.

All at once, smiling warmly in the cold air, she remembered that the Haymarket was the very theatre where she and John O had finally decided to make a go of it together. She was still a relatively unknown actress in *The Seagull*, playing the role of Masha, often with no desire to go on living and in mourning for her life. Masha was unable to love and be loved and there *he* was, just sitting there on a chair in the wings, his possessions in a carrier bag he had packed that afternoon after telling Penelope that he was leaving her, and sitting there, watching her every move and listening to her every word, the most famous playwright in the world just sitting there waiting for Lisa Moran.

When she wasn't actually on the stage she sat on his lap canoodling until her cue and then she kept getting emotionally confused as she spoke her lines about loss. 'I shall tear love out of my heart by the roots,' Masha had cried as she gazed at John with her heart overflowing with longing and, yes, yes, love.

So they went to her Shepherd's Bush flat together and practically made its walls sing as, in two weeks, she managed to take a stone off him in sheer pleasurable exercise and he not only became the most famous playwright in the world but also one of the slimmest and, for a while, the happiest. Oh John it was so good once. Where did it all go wrong? How had Masha 'of dubious descent and resident in this world for reasons unknown' gone and fucked it all up again?

Yet despite everything their marriage had lasted thirteen years, encompassing his major successes in which she had so often heard her own voice. All his big plays had come from her, she had inhabited all his leading female roles, even the ones she hadn't played herself, and it was no accident that he was now embittered and silent, living with his usherette with fat ankles in the country and, apparently, unable to get out of bed unless he had half a bottle of champagne chilling.

'Never get involved with a man who hates his mother because he'll always end up hating you,' she had told a hack. 'And ask him if he is ever going to write another play or does he want me to go over there and tell him how to do it?'

And frigid? Her? Frigid! She had taken him on sexual roller coaster rides to heaven and back often enough. She knew exactly what kept John O happy and, if he wasn't careful, she was going to spill the beans on him in the public prints in full.

She strode down to Trafalgar Square, its wide open spaces – this 'front room' of London – looking simply lovely with the huge Christmas tree lit up like a million glittering dollars and the shiny black Landseer lions stretched out peaceably on their plinths around Nelson's Column. It was unusually quiet for this time of night and year, just a few insomniac pigeons clockworking around looking for something to eat. Most of the revellers must be enjoying the livelier flesh-pots of Piccadilly or Soho, she thought. For a while, she watched a man cooking chestnuts on a brazier then, half hoping to flag down a taxi to take her home, crossed the square to St Martin-in-the-Fields, where Midnight Mass was in full swing.

The Church was packed, so she stood in the porch to listen to the triumphal singing. Christmas, she knew, was supposed to be an affirmation of life yet she had never really understood why all she had ever got out of it was loneliness and loss. It had always been the same for as long as she could remember. Everyone was happy at this time of goodwill — or at least *pretending* to be so — and there she was boiling over with angry gloom. She could not remember one single Christmas that she had ever enjoyed. Not one!

After the Mass finished some street people were making their way down into St Martin's crypt where many of them would spend their Christmas. 'Excuse me,' she shouted at no one in particular. 'Would any of you know where I might find Ironing Board Dave?'

'Probably over at the Maple dance for dossers in King's Cross,' a voice shouted back. 'Goes there every Christmas Eve. Right behind the station.'

TWELVE

The taxi dropped her opposite King's Cross. A woman with her leg in plaster limped past pushing a supermarket trolley. The black, disjointed mass inside the trolley was a folded-up man with the lower half of his body dangling over the end. He was so drunk he could barely locate his mouth to shove his bottle of VP sherry into it.

'Look at this bastard here,' the woman said to Lisa, stopping to catch her breath. 'My 'usband. Huh! Look at the bleedin' state of 'im. I breaks me leg in a fall. 'E offers to take me to the Maple party in a trolley, goes an' gets one from Tesco's an' comes back so bleedin' pissed *I*'ave to push *'im* to the bleedin' party.'

'Evening,' said the drunk, waving his sherry bottle around in greeting. 'Fancy a swig of this do yer?'

'Here, I'll help you,' Lisa offered. 'I'm going to the Maple party too.'

''E's always doing this to me,' the woman grumbled. 'Story of me life, really.'

'I'd get rid of him if I were you,' Lisa advised. 'There's not a man alive who's worth a tuppenny wank. Not one.'

On the next corner they bumped into three Irish dossers with wild tangles of hair poking out from beneath the rims of their woollen bobble caps. They were also on their way to the party and, it being Christmas, offered Lisa swigs from their whisky bottles. Soon all five were making their way up the pavement in a cloud of riotous, drunken laughter and chinking bottles. They cleared the railway station, passed the Midland goods depot and headed for the giant iron gasometers which were floating in the silvery blue night like a squadron of Stone Age flying saucers.

In the absence of anything more intelligent to do they began taking it in turns to give the supermarket trolley a good shove, sending the drunk careering forwards in rattling surges with a left-handed bias until the trolley, for no apparent reason, veered sharply right, shot off the kerb and fell on its side with a bright musical clash of wires as it hit the side of a parked car. Its drunken occupant bashed his head on the car bumper, broke his sherry bottle and, judging by his heart-felt, foul-mouthed oaths, was not best pleased.

He was being helped up when one of the dossers began shouting the compliments of the season at a couple of beefy tarts in ocelot coats, half-frozen as they tried to drum up a bit of last-minute business before the Christmas close-down. 'Never mind about those clapped-out bodies tonight. The Maple party should have started by now.'

'Who you fucking calling clapped-out? You can try it if you want.'

'Not fucking likely. Never been that desperate.'

Everyone joined in the laughter as the banter continued and Lisa could never remember having so much fun as here with all her new mates, all gladragged up for the Maple. These were *her* people for sure and she felt a lot more alive with them than at Langan's.

Lisa's gang was about a dozen strong when they clattered into the warehouse arm in arm. Two tough-looking bouncers were on the door, put there, she guessed, to throw out anyone who looked too respectable. She had put on her sunglasses and, head bowed, flapped her hands a bit suggesting some kind of street idiocy to tell the bouncers she belonged too.

Inside several hundred people were milling about beneath the criss-crossing iron girders, many with a bottle in one hand and a chicken leg or French loaf in the other as a rock band was tuning up on a makeshift stage at the far end. Various organisations and churches in the city took in dossers over Christmas providing there was no drink or drugs but for this highly alternative party, organised by highly alternative people, almost anything was on offer which would guarantee you total oblivion for Christmas. The first man Lisa bumped into was carrying a tray of illegal substances and smokes. 'Get your drugs here. A bit of blow. Uppers. Downers. Get your drugs here.'

She picked a hand-made joint out of the various pills and capsules and the waiter lit it with a long flare of a butane lighter. He looked a good advertisement for the drugs he was giving out: as dirty as a dustman, hair all over the place and dried blood splattered across his left cheek. 'Happy Christmas,' he said, squinting at her so hard it was as if he had seen that face before but said nothing.

'And to you darling.'

Her first long toke rifled every corner of her brain and she felt amazingly light-headed as she threaded through the jostling throng. The Black Tarantula was there as was One-Eyed Jack, oddly well-behaved with a couple of painted whores, his mouth full of mince pie. A woman in a Yankee baseball cap gave Lisa a kiss full on the lips. It was a bit like French kissing a dumper truck, she decided but, by now, she had acquired yet another joint and was too stoned to care. Miss Yankee could have another kiss at any time.

The rock band were clearly on all manner of banned Class A drugs too since, after the most perfunctory of tune-ups, they began tearing into number after number as if they had to perform somewhere far more important in about five minutes' time. The well-zonked party was already getting higher and higher while the singer must have taken everything on the drugs tray in one big cocktail, the way he slurred his way through most of his largely incomprehensible lyrics. One of his arms was tied up with bloodied bandages, he had a hump back and, the way he was standing, it looked as if one leg was a good six inches shorter than the other. He was a complete mess so there was a fetching irony in his rendition of Free's *All Right Now*. They continued with *Everyone Wants to Shag* followed by an equally tender working of the Rezillos' *Someone's Going to Get Their Head Kicked In Tonight*. The light show was furnished by a few lines of winking traffic bollards while occasionally – and only occasionally – they did a slow country'n'western number like the gently satirical *Take Your Tongue Out of My Mouth Because I'm Kissing You Goodbye*.

This was shaping up to be the only Christmas Lisa had ever enjoyed as she held her special fag up high and jigged around and around in this seething, skirling sea of dope and stinking bodies. She had no idea who she was actually dancing with – sometimes it was the tart in the baseball cap, who seemed to have taken a fancy to her, sometimes a lively little whore with a Dolly Parton bosom. The Black Tarantula bobbed up at one stage, dealing Lisa a painful jab in her side with an elbow. Another sadistic nutcase, Lisa thought as she pogoed off to safety – only to fall into a jigging twosome with a bombed-out, slavering, overcoated tramp. No one took their coats off in the Maple, no matter how happy or hot they got and it might have been the first party she had ever attended where everyone wore at least three coats. The very air dripped with sweat.

The band swept into *Jailhouse Rock* and the dancers were but a community of stoned joy when, with the next number, the Monkees' *Daydream Believer*, the band took everyone even higher. The Black Tarantula was edging alarmingly close to her again, now hoisting up her skirt with both hands and showing she had no knickers. A man collapsed on the floor, exhausted, legs and arms akimbo as others tried to revive him by pissing over him steamily.

Just then a gap opened up in the dancers and, rather like that classic, enchanted moment in *West Side Story*, when Richard Beymer first spots Natalie Wood in the dance in the gym, everything went still for Lisa and she took off her sunglasses to get a better look. *Right there* was Daniel Jenkins, the Missing Link, The Great Visionary from Dalston Lane, with wild, dishevelled hair and dressed in an old coat, jumping around in the spotlight with a French loaf sticking out of his flies like the largest dildo she'd ever seen. He was so drunk or stoned his blue eyes were but tiny red buttons and, as he waved his loaf around, he bellowed in a drunken, Welsh accent: 'Come on and get it boys and girls. Come and grapple with the monster of the deep.'

The dishevelled and drunk nutcase dancing with him was presumably Ironing Board Dave.

Stock-still, she pondered, as she took another long toke on her joint, love's bizarre malice. How could she have gone and fallen for *that?* All her friends frequently said *she* was potty but *he* was far pottier than her at her pottiest. He didn't even have a shilling, didn't own a thing of value. 'As soon as you own something everyone wants to take it off you,' he had once said. 'Possessions are prisons. Destitution is the only key to freedom.'

Extremely shy, Natalie Wood finally walked over to her handsome Richard Beymer, stood in front of him and hoped he would recognise her. But he didn't.

'What I need is another drink,' he grumbled to no one in particular. 'Why can't we ever get enough to drink? No serious drinker *ever* gets enough to drink. Two hundred drinks is never enough if you are a serious drinker. Bladders to it, I say.'

'You've had enough, I'd say.'

'Tell her Dave. Tell her I *need* that drink. Just tell her.' Daniel was doing a lot of swallowing now, interspersed with hiccups. His unshaven face was ghostly pallid and she took a step backwards in case he decided to throw up all over her.

'Give the man a fucking drink,' Dave told Lisa as if she was some kind of waitress. The band was making such a noise they had to shout straight into one another's ears.

'I think he's had enough already. You shouldn't give him all this drink you know. He's not a well man and I think he should come home with me now.'

''Oo the fucking hell are you then?'

Daniel was swaying dangerously as he began patting his overcoat pockets, perhaps hoping to find a bottle in there somewhere. The band began *Heard it on the Grapevine* and a fight had broken out about ten feet away. 'Got to have a drink. Jus' one drink an' I'll feel fine,' Daniel said as he cupped his hand under his chin and coughed up blood into it. Another cough brought up more blood and he held it out for Lisa to examine. Richard Beymer hadn't acted like this in that West Side gym.

'See? If you'd given me that drink this wouldn't have happened,' he told her in deadly earnest. 'Ah,' he added, cocking a ear. '*Heard it on the Grapevine.* One of my favourite records of all ...'

He choked on something, his body whirled around and he let loose a torrent of blood spattering everyone in sight. *West Side Story* had turned into *The Texas Chainsaw Massacre*. Lisa started to scream for someone to ring for a fucking ambulance as he fell forwards into her arms and brought up another stream of blood which gushed straight over her shoulder and ran, monstrously, down the back of her coat. 'Get a fucking ambulance,' she screamed again as she laid him on the floor, noticing that his trousers had also gone red with blood. *Who would have thought the old man to have so much blood in him?*

'Ah ... it's you, Lisa, isn't it?' he asked, chewing on some more blood. 'The most beautiful woman in the world.' More coughing, spattering red sprays of spit everywhere.

'Daniel, darling, I've told you a hundred times drink just isn't good for you. Look at the mess you've gone and got yourself in now.'

'It wouldn't have happened if I'd had another drink,' he persisted. 'One more would have settled my belly down a treat.'

'Your drinking days are over you dull cunt. You've drunk your last.'

Lisa fluttered anxiously around the paramedics as they stretchered Daniel into an ambulance. He looked so blank and still, close to snuffing it for all she knew and, when Ironing Board Dave climbed into the ambulance with them, she ordered him out. 'Haven't you done enough damage?' she shouted with a motherly outrage. 'He's never going out with *you* again. I suppose you're Welsh as well are you? You're all raving pissheads every single one of you. I know about the Welsh.'

She kneeled by Daniel's side and held his hand as the ambulance, lights flashing and sirens wailing, sped to St Bartholomew's Hospital. As soon as it stopped she hurdled out, screaming for help, rushing around Casualty, buttoning anyone unlucky enough to be wearing a white coat. Fuss like this always works in hospitals, she knew from old. The meek might inherit the earth but they'll never get so much as a dud placebo out of Margaret Thatcher's National Health Service.

Within minutes she had duty doctors and medical orderlies, some with mistletoe or tinsel in their hair, wafting from distant parties and all agreeing with her that the NHS had gone to the dogs as she directed to them to the corridor where Daniel was stretched out on his trolley.

He was examined quickly but thoroughly, then taken away for a transfusion. A whole line of hospital workers, led by Lisa, pushed him across the courtyard, past a fountain and under a canopy of bare branches. In the ward a nurse took a blood sample as Lisa made a quick inspection of the place, discovering bodies collapsed on beds all over the place. One called out constantly for Kevin; others had broken legs pullied up into the air, heads swathed in bandages and tubes up their noses. The smell of disinfectant began to get to her and no sooner were they putting up bags of blood for Daniel than she was tapping one of the doctors on the shoulder. 'He can't stay here. It's far too noisy in here for someone as sensitive as Mr Jenkins. Haven't you got some sort of *private* ward?'

THIRTEEN

Daniel stayed in a private room for a few weeks and, after the doctors had done their rounds and lunch had been served, Lisa found she could flick the latch on the door, take off some clothes and just jump into bed with Daniel and enfold him like an old shawl for a few hours.

There was none of the old malarkey and they simply enjoyed holding one another, listening to one another's heartbeats or shifting their bodies around together. She never told Daniel but she had done this once before with Joseph Creasey, the film director, during his final days when he was dying from cancer. She would wander around to his Chelsea house in the afternoons, climb into bed with him and they merely held one another, not saying anything at all because, when you are dying of cancer, there is nothing to say.

Even after a lifetime of great achievement, with so many films that captured the *zeitgeist* so accurately and portrayed relationships with a sensitivity rare in the cinema, all dear old Joe wanted was some simple love and affection to ease his way out and she provided that right up to his final hours.

Daniel was hardly dying, of course, and was making a clear recovery but the doctors had warned him to take it slowly and carefully. The endoscopy test had shown that the exploding ulcer was on the mend but, on the one time during their long embraces, when he became sufficiently aroused to put it inside her, his belly became so sore and painful he had to pull it out again.

But she was relaxed about that: didn't even think of staging a horror show as she might have at other times in other circumstances. The ghosts weren't playing her up too much these days; they only tended to give her grief when she was unhappy or lonely and she wasn't either of those just now. She was simply a girl in love as her ghosts snoozed quietly.

She brought him little gifts every day or the seafood sandwiches he liked so much and she didn't indulge in any unruly, starry behaviour either, not picking on the doctors or bullying the nurses, signing the odd autograph for the patients and even flirting with a few of the men there if she thought they might be of any use to her.

Unlike Harry Kirby, who was looking increasingly stricken every day, this other man in her life was going to get well and she didn't care what she had to do to get him the best treatment. This time she was going to clear the decks and build a stable and secure love before it was too late. No more juggling with other relationships. Just this one, on this bed, where she could see him and keep her arms around him in case he made a run for it.

She did understand and appreciate the grave risk in trying to build anything at all on the most insecure foundations of Daniel Jenkins but he seemed worth the risk and had so much that appealed to her on every level. He was brave, an artist, committed to his work. Few were as good as him in bed – except when he was recovering from a burst ulcer – and she adored chatting with him when he was in the mood, particularly about his curious relationship with God.

And then there was Daniel's obsession with London which made even less sense to her, particularly as he was from fucking Wales. Of late he had again been telling her how he planned to explore the whole sewer system of London in a solo expedition which could take up to a month. He had even obtained maps of the metropolitan sewers and was trying to work out his route which would form the keel of his ship which he wanted to build like a huge liner. But would this liner actually ever sail, she often wondered, even if Kennington had been sufficiently impressed with the bit they'd read to give him a small advance. Perhaps mercifully you didn't come across anyone like this every day. Yes, there was only one Daniel Jenkins.

His one rather odd, if not unique, feature was that he was unattached. Chekhov had said that love wasn't worth having if you didn't steal it from someone else and she'd done a fair share of that in her time but had never been convinced it was right. She was also enjoying the fact that she could conduct this affair in the open or at least as open as you could ever be with those bastards from the Press lurking in every shadow.

The nature of their relationship appeared to have changed again. Where she had often found herself malleable and smitten, she seemed to have a little control over it now, making decisions which he – never the most co-operative of men – seemed happy to go along with. Perhaps he simply needed to rely on her when he was weak and uncertain, and he didn't even seem to need to write in this state, was just happy to hold her in the afternoons – which pleased her more than she could say.

'Daniel, come and stay with me for a while in Chelsea and get on with your book. I could give you all the safety and security you need for your work. You could take the spare room at the top of the house and maybe we could even find ourselves a little hideaway house in Suffolk for weekends.'

'You're talking like someone who's just got their hands on some money. How could we find a little hideaway house in Suffolk if you're as broke as you're always saying you are?'

Well there was a simple reason for that, she had better admit before he found out elsewhere, which was that she had finally accepted that Israeli crock: six weeks' work, two on interiors in London and four on location in Israel. After a lot of humming and haahing, between herself, Karen Duffy and the producer, she had wrung a huge fee out of them, an insanely high fee for lates – so high there certainly wouldn't be any lates – and her own hairdresser and wardrobe mistress. She had also managed to get them to agree to take her name off the credits and, although she hadn't yet told Daniel about this bit, they had agreed she could take her boyfriend with her to Jerusalem, at their expense.

Nothing had been too much trouble. They would even let her look at the dailies if she wanted *and* were even prepared to negotiate further on a slice of the box-office profits. But Lisa had told Karen to forget about that because, as certain as night follows day, there wouldn't be any. 'Karen, believe me. I've read the script. This might even become the biggest turkey of all time and it won't make a fucking penny.'

The story concerned a young Israeli psychopath *fighting for the Arab cause* who keeps bombing and shooting everyone in sight until, for purely symbolic reasons which she couldn't even start to fathom, he ends up on his own in the cliff-top fort of Masada fighting the whole Israeli army. The working title of the film was *Rebellion*.

Fortunately she wasn't having anything to do with the Masada mayhem but she was the mother of the nutty terrorist who kept tracking him through the Negev desert in some desperate, if doomed, attempt to get him to see the error of his ways. The mother was pretty demented herself but Lisa was quite relaxed about that: she often quipped she had graduated with an honours degree in dementia.

But she did feel rather odd and even invaded when, fully recovered, Daniel was finally discharged and she took him home to Cheyne Walk. She had been living on her own for about ten years now – and had got perfectly used to it – so it didn't look quite right seeing him sitting in her living room, feet up and reading a newspaper, with Juliet, Hedda and Regina gazing down. He didn't have to feel imprisoned at all, she kept insisting; he could come and go as he pleased and, if he wanted to go back to Hackney, that was all right too.

Yet, despite such reservations, she was still very keen for it to work between them and had even sent the dog for a long holiday in kennels so he didn't get too much under Daniel's feet until he had settled down. There were only two rules, she decreed: he shouldn't drink and wasn't to bring any floozies back here when she wasn't around.

'The doctors didn't say I couldn't drink again,' he pointed out. 'All they said was I should drink in moderation.'

'Your drinking days are over, my love. Lost and by the wind mourned.'

'I really do need a few drinks, Lisa. It relaxes me and I need to relax or I don't perform too well at you know what.'

'You seem to be doing all right,' she lied since he hadn't been performing too well at you know what lately, all nerves and shortcomings. She'd guessed what it was and had once crushed a few tranquillisers with a garlic press and dropped it in his bedtime cocoa without telling him. But all that had done – had she put in too many? – was put him straight to sleep.

'I don't think so and anyway I always do it better after a few drinks. Always have done really.'

This seemed a pretty unassailable argument for the joys of alcohol so they soon found themselves having a few gin and tonics before going out in the evening then quickly falling into much the same routine of first going out to see Harry Kirby, having dinner somewhere and then wandering into some pub for an hour or two before going home and falling into bed.

Harry was still going down with some stupid infection or other but at least he seemed to accept – and even approve of – Daniel which was more than can be said of most of her men whom he had often actively hated without even meeting them. 'But this one actually seems to be bringing you out in a nice glow,' he had told her. 'You should hang on to this one.'

Well that was precisely what she was hoping to do as they ate at Drake's or Victor's, then strolled the length of the King's Road, hand in hand window-shopping before having a quiet pint somewhere like the Markham Arms, one of the few public houses where Lisa could relax without being bothered by the regulars. Having such a public and recognisable face, even with her sunglasses on, still kept throwing up all kinds of difficulties, with strangers telling her about horoscopes or would-be writers wondering if she fancied reading a script of theirs. But she dealt with them all calmly – there was never any point in getting angry or even showing irritation – and, fortunately, Daniel was always very relaxed about it too. But there again he was always relaxed when he had a pint in his hand, she noticed darkly. Put him in a pub and he never stopped beaming; he might even have been born in one.

They often stopped to kiss with tangling tongues in dark doorways on their walks and she particularly loved it when he managed to worm his warm hands down the back of her knickers, hoisting her up by the bum and getting her to squirm so much she looked like a somewhat upset worm on the hook of a fishing line. Then she got so excited by this she would have quite liked to have got on with it there and then except he always said it was best if they waited and just thought about it a while.

Then, when she announced she was fed up with thinking about it and wanted to get on with it, he would almost always find another pub and they would fall chatting in another corner, just gossiping away and her telling him about her men, perhaps, often about Albert who had caused her marriage to John O to break down. She had actually told John O about Albert and had left him in bed crying but then, when she met Albert, she changed her mind about him in mid-speech on one of the corners of King's Road in the pouring rain. She had never really understood why she had done that and could still recall all that pain in Albert's face as he stood there crying as copiously as the rain.

They laughed a lot until he couldn't find any more pubs that were open and they got home where, in bed, they became warm and tight, understanding one another's needs more and coming to rely on one another's bodies to relieve any lingering anxieties.

It worked well for her too, although she was becoming rather worried about the way he really did seem to perform better the more he had to drink. That was a real worry and another was that she always nodded off after they had finished but he often got up after sleeping for an hour or so and sat in the living room where she had caught him a few times gazing out at the Thames sadly, as if he was missing someone.

Maybe it was all down to her ever present insecurity but she did wonder if there was another woman threatening her newly found happiness. He had never mentioned anyone but, perhaps precisely because of that – since everyone has someone – she was sure that there was another woman somewhere and she wanted to know about her, if only to see what she was up against. But, if there was, he wasn't telling and she wasn't about to start pushing him either so she left him to his Thames vigil and crept silently back up the stairs to lie in her bed, gazing at the ceiling and chewing her lower lip.

FOURTEEN

Wearing an Arab headscarf and shouldering a bulky black bag Lisa was struggling across the desert. The winds of the Sherav, all whirling sand and shimmer, had begun to blow from the faraway Sahara and she bent low into them, her hands rearranging her headscarf as the sand tore at her eyes and wormed into her mouth. Sometimes the winds whipped up the sand into tiny tornadoes which drilled into the sides of the dunes or settled on a spiky cactus and tried to throttle it to death. This was the worst time of the year for such a trip and the sands were glowing with a furnace intensity when they were not being blown around by these furious winds, scything into everything and trying to pick a hot quarrel with everyone.

All around her, as far as the eye could see, was a savage landscape of gaping wadi and harsh ridges. Sometimes a Bedouin on his camel would appear, black on yellow, out of a gusting sandstorm, then disappear. Streams of sand went riffling around her sandaled feet; ants had bitten into her legs, bringing them out in nasty red lumps while her lips were swollen and cracked. But despite all this aggravation she somehow managed to retain an intense dignity in her bearing.

She reached the edge of the oasis and unpeeled her headscarf slowly as she looked down at the young man standing by the sheltered pool. A white bandana was wound around his forehead and two bandoliers of ammunition criss-crossed his bare, muscled chest. His face was darkly handsome with hooded eyes and a nose that could have belonged to a bird of prey. Behind him two Kalashnikovs lay next to a rucksack. He caught sight of her shadow in the pool but said nothing as he turned to gaze up at her, shielding his eyes from the romping sand with one hand.

'I knew you would be out here, Raz,' she shouted down at him. 'Mothers know everything about their sons.'

'You shouldn't have come. This is private business. All this has nothing to do with you.'

She put her bag down on the ridge carefully. 'It has everything to do with me. Your blood is my blood. I am your mother. I brought you into this country.'

'That was then. There is new business now. Private business. It's my laundry we're talking about here.' He wrinkled up his nose and bared his teeth in frustration. 'How the hell did my laundry get into all this? Oh fuck, fuck, fuck.'

'Cut, cut, cut.'

Avie Glick, the director, flung his jockey cap down and kicked it savagely. The wind machines were switched off and the Sherav ceased to blow. The cameraman lit a cigarette while the dyslexic actor, Yuri Pucket, began throwing his thick arms around in the fervent Israeli manner. 'Avie, there's too many words in this script. I'm a man of action. I don't do words.'

A young girl ran up to daub some sand-coloured slap onto Lisa's glaring face. How had this man managed to develop such a third-class brain inside his first-class body? He couldn't learn the simplest lines and she had already advised him to cut out all dialogue and stick to shoot and splatter films. Just concentrate on the bullets, Yuri, and leave the words for someone who can use them.

Yet, just for now, she was being the consummate professional and she picked up her bag for the fourth time that morning and trudged back out into the desert, tracked by the boom camera, until the signal came for the clapperboard to crack, the tiny tornadoes to resume, the Sherav to begin blowing again and for her to restart her Lawrence of Arabia gig.

'I knew you would be out here, Raz. Mothers know everything about their sons.'

'You shouldn't have come. This is private business. All this has nothing to do with you.'

She put down her bag. 'It has everything to do with me. Your blood is my blood. I am your mother. I brought you into this country.'

'Then was that. There is new business now. Private business. We've all got to do our own laundry now. *Then was that? Doing our own laundry?* Can someone please explain to me what the fuck I'm talking about? I can't understand these lines. There's too many words and I don't understand any of them.'

'Cut, cut, cut.'

Avie Glick's luckless jockey cap got thrown to the ground yet again and, by way of a change, he jumped on it. 'Take five everyone. We'll rewrite Yuri's lines. Just give him two lines and stick them on idiot boards behind those palms. Reading you can do, can you, Yuri?'

The Mercedes dropped Lisa off at the American Colony Hotel, just next to the Garden Tomb outside the walls of Old Jerusalem, and she rushed shrieking silently into her suite to find Daniel sitting peaceably on their bed, smoking a cigarette and looking out onto the dusty city where the late afternoon traffic was battling its way home after another hard, hot day in the Holy Land.

'You look as if you could do with a stiff drink,' he said.

'Make that half a dozen,' she cried as she began taking her clothes off for a shower.

Well at least he was happy enough here, she thought as she pushed her face up against the sprinkling water, trying to wash off memories of the day and untold lumps of the Negev which seemed to have got into every orifice. She could never remember seeing him so happy and relaxed. After he had agreed to accompany her here he had immediately started worrying that, being in Jerusalem, God might start chatting to him again. 'Don't laugh, Lisa, this is God's home town and, if he's going to start talking to me again, it is almost certainly going to be here.'

'Don't be so daft. If we know anything at all about God we know he's not predictable or clichéd. He's only ever a force in his own right and he'd never talk to anyone here, least of all you.'

'You wouldn't find much support for that view in the Bible. He was always talking to *everyone* here, out in those very streets.'

'That was all ages ago and anyway they're all now too busy fighting one another to listen to a God of love. Anyway I keep telling you. God has got fed up and has moved on to another project.'

And not only did God not talk to Daniel out here, as he had been fearing, but he was absolutely loving being here, exploring the city on his own while she was out in the desert having her very arse boiled by the heat and all that stupidity.

Without even drying herself she fell straight onto the bed next to him bumping her face up and down onto the pillow as he began to massage her shoulders. 'I've never felt you so tight and bunched,' he said, kneading her pain. 'Look, there's a nice gin and tonic here, fizzing away and asking to be drunk.'

She sat up finally, uninterested in the drink, her face slippery with tears. 'Oh Daniel, I've been in some messes,' she wailed. 'But I've never been in a mess like this. They're all kids. They don't know *anything*; they don't know anything at all.'

Slowly, punctuated by much nose-blowing and sighs, she explained how this prize prick of a director had got a lot of money from the Israeli government as well as the co-operation of the army. But now government officials had discovered that the film was about an Israeli fighting for the Arabs. So the money and the army, if not the film itself, were in danger of being stopped forthwith if it was going to be one long advertisement for the fucking Palestinians.

Then it had turned out Avie Glick had shown one script to the government, which they had approved, but was working from a completely different one, which he wouldn't show them because he wanted to make some obscure fucking point about artistic freedom. All day long they had been trying to do a few scenes while a million big-mouthed executives were busy arguing the toss about the script, who was exactly on whose side, the meaning of patriotism, who was pissing on the flag and God alone knew what else.

Daniel got up off the bed and held out his arms wide. 'Well, it's very easy isn't it?' he said softly. 'Let's just go home. You're a distinguished actress and you don't need all this crap. Let's just go home and forget all about it.'

She shook her head vigorously and continually. 'If only it was that easy.'

'It is. We can pack our bags. Go straight to the airport and take the next plane to London. I'll ring the airport now, if you like.'

She sat down at the dressing table, moving her lips around in the mirror before picking up a powder puff and patting under her eyes, still bloodshot from tears and sand. 'Daniel, you just can't walk out of a contract and, anyway, I really do need the money.'

'Lisa, I can get work. I haven't worked since my illness but I'm sure I can get some work – well-paid work for a magazine or something.'

She regarded him coldly. 'What do you mean by well-paid work? I don't want you to get work of any kind. You've *got* work. Your work is writing books. You have the noblest calling known to man; you are the last of the free men. I love you because you're an artist and I don't want you going out to look for any work. For money. You are a real writer who has yet to find his way and I wouldn't dream of asking you to work. For money. I believe in you. Money's my problem and we're not going to solve it by running away on a plane.'

He was so overwhelmed by what she had said he sat down on the bed and couldn't say a word.

'I've never made any real money,' she continued, turning to powder her face in the mirror again. 'Stage actresses never do. I might *seem* to have a lot but the truth is I'm poorer than a church mouse. If I lose this film I'll probably end up penniless. We just can *not* go home.'

'Well, at least we've got something in common. Being broke, I mean.'

'Yes, we do have that.'

'So then.' He clapped his hands, a mannerism he had picked up off her when it was time to change the direction if not the tenor of the conversation. 'We'll just have to stay. Israelis are famously argumentative so they're bound to argue their way to some compromise in the end. I'll stay and help you in any way you want: carry your bags, do your toenails, write you some decent lines. So, what's modom's pleasure?'

'Daniel, it would be almost bearable if you weren't so happy here. What's going on in that stupid brain of yours anyway?'

'Oh, I just love it here and maybe, perhaps for the first time, I feel we're equals; a pair of broken bums in the Holy Land.'

'Don't put me on the same level as you, you smug bastard.'

'Yes we are, a pair of broken bums in the Holy Land. Now I'm getting hungry but I'm not quite sure for what, if you get my drift. So are we going to have a bit of the oh-be-joyful now or are we going straight to dinner or what?'

She gave one of her best chipmunk smiles to the mirror, almost her first that day. 'I tell you what. Let's have a bit of the oh-be-joyful and then go to dinner.'

Right through dinner she could not stop herself smiling at him through the candlelight. She didn't want much food – just two plates of *hors d'oeuvres* – and kept smiling at him goofily like a schoolgirl smitten for the first time. She laughed often and loud as he described his wanderings through Old Jerusalem, his encounters with obnoxious traders, his visit to the nearby Garden Tomb where the angel rolled away the stone and his idea that he might do a small book about the city since he didn't see how he could write a book about London while he was here in Jerusalem. She laughed at his every quip. In her present mood, she would have laughed if he had read her the Israeli telephone directory.

'So, when you were out walking around Jerusalem today, what I want to know is did you miss me a lot, sort of half-way or not at all?'

He put down the knife and fork with which he had been dismembering a steak to have a little think about this and a couple on the next table were also clearly interested in how much had he had missed her. 'To ... be ... perfectly honest. I'd say about half-way.'

'Your trouble is you never quite say the right thing. It would also help if you weren't quite so honest. So then. Why can't you just say you missed me a lot?'

'All right. I missed you a lot.'

'But you don't really mean that do you?' Her voice was rising. 'You didn't miss me at all did you? I'm standing out in that desert storm dying to see you and there you are, having the time of your life walking about ... looking at things. Never mind about writing a book about Jerusalem. It's me you should be writing a book about. We're going to have a long talk one day about this book you're going to write about me. Now: tell-me-how-much-you-missed-me.'

He picked up his knife and fork again only to put them side by side on his plate and push it away. A lot of other diners were also becoming enthralled by the unfolding scene, catching her every word.

'Lisa, keep your voice down will you?' he replied in a sort of panicking whisper. 'Look, you're always there with me. I'm always talking to you and telling you about things I'm looking at. Even when you're not there I'm always talking to you.'

'Better. Not by much but better anyway.'

'Also I've been trying to work out exactly what we're going to do on your next day off.'

'If I ever get one.'

'We're going to get a car and a guide to see the very best the country has to offer. You and me.'

'And a guide. What do we need a fucking guide for?'

'We need a guide so we can sit in the back of the car and smooch between the places we visit.'

'Better still. Full marks. I'll make a decent lover out of you yet. So Dopey Daniel, are we going to sit around here all night waiting for you to have dessert while these two twerps listen to every word we say? Or can we go straight back to bed and try out a bit more rumpy-pumpy?'

'I'm worn away,' he cried. 'My body needs to recover. It *demands* a dessert. And keep your voice down will you? It's not just these two, it's half the restaurant listening.'

'Oh bollocks to them all,' she roared. (Henry V before Agincourt.) 'They can listen if they want. I was only asking you if you really *had* to have a dessert. I can never eat anything when I'm in love myself. Come on then, have your fucking dessert and we'll get back to bed. I need at least half an hour's sleep before I start work in the morning. And it's ages since you told me you loved me.' She raised her voice even higher. 'These two here would be *most* interested to know how much you love me.'

Without a word the red-faced eavesdroppers left the dining hall. A few others were drifting out too. 'I *might* tell you I loved you if you kept your voice down a bit,' he mumbled. 'Just keep your voice down will you?'

'Don't be so fucking working class. Come on now. Tell me how much you love me. Is it a little, a lot or sort of half-way?'

'And watch your language too will you? Those lips of yours once kissed your mother. Try and remember that sometimes too will you?'

'I knew that you would be here, Raz. Mothers know everything about their sons.'

'All this has nothing to do with you. This is private business. You shouldn't have come.'

'It has everything to do with me. Your blood is my blood. I am your mother. I brought you to this country.'

Idiot boards bobbed up behind palm trees in the manner of ducks at a fairground shooting range. 'But this is a new time for us now. The conqueror has become the conquered. Don't you see that?' The idiot boards bobbed down again.

'I just see my own son, that's all I see. I want him back in my arms again, not fighting the whole world.'

The great man of action sank to his knees and raised his hands, as if about to further implore her to leave him in peace, when he lost his balance, fell sideways and bashed his head on a rock. 'Oh shit!' The idiot boards bobbed up again and hovered indecisively before disappearing behind the palms.

'Cut, cut, cut.'

Mid-morning and it was raining hard on the streets of Old Jerusalem. Huge black clouds sweeping in over the Moab mountains disgorged buckets of rain on the city. Raining on Arab and Jew alike, on Lutheran and Mormon, on women and children, tethered donkeys and wandering cats. Everyone was soaked in equal measure by this impeccably democratic downpour. Raining impartially on dome, spire and steeple, raining on the Hyatt Hotel and the Hebrew University, on Mr Whiskers' Café and the Church of the Holy Sepulchre, on the Hadassah Hospital, the police station, the Mount of Olives and the Dome of the Rock.

It was also sheeting down on the Via Dolorosa where Daniel and Lisa were standing, hand in hand, looking down it. The pipes and drains kept constantly gurgling with water; it came gushing over doorsteps and seeping out of holes in walls. Rain drummed on corrugated roofs and made waterfalls of the awnings covering the Arab spice stalls. At each junction of the alleyways torrent after torrent went flooding down the storm gutters, picking up the street rubbish and sweeping it away.

They moved a few steps down the sodden slopes and stopped again, soaked to the skin. Liturgical bells sounded through the swarming damp and spicy odours. Israeli soldiers in khaki oilskins kept up their ceaseless patrols and, from time to time, the droning call of the muezzin broke, with startling clarity, through all this pluvious turmoil.

The rain and continuing argument about the script had given Lisa an unexpected day off from filming so Daniel was showing her the sights and they had begun working their way along the Stations of the Cross in the Via Dolorosa. A few other wet pilgrims appeared occasionally but mostly it was just the two of them with raindrops chasing one another off the ends of their noses. 'This is the first Station of the Cross, where Christ was condemned by Pilate,' Daniel explained. 'There's a Roman cistern down there and a stretch of the road where Christ is supposed to have walked. Somewhere near here a crown of thorns was fastened on his head.'

Lisa was a country child on her first visit to the big city, happy to let Daniel show off even if, in truth, all this Route-of-the-Cross stuff, with all these plaques, was extremely disappointing and all got up for pilgrim money, no doubt. But it all came down to money in the end didn't it? Even the death of Christ, as old Judas would have undoubtedly attested. Nothing and no one had ever broken the power of money.

They came to the final station, the Church of the Holy Sepulchre and this was an even bigger disappointment, its floors covered with vast puddles from the leaking roof. Even holy old Daniel hated it, she was pleased to learn: run by half a dozen quarrelling sects, each with its own patch of religious icons and collection plates. Never forget the collection plate, best beloved. 'There's more spirituality in my lavatory,' she whispered to him. 'And I would never trust that priest there; just look at the old git eyeing up that woman's knockers.'

'The priests don't just eye them up either. I've been in here when they've been grabbed.'

But other parts of the city, which Ezekiel once called the centre of the world, were inspiring in the extreme: the Wailing Wall with its great grey oblong of free-standing stone, once part of the Temple of King Solomon and the Moslem Dome of the Rock, built over the actual rock from which Mohammed allegedly ascended to heaven. This whole building throbbed with centuries of believing prayer and, looking up at the great shadowy rafters alive with hurrying birds, Lisa said: 'Now this is what I call a real church. I might even get to church regularly if I had a church like this in Cheyne Walk.'

The two of them came down the rock-strewn slope with Yuri walking determinedly with his Kalashnikovs and her struggling to keep up with her black bag. The sour look on his face suggested he didn't want her around but she wasn't having any of it, clearly prepared to shadow her errant son right to the grave if necessary.

He dropped one of his guns and turned around. 'Go away,' he shouted as he raised a hand, poised to strike her.

'You would hit your own mother now would you?' she asked raising her chin defiantly, daring him to try it.

His hand faltered and fell. 'Just let me do what I have to do. How many times do I have to tell you? All this has nothing to do with you.'

'There are some things which are written in the very wind and one of ...'

She stopped speaking as he dropped his other gun and began dancing around the sand and shaking himself like a demented leprechaun.

'Cut, cut, cut.'

She put down her bag and glared, hands on hips, as he continued dancing around the desert smacking his arms and legs with his palms. 'Avie, there's some fucking thing biting me here. Some fucking insect. Oh shit.' *Smack, smack, smack.* 'It's got fucking big teeth and ...' *Smack, smack, smack.*

The moment he stopped dancing she walked over to him and leapt into the air to grab him by one of his ample sideboards, bringing him down to one knee and twisting the hank until he was yelping with a lot more pain than the insect had given him. 'Now listen to me shit-for-brains,' she spat, venomously but quietly, her mouth about two inches from his ear. 'We are all professionals and we have all had enough of this fucking desert and we want to go home. We are *all* being bitten by insects. Not just you but all of us. Hear me?' He nodded. 'It does not *matter* if some fucking insect is eating you. *It does not matter.* You just get on with your work because *you*, darling Yuri, are a professional and everyone wants to go home. Now get back up there and let's have no more crap about fucking insects. Never mind about insects. Insects can look after themselves and it's time for *you* to look after *us*. So get back up that hill and start being a professional actor for fuck's sake.'

She neither raised her voice, nor even modulated her tone, just spoke quietly and lethally into his ear, the way you do with sick horses. But her words seemed to have worked since everyone from the clapper boy to the director stood in quiet wonder as Yuri picked up his Kalashnikovs and, head bowed and sniffing a bit, trudged back up the rocky slope followed by Lisa to their marks. 'Sorry about that,' he shouted at them all. 'Ready when you are.'

FIFTEEN

It was almost two weeks before Lisa and Daniel had their next day off together and they hired a white stretch Mercedes with tinted windows and a melancholy, chain-smoking Israeli chauffeur, to see the sights of Bethlehem, Nazareth and the upper reaches of Galilee.

Lisa could relax now that the back of the film had been broken and one of the line producers had even talked of making a *Rebellion II* and had asked her if she might be interested but she had told him that there wasn't enough money in the world to get her to go through all that again. It wasn't the work that had got to her, nor even having to hold Yuri's hand all the time, but the fact that this was yet another stinking story about death and destruction, aimed at the teen market and unredeemed by any artistic merit.

But this was all between herself and the line producer. He mustn't say anything about this to Avie Glick or the others. And well, at least it was work. Hadn't Richard Burton always said he had appeared in all those turkeys because they had given him a reason to get out of bed in the morning? She liked a reason to get out of bed too, particularly when there were *good* reasons. Yet money was always a good reason, she had to keep reminding herself. It was no use covering yourself in glory with awards if you couldn't pay your rates bill. She'd known enough in her trade who couldn't even do that.

She was wearing a light white cotton dress with a simple gold choker and felt all of sixteen as she pawed Daniel the dusty few miles to Bethlehem and her sunny, sexy mood wasn't even dissipated by this sour, tacky town, awash with souvenir shops and beckoning traders. Three armed soldiers guarded the entrance to the Church of the Nativity inside which hundreds of pilgrims were being herded by policemen down to the grotto of Christ's birth. *Keep moving down there, Move right along there please.* A group of nuns came scything through the crowds, all starched smiles and scimitar elbows. *Get a snap of him Albert. Get one of that monk talking to Robert.* A policeman began pushing the backs of some of the visitors, urging them to move faster. *Move along there please.* A smiling monk, cigarette in hand, stood over a collection plate, removing some of the larger bills. *Please keep moving. Say your prayers later.*

Later they drove to Nablus and stopped for ten minutes to look at a crocodile farm. Lisa always brightened up when intrigued – like the bright, naughty child who only misbehaves when bored – even chuckling when she picked up a baby crocodile which squirmed violently in her fingers. She offered it to Daniel who just shook his head and shoved his hands straight down into the pockets of his jeans. 'I should take one of these to Yuri but it would probably scare him stiff,' she said only to learn the baby croc wasn't for sale.

She was cheered by a flower farm too where she learned how the clever Israelis shone lights on the beds at night, confusing the life cycles of the flowers and making them grow twice as fast. But she did start feeling distinctly scratchy when, loaded up with all kinds of blooms, they stepped out into the bright, dusty sunshine and she whispered a few words to Daniel through her flowers.

'What did you say?' he asked, acting the goat since he'd heard well enough.

'I said all this sunshine is making me randy. It's something to do with the heat and I always get like this in a certain kind of heat particularly if there's someone to get randy with.'

When he continued to pretend he didn't know what she was talking about – or, if he did, wasn't about to do anything about it – she drew closer to him and spoke like a little girl sheepishly telling her mother that she had just wet her knickers.

'A fuck, Daniel, I need a fuck.'

'Oh that's what you're muttering about. Well, I'll have to have a talk with our man here and see what we can do.'

She hung back coyly, hiding her face behind her flowers as Daniel explained to the chauffeur that perhaps he'd like to go for a walk for ten minutes since he and Lisa needed to do something private in the back of his Mercedes. 'We won't make a mess and I do, er, hope you don't mind.'

'Mind? I should mind? I fought in two wars,' said he. 'I should mind about these things? Take as long as you want.' He went to sit on a distant wall, lit a cigarette and watched his Mercedes shaking on her chassis for a full six minutes until the back door opened again. It had put the lady in a very bright humour too and she was chortling a lot and kept insisting that the chauffeur took all her flowers home to his wife.

'That I cannot do. She knows when I buy flowers I am ashamed of something I've done. I never admit anything. Never have. Never admit to fuck all, I say. Even when they catch you on the job. Just keep lying through your teeth.'

'So what happened to honesty in relationships,' Lisa asked as he drove off.

'You tell us,' said Daniel, smiling broadly. 'Lisa Moran is now going to tell us how to conduct an honest relationship.'

'There's nothing to it,' she said breezily. 'I'm always honest with you. You're the one who keeps telling lies.'

'Lisa, who are you trying to kid? You are the most breathtaking liar I've ever come across. You're at it all day long.'

Nazareth was a splash of lively Arab music set in pine-encrusted, sun-soaked hills. They walked around the streets hand in hand while yet more charabancs, run by Mount of Olives Tours or Egged Tours, stopped to disgorge yet more pilgrim crowds. The traffic jams in every street were constant, honking cars stuck nose-to-tail with yet more honking cars.

She was amazed at how secure she had begun to feel with him. He had even managed to accuse her of speaking with a forked tongue without her getting into a strop. She was being very good and quiet, staring dopily at him as he spoke and giving him the occasional kiss on the side of his neck as they wandered through the church marking the spot where Christ had once lived. Shafts of sunlight slashed boldly through the shadowy crypt with thousands of dust motes dancing in them like angels on the point of materialising.

Later they strolled through the crowded market where Lisa kept pulling wads of shekels out of her purse, busily buying piles of stuff for the chauffeur's wife. She had no idea why she had taken such a shine to the chauffeur's wife but Daniel soon found himself carrying an ever-increasing pile of blouses, sandals and rugs. She had to be the worst haggler ever to hit Nazareth. Some of the traders couldn't believe their ears – a few even asked her if she understood English – because when they set a price of, say, twenty shekels for a shirt, she might offer thirty – thirty! – or else give them a fifty shekel note and wave away the change.

But she was solvent again, thanks to this stupid film, free to fritter away her money in any way she chose.

Later, sitting in a restaurant in Tiberias and looking out over the Sea of Galilee, with most of their meal of fresh, spiky fish still untouched, he told her that he had decided it might be a good idea if they got married. She had suggested it often enough in the past, particularly when she had begun fretting about the possibility of another woman in his life, but this was the first time *he* had shown any enthusiasm for the idea and, if she remembered rightly, he had even said when they were in Paris, only do it with your best friend and for money.

She swallowed hard and stared out at the water where a launch, packed with pilgrims, was returning to a jetty. On the other side of the jetty was Gabriel's Café adjoining a small amusement arcade. A few mangy cats were slippering around the dustbins on the side of the Koh-I-Noor Indian restaurant and just over the road was a derelict mosque. She forked up a piece of fish from her plate and fed it to Daniel.

When she looked back out of the window the silent sea was glazed by orange flames of sunshine and dotted with the smudged reflections of single passing clouds. Her head nodded, teardrops sliding silently over her famous cheekbones as she forked up more fish. 'Can we get Percy out of the kennels the very minute we get back?'

'Of course. I don't mind him around. I just don't like patting him, that's all.'

'Well, couldn't you pat him just *once* a day? Just once, for me.' A silent Niagara of tears was now gushing down either side of her bobbed nose and she hadn't a clue why she was blubbing so much. 'That's not too much to ask is it? Just *once* a day.'

'I could manage it once I suppose,' he granted, most begrudgingly, she thought.

'All right. Once. But let's be clear about this. Love me, love my fucking dog. We come together. A fucking package deal.'

'That mouth of yours again. Look, we're in Galilee. Jesus walked on that water out there. He stilled storms and healed lepers on that very shoreline. So do you *have* to use bad language *all* the time, particularly out here?'

Her tears stopped, her eyes turning coldly grey. 'Don't change the subject. If you want to marry me you've got to become a decent and proper father to the fucking dog as well.'

'I've said yes, haven't I? I said I'd give the thing a pat. Once a day. *Once.* So are we going to have a quarrel about this now, or what?'

'We might.'

'So is it a yes or a no?'

'Yes or no to what?'

'Marriage. Are you going to marry me?'

'It's a maybe. I want to see how you get on with the dog first.'

'Oh, I get it now. You're going to blackmail me into getting to love that dog of yours aren't you? That's your little game here.'

'Look, are you going to eat this fish or am I going to sit here forever waving it in the air?'

Some days are a perfect, ascending scale of musical notes and that day just kept getting better and better although nothing could have quite prepared them for what happened at Yardenit, a pilgrim baptismal centre run by a kibbutz on the banks of the Jordan. Somewhere along here John the Baptist had announced the coming of the Messiah and, nearby, this Messiah had been baptised by John, so the enterprising kibbutz was now providing baptisms for pilgrims on much the same spot – for a fee.

There must have been three hundred pilgrims already there, all dressed in white as they filed down a series of concrete steps to be baptised alongside a series of railings in the turgid, brown water, either by their own minister or one with Christian qualifications laid on by the kibbutz.

Many were queuing up to enter the water and others were climbing back up the bank, soaked but smiling blissfully when the afternoon calm was broken by the insistent hand-clapping and get-up-and-dance drive of a Negro spiritual. Daniel tugged Lisa around the back of the crowds until they found a space where they could look down on some thirty black Americans singing *It's Hard to Stumble When You're on Your Knees* as they prepared for their own mass baptism.

One after another they went up to their pastor, a huge man seemingly built out of piles of inflated black inner tubes, and he took hold of each one, asked if they believed in the Father, Son and Holy Ghost and immersed them in the river. No sooner were they out of the water than they were back clapping and singing, making that astonishingly joyful noise which spoke so vividly of revival meetings in the church halls of the cotton fields of the Deep South. The song attracted all others to it; everyone along the bank swayed and clapped with the same driving fervour. They had the power of an advancing army on the edge of battle and the constant smiles of their huge white teeth spoke of an infectious happiness, as warm as the Israeli sun.

Unnoticed by Daniel, Lisa picked her way down the slope, waded into the river and asked the black pastor if he would baptise her. His hands shot up into the air and his mouth erupted in a golden gale of laughter. What could he say to this small white woman dressed only in a cotton frock? Never in a thousand years? You're not black enough for me? Your nipples are showing through your wet bra? I'm not paid to baptise poor white trash?

So he took hold of her and everyone was clapping and singing another hymn as Lisa loudly affirmed her belief in the Father, Son and Holy Ghost, held her nose and was plunged backwards into the River Jordan where her many and various sins were duly washed away.

The sun was sinking over the hills of Judea as they drove back across the plains of Armaggedon, east of Haifa. These huge plains were yet another Israeli bread basket and, in the continuing yellow explosions of the sunset, the very earth trembled and the lush parallelograms of corn shivered beneath a golden quilt of light. Water guns were spraying the crops, making hundreds of tiny rainbows and holding them up in the air with an improbable and almost vulgar gaudiness.

Lisa' s mind was dizzy with beautiful things. Swathed in a blanket, only in her bra and knickers because her dress was hanging up to dry, she was curled up in

Daniel's arms as the Mercedes hummed expensively over the rainbow plains. Just now, with her sins freshly washed away – and in the River Jordan, at that – she was thinking it might not be too late to lead a half-decent life. She had often felt the need to settle down and play it straight so perhaps it might be a good idea to marry Daniel and at least *try* to act the dutiful wife by doing whatever it was that dutiful wives were supposed to do.

Small dust storms, made by goats being herded back to their pens after a day grazing, moved slowly over the plains. Bedouin encampments also dotted the area, their tents aglow with the pale blue lights of televisions operated with heavy-duty lorry batteries.

'The Bible tells us that it is here on the plains of Armageddon that Christ will come again,' Daniel mused. 'It will be a time of great upheaval, war and rumours of war. The Sons of Darkness will engage in the final great battle with the Sons of Light. Every eye will see him when he returns with a shout, with the very trump of God.'

'Perhaps he's already out there, hitch-hiking to Jerusalem,' Lisa said, showing, perhaps, that the effects of her baptism in the Jordan might be wearing off quicker than expected. 'Do stop if you see anyone out there kissing lepers,' she shouted at the driver. 'Or if there's anyone walking on water. Oh Daniel, what a party we could throw for him if he turned up right now.'

'I don't think the time's ripe yet. Cities have been destroyed and rebuilt on these plains twenty times since Jesus was around. But I'm sure he can't be too far away. And the Sons of Darkness are gathering. I *am* sure of that. God is always going on about that.'

'So what do we do if Christ is out there and on his way?'

'We just make sure we're ready. That's what St Paul was always telling us. Be ready. Be prepared. Don't get caught off guard.'

'Mmm. Well I'll be ready enough if he comes tonight. I don't think I've committed too many sins in the past few hours so I'll be as ready as I'll ever be.' She pulled her blanket up around her shoulders and snuggled down into his arms again, looking away from this strange and vibrant landscape as it waited for the return of the Son of Man.

She would always look back on this day of complete and perfect happiness as *their* day. Her eyes had been filled, and her heart, and her ears. This baptismal day in Galilee she had been born again.

SIXTEEN

After an unusually cold and prolonged winter the white and purple splashes of the crocuses in the London parks gave way to ragged yellow carpets of daffodils and burly steeples of roses. Beds of tulips, hyacinths and wallflowers were dug up to make way for exuberant storms of cornflowers, begonias and busy lizzies. Trees came into full leaf and willows wept voluminously on the edge of lakes as the whole of the natural world came together to sing the psalms of summer.

In Hyde Park children sent model boats whizzing around the Serpentine and the Sunday afternoon sunshine became plump with the music of brass bands between three o'clock and five. In Regent's Park old ladies sat knitting in floribunda pergolas next to dog-collared punks with safety pins in their lips. In St James's Park fluffy lines of goslings followed their mothers across the lake, all cheerful today as they paddled along in erratic lines, unaware that they, the first babies of the city summer, would soon be eaten by rats or seagulls.

The skirts of the office girls had got tantalisingly shorter as the queues for the healing cones of the sweating ice cream man grew longer; tea rooms became alive with chinking cutlery and rattling silver in a cloying stew of over-brewed tea. Burglars took advantage of open windows to steal televisions or anything else that wasn't actually nailed down, making off down back lanes or through allotments while the house-holders were out and neighbours dozed peacefully in sun-baked armchairs in their gardens, wondering what that sudden noise might be but doing nothing about it.

Lisa let herself into Harry Kirby's flat with a great deal of difficulty since she was carrying several bags bulging with shopping. She dumped the bags on the kitchen table and began sorting out the items that needed to go straight into the freezer, only to pause in mid-scrabble to pour herself a glass of flattish champagne from a bottle in the fridge that she always kept for herself. The glassful did something to calm her edgy humour after negotiating the multiple frustrations of supermarket trolleys that wanted to go in the opposite direction to the one they were being pushed, traffic wardens who were forever sticking tickets under her windscreen wiper and the traffic itself which never seemed to be going anywhere.

After pouring herself another glassful she walked into the bedroom where Harry, propped up on a pile of ornamental Indian cushions, was watching a small portable television at the foot of his bed, its volume turned down low. He lifted a hand to acknowledge her arrival but his eyes remained glued to the screen.

'Harry, darling,' she said, kissing him lightly on the forehead and sitting down next to the bed where she took another few sips of her champagne. 'It's the same mad story at the Old Vic: they ought to throw a bomb into the dump and be done with it. Barmy direction, no one knows what they're doing and Larry never makes his mind up about anything at all, just keeps giving notes to all and sundry. I'm simply just going to have to fuck him to try and calm him down. He's just not getting it these days. I know it. He always said that you should never have your wife in the morning since you might come across something better in the afternoon but I know he's not getting anything in the morning or the afternoon. He's so tense all the time so, if that's what it takes, that's what it takes. He just needs *more*.'

Her lips spluttered a bit before she wandered back to the kitchen to re-fill her glass. 'I wouldn't be doing this play if it wasn't Ibsen, you know. We've always had it drummed into us we must drop everything for Ibsen but why won't they give me a decent Stoppard? Just something – *anything* – new. That's what I'd really like. And my part is so big – I'm just talking all the time and often can't get out of the way to take some water for all this heat.'

She sat down next to him again. 'Anyway … enough of my ravings. How are you, my darling? You look a lot better; in fact, I'd go so far as to say you are looking pretty terrific.'

Empty words she knew, since it was difficult to imagine how he could look any worse. She would have just done a Hedda and shot herself if she had been told that this strange new disease was bearing down on her. Now the doctors were saying it was some form of virulent gastroenteritis which his immune system was unable to fight properly but, whatever it was, his body had become skeletal and his hair had thinned alarmingly. Even his hands seemed to be shrinking on wrists as thin and brittle as lollipop sticks. Only his large brown eyes seemed to retain a little of their old lustre when he decided to look up at her and that wasn't often.

To make matters worse he was using a little slap to put a more presentable front on things. Eye-liner and mascara had been used sparingly but he had been lavish with the lipstick and used a lot of rouge. Quite frankly, these embellishments made him look ridiculous but, if they made him feel better about himself, that was all that mattered and it was not for her to comment. At least his pride hadn't capitulated. It's pride that makes us what we are isn't it? Good old-fashioned pride had a lot going for it. *My high-blown pride / At length broke under me, and now has left me / weary and old with service.*

'I *am* feeling a lot better,' he said finally, giving a wan, meaningless wave of his hand but keeping his eyes glued to the television screen. 'The doctors say I'll probably be on the mend in a few weeks' time. I wouldn't miss your first night for anything.'

She lifted his hand and kissed it lingeringly in the middle of the palm, feeling his tiny fingertips touch her closed eyes. 'Yes, my darling, you'll have a front seat and I'll make a special bow at curtain call just for you.'

'I never remember you bowing at any curtain call. You always just stand there scowling at everyone.'

'I told you. I'll do one *for you.*'

His shrunken features smiled at the thought and he even looked away from the television for a few moments, not at her but at the wall, as if savouring memories of other curtain calls and standing ovations. 'And afterwards we'll go to Joe Allen's like the old days,' he added, becoming unusually animated. 'But, oh my gosh, don't go shouting at the waitresses again will you? Or try and fill one of them in. I've got my image to think about.'

'Pah! Who worries about that lot? You're not in the mood for a glass of fizz I suppose? I've just a few more bottles and your groceries.'

'No fear. The doctors said alcohol might affect these new pills I'm trying out. They say it'll only be a few weeks now before this old body starts rallying. They say.'

Poor old Harry. The doctors were always coming up with new wonder pills which were just like the old wonder pills, forever promising he was going to get better in a few weeks. But they weren't even too sure what was making him go down with infection after infection so how the hell did they think they were going to cure him in a few weeks? She kissed the palm of his hand again and picked up her drink. What was so engrossing on the television? As far as she could make out it was some BBC2 programme about gardening. Since when had he been so interested in gardening? Everything in his window box had always died and he had even given his lovebirds in their Taj Mahal away, which she had found an unimaginable relief. Their singing had somehow mocked the spirit of the place, almost satirised the encroaching darkness in the flat.

Yet she wasn't upset at being ignored like this: she had a mother's compassion for her poor, sick Harry and, if he preferred to watch a television programme about gardening rather than listen to her battles with Larry, that was fine by her. She could sit here in peace and drink enough fizz so that she could go home and face that boring Welsh sod she was living with who was probably even now lounging around there and being beastly to her dog. She had never known anyone be so mean with their affection as Daniel was with Percy. He did occasionally give him a token pat – but only if he thought she was looking – otherwise the cold-hearted swine ignored the dog completely, even complained about his snoring if the mutt was lucky enough to sneak into their bed at night. He wouldn't take Percy out for a walk in the daylight either, claiming that people would laugh if they saw him walking a 'snivelling Pekingese'. Typically, he'd said he wouldn't have minded a normal dog. 'You know, all ribs and big bollocks. Now that's what I call a dog.' Working class Welsh git.

Within a few months Daniel had become one of the big disappointments of her life. He had stopped drinking again which meant that he wasn't nearly so much fun as he used to be – he roared with comedy when drunk – and, even more disappointingly, he wasn't a lot of use to her in bed either. Drink had relaxed him in bed in the past, made him more thoughtful and lingering, but she had often barely got going these days when he had finished, leaving her struggling with herself in some dark room as she fought with the ghosts who were beginning to show up in her life again, not actively menacing her but growling around on the edge of her consciousness as if trying to sniff out a way in.

Furthermore there he was in her house. He could have been a paying lodger for all the notice he was taking of *her*, often going out at lunchtimes without telling her where or else sitting in his room at the top of the house with his ever-growing collection of books about London as well as three maps of the metropolis which he had somehow acquired from the North Thames Gas Board, the London Electricity Board and the Public Health Department of the Greater London Council and had pinned up on the walls.

She simply didn't understand how anyone could be so obsessed with something as large, smelly and complex as London but there it was. Even more intriguingly he had photocopied a blown-up section of the A to Z of London on the wall, the Brixton page carefully annotated with arrows and lines. Was he a medieval necromancer trying to put a hex on this part of London? Maybe he was mad and she hadn't yet seen it – but he had always dismissed all that kind of stuff as so much piffle. So what was he up to? What was he planning and, more to the point, was he actually thinking about leaving her and, God forfend, going to live in fucking Brixton?

It was always possible, of course, that she could have put these questions to him directly except that would mean admitting that she had been nosing around in his room whose privacy, she had repeatedly assured him, was sacrosanct.

But at least she had cracked the mystery of where he had gone at lunchtime because he had finally told her. Far from shagging some local floozy rotten, as she had suspected – if only because that's what she always expected from her men – he was, he said, going to Alcoholics Anonymous meetings. He had even had the temerity to suggest that she might benefit from going with him. Well, he could stuff that for a lark. She had never had a drink problem; she could pick it up or leave it alone whenever she felt like it. Anyway she wished he *would* take a drink from time to time, not only to improve their sex life or turn him into a roaring drunk but so they could have a decent argument, with lots of extravagant statements, slammed doors and even a few wild punches too. Yes, that's what she was missing, a really good row. The sex always got really whizzy after a good row.

Daniel Jenkins would just have to go; she couldn't put up with all this any longer. As of tonight he was out on his ear. He could take all his maps and books back to his Hackney hovel. At least she had made sure to keep up the rent on that.

'Have they actually found out what's wrong with you yet, Harry?' she asked finally.

'Yes and no. They keep changing their minds but they reckon, for sure, that it's Karposi's Sarcoma. My immune system's buggered. Not to put too fine a point on it, I'm rotting away. Done for.'

'Oh Harry, don't talk like this. It upsets me to hear you talking like this. I can't bear it. Perhaps I'd better go and leave you to your television.'

'Don't go. Finish your drink. I'm so alone, dearie, so alone. We're two of a kind you and me. Very alike and always alone. That's why we've stuck together for so long.'

Then Harry uttered a sentence which exploded inside her like a lighted match on a pool of petrol.

'I can't help wondering if this isn't some sort of punishment from God for the way I've lived.'

Her head snapped back so suddenly she saw a cluster of twinkling stars. 'Harry, don't talk *crap*. I really am going to go now if you are going to talk so much *crap*.'

'Lisa, I can't help it. Every time I've bent over or taken it in the mouth I've always felt God frowning down on me. I've always felt like that. Guilty, furtive, a scuffling rat in the shadows, forever pursuing sex. That's been the story of my life really and now God is punishing me for it.'

'*Crap*, Harry. I can't sit here and listen to all this *crap*. You did what you did. That's all there is to it. God doesn't give a damn where you stick your sorry dick. He's got far more important things to worry about.'

'God cares about love doesn't he? He must care about love and love is not snatching at it in the dark, in some cottage, from a total stranger. Whatever else that might be that's not love. That's lust. That's thinking with your dick.'

'Harry, you did what you had to do. You did what made you happy and there is no point at all in now thinking that God's out to get you because you're the way you are and you did what made you happy. Why should he now want to take some revenge on you because of the way he made you?'

'Perhaps he made a mistake?'

'God doesn't make mistakes, you stupid bastard. I've had enough of all this. Let's have another glass of champagne and talk about something interesting.'

'You don't find God interesting? You'd find him very interesting if *you* were dying.'

'Now you just listen to me, you silly cunt,' she barked, her mouth frothing up with spit. 'In case you haven't noticed we are all dying and that has nothing at all to do with God. *It is just the way we are, Harry.* Our profession is to die; that's the reason we live and it's the same for all of us. Now if you're going to keep blubbering about how God is punishing you ...' Her hands wandered around the air and she lost the thread of her argument. 'I've got another stupid bastard living with me who's always worrying about what God's going to do with him and I've told him what I'm telling you. God can look after himself. All you've got to do is show some balls and stand on your own two feet.'

'In case you haven't heard, my balls have shrunk away. There's nothing ...'

'You stupid faggot.' She slapped him hard on the top of his bald head with her open palm and he yelped like a stricken puppy before taking cover under the bedclothes. She stood up slowly, stepping backwards with her hands taking hold of her own hair. Shadows hardened in her mind and she heard a distant shriek of laughter in there. One of her cheeks stuttered with a facial tic which became more and more pronounced as she spoke. 'This is just a terrible delusion of yours, Osvald – only a delusion. All this excitement has been too much for you; but now you shall have a rest – at home with your mother, my dearest boy.' *Another step backwards, Lisa. Let your hands down carefully now. Watch the breathing.* 'There! It's all over now. You see how simple it was. Oh I knew it would be. And look, Osvald, we're going to have a lovely day – bright sunshine. Now you'll really be able to see your home!'

Mother, give me the sun.

SEVENTEEN

Nine days later Lisa was sitting in her drawing room in the afternoon gazing out of the French windows at what she sometimes saw as her own personal riverscape: Old Father Thames flowing behind the softly rustling elms of Cheyne Walk.

She had always loved and knew her paintings but this was an incomparable, even priceless, painting of what Spenser once called 'the silver-footed Thamesis' bowling down through the city. Everywhere she looked something was happening: here a speeding police boat, there a lighter full of rubbish, often a small cruiser throbbing with disco and drunken laughter. So much movement and light, particularly when compared with the static shafts of light of a Canaletto or the Thames dreamscapes of a Turner, even if the old master had filled them with misty beauties and half-formed images of life merging mystically with death.

Her house was far too expensive for her, she knew; it didn't make any economic sense for her to be sitting on this vast pile, particularly as it was now probably worth a small fortune, but she couldn't quite see how she would manage without this view to sustain her if she sold up and found something a little more sensible, didn't quite know how she could carry on without watching this constantly changing drama outside her window.

The Thames spoke to her on all kinds of levels, not only telling her about her past and how she had grown and loved on these banks but about death: the rotten spars and the bodies of the dead dogs which floated by, not forgetting all the skulls they kept finding on nearby mud banks since the river was once used as the city's cemetery, the place where a pagan citizenry had flung their dead to get rid of them.

Daniel had got her thinking a lot about London, about the city's immense complexity and history and she shared his fascination for its inner workings. As she had guessed from all the maps in his room his plans for making a long journey through its tunnels and sewers, pipes and corridors, were being firmed up and she secretly thought she would like to do that herself, to get away from the harsh and unrelenting gaze of the spotlight and hide somewhere in a medieval darkness, to escape the publicity and the essential triviality of the theatre and venture down into the hidden city to bask in its longevity and explore it anew.

Her relationship with Daniel was still fraught and delicately balanced; neither was in control of anything and it might collapse at any moment but, sitting here looking at the Thames, she had to grant that he had brought a lot to her interior life: he had made her more serious-minded about issues for one; got her thinking about God for another and also prompted her to become more inquisitive about the capital where they lived. These were all bonuses at her time of life, she decided, as she watched the first signs of the evening mists beginning to gather on the surface of the Thames like a convention of baby ghosts.

She heard the rattle of keys and Daniel coming up the stairs so she called out his name, telling him she was in here in case he went straight up to his room. She had never known anyone work as hard: he didn't seem to want to eat and was so *driven*.

'Hello girl,' he said breezily coming into the living room. 'I thought you were supposed to be at the theatre. Nothing wrong is there?'

He looked furtive, slightly nervous, as if expecting trouble from her, but, not for the first time, she confounded his expectations by asking him if he would like a cup of tea. She never offered that if she was about to start trouble. He knew the signs. Relaxed, he smiled that brilliant, blue-eyed smile that she had once fallen so hopelessly in love with and sat in a chair opposite hers as she pottered noisily around the kitchen, returning with a tea tray and a plate of biscuits before setting it down on the small table between them.

'I'm so glad you're here now,' she said. 'I love this time on the Thames with the sun beginning to settle down on the rooftops and it's always that much more enjoyable when you're here to share the moment.'

He picked up a biscuit and bit into it, his back stiffening slightly, eyes locked on her. She saw he was wondering what was going to come next and almost fearing what she was about to say. This was no good, this was no good at all.

'You've been to AA, I guess. Anyone interesting there?'

'I've been walking around Brixton as it happens.'

'Really? What's going on in Brixton?'

'Not a lot.'

She looked at him for a while, smiling curiously but, when she saw he wasn't about to offer any more information about Brixton or AA or anything else, she took the initiative.

'Daniel, these have been very difficult times for me so I've had to make a few hard decisions.' She poured the tea, handing him the cup and saucer whose quiet rattling when he took it betrayed his nervousness. Oh this had become really hopeless but she swallowed hard and ploughed on. 'I've told Larry I can't carry on with the play because Harry Kirby is going to die at any moment. Larry has been unusually understanding, for Larry, and he's let me go without any fuss although that may be because he's shagging my understudy.' She regretted that stupid amplification almost immediately not only because it was wrong but she had been trying to be serious. She picked up her own cup and took a few sips. 'I don't know how long it's going to take Harry to die but I *must* be there with him. You do understand that don't you?'

'Absolutely. He's been your best friend for ever. I understand that well enough.'

'No, Daniel. *You* are my best friend. Harry is a very old acquaintance of whom I am very fond but, when he does finally go under, I know I'm going to be in a very bad state. I'll need somewhere quiet to recover and I want some time for the two of us to get away from all this. None of this means anything. Just look at all these posters of me – *of me*! – and those paintings hanging there getting more and more expensive. And this huge house. Who needs all this?'

'Where did ...'

'Please, Daniel, let me finish. I know we've not been getting on too well lately and there's something not quite right between us. These things happen but I *do* love you.' A tearful look and a lot of slow breathing and heavy emphasis on the next few lines. 'But before it all falls apart I want to make a real effort for a change. I don't want you to just pack a bag and flee. We must work at it so I've decided we should find a country cottage where we can have a quiet life together. The two of us. I've got a little money left from that poxy film and I'll sell some of my paintings if necessary. What we need is somewhere to escape to; somewhere to patch it up between us. I also want you to have somewhere you can get on with your work. Your work is very important to me.'

'What about Suffolk?' he asked with suspicious cheeriness. 'I've had some great weekends in places like Southwold in my drinking days and I've always thought I'd like to live around there.'

'Suffolk would be wonderful. Oh Daniel let's do that. Let's just do that. I mean *after* Harry, you know ...'

'I'd work well out there too but, before you go on, there's also something important that I need to tell you.'

Her eyebrows gave a startled twitch and with those two dread words 'something important' she immediately expected the worst. She always expected the worst and this sounded as if it might be somewhere beyond that.

'I'm not sure how to put this but I'm going to have to go and live in Brixton for a while. I've been over there looking for a room.'

Her already wobbling scaffolding began collapsing inside her. There she was making a real effort, a genuine sacrifice to keep their love going and there he was wanting to go and live in fucking Brixton. So he was going to leave her after all. She couldn't put up with much more of this and threw a despairing glance at the river. Then, unable to think of anything better to do, she sank to her knees and began sobbing into her upturned hands.

'It's not like that, Lisa. Stop it. It's not like that at all. I'm not going any-where. I just need to be in Brixton for a while just as you need to be with Harry.'

'What's the matter with this place? Isn't Cheyne Walk good enough for you? What's in Brixton anyway? Is this another chapter for your book?'

'Not really.'

Her sobbing slowed as she thought for a bit while still staring down into her tear-stained palms. 'If it's not for your book you must be leaving me.'

'It's a lot more complicated than that.'

'It doesn't sound very complicated to me. You're leaving me here in Cheyne Walk to go and live in Brixton and that's all there is to it. That's not in the slight-est bit complicated is it?'

'But I'm not leaving you, girl. It's God again. God has told me I've got to go and live in Brixton.'

She sat up on her knees, placing her hands on her hips, her bloodshot eyes looking at him as she tried to work out whether she should start crying again or merely laugh. God really must have had a good, long snigger to himself when he decided to pick on Daniel to talk to. You couldn't even really work out what kind of man Daniel was, one minute rolling in the gutters pissed-drunk with all his disgusting mates and the next some cracked prophet, stone cold sober and talk-ing about how he had just been given his marching orders by God to go and live in Brixton. Yet this was why she truly loved him, she knew without a shadow of a doubt; no mere man had ever exercised quite this much power over her and she did not want to break up with him. He might well have been as mad as a lorry wheel but he was always gentle and loving with it, never dangerous or threaten-ing in any way and was even beginning to put in a decent performance in bed again which might have been something to do with the odd valium she was drop-ping in his cocoa.

And it didn't matter to her if he was merely mad. The world was full of mad people so one more wasn't going to make much difference. She was the only sane person on her block although most of her men had clearly thought otherwise.

So yes, she wanted this thing with him – whatever this thing was – to last and, the sooner she got him to that cottage in Suffolk, where she could keep an eye on him, the better.

'But you still haven't told me what's the matter with Cheyne Walk,' she cried inanely. 'You can be looked after here. You're safe here so why doesn't God tell you to stay here? What's God got against Cheyne Walk?'

'God hasn't got anything against Cheyne Walk. He just wants me in Brixton.'

'How do you know?'

'He told me.'

'What? Did he say "Daniel Jenkins, pack your bags because I want you to go and live in Brixton?" Is that how he put it?'

'Not really. But I've told you before he doesn't converse like normal human beings. He's only ever like himself and, if he talks to me in any way at all, he does it through pictures, images, *feelings*.'

'And what about me?'

'What about you?'

'Me. Lisa Moran. The woman you live with. Remember me?'

'Lisa, I know who you are but what about you?'

'Well, did he say anything about me? Any suggestions that I might like to go and live in fucking Birmingham or somewhere?'

'Aw, you're just being daft now.'

'I'm being daft? *Me?*'

'Look, how can we have a serious discussion if you keep being daft all the time? I know it's hard to explain and perhaps even harder to understand but the long and short of it is that he wants me to go and live in Brixton and that's it.'

'For how long?'

'He didn't say. All I know is that he wants me there as a witness.'

'A witness? Not a fucking Jehovah's Witness, I hope.'

'Naw. He wants me to see something for myself. I tried ignoring him but he kept going on about it so I'm just going to have to go. I've already found a room over there. Nice landlady. Fat and black. She'll look after me a treat. You can always come over and see me there.'

'Oh well, thanks for that.' The offer slightly mollified her; at least she hadn't been banned from Brixton, not that she was terribly sure where it was. 'I don't suppose God has any good country cottages in Suffolk on his books has he?'

'You're being silly again, Lisa. Look, this is serious business we're in here, very serious business. God is worried about a coming spirit of destruction in the cities. He's scared of what's going to happen to them and he was telling me much the same thing that time we were in Paris. We're living in a long season of black rain and there's an attack going to start that no one's yet understood.'

'You know Daniel I am sure there must be pills that can help you with whatever it is you're suffering from. There must be something for it, whatever it is. But, to move along slightly, tell me one thing. Is there any danger at all of us having a decent fuck tonight? I'm starting to feel really scratchy and I really need one, you know. God's got his problems and I've got mine so, Mr Prophet, what about it?'

EIGHTEEN

After a long heatwave it rained on the streets of Brixton for four days, keeping everyone indoors until it abruptly stopped, not making way for more blue sky and sunshine but a grey sky with muggy air in which nothing happened except for stray thunderheads which rumbled like distant cannon but never actually broke into proper thunder.

And this became the daily pattern as shoppers in The Electric Avenue moved from stall to stall, wishing the thunder would actually make up its mind and behave like thunder or that it would rain properly, as rain should, or even that the sun might shine on them all again, nicely and cheerfully, as sun is prone to do because the sun is always in a nice and cheerful mood.

But nothing stirred in all this sweating greyness as Daniel mingled with the shoppers around the stalls, sometimes making a furtive note as he tried to identify the various elements that made up this predominately West Indian market – the pungent smell of goats' meat and the salted pigs' tails: the jackfish and snapper: the mangoes and plantain: the open sacks of black-eyed beans and pounded yam: the pyramids of heavy Jamaican loaves, tins of breadfruit and callaloo. You name it ...

He often stopped at the corner stall for some iced sarsparilla or to buy a copy of *The West Indian World* but mostly he kept moving, very slowly, mostly watching, looking, trying to get the measure of this area where melancholy young blacks gathered on disaffected corners feeling a shared sense of menace. They sometimes glared at Daniel but he usually managed to defuse their antagonism with the bright smile which had long been his most valuable asset. People almost always relaxed if you smiled at them brightly enough.

He ate in a small café near Railton Road that night – a plate of egg and chips, his favourite, with tea and a pile of bread and butter – sitting in the window and watching the people passing by. The rumbling thunderheads changed to a sharp crackling just after nine o'clock and there were squirmy flashes of lightning.

This tension, this inability to decide on anything seemed to be stalking the very streets and, as he left the restaurant, a dozen or so dread-locked youths ran across the road and down towards Coldharbour Lane, past corrugated zinc fences and derelict houses with rubbled, sometimes blackened interiors which smelled of recent fires. Some of the shops were boarded up and, on a patch of waste ground, three burned-out cars were piled up on top of one another like monstrous, metallic, mating toads.

Daniel rang Lisa from a call box and gave her his news - which was no news at all really - and told her he loved her. She said she loved him too but she didn't have time to chat because Harry was going through a bad patch.

Harry Kirby was lying naked, apart from a cloth to cover his modesty, on top of his bed, motionless but occasionally shivering like leaves being rattled by stray gusts of wind. Sweat was pouring from every part of him and even the biggest fan Lisa could find in Harrods failed to cool him down; the fan throbbed ceaselessly but seemed to have no effect on all this malarial sweat. Her main concern was his dehydration and she kept trying to pour water between his cracked lips but, even after losing so much fluid, he didn't seem to want to take the water which made him cough and splutter a lot. Her hands wrung out another cold flannel and laid it across his forehead as he began muttering the name of some man over and over.

Sores were breaking out before her very eyes but she was not afraid of whatever it was that was killing her friend: she would have kissed and licked his every sore if she thought it would make them go away. Death had never held any fears for her. Whenever it threatened she would just inch closer to it, ready, willing and able to take its icy, welcoming hand. He cried out that man's name again – Chris? Fish? Tish? – and she moved closer, blowing on his fevered cheeks in some forlorn effort to cool them. Accumulated mucus made his breathing more difficult and sometimes he had to cough and splutter it clear before he settled down again.

The doctor had come and gone but there was little he could do. Harry could have gone to a hospice to die but Lisa had decided he should stay here, in his flat, surrounded by his things. The doctor had returned with an oxygen cylinder but Harry had never quite taken to it, never felt happy if his mouth was covered. This latest in a long series of illnesses was simply pneumonia and she was just going to sit there with him until the end, take him by the hand and help him step out of his miserable, pointless life.

'I always remember my first love,' she told him, unsure if he was listening. 'Sebastian. I was thirteen. I kept following him around but he hated the sight of me. I stood on corners after school where I knew he would come past. I was outside his house in the mornings. It drove him mad and he threw things at me and told me to go away. But I was obsessed. We never did anything, never even kissed, but I still find myself thinking about my handsome Seb. That fine hair. Those shoulders. I still wonder what became of him.'

Harry dozed off again and, unable to sleep herself, she picked a book off the shelf, DH Lawrence's *The Rainbow*, a work which had once been a good friend to her although she could not recall quite when. She opened the first page and took it in as a whole, a trick she had picked up when young. She only had to look at a page for a few moments, not the actual words, and her mind took in the lot. It was never clear to her – or anyone else – how this worked but it had been a great ally to her as an actress when she had to learn her lines. She could also live inside a book as strongly and imaginatively as in one of her dramatic roles; as long as she liked the characters she could take them and become them.

Thus, very quickly, she slipped into this world of Lawrence's, so perfectly evoked, in which the people lived close to the land and there was a blaze of sensitivity about them and they were always ready to respond to what they found attractive, a little like Daniel really; he would have sat well in a novel like this. Like the fiery Brangwens he also had subterranean leanings in which nothing made much sense: the way he was so spiritual yet so part of the grubby world too; the way he flinched at the sight of cruelty but could also hand it out. She had often found him positively callous in his dealings with her; going missing for ages without any explanation; not so much as a wave or a goodbye, just taking off into the mists of another lonely day and leaving her to guess when she might see him again, when he might hold her in his arms and whisper new promises of the resurrection.

Tom Brangwen was so alert to his emotions and so aware of the heavy demands of his sexuality. 'She was too living to be neglected.' Lisa liked that. Daniel shouldn't neglect her either; she was too living. 'And then it came upon him that he would marry her and she would be his wife.'

When Tom kissed Lydia he was overcome with an agony and it became dark and, sitting down, he fell asleep for a few seconds. He awoke newly created, a new birth in a womb of darkness. Everything was as new as morning, fresh and newly-begun. 'Like a dawn the newness and bliss filled in. And she sat utterly still with him, as if in the same.'

They married, Tom and Lydia, and there could be a tension and antagonism in him which might burst 'and the passionate flood formed into a tremendous, magnificent rush ... and he would create the world afresh.' Lisa liked all this talk of newness and freshness, this preparedness to start again. All the emotions were refracted through a naked honesty; one moment they were murderous to one another and the next they were overcome by an aching tenderness. The relationship always evolved too, sometimes taking a step backwards but never stopping still. That's what she was looking for with Daniel: an honest, evolving relationship which would finally develop into an almost mystical union. Yes, that would be the blueprint.

She had to leave her book when Harry began coughing again and she decided to give him a body wash to try and relieve some of his burning discomfort.

Daniel took up a new position, deep in the darkness of Coldharbour Lane as a group of young blacks came sauntering along before gathering on the pavement outside a chip shop. They moved around one another slowly in the light of the shop window, not saying much although a few did break away briefly to kick a tin can around, which clattered with dead laughter, before being kicked over a wall and disappearing into the darkness.

A short while later a ball of fire came romping out of the window of a derelict house and they all ran to look at the hungry flames, remaining there even when the fire engine finally turned up – just as the fire itself was on the point of burning itself out. A few picked up bricks and threw them through the still smouldering windows. The thunderheads had fallen silent, leaving just the heat. News of another fire, on the corner of Atlantic Road and Mayall Road, could be heard clearly on the fire engine's radio. The unit should get over there as quickly as possible. A police car came past slowly but didn't actually stop as the youths jeered it on its way. Soon the fire engine left also.

Daniel remained well out of the way when he noticed a couple of the youths going into another derelict house nearby. A flare of a flame caught in one of the broken windows and they both came running out before a fire began going up in that house at surprising speed. More people came along and there was a loud argument between them and the youths. Some were residents worried about their properties. Yet more turned up together with a police car and Daniel stiffened when he heard a noise which sounded like a squealing mob riding along atop a medieval siege machine.

The squeals and creaks were becoming louder and louder and, as this huge truck began approaching, Daniel had to shield his eyes from its brilliant and vulgar dazzle. The wheels of the truck seemed to be made of fire and several separate lights turned and turned again on its roof, all glaring with incandescent whiteness. The silhouettes of three men were moving around inside these swirling white lights and they all seemed to be working a sort of giant television camera which was soon focused on the blazing house with the crowds gathering and quarrelling all around it.

A policeman tried to arrest one of the youths and the separate lights of the truck came together and focused on the youth as he struggled in the merciless spotlight. A lot of shouting and pushing followed when the truck's spotlight jerked up abruptly and focused on another fire which had broken out in another derelict house a little further down the road. Those screams straight from hell started up again as the truck creaked forward to that fire and everyone was busy roaring and cheering.

'Did I ever tell you how much I've always enjoyed DH Lawrence's work,' Lisa told a plainly uninterested Harry as she washed down his scabbed chest. 'I don't think anyone has ever put together sentences like him, so long and fluent. There's almost a condition of singing in some of them and, when you're reading it, you often feel as if you are holding a hymn sheet and you want to sing out all the beautiful phrases. I so wish I'd met him. I've met a lot of famous men in my time but I would have loved to have met the old Nottingham nutter with his funny beard and even nuttier wife. Ah yes, Lorenzo, lover of my soul.'

She was washing around his neck when she noticed images from the television flickering soundlessly in his eyes. Groups were gathering around some house fires but, without the sound, she couldn't quite work out where these fires were and, in the event, merely leaned across the bed to turn off the set. 'You're never going to get better watching all that crap,' she told him.

'And all your sufferings will drown in the mercy that will fill the earth; and our life will become as quiet and gentle and sweet as a caress. I have faith, I have faith ... '

Daniel followed the truck with the wheels of fire from a distance of about twenty five yards, stopping when it stopped and starting again when it moved on. He couldn't quite make out what it was supposed to be doing except that it was clearly some infernal force for disturbance since trouble was breaking out all around it. Gangs of youths sprinted alongside it, some peeling off to smash windows and, as each window shattered, smaller groups scurried across the street, picking up small items at first then becoming bolder, carting off fully-clothed mannequins, piles of this and boxes of that as yet more windows were broken.

The most peculiar feature of all this mayhem, for Daniel, was that all these hooligan acts seemed to be carefully framed in the intense white glare of the truck's spotlights and it was almost impossible to work out if these acts *only* happened in the spotlight or were actively encouraged by its attention.

Gangs bowled down through the white spotlight, hotly pursued by police. All along Railton Road muggers snatched handbags and wallets, striking down anyone who resisted. A large woman, walking down an alley, spotted a gang running towards her, turned to run away and then noticed *them* running away from *her*.

With more people running out of doorways into the streets, which had become alive with police sirens and the baying cries of looters who had lost control of themselves, the truck pressed on, its white spotlight picking up a policeman falling backwards clutching his face which had become a mask of blood. A petrol bomb smashed into the front of the Post Office, then another. A police helicopter whump-whumped overhead. A phalanx of police with riot shields marched into the fray, beating their shields with truncheons in some hopeless effort to scare the rioters into behaving themselves. Smoke eddied one way and another as another group went running past the truck. A horse whinnied and metal-shod hooves clomped along the road. More white smoke swept around the advancing horse and the drumming of truncheons on riot shields reached a new crescendo.

The truck continued picking up all this savagery in its white glare and, despite its awesome presence to those with eyes to see, Daniel marvelled that no one seemed to be taking any notice of it at all: that, in all the mayhem foaming all around them, it could be almost *invisible*. Police cars were being surrounded with fists drumming rhythmically on the bonnets until the terrified police somehow managed to escape and their cars were overturned and burned.

Another petrol bomb sent a sheet of flame steepling sharply up out of the road and a police horse reared up on his back legs in screaming, eyeball-popping terror. 'Calm down, Beth. Stop it, Beth,' the police rider kept crying as, all flailing arms and elbows, he fought to control the horse in the unblinking gaze of the white light.

Further down the road the white light found another police phalanx trapped on a building site by a stone-throwing mob. Bricks fell on them, exploding against the walls or on their plastic shields which they held up over their heads to protect themselves against this punishing rain of mayhem and violence.

And then Daniel saw something, as terrifying as it was amazing, since all manner of strange colours were trembling and liquefying around the truck with the wheels of fire. All at once, these colours seemed to rush into one another and then shoot straight up into the sky like some strange, malevolent rainbow, black like sin and red like blood and yellow like pus, scorching a rising arc of evil into the very sky. Then, after a series of small explosions deep within it, the rainbow's arc broke into thousands, perhaps millions of smaller rainbows which broke from the others, only to join them again until the whole sky was but a criss-crossing mesh of conjoined rainbows.

Lisa was sitting next to Harry and began fearing the worst when she couldn't hear him breathing. Indeed she was on the verge of panicking when he spluttered a small cough before settling back down into his sweating discomfort again.

From somewhere outside the open window a strange voice was singing on a distant radio. It was a voice wrenched out of a place of bitterness and pain, a voice that you might hear at the end of a funeral service which instantly made you want to weep, a song without any discernible words, just pure, carolling anguish. This voice said that our time was over and the intensity of its pain made the coming death no bad thing. No one should suffer such pain for so long. It only takes fifty seconds to die in an electric chair, she had once heard.

Now she was getting into a real lather and wishing that Daniel would come here soon to deal with her ghosts. She could feel all their hands at her heart and, in the absence of a better idea, she decided to clean the flat, stacking up the chairs on the kitchen table before getting down on her knees to wash the tiles. But they weren't particularly dirty. She had washed them only the day before but she set to it with a will, finding it a strange and soothing therapy for her frayed nerves as she worked her cloth vigorously into corners where there might have been some dirt which she had missed the last time.

When she had finished she went to stand at the open window, taking off her rubber gloves and looking down at a boutique doorway in the Old Brompton Road where a young couple were arguing loudly. The boy struck the girl to the ground and the girl got up and struck down the boy.

Even though it was just past midnight a blood-coloured glow lit up the distant sky as if the sun had decided to come up several hours early. The warm night carried the noise of helicopter blades as the metallic birds hovered, black on red, in this furious new sunset. Harry was coughing again and she was about to take him some fresh tissues when a news bulletin on a loud nearby radio made her belly churn.

'Following the disturbances in Brixton we now understand there is also trouble in the streets of Battersea, Dalston, Hackney, Chiswick, Acton and Southall. Within the last hour police have been called to attend riots in Birmingham, Chester, Ellesmere Port, Hull, Liverpool, Newcastle, Wolverhampton and Preston and Wolverhampton.'

Her mind could barely connect with anything and she just wished Daniel would come home as soon as possible. *God is worried about a coming destruction in the cities. He's scared of what's going to happen to them. There's an attack going on that no one has yet understood.* All his words about the cities heading towards the brink were true and she didn't want him getting caught up in any of it. The sooner they both girded up their loins and got to a cottage in Suffolk the better.

Daniel simply walked straight out of the troubled streets of Brixton on his own two feet, his brain still throbbing and even broken by the shock of what he had just seen, almost totally unaware of what was going on all around him as he followed the pavements to he knew not where. A seagull came fluttering down through the sodium glow of the street lamps and screamed at him accusingly, almost as if trying to blame him for all the disturbances which were so busily spreading through the land.

Had he been aware of what was going on all around him he might well have heard various radio and television bulletins keeping people up to date with the latest outbreaks. Even at such a late hour one or other was operating in almost every open window, busily reporting the sharp blows and fiery explosions of lawlessness. He was walking through a deep canyon with violent imagery breaking out of its very walls, surrounding him in a flickering neon anger.

He could have been walking down those angry canyons for several hours when he stumbled into a field – a public park? – where he lay down on the grass and, after sighing a while, stayed there, almost motionless as the early mist settled over his closed eyes before being dried by the rising sun.

His mind was in a state of blind confusion although one coherent thought did manage to fight its way through everything which was how nice it would be if he could only get to a pub and have a good drink. That's what he had always liked about a good drink, he now remembered. No one, no one at all, could talk to you about anything, anything at all, when you'd had a good drink.

Lisa was so pleased to meet her old chum Ursula Brangwen again that she didn't actually notice that Harry had finally slipped his leash and drifted off into the long darkness. Ursula was the one woman in the whole saga who actually managed to break free from the rural life and become sure she can now make a full life for herself. This was a woman with whom Lisa could identify; a sensual, free soul who 'had a passionate craving to escape from the belittling circumstances of life, the little jealousies, the little differences, the little meannesses'.

She falls for Anton Skrebensky and 'she reached him with her mouth and drank his full kiss, drank it fuller and fuller. And it was good. It was very, very good. She seemed to be filled with his kiss, filled as if she had drunk strong glowing sunshine.'

Her relationship with Anton failed and then her sexual life fanned into a kind of disease for her; finding herself attracted to the teacher Winifred, undressing and holding one another in the rain. Then there was a dalliance with Anthony, the handsome gardener and then going to college where education fully and finally released her from her past.

Delights kept spattering Lisa's heart as she read on since, in Ursula, she saw the history of her own warm and cold loves: the giddy highs, the dull celibate lows and this abiding expectation that when things could get no worse they could only then get better. For all her cynicism and wanton waywardness Lisa had always believed in love, had always thought that, without it, life was some pointless, Beckettian journey from nothing to nothing. She had known men without number and turned down even more but, sexually, it only ever worked when she was in love, as she was now, greedily and desperately with Daniel.

Loveless, drunken fucking was all right in its place but it never really got you anywhere. Many was the morning when she had just told them to go and, sadly, never saw them again. That was the real trouble with loveless, drunken fucking: you *never* saw them again, not ever.

But DH Lawrence's greatness, she still believed, was that he alone seemed to have that one great and early insight that women had sexual desires and needs too; they too could look at a man and feel a darkening of desire, an urgent throbbing between their legs. Lisa had spoken for *Lady Chatterley's Lover*, as a witness for the defence, when the publishers had been prosecuted in the Old Bailey. She had got up there in that lonely dock and said that Lawrence was almost alone in understanding a woman's needs and it would be a grave crime against all womankind to ban the book again. Lawrence had brought women out of the medieval darkness and, almost alone, set them free. Her words were thought to be a powerful argument in the publisher's subsequent acquittal.

She finally came to the end of *The Rainbow*, feeling almost inspired by the final few words when she noticed that Harry was quiet and still. He was gone, gone, gone. Poor Harry. He had been such a handsome man and now he had shrunk to this. She was sad, but relieved too that he'd finally thrown off his mortal coil, that he'd gone home at last. Life and these lips had been separated.

With tears pouring silently over her cheekbones she looked especially gaunt and stricken as she lifted up her book and read its last few lines aloud to Harry. 'And the rainbow stood on the earth,' she said, enunciating the words carefully, working hard to control her shaking hand. 'She knew that the sordid people who crept hard-scaled and separate on the face of the world's corruption were living still, that the rainbow was arched in their blood and would quiver to life in their spirit, that they would cast off their horny covering of disintegration, that new, clean, naked bodies would issue to a new germination, to a new growth, rising to the light and the wind and the clean rain of heaven. She saw in the rainbow the earth's new architecture, the old, brittle corruption of houses and factories swept away, the world built on a living fabric of Truth, fitting to the over-arching heaven.'

PART TWO

1985

IF IT BE LOVE INDEED

'Make me a willow cabin at your gate,
And call upon my soul within the house ...'

WILLIAM SHAKESPEARE: TWELFTH NIGHT

NINETEEN

The yellow Rolls-Royce purred through Lisle Street in Chinatown and even some of the Chinese – not especially known for their subservient attitudes – stopped to admire its flashy trumpery. It was the ultimate car in any city, the *one* triumph of the English class system, with its uniformed chauffeur in a peaked cap and black leather gloves.

The bustling crowds forced it to slow down but always made way for it. Even other cars gave way before the glittering silver figurine on its bonnet and passers-by asked one another who the small blonde figure in the back might be, in her chic black suit, white silk shirt and Rayban sunglasses. A few even waved at her but she ignored them, as she ignored everything else, including the brumming car telephone.

'The phone is ringing, Miss Moran,' the chauffeur pointed out.

'I know, Peter, I know. But I really don't feel like talking to anyone just now.'

'As you wish.' He reached behind him and switched it off – to Lisa's enormous relief since she didn't know how to do so herself. She had always been hopeless with knobs and switches, often just fiddling with them at random, all fingers and thumbs. She wasn't at all sure about this Rolls-Royce lark either. The car was lovely enough – particularly as she had acquired it and the chauffeur for nothing – but these people gawping at her all the time were beginning to fray her already threadbare nerves. Albert had once bought a Roller but had got so fed up with all the attention it attracted he soon sold it again. It had never bothered Michael Winner though. 'I just give 'em a wave and a smile.'

She poured herself another glass of champagne to calm herself down. She was on her way to speak to the media, always a big trial, and they had been hounding her mercilessly of late but Charlie had insisted that a Press conference was the answer and she had to keep Charlie happy or the yellow Roller – along with a good many other career benefits – might roll out of the door as quickly as it had rolled in.

They passed yet more Chinese restaurants and shops, some with papier mâché lions and envelopes stuffed with phoney money dangling on string in the doorways. The Chinese were about to celebrate The Year of the Ox, the year which demanded hard work from everyone.

Well, they were going to get their share of hard work from Lisa Moran. She was opening in a one-woman play, *A Series of Surrenders,* the following Monday. Sean had written it especially for her. A small theatre, The Spot, had been refurbished and a fortune spent promoting her return to the boards after six years. *Six years!* Where had all that time gone? She couldn't point to anything remotely useful she had accomplished in that six years and the media monkeys were certain to ask her what she had been up to in all that time.

There were going to be separate interviews with radio, press and television, in which she would talk about any trivia she felt she could get away with. Ugh! She poured herself another fizzy stiffener. The monkeys had been informed, in unequivocal terms, that they were not to ask anything about her private life in general or her men in particular: any questions about her men and the interview would be terminated immediately.

She was also most touchy, she had told the public relations girl, about her old role in *The Rebellion* films. The first one had become a major international success, making Yuri Pucket one of the richest actors in the world since it had spawned violent sequel after violent sequel in a series which had generated a billion dollars. She had only ever appeared in the first but they were still calling her the mother of this appalling industry, so questions about that wouldn't be welcome, particularly as she hadn't got anything out of it after her initial fee. *Karen, it won't make a single penny at the box office.* Every muscle seemed to stiffen when she recalled speaking those few words which had cost her a small fortune. She even threatened the studio with an army of lawyers and accountants but that didn't get her anywhere either. And as to whether the film was a crock she still didn't know since she had never once bothered to see it.

The Roller finally pulled up outside The Spot and a small group of photographers practically fell over one another trying to catch her getting out of the car. She refused to pose on the pavement and merely hurried in through the stage door with her head bowed. It wouldn't have been so bad if they'd been solely interested in her long-awaited return to the stage, but she knew it was her affair with Charles Judd, chairman of the third largest property company in London, that was getting them all on heat. Most, but not all, of her affairs had been meat and drink to the tabloids, particularly after the world-wide commercial success of the *Rebellion* films, but this one seemed to be an unusual circulation-spinner with its combination of fame, glamour, money and the ritual aggrieved wife sitting in her luxury home in Totteridge Lane howling her betrayal at any reporter who cared to knock on her door.

'Oh Lisa, you look absolutely fabulous,' the PR girl swooned, kissing the whereabouts of Lisa's cheekbones three times. 'You're the only woman I know who manages to lose two years every time I meet her. I just don't know how you do it. And what a fantastic suit.'

'Phillipa, darling, just make sure those bastards ask the right questions. I'm feeling a bit delicate today and I don't want them pressing all my buttons. Poor Charlie's got enough to put up with without them climbing on his back yet again. Fucking jackals. The whole lot should be shot at dawn.'

'Lisa, these are just arts hacks who write about the theatre and they've been warned and double-warned. I've made them agree to everything except a blood test. They won't be asking you about *Rebellion* or your men. They just want to talk about your work. I thought we'd do the interviews on the stage. The television cameras can work easier up there and we can get them out of the way first.'

She sat in her armchair on the stage, playing nervously with a cigarette as the technicians from Thames Television moved around her, setting up the lights and cameras for the first interview. The interviewer was checking through his prepared questions which he hid down the side of his armchair. Lisa was always nervous on such occasions until she decided she liked the interviewer and the drift of his questions. Then the problem was not so much keeping her talking as getting her to shut up. Otherwise longer and longer silences would be punctuated by a lot of irritable fidgeting, often followed by a torrent of foul language and a declaration that the interview was over. It was almost impossible to tell which way it was all going to sail in a Lisa Moran interview, if it sailed anywhere at all.

Yet the first interview with Thames went well enough, partly because the interviewer kept losing his questions down the side of his armchair and that amused her. The second, with some BBC television arts programme whose name she did not catch, also went well but by the fourth interview, with Capital Radio, she was beginning to flag: the questions were repeating themselves and she was giving much the same answers.

'This play, I suppose, is about a woman who is coming to the end of her life and beginning to add up what she's got and hasn't got. Everyone assumes she has everything but love is missing and so she describes how she deliberately sets out to find it. It's an old quest, of course, but no one has ever tackled it quite like her. The title is ironic since she does keep surrendering which is how she finally gets what she wants. Quite how she does it people will have to discover for themselves by coming along.'

'All rather different to the role you played in *Rebellion* then?'

She winced visibly but took it in her stride. They never listened, did they? Wild animals, when you got down to it, forever sniffing around where they had been told not to go. 'We don't talk about that film. It wasn't exactly the highlight of my career and that's all I'll say about it. Put it another way, actresses have to pay their bills too. I *needed* to pay my bills when I made that.'

'Is it likely that your ex-husband, John Orland, will ever write another play for you?'

Another tightening of the mouth. This one seemed to be actively courting trouble. He was also ugly with thick, deformed lips but she ploughed on. 'I was wondering when dear old John would crop up but I'm not privy to his writing plans and, rather like Rhett Butler, I don't give a damn. I'm not even sure if he can tell one end of a Biro from another these days. Is he still writing? You'd better ask that usherette he's living with. Or has he left her too?' She forced a sickly smile which was more a rat-like baring of her teeth. 'I can't tell you anything at all about him I'm afraid.'

Interview followed interview with some of the questions sailing close to the wind but she was still somehow managing to hold on to her legendary temper when the interviewer from *Time Out* eased himself down in front of her. No sooner had he switched on his tape recorder than she found herself telling the most whopping lies if only to ease her thickening boredom. Rather like Hedda her only real talent was for boring herself to death and she even started rewriting the theme of the play, claiming that it was how innocence could, in certain circumstances, be a crime; how naivety could be a bigger sin than sophistication.

'Do you see any echoes of your own private life in this play?'

Again she bridled a bit but she quite liked the look of her new inquisitor's lean and hungry features. 'Well yes and no. I've often found life disappointing and had my own problems coming to terms with what Shakespeare called 'the perfect ceremony of love's rite'. There have been many men in my life – too many perhaps – and I have received many intimations of love but never found the real thing, never really found that emotional holy grail we girls are always looking for.'

This was going well – he had checked that the spools on his tape were working properly, as they always do when you are telling them something they want to hear and do not want to forget. 'I know I'll find real love one day,' she went on, dropping her voice a shade and leaning forward slightly, as if enjoying herself at last. 'I've always had the feeling that everything so far has just been a series of rehearsals for the final big production. I'm very Russian about love. I believe in it absolutely. One day the clouds will part and the grail will be sitting there waiting for me to pick it up and I'm sure I'll recognise it immediately.'

'You wouldn't say, then, would you, that you are in love with Mr Charles Judd?'

The question fell with all the grace of a big stone being dropped off a bridge onto a passing train. She stiffened and sat upright, staring hard at this positively repulsive interviewer from that desperately unimportant listings magazine.

There was always one bastard around ready to spoil the party, wasn't there? She looked down at his circling spools of tape and up again at him, his eyes wide with anticipation of a juicy reply and the watchful mien of a dog unsure if he was going to get fed or kicked. He wasn't remotely interested in her play or the arts, she knew; this one was on another mission altogether.

'Charles Judd?' she echoed weakly, her eyes wide with ignorant innocence.

'Charles Judd, yes. He's a very wealthy man who's big in property in the city. We've been told he's financing your comeback in this play.'

She blinked several times, swallowed a mouthful of saliva, blinked again. Plates groaned. Spots flamed and spat. A low rumble of uneasy lava. 'You've been reading the wrong gossip columns,' she snapped.

'Oh come on Lisa …'

'Miss Moran to you.'

She was going to give this skinny jerk a good clip around the ear if he didn't watch it. She'd had trouble with hacks from *Time Out* before; that review back in '65 for one. *Wooden lines don't come any more wooden than in the mouth of Lisa Moran* indeed! Why did these bastards always come from *Time Out*? Did they have some factory in the basement of *Time Out* manufacturing illiterate creeps like this? A few more loud, lumpy gurglings of lava. 'So then. Have you got any questions *about my work?*'

'Miss Moran, we have been probing the business dealings of Mr Judd for a long time now and I have to put it to you that he has made millions out of the misfortunes of others. What he is doing now is not actually illegal but he has caused a lot of distress to his tenants in the past and an actress as distinguished as yourself should not get caught up in any of this.'

She was so confused by this attack on a man who had always been kind and supportive to her that she couldn't actually see through the gathering fog of her rage. Then her armchair moved backwards sharply as she leaped to her feet. 'Get out of here you little wanker,' she managed to gasp finally. 'Get out of here right now or you're going to get your bollocks shaved clean off.'

'I'm only warning you for your own good, Miss Moran.'

'Out! Out! Out!' She stormed across the stage and disappeared, stage left, pursued by a PR girl.

'At least read the dossier I've compiled on him,' the *Time Out* hack shouted after her. 'At least read that. You should know what he's done to his tenants, the methods he's used to winkle them out of their homes.'

Lisa reappeared, almost at once, stage right, still pursued by a PR girl. The movements of her hands suggested the *Time Out* hack was going to have quite a lot of dark bruises to attend to quite soon. Those boards were her jungle; this was where she ruled and tore apart those who upset her.

'You snivelling piece of crap,' she screamed, sprays of angry spittle flying from her mouth, her hands tightening and loosening as she bore down on him, one slow step at a time. 'You come in here, spreading your filth and lies when we're trying to put on a play about innocence and love. You come in here poisoning the name of a good and kind man. Well, I'm not having it, do you hear? I am just not putting up with it.'

The hack tried to grab his tape recorder to leg it but she got him by the collar with both hands and pulled him backwards across the stage where he fell over and she set about him with her fists, whacking him around the head five or six times while the tape recorder he had dropped screeched like a baby Dalek which had lost its mother in a fog.

There were still Press photographers at hand and, far from coming to their colleague's rescue, the rotten sods merely stood there taking photographs of the attack. The front page of the *Evening Standard* that afternoon carried one of its liveliest photographs for many years and the headline wasn't too bad either: TOP ACTRESS BOUNCES HACK.

'I'm sorry, Charlie, I just couldn't help myself. I've always been loyal to my friends and, when he bad-mouthed you, I just had to let him have it.'

'Nuffink to be sorry abaht, Duchess. All I'm saying is, you want to 'ave someone beaten up, just let me know an' we'll get it sorted. That's all I'm saying. I'm not getting at you or anyfink like that.'

'I just lost my temper, Charlie. It happens sometimes. Something snaps and my brain goes walkabout. My bad temper is going to put me in prison one day. I just know it. You *will* come and visit me there, won't you Charlie. I could manage any sort of stretch if you'd come and visit me just once a week.'

'I'm sure me missus would be pretty 'appy to see you locked up but you're not going anywhere. 'Ere, you want any more of this plonk?'

Lisa was sitting with the new man in her life at a candlelit table in the corner of The River Room in the Savoy. A pianist was tinkling the ivories somewhere in the distance and the waiters hovered on the edge of the candlelight, poised to anticipate their slightest need especially as Mr Charles Judd was one fantastic tipper. She had barely touched her lobster but Judd had all but eaten the claws and whiskers of his and was now quietly belching as his eyes ran down the menu and he tried to decide what he was going to fill his fat little face with next.

The wine waiter refilled Lisa's glass with the deliciously rich Romanée-Conti and she relaxed more with every sip, happy at least that she had managed to apologise to him for duffing up that jerk from *Time Out*. Not that he seemed to give a tuppenny toss as he concentrated on the menu and decided on one of the Savoy's celebrated milk puddings.

Yet even with the wine calming her down she didn't feel entirely at home in this place varnished by so much money, unable to relate to anyone or anything, where no one seemed to walk past you so much as waft through the candle-lit murk. Women always left a trail of expensive perfume in their wake here while the men might give you a discreet nod if you caught their eye. Occasionally the candlelight caught in a necklace and the very glitter – like stars falling from a fairy godmother's wand in a Disney film – said that the bauble was not paste.

Lisa studied her Charlie carefully as he turned to beckon one of the waiters with an elegant 'Oi, you.' Of all the cock salmon which had leapt up the foaming rapids of her river this, the chairman of Judd Estates, had to be the oddest and most colourful. Short and squat as a sack of potatoes, there was barely a hair on the billiard ball of his bald head. His accent was pure East End but somehow he had managed to clamber out of there – and an early business association with the Krays before they took up lodgings with Her Majesty – to build up his property company into an empire which seemed to make as much money as the Royal Mint but with far less effort.

He had always insisted to her his operations were entirely legal and it had been many years since he had owned residential property, let alone hired thugs to winkle the tenants out. 'All right, there might 'ave been a few dodgy dealings in the early days but we're all legit now, Duchess. No need for any dodgy dealings now. Nah.'

Yet she often hoped that he might be into something dodgy since she really liked the idea of being a gangster's moll. She also approved of the way Charlie was forever reaching down into his bottomless coffers and showering her with furs or jewels or taking her to meet his shady mates. They had gone to Walthamstow Dog Track on their first date and she had never met so many wonderful villains in all her life.

They could have wandered straight out of the pages of Damon Runyon, flicking the cuffs of their double-breasted suits, discussing property deals worth millions in their incomprehensible argot and then bickering like poverty-stricken kids about whose turn it was to get in the next round. Their names were extraordinary – The Penguin, Jo-Jo the Nutter, The Minister, Bob the Sledge – and Lisa was a big hit with them all, entering straight into the world of the dog track and forever tarting it up with plenty of leg and cleavage, not forgetting the furs and the bejewelled turban formerly favoured by Joan Crawford. Her very appearance caused great delight for all her boys, as she called them, and mounting dismay among their peroxide floozies who hung around in the background, with their own sparkling jewellery and gilt, waiting for the bar to shut so they could then be noticed. The boys even gave Lisa the ultimate East End title of 'The Missus' but Charlie liked to use the even bigger honorific of 'The Duchess'.

All her boys were graduates in crime and violence, the bright new stars of Margaret Thatcher's booming, greedy London, who had abandoned the rats-through-the-letter-box and muscle stuff and moved into legitimate property deals en masse. Property was the key to a brave new world where every gangster's dream was borne up on a tidal wave of borrowed cash. Anyone selling a couple of sizeable houses in London could become a millionaire almost overnight. This cash then started running through computer terminals with people adding noughts to it for no sound economic reason that Lisa could see.

Any developer who could find his own way to the front door of a bank was showered with money and every vein in the city had millions of pounds of ever more useless money coursing through it. Everyone knew there had to be a crash. But not just yet. Not today when everything was one long celebration, complete with champagne and milk puddings in the Savoy and you bought whatever you fancied.

Many of her boys at the dog track were still small fry, turning over derelict houses or the odd block of flats but the high rollers like her Charlie had got into offices and shop development. All you had to do was find a bit of land in the city – any old bit of land, it seemed – get plans drawn up, grease a few palms and then borrow a million or three. The more you borrowed the more secure you became: the more you owed the less likely the banks were to touch you for fear of upsetting the overdrawn apple cart and losing the lot. That was the part that Lisa could never understand. Her bank always came charging after her like a wounded bull if she ever got slightly overdrawn.

Yet, in all fairness, Charlie had been more than generous with her. He had paid for The Spot to be converted from a strip club when they could not find a suitable venue for Sean's new play in the West End. She could buy anything she wanted in Harrods and charge it to his account and, only a few days earlier, she had found the yellow Rolls-Royce, complete with chauffeur, parked outside her house in Cheyne Walk. He also had an unusual way of actually giving her money, not with a fat envelop next to her bed or anything vulgar like that but by handing her a small roll and telling her to whack it all on a certain dog at Walthamstow, usually in the knowledge that the favourite had just been fed a dozen pork pies and a bucket of water or that the trainer had given its knackers a good squeeze before it got put into the starting box. She adored all this low-level villainy and the bookmakers soon came to hate the sight of her huge laughing mouth and turbaned head, particularly when she came back to their pitches to collect wodges of money the size of lavatory rolls. She didn't always win but it was getting so bad they had tic tac men monitoring her every move so they could lay off her bets in plenty of time.

Charlie had also given her the keys and deeds of an apartment in Puerto Banus in Marbella and even arranged membership of the beach club for her there. She had never wanted an apartment in Puerto Banus which, as far as she could make out, housed half the criminals in the East End, still less belong to a club with Jimmy Tarbuck and Bruce Forsyth on its membership list, but Charlie had insisted she could probably sell the place at some time in the future if she was strapped for cash.

In the light of all this she wouldn't have been too surprised if Charlie had asked her to ride shotgun on a bank raid or uncouple a few carriages on the Royal Mail train but, apart from frequently objecting to her foul language and once complaining that she was showing too much cleavage at Walthamstow Dog Track, he appeared happy for her to do anything she liked without paying any dues. In his simple, working class way he kept saying he was happy and honoured to have her around. "Appy an' 'onoured, Duchess.'

'Has your wife been giving you any grief lately Charlie?' she asked when he had finished slurping his way through his milk pudding.

'Nah. But I s'pose that fuss in the *Evening Standard* will get her in a lather again.' He blew his nose loudly into a table napkin. 'She's got 'er dream 'ouse in Totteridge Lane wiv Frankie Vaughan living next door. Full of white carpets which cost a grand a month to get clean. Then there's the Jacuzzi she once had filled with champagne an' made enough bubbles to fill the bathroom. Then there's the six peacocks in the grounds who make enough racket to keep half of North London awake at night. She's got the lot so what does she want me for?'

'Perhaps she loves you?'

'Loves me? Nah. All she ever loved was that big 'ouse of hers. Lost interest in me, she did, the day she moved in.'

'So, are you coming back to stay with me in Cheyne Walk tonight Charlie? A girl can get awfully lonely you know and it would be nice to have you there. You don't *have* to stay with your mother in Stoke Newington all the time. I'd have thought your mother would have been glad to be shot of you.'

He jumped slightly as a waiter's hand came over his left shoulder to light his Havana. 'All right, Duchess,' he said between puffs. 'S'pose Mum won't mind for one night but I'll have to give her a bell to tell her 'cos she'll probably be making me somefink for me supper an' she'll be worrying if I just don't show up. But she's well pleased to 'ave me back 'ome. Well pleased she is. Never thought she'd have her little Charlie back 'ome did she?'

'And you are going to sleep with me tonight, aren't you Charlie? In my bed. You can roll over and have a nice little kip if you want but I get even more lonely when I hear you snoring in the spare room.'

His lips spat out a few bits of stray tobacco and a look of abject woe spread across his fat features. 'Aw, we're not getting back into all that again are we Duchess? I've tole you before. I've got too much respect for you. I've tried 'ard enough an' you've tried 'ard enough but you're a star an' I don't know 'ow to start wiv you let alone finish.'

'I know how to start, Charlie. You just leave it to me.' She took another big

130

sip of her Romanée-Conti and it gave her such a divine whack on the side of her brain that Charlie's bald head actually dissolved into an alcoholic mist before materialising again. 'I know how to start *and* how to finish.' This wine was making her more and more horny but she couldn't remember the last time any man had put much of a smile on her face and she had long dismally concluded that Charlie would never do anything on that front; that he would just become an amusing friend who showered her with lots of jewels and money; a diversion coming at a time in her life when she needed all the diversions she could lay her hands on since, in private, away from the spotlight, her ghosts still bayed at her in the middle of the night.

'An' it's your posh voice an' the way you look an' all ... it's difficult to explain really.'

'Oh fuck this upper class thing. I am not upper class. Where did you get that daft idea from anyway?'

'Your language, Duchess.' He looked around anxiously. 'And we are in the Savoy ain't we?'

'Charlie, there must be other ways we haven't tried,' she began whispering with some urgency because that wine was stirring frothily in her loins. 'All right it hasn't worked so far but there must be other ways. Just tell me who you really love, who you find really sexy.'

'Well there really is one,' he said as his face bloomed into a big grin. 'The most lovely woman in the world is me dear old Mum but it has even less chance of working wiv her ain't it?'

TWENTY

Another day of humming anxiety and ghosts loomed in Cheyne Walk. Lisa had got up around midday feeling reasonably bright and collected but a letter from the local residents' group had knocked her straight out of kilter.

The trees along Cheyne Walk were dying from some mysterious disease and Chelsea and Kensington Borough Council was proposing having them all cut down, the letter said. Patches of yellow fungus were speckling the trunks and many of the young buds were turning brown, dead before they had come alive. There were possible treatments for this disease but they might be expensive, the letter continued. But in any event it was felt that every option should be explored before the council resorted to the axe. *Resorted to the axe*. The phrase had a certain Shakespearean chilliness about it.

So, as she stood in her living room, still in her nightie, looking down through the open window at all the palsied and condemned trees of Cheyne Walk, the ghost of Ranyeuskaya in *The Cherry Orchard* came to visit, standing next to her, looking through the window and sharing in her sorrow. Lisa had always loved those trees and had often seen her own cycles of life in them, had seen the way they had often reflected her moods and temper from year to year, sometimes appearing wan and dead but then energising in the spring before bursting into defiant life.

'Without the cherry orchard I can't make any sense of my life,' she said aloud 'and if it really has to be sold then sell me along with it.'

The trees in the cherry orchard, she recalled, were actually warm and bright with blossom when they had been cut down. They had suffered from no mysterious fungus but had been cut down when they had been full of the brightness and vivacity of life itself. Chekhov had always been calling on us to find the courage to endure and enjoy our lives but what was the point of enduring all this crap? Just *what* was the point?

'Yet the earth is brown and beautiful,' said Ranyeuskaya, putting a consoling hand on her shoulder and offering her a small lace handkerchief. 'There are many marvellous places.'

'But remember the new railway line running through the cherry orchard will save the family. And there will be a fair income from leasing the land for summer cottages.'

But Lisa continued crying and began pacing around but then decided on a long, hot bath in the hope that it might calm her down a bit. She shouldn't get too sad and there were, after all, many reasons to be hopeful these days and certainly she could draw a lot of consolation from the success of her play at The Spot.

A Series of Surrenders was not another *Hedda Gabler,* and didn't even come close to another *Little Foxes* but it had been a creative and critical triumph, a string of mood cameos each with the bite of real truth in them. For one hour and eleven minutes each night these cameos had brought her thrillingly alive as a mature woman moving gracefully to the end of a difficult and stormy life but still full of beautiful ideals. She was scornful of the men who had tried, but failed, to put her down; not in the least regretful of her many mistakes and, in the end, defiantly proud that she had always put love first. Most of it was drawn from her own story, of course; she had spilled the beans of her life to Sean who had then embroidered in his own bits. But no critic had actually caught on to this.

Every seat in the house had been sold out *before* any critic had clapped eyes on it, largely thanks to that assault on the hack from *Time Out.* With a flurry of brisk punches Lisa Moran had immediately become the new champion of everyone from feminists to the old-age pensioners and anyone else who had ever dreamed of beating the shit out of one of those monsters from the media. *A Series of Surrenders* received near-universal acclaim and her career was on one of its mysterious upswings after lying fallow for so long. Even *Time Out* put that by-now famous photograph of her on their front page. GREAT ACTRESS HITS HER PRIME, they had headlined generously, with a bracketed strap line: And Our Reporter.

Offers were coming in daily although nothing truly original had turned up which would take her off to fresh fields and pastures anew. Yet it was the way of the world wasn't it? You give your life to some classical roles and act right out of your skin, leaving your very blood on the boards but then you actually punch someone and ...

So there was much to be happy and positive about as she wallowed in her bath except that the sheer fretting evil of her earlier mood returned with some force when she lifted herself out of the water and paused long enough to catch sight of her body in the full length mirror. Wherever you looked and whatever you looked at there was something not quite right from the thinning thatch of her hair to the way the flesh on the inside of her arms was withering. She had always taken care of what she ate and had never been fat in any way but parts of her had lost their suppleness and it wouldn't be too long before everything was withering and all she'd be good for was playing a hag on a blasted heath. She also began taking special care with her make-up because of the spreading crow's feet around her eyes and not forgetting the tucks under her ears which, by the look of that slight sag on her jaw-bone, were going to have to be tucked again very soon. What man would want to feast himself on this ageing and withering body? She might have a few chances if he were blind but, as it was, none.

She dressed hurriedly, still feeling the intrusive presence of Ranyeuskaya, before stretching out on the chaise-longue gloomily watching the sun stream dust-motes across her living room. Sometimes she liked to blow into them, causing small storms of turbulence which took ages to settle down, no matter how small the puffs. The lunch-time traffic was grinding away outside, further poisoning the trees of her cherry orchard.

Her real problem, she knew, was that with her career on the rise and, thanks to Charlie, a healthy bank account, her love life was one fat zero. Contrary to the message of *A Series of Surrenders* she had got just about everything right *except* love and, stretching out here on the chaise-longue, watching the dust eddying around in the sunlight, she was very close to weeping about it. No love, no sex. What was a girl to do? She walked out to the kitchen and returned with a glass of fizzing champagne, putting it down next to the telephone. She also picked a book from the shelf and sat back down with it, putting on her reading glasses. Her dog, as usual, was snoring beneath her. That's all he ever did these days, only ever waking up for something to eat and then sleeping again. But, there again, he was getting old too; we needed all the sleep we could get these days.

No love, no sex. This refrain kept humming away in her mind like the hook of one of those cheap pop songs which would never leave you alone. She had always been so useless at handling sexual frustration too. Her nose went hollow, her belly kept turning over and over and all her blood seemed to flow the wrong way when she wasn't getting any. A good drink could often settle her but, no sooner had she sobered up, than her insides were in another mess again. She'd gladly take any pill to get rid of all this frustration but they didn't exist; the only pills her doctor had were for perking up your sexual appetite which was about the last thing she needed in this state. She put down her book with a loud sigh, causing the dog to open a sleepy eye before closing it again.

It would have been far easier if she could just have put her ageing body around a bit but she liked to have some sort of feeling involved in the transaction. There was never a shortage of offers after all – although she was sure that all they ever actually wanted to do was fuck her fame rather than her – and almost all the men of her age these days, rather like her dear Charlie, couldn't get it up or at least not with her — yes, age *could* wither it! — body. She wouldn't have been at all surprised to learn that Charlie actually paid for young whores: dim girls with firm, creamy bodies which went in and out in all the right places.

A lot of the younger men were getting most particular where they put their sad little dicks in this the age of Aids. She was wary of Aids too, which further reduced her chances, particularly now she understood what had wasted her dear old pal Harry Kirby. Many others in her theatrical profession were going down with it and, while it mostly seemed to threaten the gay community, she had been told that everyone was at risk. There were more — far, far more — people dying of Aids than was being officially admitted. Celibacy was back in a big way. Not for her though. Not for her.

It had never really crossed her mind that she should give up sex altogether. Good sex was the one thing that had always given her certain relief from the permanent gridlock of her humming anxieties. Good sex kept her ghosts quiet and under control and, sorry as she was to admit it, you would never catch her insisting on a condom. She would still have taken any bare-back chance with the right man, if she could find such a mythical being. But where was her knight on a white charger? *Where?*

Andrei Barapov still sculled over the herring pond occasionally but he had never been up to snuff between the sheets, even when all his muscles and joints had been working for the same common purpose, which they mostly weren't. They did try it from time to time but only when she was in between 'headaches' and, to further discourage him, she would insist he brought current certification that he was HIV-free. She had never quite managed to call it off with him, just as she had never managed to call it off with any man in her life. But he was getting on her nerves in a big way these days, fathering yet more ballet dancers in Manhattan and becoming more and more maudlin about the prancing little bastards. If any man needed to discover the joys of the condom it was her little Andrei.

She emptied her glass in two quick gulps, her inner furies rising thick and fast as she hitched her skirt up across her thighs. Her fingers began feeling around inside her knickers, rubbing her stubbly bush around and around, finding her clitoris hard and aching, desperate for some proper attention. Oh what a sick joke all this was. There were the gossip columns going on about urchin, elfin looks and that gamine sexual magnetism and how men found her irresistible and look at her now! This would have made a pretty picture in Nigel Dempster's column wouldn't it? Or on the front cover of *Time Out*. Oh how the hairy readers of *Time Out* would have laughed if they could see a picture of the great actress hitting her prime now. GREAT ACTRESS HAS A BIT OF A RUB. Big picture of her with her hand up her skirt. IF ONLY SHE COULD FIND IT.

She stood up unsteadily, her legs staggering one way and another as a few hot flushes of her favourite old lovers flashed through her consciousness – oh not Daniel again! – when she fell back onto the chaise longue, continuing to massage the inside of her legs hard, her body arching up and up, her legs rising ever higher as if she was trying to ride a bicycle upside down, her reading spectacles slipping further and further up her nose as her mouth opened wider and ever wider. Her dog, now firmly awake, was up on his hind legs and sniffing her, whimpering softly, uncertain what was going on even if he was certain *something* was going on.

The pattern of her breathing was changing and Daniel came wandering back across the roof of her mind again – oh Daniel baby! – and she kneed the dog away as he tried to climb right on top of her. She abruptly stopped what she was doing and flung her hands into the air with a muted cry of surrender before sitting upright again, putting her glasses back on her nose properly and wiggling her bum around a bit as she put her skirt back into place. Her eyes flashed around the room, as if checking that no ghosts had been watching this truly appalling and disgusting performance. She took a deep breath and held it, trying to recover her composure as she felt that old hollowness in her nose, her belly churning over and over and all her blood flowing the wrong way. She never learned did she? Far from settling anything all this had merely made it all worse. 'Why does everything I touch become so mean and ludicrous? It's a curse!'

Oh dear this was no way for the greatest Hedda Gabler of her generation to carry on. This was no good at all. She picked up her book yet again and realised she didn't have a clue who had written it – let alone what it was about.

As the afternoon yawned interminably before it was time to go to The Spot, she had a few more drinks and found herself becoming increasingly miserable and practically weeping for Daniel. Even after being apart for close on six years there was only one face she ever saw when she took herself in hand, only one pair of arms ever enfolded her and it was always the same pair of bony hips wedged between her thighs. It was hopeless, so utterly adolescent somehow, but it was always that enormous nose and long hair she missed in her panting shame. He had left a despairing, sobbing hole right in the middle of her which, it was becoming increasingly evident, he alone could fill. Ever since he had gone missing in fucking Brixton – only sending her a postcard of the Thames saying he was all right – no one had ever come close to calming her down, not even for five minutes.

In all this time Daniel had somehow managed to get going as a writer and had sent her three of his books with amiable, if not particularly loving, inscriptions on the title pages. She had fallen on them and read them like a greedy thing, astonished at how clearly she could hear his voice in the words and laughing loudly and often, particularly when she recognised a few of her own little quips.

The books were quite clever in their own way, with sharp characterisation and stories which moved forward briskly but she couldn't quite see their point, if indeed they had one. The first was a quite interesting story about retrospective jealousy with the focus of the man's passion on the woman's previous loves: a theme which sort of rang a bell with her. The second was about the search for a young girl in an England set in the future which, after a few twists and turns, became a chase. The third was a quite interesting story about two lovers going to the Lakes to live together and it not quite working out until a truck driver intervened.

Yet the big puzzle of all these books was not just that they were so *little* but that they didn't seem to reflect Daniel's depth of feeling or metaphysical encounters. The books had picked up a few decent reviews, which had been reproduced glowingly on the dust jackets, with none, as far as she knew, troubling the best seller lists, but it was as if Daniel had turned his back on himself and was merely turning out stories like so many pancakes hot off the griddle.

She wouldn't have allowed that had she still been with him; she had always wanted him to dive deep and then go deeper. He should go where no writer had been before which was why she had always been so keen on his Cockney *Ulysses*. The very concept had a thrilling ambition and she was convinced that Daniel, like Joyce, should give up all compromise to engage in a long, complex and difficult struggle to realise his artistic dream. And fuck money, she had always screamed at him. Any fool can make money. Get in there and become a real writer.

She'd had similar feelings when John O had been working in the house in Cadogan Square: feeling that gorgeous tap-tapping coming down from upstairs and filling her whole being with a magical delight. You could smell John's defiance wafting through every room. In his prime, when he had been writing his best plays, he had been the Prince of the Nay-Sayers and Daniel had that in him too. But not any more he didn't. Something awful had happened to him. He had gone all soggy, writing just like the rest of them, treading water, going nowhere.

Daniel hadn't even once mentioned God in his books either. And why was he still so reluctant to write about all those shimmering visions of his? God didn't get a look-in anywhere now. It was all alienation, cruelty, perversion, violence or the fucking environment. A whole generation of children was being destroyed by a corrupt media's obsession with crime and violence. Northern Ireland had been splattered apart by a violence-obsessed media for thirty years and they were still blaming the terrorists. She was right with Daniel on that front so why wasn't he writing about that? What was the point of a prophet who didn't want to prophesy? What was the point of having God talk to you about how he was so upset by everything when all you wanted to do was keep shtum about it, particularly when the world was full of oafs with empty voices all clamouring for our attention. There wasn't one writer saying one fucking thing that was worth listening to. Stoppard was undoubtedly clever and entertaining but what, if anything, was he saying?

She had always sent Daniel letters c/o his publisher, Kennington, because she no longer knew where he lived, thanking him for his books and saying how much she had enjoyed them – even when she hadn't but she knew all about the fragility of writers – and suggesting that it would be pleasant for them to have lunch together one day. But he had never replied – not even to refuse her invitations – and this resolute, bad-mannered, cold-hearted rejection was making her more and more despondent and ever more determined to do something about it. Daniel Jenkins was the only man who had ever walked out on her and she wanted him back, if only to be able to dismiss him properly. It was that adolescent thing again, she knew: wanting to get in the killer punch first. Even with old and withered bodies we never really seem to change; we still act as if we were in the first flush of our youth.

At one particularly low period a few months ago, on discovering that Charles Judd and his yellow Rolls-Royce were far from answering any of her real dreams or needs, she had hired a private detective to track Daniel down and tell her what he was getting up to.

The truth had turned out to be every bit as appalling as she had feared. Daniel Jenkins, the detective reported, was living in a flat above a Greek kebab house in Portobello Road with a young girl by the name of Helen Grantby. This girl made a living of sorts selling her charcoal sketches from a stall in the weekend market and Mr Jenkins spent his time working on his books. Yet, perhaps predictably given their occupations, they were as poor as church mice, often seen scavenging for food behind the stalls after the fruit and vegetable market had closed.

On some nights they attended meetings of Alcoholics Anonymous in the nearby Methodist Church and the detective had discovered, merely by sitting in on a meeting there, that Mr Jenkins was the Thursday night secretary of the group and Miss Grantby, who also had a long history of alcohol abuse, made the tea and provided the biscuits. The couple seemed reasonably well-adjusted and Mr Jenkins had mentioned God a few times in his 'share' and was even thinking that now he had put his 'old life' behind him he might try to become ordained in the Church. *Ordained in the Church?* Surely the Church wasn't so hard up they'd allow him into their midst. The Rev Daniel Jenkins indeed. He was even more certifiable than her.

Lisa had been so keen to learn what this sketching, tea-making tart, Helen Grantby, looked like she sent the detective back to snatch a photograph of her.

Helen Grantby looked remarkably plain to Lisa, who studied her face long and hard – a touch of Helen Mirren perhaps? – but hardly what you would call beautiful. Yet what really got up Lisa's trumpet was that this plain Jane was undeniably *young*. The bitch was hardly out of her pram and how she had found time to get all that alcohol down her neck Lisa couldn't even start to imagine.

So was this Miss Portobello listening to his religious insights into life now? And, if she was, would she appreciate them as much as Lisa had? She had always been in awe of them. Yes, in awe. That's why she so desperately wanted him back, not just for all that thrumming sex – well, maybe a bit of that – but to know more about his extraordinary encounters with God. That man was building a private stairway to heaven and she wanted to be next to him while he was at it. Even to think of him holding Miss Portobello made everything inside her tighten with coils of real fury. He was hers, damn it. He didn't belong to Miss Portobello or the fucking Archbishop of Canterbury. She had given up a lot for him and he owed it to her to come back. Oh there she was, going nutty again, but that was the effect he'd always had on her. The ship of reason was never cruising anywhere in Lisa's personal high seas when he came into view.

Then, really stupidly even by her stupid standards, she decided to go down there to see for herself, carefully disguising herself in black clothes, a woollen hat and Raybans and standing over the road from the Greek kebab house in the deep, dark doorway of a record shop to wait for the gilded couple to come out.

She'd been to the antique shops up the posh end of Portobello often enough but hadn't been down here before, a little way from the arches of Westway motorway and with strange surges of people moving around even at this time of night. The odd dread-locked Rastafarian shuffled past in a cloud of sweet-smelling pot and there were even odder heavy metal fans with tattoos and lots of silver studs in their denims. Hippies and drunks pitched around the pavements and shuttered stalls – many seemed to be local working class people, plainly bewildered by that was happening to their little area. As a llama went past on a lead Lisa thought she liked what she saw, that this might be the place for her now that her cherry orchard was due for the big chop and now that *he* lived here. He surely wouldn't be able to resist her if she was around all the time, would he?

Lisa had to swallow an involuntary squeal of surprise and the blood drained out of her face when the two did come out finally, probably going to Ma's in Acklam Road, run by a huge West Indian woman, for their dinner, according to her private dick. Daniel had had a severe haircut since she'd last seen him and he'd got slightly fatter too. She didn't like him fat; she liked him lean and hungry *and* she preferred his hair long.

But, as she followed them from a suitably discreet distance, she could tell by his body language that he was upset about something. She didn't dare get close enough to hear his words but, even from this distance, she could tell he was really worked up about something, particularly in the way he stopped occasionally to hold himself.

Oh this was hopeless. She was a famous actress for fuck's sake; she had one of the most-photographed faces in the world and here she was stalking a writer with short hair and a big nose who no one had ever heard of. How could one man sling so many hooks into her? Here she was being dragged along Portobello Road like a trout desperately trying to break free from all these ensnaring lines and fall back into the safety and anonymity of the dark night. But she couldn't escape, couldn't even loosen that which was driving her forward behind them. Love was a curse indeed: a curse which was no less bitter because it refused to go away, refused to die even when its summer lease was up.

She took to the other side of Acklam Road and found another doorway from where she could see the two of them in the window of the restaurant, both still locked in argument, hardly bothering with the food that was put in between them. She would have loved to have known what they were quarrelling about, maybe she could even have sorted it out for them but she still didn't dare to try and get close enough to them to hear the words. Then a fat West Indian woman, who was probably Ma herself, joined in the discussion, which had clearly become really heavy, since there were no smiles anywhere and just a lot of air being poked with angry fingers.

Later the two left and walked up to the arches under Westway where they stopped and began shrieking at one another again outside some travellers' caravans. Lisa found the area slightly threatening and became ever more careful to conceal herself in the darkness. Trucks growled overhead like aeroplanes coming in to land and the ground was littered with supermarket trolleys, broken drug ampoules and orange bread trays. A little like the rubble of her romantic dreams.

Then, all at once, their words were strangely amplified by the concrete arches. 'So you want all that back again,' Daniel was yelling at her. 'Just a few clothes in a black bin-liner? Pissing yourself in the street and waking up in detox.'

'I don't know how many more times I've got to tell you Dan. I can't think of any other way of dealing with all this pain.'

The row was interrupted by a burly man with hands the size of shovels emerging from one of the nearby caravans. 'You're waking the fucking baby so you are so fuck off the pair of you or you'll be getting something in your fucking ear.'

A woman with wild black curls and a billowing nightie came hurdling into the discussion, dragged there on a lead by an enormous slavering dog. 'If you two noisy bastards don't piss off this dog gets an early breakfast.'

The quarrelling pair left quickly and Lisa found herself running into yet more distant darkness to avoid them. Well at least she could take some comfort in the fact that, far from being serene lovebirds, there was a deep dispute between them about something important. She could never remember Daniel ever getting worked up like that over anything. Most of the time he was so laid back he was practically asleep.

Perhaps she could even exploit that dispute and find some way of stealing him back. She had no reservations about trying to do that: she would have to do something to get all these hooks out of her, forever pulling her around in ways she didn't want to go. She couldn't keep bleeding like this all the time: day after fucking day, month after fucking month, year after fucking year.

TWENTY ONE

The following Monday Lisa received an unusually high number of letters which her new part-time secretary, Josey, had sorted into the usual three piles: junk, money and glory.

Lisa binned the junk without even looking at it, scanned the money pile quickly which, yet again, invited her to do ads for quite stupid sums of money that she always refused and then flicked through the glory pile – would she become a patron of this, would she open that, would she perhaps find time to visit so-and-so?

It wouldn't have been quite so bad if they ever wanted her for herself but all these people were still doing, she knew, was merely reacting to her latest bout of publicity. No one offered you anything for years then, after a headline or two, they were all after you. Maybe it was the way it had always been but she still did-n't like it and she kept writing no, no, no on the various letters. *Who do we get for this? Oh, Lisa Moran is in the news, let's try her. What's she in the news for? I'm not sure now I come to think about it. Didn't she punch someone?*

Yet buried in the glory pile – which Josey perhaps should have put in the money pile – was yet another letter from a publisher wondering if she had ever considered writing her autobiography. The book had every chance of being highly successful, the letter drivelled on optimistically – in the predictable way all publishers' letters drivel on optimistically even when the book's real commer-cial possibilities were well below zero – and, given the strong chance of a news-paper serialisation, the advance could be substantial. They could also suggest some of the best ghost writers in the business, if she needed one.

She had received many such offers over the years – particularly after the col-lapse of her marriage to John O – but had turned them all down because it would mean ratting on all her men, especially the married ones. She had never quite liked the idea of spending all that gloomy introspection writing a book about herself who she didn't find all that interesting. She was just an actress after all who couldn't really do anything properly.

Lisa was about to scrawl 'No' on the letter when her heart took a little tumble as she noticed the letterhead, Kennington. Unless she was mistaken those were Daniel's publishers and she got up to her bookshelf to check on one of his novels. And there they were, the self-same. She sat down again and, as she re-read the letter carefully, Regina Giddens, the manipulative bitch to beat all manipulative bitches, came to sit down next to her with a small cough. Lisa looked up at her and back at the letter with a widening smile. A plan began falling into place, clicking like the tumblers inside a safe. 'I've been lucky before, Horace, and I'll be lucky again,' she said reaching out to pick up the telephone.

That Thursday the yellow Rolls-Royce swung around the traffic island in front of Buckingham Palace with such purring majesty that some of the tourists, waiting for a glimpse of the Queen, began snapping their Instamatics at the back of Lisa's head. A few waved at her and even the patrolling police seemed to stand to attention as it slimed up The Mall.

It was a strange city day with the sky curdling with dark winter clouds as spring sunshine swarmed over the towers and domes of Whitehall, making them glitter like the skyline of Istanbul. A ragged, saffron line of young people from the Hare Krishna temple came jigging down the pavement, doubtless heading for the palace to annoy the Queen with their banging bongos and crazed mantras. A policeman was interrogating a van driver who'd had the temerity to drive his scruffy heap down The Mall and a man in a bowler, about to step in front of the Roller, stepped back on to the pavement and gave Lisa a small bow.

By the time she had reached the end of The Mall the sky darkened again and the rain came tearing down in silver, cold sheets. Yet when they finally pulled up outside Le Caprice, at the back of The Ritz in Arlington Street, the sun had shouldered all this rainy darkness out of the way, framing the restaurant doorway in a dazzling archway of welcome. Lisa stepped out of the car like Aphrodite on a quiet stroll down Mount Olympus and was kissed three times on the cheeks by Timothy, the greeter.

'I say, this motor's a bit of all right. It can't have been long since you were offering to wash the dishes in here for the price of a meal.'

'Yeah, fucking ridiculous ain't it,' quoth Aphrodite in her best Walthamstow dog track Cockney. 'To be honest, Timothy, I hate the thing. Everyone stares at you all the time and they even salute you. If I could keep the money I'd sell it in a flash.' She winked and lowered her voice confidentially. 'Ain't mine, I'm afraid. Bit of a legover job, if you follow my drift.'

'You must give great legover, if that's what you get for it.'

'The best legover, Timothy. Take it from me. The *very* best.'

She was almost half an hour early for her lunch appointment and sat at the table next to the window, where she could see all and be seen. It didn't matter to her that she was being used as a decorative advertisement to raise the tone of the joint. The food was always good and not too expensive; she could have a couple of plates of *hors d'oeuvres*, all she usually wanted, and they always made a pleasing fuss of her when she was on her own like this, watering her with as many free glasses of champagne as she cared to drink. She also liked to talk to the waiters, taking an avid interest in their love lives and freely dispensing advice. 'Foof! I'd just get rid of him if I were you. Tell him to sling his hook and find another.'

It often surprised her lunch dates that she always arrived early but that was her way. The champagne helped to settle her for what might be a sticky bout of negotiations and, anyway, her career on the stage had long drummed into her that you should never be late for anything.

The people from Kennington were on time, not one but three. They were clearly taking this possible deal *très serieusement* and Lisa had done her own bit of power dressing for this one, the Cleopatra-On-The-Nile-In-Her-Barge look: heavy Cartier costume jewellery and one of her Seventies Yves St Laurent suits with ivory trousers and matching shoes. (I'm hoping for a lot of money so don't demean me or my couturier with talk of tiny advances.) The two men were dressed in sombre, cheapish suits, which may have been Burton, and the young bespectacled woman wore a spruce navy jacket and matching skirt. (We're pretty broke but we hope you'll go along with us if only because it will be great for your image.) There was always a lot said at publishers' lunches long before anyone actually managed to open their mouth to speak.

Lisa read the trio immediately. The smiling man with the silver hair, already corkscrewing his finger in the air for large gin and tonics all round, was the daffy chairman who would keep smiling even if someone managed to throw up all over the table. The younger man, giving her lots of eye contact and going on about how really pleased he was to meet her finally, was almost certainly the editorial director who took all the final decisions, while the young girl was either the proposed editor of the project or the number-crunching accountant there to explain why the publishing house could not afford whatever whopping sum Lisa was going to demand.

It all started well enough, after their G & Ts, with long muttering studies of the wine list before the smiling chairman announced that the house wine was probably as good as anything so why didn't they settle for that? Lisa clapped her hands cheerfully and said yes, the house wine was fine and she was sure they would enjoy it, but she intended to stick to the champagne.

'Yes, er, yes, well,' stammered the chairman, picking up the wine list again as the others looked to him for a lead. 'Yes, er, well, yes, I suppose we could simplify matters and *all* drink champagne.'

It was a good start, giving Lisa the psychological advantage and she was almost sure she could see their minds rapidly revising whatever figures and tactics they had been talking about on their way here. So, having softened up their defences, in a manner of speaking, she would now move in the heavy artillery and blow their legendary meanness into smithereens.

'John Orlan first introduced me to the joys of champagne,' she began. 'He liked to drink it morning, noon and night. The Voice of the Working Class wouldn't go anywhere unless there were a few bottles on ice. Tried to clean his teeth with it once. Poor old John always felt he'd escaped the working class if he had a glass of fizz in his hand but he never did really. Never.'

'You never did much in films, did you Lisa?'

'Not really. It was mainly stage, but I did three or four films, including that wretched *Rebellion* rubbish. But nothing for television.'

'How did you get involved in the *Rebellion* film?'

'I'd been out of work for ages and only agreed to do it because they said they'd keep my name off the credits but the bastards didn't and now I'm having to live with it. I was reading somewhere that the *Rebellion* films have grossed a billion dollars. Can you imagine it? This great mythical hero, Yuri, has generated a billion dollars and the same great man of action is scared stiff of ants.'

The table erupted in riotous laughter and the chairman called for another bottle of fizz.

'I am not joking either. That Yuri Pucket has got to be the biggest wuss I've ever come across and I've come across a few. He couldn't stand still if he thought there was an ant within six feet. We spent more money on insecticide in that film than we did on bullets. Every time I look at that poster – you know, the one of him frowning, all guns and rippling pecs – I burst out laughing. The only woman he ever listened to was his mother and someone once told me to act like her. So that's what I did in that film if only to get him to behave professionally. And I slapped him a couple of times. It worked too.'

They were on their third bottle and no one had even looked at the menu so she judged she was doing all right. She knew what sold books and, by the time she had finished with them, they would be signing a blank cheque and handing over the head of Daniel on a silver platter.

'The gossip columns say you've been seeing Andrei Barapov,' said the editorial director. 'Is that true?'

'Oh the Bouncing Codpiece comes over from Manhattan now and again and we do a little coke together. He can't dance unless he's had a good snort since, as Henry Cooper might have said, 'e's a good boy but 'is legs 'ave gorn. It's a good job they don't do drugs tests at Sadler's Wells.'

'Coke as in drink do you mean?'

'No. Coke as in cocaine. Terrific stuff. About the only thing that keeps poor

Andrei bouncing around. You should try some. It would probably brighten up your list no end.'

'It might at that,' the chairman agreed wanly. 'It might at that.'

'And you've been linked with Charles Judd who is said to be one of the richest men in London.'

'Well I'd better be careful what I say about dear old Charlie because – wink, wink, nudge, nudge – I'm quite attached to my kneecaps. We're not lovers within the meaning of the Act and he's really a father figure to me. Yes, it has given dear old Charlie a lot of pleasure setting me up in this play of mine and I do owe him a great debt.'

When they did order the food, Lisa said that she would settle for a large plate of one of the starters, bang bang chicken, and, to her mild surprise, the two men went along with her. The young girl in the suit ordered a plain rare steak with no trimmings. She had barely drunk anything either while the two men had been guzzling so much they had gone off to strain the potatoes together.

'Is that an Yves St Laurent?' the young girl asked when they were alone.

'Yes.'

'I thought so. You can always tell real style. Clothes like that last forever, don't they? I expect that Cartier brooch cost a fortune too.'

She's not an accountant or an editor, Lisa realised. Apart from their Christian names, which she had anyway now forgotten, she didn't know any of their official titles. 'So what do you actually do at Kennington, my deah?' she asked, when the two men returned, all hiccups and beaming *bonhomie*.

'If you did this book for us,' the editorial director said when he had sat down and re-arranged his elbows on the tablecloth. 'If you did us the great honour of doing this book, exactly how candid might you be prepared to be?'

'About all my men, you mean? How I once gave Picasso a blow-job and all that?'

He swallowed hard. He'd clearly not heard that one. 'Yes, all that.'

'Oh, I'd be very candid indeed,' Lisa lied. 'Yes, I'd tell all. As I hope you can see there's nothing mealy-mouthed about me. What you see is what you get, although it might have been a bit of a wank with Picasso to be honest. We were all so drunk on absinthe I'm not really too clear who did what to whom and when. I do remember old Pablo's hands suffering from permanent wanderlust.'

'Well, we've had a little chat in the lavvy and decided we could probably go to two hundred thousand if you'd tell all. The truth, that is. There would be a lot of other residuals and, of course, this sum is not finite because it's merely a *guaranteed* advance against earnings. You would not exactly get two hundred thousand up front but I wouldn't be surprised if your story, told in the right way and marketed in the right places, couldn't net you half a million. Or maybe even more. It all rather depends on what you're prepared to reveal. In general let's say we'd be interested in your work, your relationships with your men and, er, a little bit of drug-taking wouldn't come amiss either. Let's say, er, the more indiscreet you got the more you would be likely to make.'

They were all quite serious now, waiting for her response and she knew better than to agree to – or haggle about – anything at this stage, content to let her agent Karen sort out all the grisly stuff later but she could at least settle the one crucial condition now. 'That's a lot of money,' she said, lowering her eyes, biting her lower lip and taking her time. 'A very great deal of money and I could start on the book quite soon. I've got no real commitments after my present run in The Spot which ends next Saturday. But I couldn't do it on my own. I'd need a ghost writer.'

The men's bums rose a good inch off their seats as the chairman called for another bottle of champagne and the editorial director re-shuffled his elbows. 'Miss Moran, for a book like this a ghost writer would be as easy as winking. We could get the very best, perhaps even try, say, Tony Holden, who did very well with his Prince Charles book. Or, let me see now, we might even try Kitty Kelley who did the Liz Taylor biography.'

'Ah now we've got into difficulties already,' Lisa said. 'There's only one ghost writer I could work with.'

'?'

'Daniel Jenkins.'

'!'

'He's not very well known but he's a brilliant writer who I also happen to get on with. I mean how could I work with Kitty Kelley after what she did to Liz Taylor? We'd end up killing one another.'

'Kitty Kelley was only a suggestion,' the editorial director said, a little icily. 'There's nothing in stone. We could even try David Holroyd if he was looking for a break from his Shaw. But Daniel who again?'

'He's one of ours,' the young girl broke in quietly. 'He's done three novels for us. They haven't exactly set the world alight but they *were* well written.'

'Oh that Daniel Jenkins. Yes, yes. I remember him now. But I'm not fiction you know. I'm biographies and travel.'

The young girl turned to Lisa and continued in much the same quiet monotone. 'Miss Moran, you asked earlier what my position is with Kennington and I'm afraid I didn't get a proper chance to explain. I'm one of those people who likes to listen to everything before I make a decision and, in such circumstances, I'm always happy for the men to do the talking – it's what they're best at, after all. My name's Miranda Haworth and I am the managing director. *I* am the boss. Eric here is in charge of biographies and Billy is our senior editor. I'm sorry we didn't make this clear at the beginning but lunch seemed to gallop off on its own.'

Lisa shook her head, amazed that she had so misread the situation. None of them had eaten much food but Ms Haworth told the waiter to clear the plates away and bring another bottle of fizz.

'There's still much to discuss,' Ms Haworth went on, moving her glass carefully like the first piece in what could be a long game of chess. 'But let me say now that I'm certain this book could be a brilliant success and make a lot of money for us. I also think Daniel Jenkins is a very good writer and, as you get on with him, he would indeed be ideal for the job. We'd anyway need someone who was relatively unknown because he'd only be ghosting it. Why Billy was talking of Holden or Kelley I can't imagine. They'd probably want a bigger advance – not to mention credit – than you and we don't want to share the money or glory around too much do we?'

'No, we most certainly do not.'

'So yes, let's get young Mr Jenkins on the case and, if he won't do it – he's almost one of the oddest writers I have ever dealt with – we'll talk again.'

'No, Miranda.' Lisa held up her right hand. 'If Daniel won't do it, it doesn't get done.'

They knew that she meant it and were clearly trying to figure out what the hell was going on between Lisa Moran and Daniel Jenkins but, in the delicate circumstance, not one of them dared ask for any further detail and all that could be heard against the rising, increasingly raucous, late-lunch chatter of the crowded Caprice was the furious fizzing of freshly poured champagne in four untouched glasses.

'Miss Moran? It's Miranda Haworth.'

Lisa took the receiver with both hands in her living room as the whole of her belly lurched forward like a drunk stumbling into the cold night air.

'I've spent some time with Daniel Jenkins on your behalf, Miss Moran, but I'm afraid we're clean out of luck. He's clearly very fond of you and did take a long time to make a decision. But his final answer was no. As I suspected at the outset he wasn't interested in the money and we offered him a great deal. It seems his girlfriend put up a lot of objections and there's an added complication. I didn't know this when we met for lunch last week but Daniel now tells me he's about to enter holy orders and won't be writing a book of any kind for at least three years.'

Lisa clutched the receiver to her bosom and let out such a wail of pain that the dog came scurrying across the room to snuffle worriedly around her ankles. 'Miranda there are some men who are just not worth bothering about. I can't do anything with him at all. He's like a disease that won't leave you alone. That's what he is, worse than Aids. And he's probably only going into the Church to spite me. Some big deal to make me jealous of God. That's all this is. So God wins again. He always does doesn't he? I am so upset. Just what am I going to do now? Tell me, Miranda, darling, just *what* am I going to do now?'

'You're in love with him?'

'Yes, yes, yes. Desperately. Absolutely. But I don't know why. I really don't. Miranda, I'm a grown woman ready for a free bus pass and I shouldn't be going around behaving like this at my age. We've talked about my other men but he's the only one I've ever really loved. Him! Can you explain to me why I'm throwing away my heart on someone as stupid as him? Because I can't. I just haven't a fucking clue.'

'Love takes us all differently. You should see my man.'

'What's he like?'

'He's big, black and beautiful. He's got six kids – not by me, I hasten to add – and whenever I go to see him I come back covered in bruises. He's lovely.'

'Miranda!'

'Isn't it strange? But no one knows anything about this. This is just girls' talk now. *Entre nous.*'

'Oh absolutely. *Absolument.*' Her tone changed to the soft and intimately friendly. 'We must get together soon, Miranda. We'd have much to talk about. Come around any time. Afternoons are good for me – I usually go to the theatre about four.'

'I'll do that, Lisa, if I can call you that now. Yes, I'll almost certainly do that. So what do you think we should do about Daniel?'

'We could always poison the bastard. Gas him. Hang him up by his holy balls. Oh, I don't know. There's going to be one big fucking row in the Church when he gets in there. It's going to be the end of the Church as we know it. Does the Archbishop of Canterbury know what he's letting in? Oh my God, the poor old fucking Church is falling apart fast enough without any help from him. Oh Miranda, I'm really, really heartbroken. I know it sounds silly but I'm that desperate to get him back I just don't know what to do.'

'So did you really want to do a book for us or were you just trying to get him back?'

'Both. *Both!* I've always wanted to do a book and this seemed a neat way of getting him back at the same time. But life's never neat is it?'

'No, it's never that but, if you do want to continue trying, I've got an idea. Daniel is very fond of you, there's no doubt at all about that. He spoke of you with a great deal of affection so, if you're as anxious to get him back as we are to get your biography on our list, what I suggest is that you allow me to tell him you're terminally ill.'

'Miranda!'

'Lisa, Daniel Jenkins is one big softy. You can tell that from his writing and I

149

just know it will work. I'll ring him and say we were hoping not to have to tell him this – we were hoping he would agree to do the book without knowing about it – but the sad fact of the matter is that you've recently been screened and they've found a cancer which is only giving you six months. I'll tell him you're devastated and everyone is hoping he'll do the book as one last favour to you. Your final testament, if you like. I just know he'll fall for it.'

'Miranda!'

'You could both go off somewhere and work on the book. I've got a farm-house in Provence if you fancy borrowing that. You can have it for as long as you want. Why don't I fix up a date between the two of you and you can talk about it properly? You're our greatest actress, Lisa. I know you can do this.'

'I can do it all right but there'll be one slight problem. He's going to expect to start seeing me die so what happens in six months' time when I'm visibly full of beans and demanding to be fucked all the time? Even his holiness is going to smell a rat then.'

'Ah, I've thought about that too and the answer's simple. Just tell him that you prayed a lot for a cure and God granted it. You can also be sure that Daniel will also start praying for God to cure you so it won't be all that unlikely. Better still, you can go to Lourdes for a weekend and claim a miracle. He'll never leave you then.'

'Y-e-e-e-s. But I've just thought of another problem. Daniel never believes a word I say.'

'Why's that?'

'I'm usually telling lies. Well, not quite lies. Exaggerations. He's always catching me out.'

'I know a doctor. He's a real pussycat and he'll fix up the paperwork. You can leave it around and Daniel can read it for himself. Lisa, it *will* work. Shall I arrange a date?'

A long, thoughtful pause. She had always known that publishers were a bit sharky but had never realised that they would stuff a poor, young writer quite so thoroughly. Miranda was an even greater bitch than the great Regina Giddens. 'Do you know, Miranda, I haven't felt quite this cheerful for years. I really like you. Come around soon. You and I could become great friends. Between the two of us poor Daniel isn't going to have a chance.'

'We're only here to please, Lisa. That's all we publishers ever really want to do. Serve the public and keep everyone happy.'

TWENTY TWO

The city skies were undecided what they were up to the next day when Lisa walked down through St James's Park for a date on the small bridge. A cold wind blew over the lake, making the waters choppy and forcing the ducks to jump out and lie miserably, with their heads under their wings, on grass banks. On the opposite corner of the lake, near Birdcage Walk, a revolving, golden column of sunshine had broken through the black clouds and a gabbling gang of seagulls, their slate grey wings flapping vigorously, moved up and down inside it, just above the heads of two women and a child feeding them.

She stood on the bridge, hands resting on the rail, and looked across the riffling lake. Almost six years ago she had come here with Daniel and fallen in love with him on this very bridge when he told her about the secret life of this park and the duck who thought he was a dog. Six years! Yuck! He'd been missing for most of them yet it still seemed like for ever. She had always been faithful with her love and had never given out her heart on loan. When it was given it had always been given for ever.

And there he was. Even with his short hair he still looked, well, lovely although his tie was all over the shop and his suit still didn't fit. Yes, there was still that definite aura of poverty about him; the same old story of the writer whom writing had not fed. Yet he was a delight to look at – that Concorde nose and the smiling blue eyes which always made her go quite shivery especially when they were smiling at her. Yes, this was the shape of her weakness, her very own personal torturer, always at hand, when she woke in the middle of the night, to put the knife in and make her bleed with loneliness.

She could see he was ill at ease when, instead of saying 'Hello, girl' or even a cheery 'Wotcha' or even giving her a small friendly kiss, he dived for the bridge parapet and began throwing up into the lake. Romeo and Juliet it wasn't. She had been sick often enough herself during moments of real stress – usually before going on the stage – so she waited patiently for him to finish, her hands fishing

151

in her coat pockets for a tissue.

The veins on his forehead stood out in high relief as he sent yet another shower down into the water where a dozen or so ducks were already fighting over the first instalment.

'You seem to have eaten an awful lot this morning,' she said, holding out a tissue. 'Bacon, eggs, tomatoes. You never used to eat anything at all for breakfast. A cup of coffee and a fag wasn't it?'

'I never had any tomatoes,' he replied, still choking for breath while she waved the tissue up and down slowly trying to catch his attention. 'I can't stand tomatoes. Never have.'

'What are all those red bits then?'

He leaned further over the railings to get a better look. 'Ah, now then. They might be something to do with the spaghetti I had last night. Definitely not tomatoes.'

'Don't they put tomatoes in spaghetti sauce?'

'I don't know. But they might. I eat too much. Food is the only thing that calms me down now I don't drink or smoke.' He wiped her tissue around his mouth and handed it back to her. She threw it into the lake, setting off another squawking fury of hungry beaks. He opened his eyes wide and scrunched them closed again repeatedly, as if trying to get the lake and Whitehall back into focus. 'Believe it or not I'm getting fat,' he said finally. 'Look at this for a spare tyre.' He unbuttoned his jacket and patted his bulging midriff. 'When did you ever see anything like that on *me*?'

'Just a bit of flab. You're not getting enough exercise. I'd get that off you in no time.'

He buttoned his jacket before opening and closing his eyes a few more times. 'Shall we walk around the lake or something?'

'You're the boss. Anything you like. Have you finished being sick?'

'Yes, that's about it. Nothing much left for the ducks I shouldn't think.'

'Well, they enjoyed it anyway. Look, they've polished off the lot, even my tissue. Those ducks aren't fed properly. Perhaps I'll complain to the Queen.'

She let her hand dangle as they walked wondering if he would take it and, when he didn't, put it back into her pocket, feeling strange and empty. But he put his hand inside her pocket and took hold of it in there and she was surprised at how horny his touch made her feel. Happy too, if only because it felt as if they had never been apart and those missing years had just dissolved. They spoke about his new novel and her play. He had read about her ruck with that *Time Out* hack and inquired politely after her dog. She wanted to know all about where he was living and what he got up to at nights now he wasn't drinking. She knew what he was up to well enough, of course, but soaked up everything he had to offer anyway.

It was a golden, chattering few hours as they walked repeatedly around the lake, full of news and laughter although they managed to stay off dangerous subjects like the 'state' of Lisa's health. No mention of the proposed biography for Kennington either. But she did solve the mystery of what had happened to his great work on London in that he told her that he was still – albeit spasmodically – working on it. He had yet to make that long journey under the city.

A swan flew down over their heads so hard and low their hair was ruffled by displaced air from the great sweeps of its wings before it crash-landed in a tumbling, white heap on the lake. Rain speckled. They walked into a splurge of sunshine and he took her in his arms and kissed her. A warm, wet kiss with lots of saliva and tongues. Tonsil tennis. So enjoyable. So much missed. They smiled at one another briefly and played another set. His breath still had a sickly taste on it but she couldn't have cared less. More tongue-play and, at one particularly lively moment, their teeth touched. She worked her hands inside his shirt and was enjoying the feel of his body again, particularly his Michelin spare tyre. His hands found their ways into her clothing too and she was glad she had spent time that morning selecting her flimsiest Janet Reger, designed to give his hands easy access to all areas if the mood so took him.

She felt him sob once, twice and she pulled his head back by the hair, to look up into his amazing eyes, bloodshot red and flooding with tears. 'I'm sorry,' he sobbed. 'So sorry. I really am so sorry.'

The penny dropped and she felt an uncomfortable throb of warm guilt deep in her gut. In her happiness at being with him again she had clean forgotten how – and why – she had tricked him into meeting her in the first place. 'Stop it,' she said fiercely. 'Stop all that now. Enjoy the moment and cut the sentimental crap. That was always your trouble. You could never relax and enjoy the moment.'

He pulled himself together finally and continued kissing her with such passion and tenderness she all but swooned. Exquisite carnal memories of Paris and Jerusalem came crowding back into her mind and body. Those amazing hours in Cheyne Walk. She recalled how savagely, blissfully sexual their affair had often been. They had never cared where they did it either. No matter how much she tried to deny or belittle it, she had missed that more than anything and, as she felt again the terrific swelling of her most favourite bulge in the world pressing into her belly, she knew she would do anything and tell any lie to get him back. No mere man had ever made her feel the way he did. This man did not belong to that cow Helen Grantby or Alcoholics Anonymous or even the fucking Bishop of London. This man was the glory of all her love dreams; this man was hers and she would not only lie to get him back but fight, with all her strength, to keep him and, if push came to shove, she would happily die for him too.

'You'd better come home with me,' she said. 'We've got an hour or so before I go to the theatre. I want a big smile on my face when I perform tonight.'

'An hour's not very long. I don't think I could manage to work up much of a smile in an hour.'

'Well, do the best you can eh? That's all us Girl Guides ever ask for. That you always do your best.'

A little less than a week later Lisa was stretched out on the deep black leather seats of the yellow Roller, dozing with her head on Daniel's lap as the chauffeur drove them down the long road to Avignon. She had been sleeping more or less continuously for the past twelve hours, exhausted after the play's long run. Even when she had woken up she had still been half-asleep and uncharacteristically calm. She had even been calm enough to queue for coffee for the three of them on the ferry out of Dover, smiling vaguely at the other passengers and saying nothing, not even so much as a chirrup of complaint, when she was recognised and besieged for her autograph.

They passed through a small town with a crooked church spire where old men sat in sunshine outside cafés, drinking *pastis*. Children ran across school playgrounds and stooped old peasant women, dressed completely in black, looked up to raise a gnarled hand, as if honoured that anyone who could afford to be chauffeured around in a yellow Rolls should want to drive down their street. But, if the car had embarrassed Lisa, it had frightened the hell out of poor old working class Daniel and she had promised, not once but three times, that, as soon as she reached their farmhouse in Brouelle, the car and the chauffeur would be packed off straight back to London. This was merely a convenient way of avoiding taking a plane to Nice; she would rather have cycled to Provence than do that.

The car purred down yet another avenue of white-banded poplars and past yet more huge parallelograms of vines already coming into fruit. They passed a wooded hill where the roof of an ancient chateau, resplendently phallic in its sunny isolation, poked up out of the trees. Black and orange butterflies tumbled in the shimmering heat haze and, in one clacking square, men played *boules*.

He had raised the problem of her 'illness' a few times back in London but she had kept insisting that it was unimportant and that not only had she forbidden Miranda to mention it to him, but the very last thing she wanted was for him to stay with her because he was sorry for her. She'd had a few tests with a few worrying findings but now she would have to wait for a few more tests. If they found something important he would be told but, as it was, it was something she simply did not want to talk about. He must forget all about it. End of story.

But how could she expect him to forget about it? What if she fell seriously ill in the South of France? He had failed 'O' level French; he barely knew how to ask for a loaf of bread let alone for a doctor. What would he do? He must forget about it. End of story. Bread is *pain*. *Baguette* if you want the long thin thing.

That's all the French he needed to know. She would face all the problems when they presented themselves. So leave it at that.

It was noon when they eased into the drowsily seductive enchantment of the old city of Avignon with her plane tree boulevards, the high stone walls of the *Palais des Papes* and the bridge built by a boy who had an angel as a foreman. The inevitable crowd gathered to ogle the car and, leaving the chauffeur to guard it, Lisa and Daniel strolled up a winding hill and sat in a café in the shadow of the huge medieval palace where they could look down on the glittering, green waters of the Rhône.

'This palace was once the home of the Papacy,' Daniel said. 'Where the Popes took a break from Rome for nearly seventy years in the fourteenth century.'

'What's new? The Church was bent from the start. I've never, ever understood why you're so keen on it. Are you still determined to take holy orders?'

'*Determined* might be too strong a word. But they've told me to hold off for another year, just to be sure. Would *you* mind if I did?'

'Nothing to do with me. It's your life although I've told you often enough it's your destiny to become a great writer and I'm sure the Church isn't going to help you much in that direction. Great writers can only become great by acting great, by writing every day. You've got the talent and that's what you should do. But, if you do go in, you will be able to get out to fuck me now and then won't you? They don't put you in a chastity belt or anything do they?'

'Oh sure – but never on Sundays.' They chuckled together softly as the *café au lait* was put in front of them. 'I'm almost sure you can commit any sin you like as long as you don't do it on Sundays.'

'I still can't quite picture you in the Church though. Oh I can see you raving away in the pulpit well enough, but what about Bible classes and the Mothers' Union?'

'Well, it's not looking terribly likely at the moment, is it? I can't see the Bishop of London being very enthralled by my behaviour at the moment. The Church tends not to approve of its prospective ordinands running around Europe in yellow Rolls-Royces with famous actresses. Bad for the image.'

'Bollocks to the Bishop of London. It's God you want to worry about.'

'I'll have to remember that one for my first sermon. I shall say to my flock: 'As that distinguished Augustinian, Lisa Moran, once said to me: "Bollocks to the Bishop of London. It's God you want to worry about." That would be a fine text for morning sermon wouldn't it?'

'And why not? You'd keep your congregation awake anyway. Who worries about fucking bishops anyway? And, while we're on the subject, how's God been treating you lately? Been talking to you at all has he?'

'Well, no entries for the Euro-Visionary Song Contest, I'm happy to report, but there have been some strange, new developments. I'm not sure that it all adds up to the smallest row of beans but I've been hearing gunfire.'

'Gunfire?'

'I don't know what to make of it. Perhaps you've got some ideas or insights. A few times lately I've heard automatic gunfire and it's been scaring me stiff. I heard it in the countryside about two weeks ago, after I'd been to that interview in the theological college I told you about. It went off right in my ear as I was walking past some fields. But there was nobody about and it couldn't have been a farmer's gun because it was automatic. Then yesterday I was leaving the flat in Portobello Road after packing my stuff and those shots were so loud they practically ripped my ears off. I ran for my life.'

He went though the sequence of events again in some detail and although she listened in rapt attention she couldn't even offer the wildest theory as to what it all might mean. 'Automatic gunfire? I mean God doesn't pack Kalashnikovs does he?'

He also described, with a sadness which she rather resented but pretended to sympathise with, how he had finally broken up with Helen Grantby. He had told her that he needed to be with Lisa and there were reasons – *good reasons* – why. Helen hadn't accepted it, of course, particularly as he wasn't prepared to tell her what these good reasons might be. She had gone ape, as it turned out. She'd already been upset enough by his decision to go into the Church – all tears and incoherent words – before she had caved in almost immediately, packed her bags and left in the middle of the night. What had worried him the most was that she had gone back on the drink. As for himself he'd been a good little recovering alcoholic.

Their chat in the Avignon sunshine lasted almost three hours and, with the sun sinking behind the *Palais des Papes,* they decided they had better move on and paid for fourteen *cafés au lait*. She hadn't been suffering from too many hangovers since they had been together again. Plenty of indigestion, though, from all that coffee.

TWENTY THREE

The dark night hadn't yet settled her voluminous skirts over the land but everything had got distinctly smudged as they drove up an avenue of old chestnuts to the farmhouse at Brouelle. Lisa was erect and as gleefully alert as a child on a Big Dipper as her eyes took in all the detail of the new home where they could stay for as long as they wanted.

The dying sun had bathed the fields in a sea of glimmering fire and the farmhouse floated, black on red, on this blood-dimmed tide. Grey wisps of smoke curled up out of the chimney and a rusty rubble of obsolete agricultural equipment lay scattered about the farmyard among the wooden wagons and chicken sheds standing around like tiny castles on stilts. Hunting bats had already begun flitting overhead and, almost as soon as they opened the doors of the Roller, their noses picked up the welcoming smell of a wood fire; the smell of another, gentler, more innocent age.

About five hundred yards away, concealed in a small woodland, was the farmhouse belonging to Le Patron, who had sold this, the main part of the farm to Ms Haworth and who still, with his wife, maintained it in readiness for any visitors. They clearly didn't come much more distinguished than Lisa either since, no sooner had they picked their way through the cluttered yard to the door, than Le Patron and La Patronne were virtually standing to attention on the front step. La Patronne bowed several times before hurrying to help the chauffeur unload the luggage while her husband, with a ruddy, smiling face and beefy, slightly imbecilic features, windmilled his fat arms around in welcome and beckoned them inside.

Lisa had expected the usual décor of a holiday home in France – whitewashed walls, lots of Indian rugs on stripped pine floors, a few op-art prints, some tubular steel and glass furniture, fashionable for five minutes in the Sixties but then dumped in the second home abroad – but what she saw made her gasp: a huge log fire crackling in an open hearth and a bare floor of massive, grey flagstones. The furniture was largely of dark mahogany and the long refectory table was oak and recently beeswaxed. Dark sepia prints, possibly of earlier tenant farmers, were on the walls, and there was no electricity. The light, as Le Patron demonstrated with the aid of a taper lit from the log fire, came from the curving gas lamps fixed to the walls.

They might have been in the last century as they listened to the soft puttering of the gas lamps and savoured the lovely smell of burning wood, all wrapped in Provencal peasant farmhouse tradition. Lisa didn't think anything could be improved on. Her lover neither.

There was a stone sink in the kitchen and the cooking was done on a black-leaded range. Le Patron opened the pantry door to reveal bewildering piles of fresh vegetables, several birds hanging on hooks to bleed and, with a broad wink, 'le vin'; a huge wine rack stuffed with dusty bottles just sitting around patiently for year after year, waiting to be drunk. Lisa was amazed at the generosity of it all and was further charmed by the outdoor lavatory which had *two* holes in its long wooden seat. 'Oh I just couldn't,' she told Daniel. 'I simply couldn't.'

'Oh yes you could,' he replied cheerfully. 'We'll probably get our best work done sitting out here. I'll take the one on the right.'

'I couldn't.'

'Yeees. It'll be great fun with us both working on chapter four and you sitting there trying to squeeze out a big one.'

The *pièce de résistance* was the bedroom which had a china jug standing on a marble-topped wash stand, an oak armoire with a huge, unflinchingly honest mirror and a chunky four poster bed with drapes hanging off the high crossbars and an elaborately embroidered quilt covering the sheets and lumpy feather mattress. 'I hope you're going to find a lot of energy for that,' she chuckled giving Daniel a playful nudge with her elbow. Le Patron laughed uproariously, indicating he probably knew more English than he was letting on.

'Tomorrow you are on your own but, *ce soir*, you will be eating *avec nous*. At, ah, twenty hours, you eat *avec nous* and then you go solo.' Le Patron departed with a further flurry of scrapings and bowings as the chauffeur brought up the rest of their luggage and announced that, if they had no further need of his services, he was going to stay in Aix for the night and drive straight back to London.

'I'll telephone if I need you,' Lisa said, diving into her bra and fishing out a wodge of mad money for a tip. When he had gone she put her arms around Daniel and rested the side of her face against his chest. Her one real regret was that she really wasn't going to die. *Now it seemed rich to die, to cease on the midnight with no pain.*

They changed for their dinner date, she into a fluffy white chemise, all gauzy

158

nipples and bright underwear; he into a T-shirt and a pair of old Levis. It was going to be a real meal too, they could tell from the aroma of cooking as they walked up the dark path to the small wood where Le Patron lived with La Patronne.

She was most surprised to find everything in their home was modern and run on electricity – the cooker, a refrigerator, even a horrid microwave – but the welcome was traditional enough with mine host handing out cheering glasses of Pernod before introducing his mother, her grandmother, half-sister and two scabby dogs who looked up at their visitors with such deep, snarling suspicion she half-expected them to attack her at any moment.

Lisa's French just about enabled her to gossip about the weather and quite soon everyone was laughing and hugging one another. Then, with a general chorus of 'bon appetit', they all sat down for what Le Patron described as their usual simple fare. But as Lisa looked around the table she could see that this meal was going to be far from simple, noting the fresh vegetable crudités, the baskets piled high with sliced baguettes and the brown earthenware jugs brimming with roiling red wine which you could probably use to take your nail varnish off.

She smiled at Daniel, lodged between the grandmother and half-sister, when all the muscles in her face froze. He was holding a glass of Pernod in his hand. He had drunk half of it and gave every impression that he was about to drink the other half. Oh dear, that was going to go down like a cup of cold sick at Alcoholics Anonymous. They were going to hear one wild 'share' when Daniel went to his next meeting.

But it didn't really matter too much out here, she decided, even if she did feel a slight twitch of disappointment in her kidneys that he had finally surrendered after holding out for so long. Almost all her profession was alcoholic and it had been so refreshing to be with someone who wasn't even if he *was* a lot more fun after he'd had a drink. But there again he'd had a lot of personal worries to deal with. He was worried about Helen Grantby and all that automatic gunfire was another anxiety, so if a drink helped all that, it helped. He could always get sober in the morning. She wasn't going to take a stand on it; she had privately vowed that she wasn't going to take a stand on anything at all with him ever again *and* he was going to get no more arguments out of her.

Well *she* certainly didn't want to stay dry here tonight so she saw off her Pernod in one when Le Patron filled up her wine glass from the jug. She raised the glass to Daniel, to let him know she had spotted what was going on. 'I love you,' she mimed with exaggerated movements of her lips. 'I love you very much.' She then took a big sip of her wine which was as rich and robust as a good punch on the nose until the effect of the punch wore off and various earthy flavours seeped into the sides of her mouth. The chances of anyone getting up from that table sober were nil.

The first course was a delicious *soupe de poissons*, thick with lumps of rock fish, lobster and sundry other unidentifiable fragments which had lately been squirming around in the sea. Then a small plate of what Le Patron described as pressed pig's belly. In *nouvelle cuisine* England this would have been more than enough but, out here in peasant Provence, this was merely the overture. They paused for a short break to clean their palates with a light, oily salad and a lychee sorbet heavily laced with a liqueur.

Daniel was not trying to converse with the old crones on either side of him, just staring at her dreamily while also making lewd suggestions with the tip of his tongue. Oh golly! He wasn't going to show her up in front of the *domestiques* was he? She remembered some of his better performances in his drinking days: bopping with all those smelly tramps and waving that French loaf around like a dildo. And there was that time she found him outside her house in Cheyne Walk, lying in the gutter when he had just pissed himself. Did the Bishop of London really know what he was allowing into his Church? Shouldn't she perhaps drop him a line and warn his holiness?

Next a chicken *fricassée* with Le Patron filling up all glasses assiduously, while the two old women were now as silent as Daniel. At this point Lisa simply *knew* that Daniel was going to do something awful. But what? Not throwing up all his food, she hoped. Yet he wasn't looking all that bad, although his eyes seemed to be visibly changing their shape and he had clearly lost all control of his eyelids. She was full to the brim too and her knickers were beginning to feel six sizes too small. And look at that pot belly! You'd swear she was pregnant.

Just when she felt she couldn't eat another morsel the main course arrived: a *blanquette de veau* with some fungussy vegetables she didn't recognise. Daniel, drunk or not, about to be sick or not, was eating all his food with a well-mannered care although he had somehow acquired his own personal earthenware wine jug which he was setting about with some gusto. Oh well, once a pisshead always a pisshead.

She really did hope she was going to get some of the oh-be-joyful out of him on that feather mattress tonight except that she had begun feeling a bit funny herself. The half dozen different cheeses didn't much help, nor the peach tart followed by coffee and the round of highly toxic *digestifs*. Oh boy! They were going to need a block and tackle to move her now. Perhaps, if she could just get to the toilet, she could lose her knickers somewhere although, given the transparency of her dress, perhaps not.

No one was saying anything much about anything any longer, not even in 'O' level French. Le Patron had begun making loud farting noises like a diesel tractor trying, but failing, to start and Lisa took this as her cue to wobble to her feet and announce, in slow Franglais, that she was *très fatigué* and needed to go home for a *petit* kip on her feather mattress.

Daniel, however, had come to attention, likewise Le Patron, his wife, the grandmother and half-sister, all of them standing in silence around the table with the tips of their fingers resting on it, as if all about to start the meal by saying grace rather than just having finished it. At this point Le Patron put his hands together, as if about to start a prayer, and announced that it was really necessary and *très important* that everyone should sample his *pshitt*. Lisa and Daniel looked at one another, eyes wide with shock, when Le Patron explained that this *pshitt* was his homemade champagne so, as one, they all sat back in their seats.

This *pshitt*, fatally strong and with lots of strange bits floating in it, was the one real mistake of a night. Daniel kissed everyone including the grandmother and half-sister, not with delicate kisses but full on their mouths, before stumbling out into a night which was studded with millions of brilliant stars as he and Lisa tried to make their way back to the farmhouse slightly hindered by the fact that Lisa fell over three times. At one point, Daniel fell headfirst into a drainage ditch and she kept calling out his name until he emerged, around three minutes later, complaining that he had cut his finger. He then opened the farmhouse front door with a head butt and, by the time they reached the bottom of the stairs, not only was his finger dripping with blood but there was a large red lump in the middle of his forehead. 'I – am – never – going – there – again,' he mumbled wild-eyed. 'You can tell him just where to shove his *pshitt*.'

'I couldn't believe what he was offering us,' she roared. 'Didn't know *where* to put myself.'

'No more *pshitt* for me. He can keep his *pshitt*. Look at my hand. All bleeding and bloody. Drink my *pshitt* indeed! Feel this bump here. Go on. Just feel this bump.'

'But do me one favour Daniel darling.'

'What's that?'

'Promise me one thing will you? When you go into the Church, as I'm sure you will one day, and when they give you your own cathedral, which I am sure is only a matter of time, promise me you'll open the door ... by the handle?'

Incoherent with laughter they hindered one another up the stairs and, even in her bloated intoxication – or perhaps because of it – Lisa was feeling urgently horny and there was no chance that Daniel was going to get any sleep at all in that four-poster until he had managed to perform a few small duties. They did manage to partially undress one another only to fall backwards onto the bed where they quickly discovered that, whatever else a feather mattress was for, it was not for making love on.

No sooner had a bit of pressure been applied up here than everything subsided down there. One second Lisa was riding high through the very air and the next she was lost in hysterical darkness, about to be suffocated, then up high again, sitting up on her knees and trying to remember what it was they were supposed to be doing. Most couples would have given up by now but not this one while Daniel, still wondrously erect when she could grab hold of it, was humming some hymn as if he was cheerfully polishing the brass.

She did manage to get him inside her again but his shoulder was pushing so hard against her chin she was afraid of getting her neck pulled and backed away. She tried to move in another direction but, try as she might – and the longer it went on the more desperate her trying became – nothing seemed to stop still long enough or get firm and steady enough for any of the necessary thrusts to get thrusting. He wasn't much help either, allowing himself to be tossed around like a sack of coal while still humming that silly hymn.

'Daniel, darling,' she said finally, giving him a few pats on the bum like an all-in wrestler signifying a submission. 'Do you think we could finish this off on the floor?'

Brouelle could have been the one great stage for that one great role which Lisa had always dreamed about: perfectly lit, gorgeously scented and extravagantly expansive as, without any constraints, commercial or artistic, two people struggled, creatively and persistently, in search of love and one another.

They would usually go for a long walk holding hands late in the afternoons with the buzzing earth absorbing the day's heat. She still enjoyed listening to Daniel's chatter on such walks, always interested in his insights, but was amused to find he was quite scared of any kind of large insect which might go hammering past. They never bothered her and it had soon got that if he caught sight of anything big – as in hornet – looking at him in, say, the kitchen he always got her to deal with it. 'I'm English,' she would say. 'The English don't get scared of anything like that.'

'Well, we Welsh do,' he'd say with a comic shiver. 'Do you know a bite from something like that would kill a small horse?'

One day they chanced on a glade with a hurrying stream which tumbled over a little waterfall and cascaded into a deep green pool. They stripped off and played with one another in the pool, romping and splashing until the cold drove them out again. They lay in a patch of late sunlight, slowly warming one another to the music of the waterfall, rubbing and licking one another all over, a few cold inches at a time before their tingling bodies became so hungry for one another it was as if they had never done it before, her every muscle tensing and relaxing as she hung on to him, gurgling a little as she felt the whole of her being fill with overpowering surges of new life.

In the nights, well-stuffed with the dinner which La Patronne always cooked for them, they liked to sit by the fire with a bottle of wine, perhaps listening hard and trying to list the various farmhouse night sounds like the soft, hollow putterings of the gas lamps, the sudden arthritic creakings of the rafters, the breezes moaning in the chimney breast or the rustling in the eaves that might have been the pipistrelles turning over in their beds and trying to get to sleep. Daniel had begun writing down a list of all these night sounds and they had so far got to seventeen.

'So much for the peace and quiet of the countryside,' Lisa often used to laugh when she got him to read the complete list aloud.

The mornings were a favourite time for her when, after some gentle love-making and fooling about on the feather mattress, she liked to stand at the open window with the sun warming her nude body as her sexual juices dribbled slowly down the sides of her legs until the heat of the awakening morning finally dried them up. Tears would often fill her eyes at such moments since she had never believed that anyone – especially her – could have been so completely happy for so long.

On some afternoons it might rain unexpectedly, absolutely sheeting down and drowning everything in a warm viscosity. It was marvellous for her to be out in such showers, feeling the rain beat down on her head and body, making her feel as if she was weeping with freshness as her wet cotton clothes highlighted every curve and bump of her taut figure. She particularly liked kissing in these showers too, sweet sixteen all over again and loving every minute of it. Not once had she worried about any of her gathering wrinkles; not once had she looked worriedly into any candid mirror either.

These downpours often stopped as quickly as they had begun, leaving them to pick their way home across the dripping lavender fields as the distant woodlands steamed in bright, hard sunshine. None of her ghosts had shown so much as a nose out in these perfumed fields since she and Daniel had come here, not one.

TWENTY FOUR

Daniel was sitting at the kitchen table early one night, sipping wine and making a few notes when Lisa announced, *apropos* of nothing, that she couldn't keep it up any more. She was not as ill as he had been told. 'Miranda Haworth put me up to it. There's nothing wrong with me at all.'

He raised his glass slightly to acknowledge what she had said, but his face registered no surprise, anger or even relief.

'Aren't you going to say *anything*?' she asked, the nearest she had got to yelling at him for almost two weeks. 'At least say *something* for God's sake.'

'What's to say? What do you expect me to say?'

'Well, you could get mad at me for a start. We hatched up the illness as a ruse to get you back. She wanted the book and I wanted you. Aren't you at least a little bit mad about that?'

'Not really. I suppose I could be but I'm not. I'm not a half-wit, you know. I guessed all along that you'd do whatever was necessary to get what you wanted. You always have. That's how you operate.'

'You knew I was lying?' She was absolutely appalled someone had seen so clearly right through her. 'So why did you go along with it? You *seemed* upset at first.'

'Oh I *was* upset at first. Very upset. But I remembered what an Olympic liar you are and, the more I thought about your illness, the less sense it made. Your not wanting to talk about it didn't ring true and those doctors' notes you just happened to leave lying around Cheyne Walk weren't very convincing either. No proper doctor would have allowed you to go off to the South of France in that state. I didn't believe most of it for a while and then, when I really thought about it, I didn't believe a word.'

'So why did you keep going along with it? Why didn't you say something?'

'I suppose I was half-honoured that you two witches would go to so much trouble and, in the end, I also guess that I *did* want to write your story. If anyone was going to do it, I wanted it to be me. I've never stopped loving you and, when you did what you did, I knew you loved me too. If you were lying I decided you must have loved me a lot to swallow your pride and cook up something like that. Only a girl who was really in love would go to that much trouble.'

'Cocky little cunt,' she spat slowly, putting plenty of emphasis on the first letters of her words, glaring at him, not in the least amused.

'So, now we're on the subject, just when are we going to settle down and write this book of yours?'

'Oh fuck the book. I don't want to ruin everything here by writing some fucking book. There's too many fucking books in the world as it is.'

'You'll enjoy it when you get going *and* we must come up with something to show Miranda. We can't sit around here doing nothing forever.'

'And why not? Why not? I've never known what it's like to be so happy for so long. Why can't we hang on to it while it's here? Why not, pray?'

'It won't last, that's why not. We're going to have to do something quite soon. Life can't ever be all holiday; life doesn't work like that; it's not designed for that. We have to do *something*.'

'If you're so desperate to do something why don't you do me?'

'Oh not that again. Come on, Lisa, I'm a man not a vibrator. We were only at it three hours ago and now you're on about it again. Let's think about this book; let's at least *talk* about it.'

'Who wants to talk about that?' she sighed reaching out for the wine bottle. 'What's there to talk about?'

They both fell silent, he staring at the wall and she gazing down into her glass. One of the burning logs broke into a spasm of golden sparks, part of it falling down on to the stone hearth. He got up, took the tongs and carefully put the fiery fragments back on the fire, one by one.

'Too early to go to bed I suppose. But, Lisa girl, we're going to have to decide what we're going to do about this book.'

'You know I've clean gone off this book. Who cares about my life anyway? I'm only an actress. There's nothing special about being an actress, particularly one who's been half mad all her life. I've been with some interesting men and done some good work on the stage but, when you get down to it, all I'm really famous for is being in that disgraceful, violent rubbish *Rebellion*. Why can't we write another sort of book?'

'Another sort of book like …?'

'Oh I don't know. I've never wanted to write a book anyway. It's *you* who should be writing this book.'

'I do write books, remember?'

'Not *those* books. Not fiction which is only another way of escape for you. I know you, forever looking for somewhere to hide. There's only one sort of book you should be writing, the one about what God is fretting about. Those visions must mean something. *That's* what you should be writing about. What's God trying to say to us down here? What's all that gunfire about? What does the black rain mean? What did you actually see in Brixton? You've never told me about all that in any detail. That's interesting. Not loony old me.'

'Oh we're not back on all that again are we?'

'Yes,' she all but shrieked, her mouth erupting with a few flobs of spit. 'Yes, we are. I'm Lady Macbeth where you're concerned. I *really* believe in my man. I simply know that you could become a great writer but you've got to sharpen that quill of yours and write about great things like God or even that great work about London you've been nursing all these years. And writing about great things will make you a great writer. There is no other way. Look at me, Daniel. Just what is the point of writing about me? I'm half human, half nervous breakdown. All I ever really enjoyed is cleaning floors. I've failed at every relationship I've ever had except this one and I'm hanging on to that by my fingernails. Who is interested in me? Write about what you believe. I know I'm beginning to sound like a bad hiccup but that's what people want to hear about. They're fed up with everything they're being told. Everything. Everything under the sun depresses them. They want to know what's going on in God's mind and what keeps him awake at night. Now *that* is what I call interesting *and* important too.'

A long silence yawned before them which neither broke until, after a few sniffs, he said, 'So we're not making any progress at all then. You don't want to write about your life and I don't want to write about mine. We might as well just stay here and pick grapes.'

'Mmm. Why don't we do just that? Oh Daniel, I don't ever want to go back to London. I want to stay here with you for ever, to just pick grapes and be here with you forever.'

'It's a lovely thought, girl, and it's a lovely night. Let's have a stroll before we turn in.'

It *was* the loveliest of nights with the stars powdering a purple sky and the air as soft and warm as aroused flesh. Something splashed in a pond. Pipistrelles left slipstreams of shrill squeaks and fluttering wings in their wakes. Huge eruptions of fragrant lavender punched holes in the night.

Even as she walked she felt herself brimming with relief that she had finally spat out her awful lie about her health and he didn't seem to give a toss about it. This was a major step forward for her: they had come closer to that final great union she so craved: he had understood and forgiven her mendacity. All her other men, particularly John O, would have cried betrayal and let loose the dogs of war.

They walked up another gentle slope and down through yet more avenues of young vines. But, just now, nothing moved in the sensual darkness and it was one of those nights in which nothing could be heard except the noise of blood moving around inside the ears.

Much went through her mind as they kissed: the true love whose course never does run smooth; how poor she had always been at having and holding it; how sometimes she had snatched at it wildly; how often she had clumsily missed it when it had been sitting there, ripe for the plucking. Yes, she could settle for this, she could settle for this for ever. Here in the vineyards they had slipped their earthly chains and gone to live in dreams where no one could touch them. Ever. She wanted more of this; she wanted a lot, lot more.

They stopped kissing and remained on the same spot with their arms around one another, looking out over the dark, stooping rows of the motionless vines. Nothing disturbed the fragrant delicacy of the night and it was as if they were the two last lovers at the end of time. He gave a soft chuckle and skipped to a row of vines, bending and parting the leaves until he found a small bunch of grapes. 'Tonight Lisa Moran,' he said holding the bunch up high like a communion cup. 'Tonight we are going to take communion out here together and give God thanks for our love.'

'Oh yes.'

'Wine is said to be the blood of the world and Jesus called himself the Blood of the Covenant. He turned water into fine wine at the wedding of Cana and this was taken to foreshadow the use of the wine in the Eucharist. Some talk of Jesus' blood surging every year through the world in these vineyards. In each harvest we see again an annual commemoration of the feeding of the five thousand. This is a very attractive and moving concept particularly when we think of Christ as the food of life so we are going to drink this blood to celebrate and give thanks for our own love.'

He pushed down on one of her shoulders, indicating her to kneel and held the grapes above her head to begin squeezing them until the red juice dripped slowly on to her upraised, smiling face. It ran through his fingers and across his wrists and down his arms. It dripped on her face again, once, twice, three times. 'Smell and taste the warmth and humanity of the juice. Feel the blood trickle down your throat. Feel it run straight into your heart. Know that this is the blood of life as you kneel here at the communion rail of the altar of the world. Do you, Lisa Moran, believe in the father who is love, the son who is love and the holy spirit who is love?'

'Oh yes, yes I do.'

'Then take this and drink. Drink the love that is the body and blood of the Lord.'

There was one discord. Late one afternoon a few days later, when she was walking alone through the vineyard, her ears picked up an unfamiliar noise in the orchard and, moving forward softly and slowly, she soon discovered its source.

Daniel was kneeling by a stone wall in the corner of the orchard, the soft evening light falling all around him. His head and hands were raised and his eyes were closed as he prayed in tongues. She found this act truly intriguing and took a step backwards, anxious not to interrupt.

He had told her he sometimes prayed in tongues, particularly when he was not sure what he wanted to say to God. But she had never seen him do so. What on earth could he be praying about?

Nothing made sense in his continuing flow of musical syllables until she picked up on a name which made her feel patchily cold. Helen Grantby. She walked away quickly. *Helen Grantby!* She might have guessed. Daniel had once mentioned that he had been worried that she had gone back on the bottle and into the streets and now he was asking God to look after her. But Lisa knew she had keep her big mouth shut on this one. She knew all about men who loved two women and had often thought she had written that particular script herself. She had nearly always won such battles in the past but with this *young* Helen Grantby she wasn't confident at all. Not in the slightest bit confident.

Their Provencal idyll fell apart quickly and suddenly, not with a furious row or one of her insane tantrums, but with an unexpected arrival.

Daniel was in the farmhouse reading and Lisa was pegging out her undies on the washing line in the yard when her yellow Rolls-Royce came purring to a halt in the drive. Her body stiffened with alarm and didn't much relax when the chauffeur got out to open the passenger door and she recognised the balding, well-fed frame of Charles Judd tumbling out of the back seat. Just what the hell was he doing all the way down here?

'Charlie, how nice,' she exclaimed, running to him and kissing him on both cheeks as her insides clogged up with gloom. Men never gave you anything for nothing did they? There was always a tab to be picked up sooner or later.

'Don't worry, I'm not staying Duchess, but I am in a spot of bother wiv the law an' I need a bit of 'elp like.'

'Anything at all, Charlie. Anything at all. You know that. Come inside.'

The chauffeur pulled a face at her, all stretched mouth and lifted eyebrows, which said all this was nothing to do with him, and Judd limped into the farm-house, nodded at Daniel and filled the armchair with his huge bulk before sighing long and loud and proceeding to take off his shoes and socks. 'I 'ad a meal last night in Nîmes, I fink it was. Anyway it was out of doors by a river an' I 'ad me summer sandals on an' I was savaged by mosquitoes all around me ankles 'ere.'

Daniel and Lisa looked down at his ankles with comic concern, both doing their best not to laugh out loud, perhaps not so much at the bites but the way he had scratched them leaving trails of dried blood winding around his ankles.

'Oh Charlie, that's terrible. We must have some kind of ointment or something for that don't we Daniel? Take a look in the cabinet upstairs and see what you can find.'

'Do they 'ave mosquitoes down in Spain do they?' Judd asked as he began scratching his ankles again.

'I suppose so. They've got mosquitoes everywhere haven't they?'

'Well they'll never be as big as the ones who 'ad me last night. Big as flies they were. Bit into me like mad dogs they did.'

Daniel returned and kneeled in front of Judd to begin spraying the bloodied ankles. 'This is supposed to be good for itches and stuff. Don't worry if it stings a bit at first.'

'Oh that's all right. Me old Mum always used to say that nuffink was any good unless it hurt. The more hurt the better, she said.'

'It'll also help if you stop scratching them,' Daniel advised as he stood up. 'Any doctor will tell you they'll never get better if you keep scratching them.'

'You are a doctor are you? You look a bit young to be a doctor.'

'Make some tea for us will you Daniel? I think Charlie and I have a lot to talk about.'

They did indeed and, as soon as Daniel left the room, Judd began putting his shoes and socks back on again as he explained how he had got into trouble with the law back in London. Some office block had been burned down and he didn't want to go into much detail or anyfink and naturally he hadn't done it, but he had been fitted up by a few fingers, who should have known better and were going to regret it, but, with the fuzz feeling his collar, he had decided to move out of the way down to Spain which was why he had borrowed her Roller and got the chauffeur to bring him here because he was hoping he might use the apartment he had given her in Marbella.

'But of course, Charlie. You didn't even need to ask. You know that.'

'An' another fing Duchess. I know you are supposed to be 'ere writing yer book an' all but I was wondering if maybe you would come down there wiv me to Spain for a bit, 'til I get fings sorted. I mean, I'm dead upset an' I fought you might cheer me up. You're still the only woman who ever made me laugh. You know that? The only one.'

'Of course I'll go down there with you Charlie,' she said even if he must have seen she was not at all enthusiastic about the prospect. 'I've always told you that you could rely on me if you ever got into trouble.' She knew she had been checkmated and there was no way out or around it. Whatever else anyone ever said about Lisa Moran, her loyalty to her friends had never been in question.

'I wasn't born for abroad Duchess. I was born for the rain and the cold.'

'I said didn't I? I said I'd be happy to help you and I am. More than happy.'

Daniel was in the kitchen and she explained the situation to him in a brisk, almost businesslike manner. 'So the question is do you want to wait for me here until I've finished settling him down in Spain? I don't know how long I'm going to be there. I haven't even seen this apartment he's supposed to have given me. Or perhaps you might be better off going back to London? But I can't really tell how long it's all going to take.'

'I think I'll go back to London,' he replied evenly in a tone which she couldn't quite read. 'It's where I need to be really, now that I'm going to get back to work on my great London epic.'

'Ah, you're going to get back to that? Good.'

'You've fired me up again with impossible dreams. That's what I always loved about you. No one could ever be merely mediocre with you around.'

'Good.' She kissed and hugged him warmly. 'Daniel, I will make this up to you one day but Charlie's been so good to me in the past and there's no question that I can't be a friend to him now he needs me. Take the keys to Cheyne Walk and I'll be back as soon as I possibly can.'

'No. I'm going to get my own place. I'll get a room somewhere near. Look, I'm not trying to be difficult. It's just what I want to do and it'll give me a chance to stop drinking before it gets to be a problem again. I've been thinking about this a lot and a flat of my own is just what I need. You can come and go as you like and we won't be getting under one another's feet.'

Her eyes narrowed slightly as she looked at him. What was really going on in that daft brain of his? Was he about to lock her out of his life again? And how far might this room be from wherever Helen Grantby was living? But no time to go into all that now and she returned to Charlie, ready to flee to Spain as soon as he was.

Daniel stood in the yard to wave them goodbye with no discernible emotion on his face. She had become more tense than she'd been for ages. Had she yet again found love only to again throw it away? Tears welled in her eyes and she was swallowing a lot as the car, with no room to turn around, reversed up the drive. But she had to support Charlie now that he needed her. No question at all about that. She gave Daniel yet another wave before taking hold of Charlie's fat hand. 'Everything is going to be all right, Charlie darling. How are your ankles now, by the way. Feeling better after that spray are they?'

TWENTY FIVE

By the last weekend in August, in that brilliant summer of 1985, Lisa's cup was overflowing. There had been much gossip column talk that she was going to carry off the *Evening Standard* Actress of the Year Award for *A Series of Surrenders* and, while she had always maintained she couldn't care less about such awards, that was another of her lies. Granada had also bought the rights to the play and it was going to be opened out into a full-length work for television as soon as Sean could finish a new screenplay.

She had also been offered two million dollars to star as an ageing, scheming, rich bitch in the American soap, *Dynasty*. The role hadn't been all that bad – even if she wasn't too clear why they had seen her in it – and she had been wined and dined at The Dorchester by Aaron but she had turned it down in the end as not being quite her – much to Karen Duffy's clear chagrin. 'Lisa, forget about my side of the deal.' Agents always said that when that's all they wanted you to remember. 'Forget about me but, if you pick up this kind of money, you can do anything you like afterwards. Make your own films, produce your own plays ... you'll have the freedom to do anything you like.'

'But it never works out like that does it Karen? Sophia picked up big money once and then had to spend the rest of her life chasing more and more just to keep the tax man quiet. I'll stay as I am, thanks. Poor but honest.'

She wasn't exactly poor and she had never been honest, of course. Thanks to Charlie's wise advice her property portfolio was hatching pile after pile of cash and she couldn't quite believe it when she had been told what she was worth. She had never understood where this river of money had come from or indeed how it kept breaking into yet more rivers but she could probably buy a small town in the North – and be left with change. But, as far as everyone was concerned, she was close to broke. No one needed to know *anything* about her money and, if she wanted any real cash, she took a leaf out of Charlie's book and borrowed it from the bank which, like almost everyone else in that golden period, when you walked out and bought several Ferraris on a whim, seemed to have gone raving mad. Apart from her portfolio, of course, she still had Cheyne Walk which, she had been told, could now be worth a couple of million at the very least in the booming property market.

Her stay in Marbella settling down Charlie had taken a week but she was keeping in regular touch with him as he kept protesting his innocence from a bar stool in the Marbella Club. His brief however was stoutly resisting all moves to get him back to London where the Old Bill were anxious to talk to him about his alleged role in the burning down of an office block in Docklands. He hadn't actually done it, of course, but she was getting a positive feeling that he certainly knew who had.

She chatted to him on the phone once a week, usually late on Friday night, when she read him the results of the dog races at Walthamstow and he told her who was doing whom in Marbella. She had promised to go back and visit him soon but had hated her apartment in particular and the town in general. She could have pulled out all the faux marble and gilt fittings in her apartment, she guessed, but the town itself was full of cheap crooks on the lam and new high-rise flats already falling down. Then, what with the teenage hookers working the main road, the fascist police who would knock you down sooner than look at you and the English lager louts – those peculiar glories of Thatcher's England – throwing up everywhere, she doubted if she had ever been in a more hateful place. And she actually owned an apartment there! She was going to get rid of it as soon as she decently could.

She kept urging Charlie to come home and take on the chin whatever the police were going to hit him with and he had said he was thinking about it because he wasn't mad about Marbella either. The poor thing really couldn't do abroad. 'They all talk in this weird dago lingo all the time, Duchess. An' this Spanish scoff is right terrible.'

Her relationship with Daniel had taken a new turn since he had found a small flat of his own on Fulham Road and she was doing her best to give him room to breathe, which he seemed to enjoy and appreciate. At the same time she was managing to keep a more or less permanent eye on what he was up to, often popping over there with a bag of groceries or to give the place a quick clean. She had never been quite sure about this charlady act of hers and guessed it was because she still liked to subvert people's understanding of her, to show them that she wasn't the snobbish stuck-up cow she often appeared.

He seemed to like his little flat, predictably bare of everything except a bed and a desk. Somehow he had managed to become poorer as she became richer. He had lost all he had owned in Portobello Road after the Greek kebab shop owner had impounded all his stuff in lieu of back rent and she had offered to buy him a few bits of furniture and stuff but the pious prat had turned up his nose. He liked the uncluttered, monastic atmosphere of his new place, he said. A fucking monk he should have become, not a minister in a church.

But The Minister did leave his anchorite cell twice a week to come over to Cheyne Walk when he practically flew through the door, tearing off his clothes like Superman high on speed before giving her a good seeing-to and that kept her burbling with a sort of contentment. He might well have been as mad as a Mexican Wave and she was still unconvinced about his ambition for the pulpit but he remained the best lover she had ever had. He always made sex work for her; he only ever had to put one measly coin in the slot, pull her arm and there she was bonging away and delivering the jackpot every time. Amazing. And at her age too. It was also evident from his unbridled enthusiasm for her body that he hadn't been seeing anything of that Helen Grantby – she always knew when her men had been playing away – so, yes, it looked as if they were finally settling down into a form of truce.

Indeed their relationship had become so stable she feared he had begun to take her for granted. He never bothered to bring her flowers any more – 'my bloody bank manager is more attentive than you' – and, on the rare occasion when he did buy her a record it was usually some rock'n'roll rubbish that he liked. He didn't seem to want to go out on the town for a bit of a bop either. Was he ashamed to be seen holding her hand? Sometimes she got really bothered that he was treating her as some sort of Dial-a-Fuck service before going out on his own to parties full of nubile, teenage girls or even going to another AA meeting, if you please, since he was firmly back on the wagon. He cared more for that bunch of deadbeats than her. Those of us who still drink have rights, you know. We drinkers need more affection than most. We boozers have got feelings too.

She could feel her resentments building up fast during the day before he arrived but he only had to look at her with his blue, rapist eyes, give her one of his soppy smiles, then get to work with the magic sausage for her to be left gasping for air and shaking so much she couldn't even remember what it was that she had been resenting so much before he had pitched up at the door. Yes, a small miracle for our times really.

Not that anything could be totally serene, particularly where she was involved. She was always quiet and happy *après sex* but when he was due to leave – and she could see that there was going to be no more action – she sometimes got totally stupid, weeping floods, demanding to know when she was going to see him again, accusing him of not caring about her at all. 'Just look at you. You're leaving me and you don't even seem unhappy. You really don't care about me, do you? All you want is to sit in some smelly AA meeting. Well go on then. Tell me how much you love me. You haven't told me you love me for at least a year and that's all I want to hear. *Now*.

To her even greater horror she also found herself raising the subject of marriage and becoming even more wanly weepy when he showed no interest in that at all. Oh it was just the way it was when a woman was in love, she supposed. It really was horrible wasn't it? Pissy beyond belief.

At midday the following Thursday she had put on a dab of powder and a bit of lippy before fiddling with her hair, tut-tutting at its splintery deadness. Then, with a profound sigh, she looked out of her bedroom window and down at an Indian summer stretching out on the Embankment.

It was a gorgeous day and no mistake, still vibrant with all the little tricks of a summer's endgame while the Thames looked unusually smooth and full. Cheyne Walk itself was traffic-thronged, as usual just before lunch, with billowing blue fumes emulsifying in the brilliant sunlight. The trees still didn't look too bad to her although there had been several stormy meetings with the residents trying to save them from the axe which, she gathered, was getting ever closer. She doubted if she would want to remain here then. The loss of her cherry orchard would be the signal for her to sell up and go to ... well where exactly?

She came down the stairs into her living room all spruced up in pearls and a navy suit for a lunch with a few of her chums at The Ivy and had just poured herself a naughty little whisky to set herself up before calling a cab when the front door bell rang.

'It's Lisa Moran isn't it? I'm so sorry to disturb you, Miss Moran, but I'm in a lot of trouble and need to talk to you,' said a woman she had never met.

'Do I know you?'

'I really am in the most desperate difficulties, Miss Moran and I only need a few minutes of your time.'

'We're all in the most desperate difficulties.'

'Please Miss Moran.'

'Well, I've just poured myself a drink and you look as if you could do with one too.'

Lisa insisted that her visitor took off her coat before she sat down in her living room. Her clothes (solid, value-for-money, Marks & Spencer with no frills) and her accent (educated, suburban, Hertfordshire perhaps) suggested that here was one of your average English middle class women, a bit serious, faintly boring, the backbone of most of the Shakespearean audiences Lisa had ever played to. She did so hope she wasn't another fan with a textual problem from *Romeo and Juliet*.

'My name is Clare Reynolds,' the woman began. 'I know you must be very busy and I'll try not to take up too much of your time but my world has fallen apart and I thought you might be able to help me.'

'Take as much time as you need, Clare. I've got all day. And please call me

Lisa. Just take it easy and explain your problem. If I can help I will.'

Clare bit her lower lip for a while and then, taking a deep breath, 'I wonder if, by any chance, you read in the newspapers about a shooting in Edgware three weeks ago? A young boy shot three people in a shopping centre: one was killed and two seriously injured.'

'It rings a faint bell, Clare, but I don't really follow the news and I hate newspapers. As you see, I don't even own a television.'

'This young boy … oh my God … this young boy …' Clare had been clinging to her composure but now it had shattered completely. She raised her hands pointlessly in front of her face and her fingers were shaking wildly. This was no act. This was a woman who had indeed got herself into a lot of trouble. 'My husband said … he was told by the police …oh, I can't …'

'Right, Clare, stop right there. Don't say another word. You are going to drink a stiff whisky with me and you're going to collect your breath and we are going to start this all over again from the beginning. There's a box of tissues here. Help yourself. Blow your nose and take your time. Think about your breathing. Start only when you're ready. I've got all day.'

'What I'm trying to tell you is the most terrible thing that any woman can tell another woman, Miss Moran. I've been hanging around the front door of your house for hours …I've …'

'Clare. Don't say one more word. Here. Drink that Scotch. Go on. Down in one if you can. Then tell me what you want to say at your own speed and in your own time. No, not yet. Finish the drink first. I've got all the time you need.'

She drank a good slug of her whisky, then sat sniffing and blowing her nose in a tissue. The telephone rang. Lisa picked the receiver off the cradle and put it down again. When it rang again, a few seconds later, she lifted the receiver up and laid it on its side where it burred so plaintively she put the whole lot inside a desk drawer. This tiny pantomime gave Clare time to finish the whole of her drink and regain her composure.

'This young boy. He shot three people and then the police gave chase. They pursued him into a nearby wood … there were helicopters, guns, the lot. He was cornered finally and shot himself in the head. He shot himself, Miss Moran, a beautiful young boy with everything to live for, he shot himself like a dog.' She blew her nose and looked down at the sodden tissue, the tears flowing again.

'He was your son?'

'Ye-e-e-e-s. He was. Can you believe it? Could you imagine your own son dying like that? Your own son, Miss Moran.'

Lisa shook her head.

'I cry all night. The waste. I'll never stop crying over this. Never. These tears of mine are going to flow forever. The waste of a life. That boy was never a killer. *Never* a killer. I loved him more than my own life and he was never what the newspapers said he was. A mad dog and all that disgusting stuff.'

It was Lisa's turn to cry. The pain of such tragedies really was unimaginable but she remembered all too vividly those times when she had lain on the bed, her skin flaking and turning yellow, crying out in the purest anguish as lumps and clots of blood came sluicing out from between her legs and she knew she was losing another child. It wasn't the pain but the loss of a possible life which had so crucified her. 'Clare, we'd better both have another drink,' she announced still dabbing her own tears. 'But I'm not at all clear what you're trying to tell me. Are you saying that this boy didn't do all these shootings? Is he innocent? Is that what you're trying to say?'

'Oh no. Chris shot those poor people all right. He shot them as certainly as I am sitting here.'

'Well, I'm sorry Clare. I am dreadfully sorry and fully sympathise with you and your plight – *fully sympathise* – but how can *I* help you?'

Clare sipped her drink and sniffed again. 'I knew my boy. I can't explain how or why. Mothers often don't know their children at all but I knew mine inside out. He was a lovely child but I saw how forces and events changed him. I understood them all. Even as he got older I could see right through him; I always knew when he was telling a lie. You see, Miss Moran, I know exactly why Chris shot those people but no one will listen to me. The police and coroner both say that I have an interesting theory for which there is no possible proof. The coroner ruled what I wanted to say at the inquest inadmissible because it had no direct bearing on the actual shootings – or so he said.'

'But Clare I may be stupid but I still don't see how *I* fit into all this. I said I'll help you – and I will – but why me?'

'The interesting feature about my Chris was that, from a young age, he was always very impressionable. I only had to talk to him for a few minutes after he'd got home from school and I could pretty much work out who he had been playing with. He'd pick up an accent, a mannerism, any number of new identities. I never thought a child could change identities so many times, but he was always doing it, anything from Dennis the Menace to the Famous Five, depending on what he'd been reading. Dennis the Menace lasted a month and then Chris became a member of the Famous Five. He only listened to T-Rex once and his hair became like Marc Bolan's. Anyway about four years ago he found an identity he loved so much he stuck to it and totally immersed himself in it – he saw the first of the *Rebellion* films and decided he was Raz.'

Lisa stared at her visitor open-mouthed, her skin goose-pimpling coldly as she thought of various implications of what she had been told. 'Are you saying you're blaming this one film for your son shooting those people in Edgware? Surely you don't believe your boy saw that one film and then did this terrible act. That just wouldn't be possible, would it?'

176

'Not that one film, Miss Moran. *All* the *Rebellion* films, he saw them all, perhaps a dozen times each. He read all the novelisations of the film scripts over and over again, played the sound-tracks of the films night after night. The posters, the clothes, the desert survival kit ... Miss Moran, my Chris had them all. In his mind he *became* his great hero Raz and although I could see clearly what was going on and kept worrying about it all the time, I decided that there was nothing I could do about it and that it would pass, kept telling myself that there was at least one important thing he didn't have – the weaponry. But he got hold of them too. He acquired the guns somehow and went shooting people in that shopping centre precisely as happened in *Rebellion 3*.'

'*Precisely as happened?* I never saw any of those films. I know I acted in the first one but I didn't even see that, refused even to attend the premier. You're not saying, I hope, that *I* am somehow responsible ...'

'No, no, no.'

'No one could have foreseen any of this,' Lisa continued quietly, hastily weaving several vague lines of defense. 'And as far as I was concerned that was just another crap film put together by crap. I thought it would sink without trace, to be perfectly honest with you, and didn't even want my name on the credits.'

'I haven't come here to blame you in any way, Miss Moran. It's just that a woman I know well in Edgware, Miss Doris Pleasant, once taught you drama.'

'Ah yes, dear old Doris. How is she? Still on forty fags a day?'

'Oh more if that's possible. But she's fine and told me to be sure to give you her best love if I did manage to catch up with you. It was Doris who gave me your address and suggested I call. She said that you had the great gift of pity for people in trouble, that you would listen and that, as you were connected with the first film and probably hated it, you might be able to advise me on what to do next.'

'Advise? Do next? Now I really am totally confused.'

'Help me, Miss Moran. Help me to explain what these films are doing to us. Our children are under attack. These films are not entertainment, they're an attack on our children and it's become a rare day when there's not someone in the world gunning down innocent people. But I feel so helpless even though I'm sure I understand what's going on. The police want to forget about it and the coroner won't talk.

'I've never trusted the newspapers so I won't go to them either. I want justice Miss Moran. If it means setting the world on fire, I want a mother's revenge on these wretched films. I want to raise hell.'

As she made her big speech, Clare's face changed markedly as she spoke, moving from nervous deference to a glorious defiance and Lisa felt a sharp flame of excitement explode deep inside her. She had always loved a fighter, always loved anyone who refused to step forward and guzzle the national swill. The only men she had ever really cared about had always shown a glorious defiance; the only men she had ever been interested in had been completely out of whack with the age.

'I told you I would help you and I will. But, Clare, this is a huge play we've got involved in here and there are many hidden themes. We've got to go over it all slowly, page by page, before we decide what to do. We've got to take the best available advice and look at the options. But first we must eat. I can't think about anything at all when my belly is empty. Put your coat back on. We're going to have a slap-up lunch, on me, with some very nice people at The Ivy.'

It wasn't until Lisa had ordered a taxi and was following Clare down the stairs that she had a thought – or perhaps it was a memory – which first darkened and then exploded in her mind with such concussive force she was afraid she was going to faint and would indeed have fallen down her stairs had she not clung to the balustrade with both hands. 'Clare,' she said loudly. 'When your son shot those people in Edgware, was his gun an *automatic?*'

TWENTY SIX

There days later several taxis refused to take Lisa and Daniel all the way out to Edgware because it was too far – as was their right apparently; a right which became firmer after Lisa had loudly abused them – so they were forced to take a tube, one of those rolling, rattling trains-in-a-drain which kept bursting out of the darkness into crowded stations like meteoric, mechanical worms.

It wasn't the clattering speed of the train which grated on Lisa's ever-taut nerves so much as the jumbles of people who kept crowding around her; the inane advertisements overhead; the long, pained squeals of the brakes and the puncturing hisses of the opening doors; the scrofulous youngsters with their chewing gum and personal stereos; the rolled-up newspapers, the discarded cartons of McDonald's chips, the gales of body odour, snowstorms of dandruff ... Oh how she missed being chauffeured around in her yellow Roller. Oh Charlie, why did you go bent and take my lovely car back off me? Oh dear Lord, it's been ten years since I've been on one of these stinking tubes so please, pretty please, make it another ten before I have to do it again.

The crowds of passengers thinned out after Baker Street and the train went overground, racing along above a red-tiled sea of semi-detached houses broken only by allotments with their humpy rows of potatoes and bamboo pyramids of runner beans. 'I've never been out here before,' she said to Daniel. 'Presumably people live all their lives in those houses?'

'They certainly do. This is your original Metroland which began opening up at the turn of the century when city folk began yearning for a bit of countryside. It was the tube which opened up the whole idea of the suburbs and anyone who wants to understand the growth of London has also got to understand the growth of the tube.'

At least he wasn't in a bad mood. It was usually a sign that he was in a good humour when he began airing his knowledge of London. He had been in an almost permanent bad mood since she had got him to agree to go out to Edgware to talk to Clare; to at least *see* if there might be a book for him in the son's story. Daniel's involvement was the best plan that she and Clare could come up with but, disappointingly, Daniel hadn't shown any interest at all in the idea and had dismissed the automatic gunfire angle as either a coincidence or nonsense and probably both.

'Don't ever try and kill yourself by throwing yourself under a tube train because such attempts are almost always unsuccessful,' he continued, his city guide hat still on.

'Really? It's just as well I didn't try it after shouting at that pig of a taxi driver then.'

'On average two people a week try and end it all by throwing themselves under a tube. London transport calls them "one-unders" and, when it happens, the station manager has to cut off the current and get under the train to find the body. Then the train has to be wound forward by hand and whatever's left taken to hospital. They usually lose arms or legs but not their lives.'

'Urrrgh! I'll have to cross that off any of my possible ways out then.' Oddly, given the subject of their conversation, she was beginning to feel quite cheerful herself, as so often happened when she was being told something interesting. Now he was going on about a man he had once met who was planning to break the record for visiting every station on the tube, currently 18 hours 41 minutes. By the time they got to Edgware they were both in the sunniest of moods; yes, it really was working for them both.

They might have been in some foreign city when they ventured into those suburban streets. The houses all looked the same, replicating one another down to the last brick. There were formal hedges and manicured lawns, foaming white lace curtains and concrete drives leading to identical pebble-dashed garages. Even the trees in the streets seemed to lean in symmetrical angles, all a standard distance from one another.

She felt no particular distaste for this lifestyle since she understood that it was precisely these people – and not her own theatrical people – who were the bedrock of English middle-class society, living out decent, blameless lives in the shadow of a heavy mortgage and the spirit of B&Q do-it-yourself-ism.

The two women embraced warmly on the doorstep of Clare Reynolds' house in Partridge Lane and Daniel sat in a plush armchair as they chatted like two old school chums. Every surface in the living room had been burnished, varnished or otherwise polished. A bunch of fresh flowers sat on top of the television and a video recorder in the far alcove. A log-effect gas fire flickered dully in the fire-grate and reproductions of famous English paintings hung on the walls. In the distance was the garden and every inch of that had been tended with loving care. There was an undeniable sense of solid continuity in the house and Lisa was already beginning to understand something of the outrageous scale of the tragedy which had so recently engulfed it. Young Christopher Reynolds had not only taken his own life and that of others, he had also undermined everything that his parents had stood and worked for. How could a middle class home like this produce such an alienated monster? That was the question she was hoping Daniel might answer in a book.

Even after everything her son had done Clare still enjoyed talking about him. She described how he had once written some quite tender poetry and learned to play a few basic chords on a guitar; how he had taken a successful photography course at the London Institute after he had left school and had even expressed an interest in becoming a fashion photographer. She took them up to his room which had been left exactly as it was. They walked in silently, as if into a holy shrine, except that this shrine had three different and distinctly unholy posters of Yuri Pucket as Raz on the walls. Daniel ran the tip of his forefinger along the spines of a row of paperbacks above the small writing desk; five were about the *Rebellion* series and a few had forest and desert survival themes. A TV and a VCR sat on the window and, when Daniel pressed the eject button, a cassette of *Rebellion 3* came whirring out.

The wardrobe was full of clothes which had been deliberately torn or inappropriately pinned, all suggesting a certain hard-headed aggression, with a stack of records on the floor, the gaudy op-art cover of the latest Marillion release on top. Daniel picked up a saucer full of cigarette stubs and smelled them before putting it back down again and looking into each of the desk drawers, pulling out one after another, finding the usual young man's bric-a-brac ... playing cards, foreign coins, notebooks, nude photographs, letters, rolls of film ...

Lisa couldn't even start guessing what might be going on inside Daniel and he wasn't letting on. Confusion? Dismay? Fascination? Intrigue? Perhaps a strong mixture of them all as his imagination reached out to a young man whom he had never met and never would.

There was an added complication for both of them in that they had been present at the making of the original *Rebellion* film and possibly shared some complicity in Chris's terrible crime. But it was impossible to square that rippling hunk of Kalashnikov-toting hulk on the posters with the insect-fearing, mother-fixated actor they knew. Who could ever have foreseen that such a nerd would become a mythic hero in the mind of a young man and turn him into a killer? The gulf between heavily-hyped myth and boring reality was nearly the most grotesque irony of the whole business. If only she had been given the chance to sit down with young Chris and explain to him exactly what his great hero was really like. Ah if only ...

'Mrs Reynolds, what was it exactly you were hoping we could do for you?' Daniel asked when they returned to the living room.

'I want Chris's story told properly,' she said with the same even and deliberate defiance that had so thrilled Lisa when she had first come to Cheyne Walk. 'I have this terrible feeling that all our children are under threat because of these films and I need someone to tell his story so that the world can read it and perhaps learn from it.'

'You *are* thinking of a book then are you?'

'Yes, a book. I *think* a book anyway. And perhaps you might be the one who'd take it on. Lisa has told me that you're a very good writer. "Brilliant" was her exact word. I'm not looking for money. There have been newspaper people here offering money for his story but they all kept writing about the monster from Edgware and I don't want to see any more of that rubbish. I want Chris's story told in context. I don't want my only son to have died in vain.'

'This book, Mrs Reynolds. It might be painful to go through all that again. Things might come out that you've never known about before and you wouldn't like them. And then there's your husband. What's he got to say about all this?'

'He hasn't been saying anything at all. He's been spending more and more time away from here, at his brother's. He wants to go away and forget. I want to stay here and remember. He wants Chris's room cleared out and I don't want it touched. I don't want to run away from this, you see. I can't. It's not in my nature. I may lose my husband because of my stand but I have to face everything and, if dealing with the truth means more pain then that's the price I'm prepared to pay. Not that anyone could possibly live in more pain than I'm in now.'

Daniel swallowed and Lisa's eyes threatened tears. There really was something gloriously wonderful, almost Shakespearean about this grieving mother.

'I will help you tell your son's story properly, Mrs Reynolds,' Daniel said after a while. 'There's an important book to be written here and I'm probably as well qualified to write it as anyone. The question of media responsibility also falls well within my range of interests. But I'll need to know everything – and I mean everything – about your son. We will have to get right into his world and try to discover and understand what was going through his mind right up to the very moment he pulled that trigger. I'm not even sure it can be done but I'll certainly give it a good try.'

'You think that this book might get published then do you?'

'That really depends on what we find out. What do you think, Lisa? You've been unusually quiet.'

'It's a marvellous subject for you Daniel. Perhaps the subject you've been looking for after hearing, you know, those shots.'

'Shots?' Clare asked.

'I was dreaming about the sound of gunfire a few weeks ago,' Daniel said vaguely while also giving Lisa a warning glare telling her to back off. 'Then I had a few recurring dreams along the same lines.'

'We can always try my friend Miranda,' Lisa suggested. 'She's the boss at Kennington, Clare. I get on quite well with her and I'm sure she'll be interested in such a book. What do you say Daniel?'

'Well, I might never get another chance to write a book like this and, as you say, it is a marvellous subject for me. Yes, ring Miranda will you Lisa? Try and set up a meeting.'

'No time like the present,' said Lisa, reaching for the telephone directory underneath the coffee table.

In the world of publishing every decision is reckoned to take six months to arrive. This can then stretch to anything up to six years – and even beyond – so it was almost a miracle up there with Caxton's invention of the printing press that Lisa not only managed to get through to Miranda Haworth immediately but, having outlined their plan, got her to make an instant decision.

'I'm not just *saying* I'm interested but can assure you that I am *really* interested,' Miranda said. 'Tell Daniel to get an outline to me as soon as possible and we can talk money. If you have the full co-operation of the mother we'll certainly get a good serialisation out of it and I can see it moving well off the bookshelves in America. They're all shooting one another in the school yards there.'

Perhaps inevitably Miranda asked if there had been any progress with Lisa's biography but it was just a ritual query requiring no more than a ritual response. Everyone connected with the book now regarded that sorry saga as being as dead as a dog. Lisa was even reluctant to talk about where she was born, let alone when.

Clare soon showed that she was a positive and willing fountain of information, taking them on a walk around the neighbourhood, showing them the parks where Chris had spent most of his summer holidays, the corner café where he had spent a lot of expresso hours with his friends, the police station where he had once been hauled in for riding two on a bike and the school where he had managed to take seven 'O' levels. They also went to the edge of the wood where he had tried to escape after the shooting in the shopping centre but, understandably, she wouldn't actually take them to the spot where Chris had shot himself.

'I'll have to get to know these places as your son knew them,' said Daniel. 'I'll need to talk to all his friends, his teachers, any girlfriends and the police. Did he ever have any special girl friend?'

'Not really, he was always a bit of a loner and that was a big part of his problem I'd say.'

'Any male friends then?'

'There was a Brian someone or other. The police questioned him about where he got the guns from but we never did get an answer to that. This friend came to the house a few times. Brian Hitchens? They were at school together.

He'll know a lot if you can get him to talk.'

'The school might be difficult,' Daniel mused. 'They won't want to advertise that they taught someone like Chris. It might help if you sent a letter to the headmaster asking him to talk to me. Tell him we're trying to tell the story of one young man which, in its turn, will hopefully tell the story of his generation. He'll probably say no and tell everyone in the school not to co-operate but it'll be worth a try.'

Lisa was impressed by the way Daniel was picking up the various threads of the story so quickly. She liked his careful patience with Clare too, the courteous respect he was giving her. She wouldn't have minded some of that for herself come to think of it. But that was the way wasn't it? On some days your man pleased you wildly, on others you couldn't stand him. She had absolutely hated him when he was refusing to have anything to do with this venture but, now that he was going along with it, she was getting quite soppy about him again. 'We are, of course, in a good position to talk about that bastard Yuri,' she chimed in at one stage. 'I'm sure the world will be most interested to know what he's really like.'

'I'm not sure it's relevant to Chris's story,' Daniel replied after a while. 'Yuri's public image as Raz was the truth for Chris and that's probably all that matters in this story. But it might well turn out that Yuri's, albeit public, role in this is only half the story. There must be other factors. Nothing could be that simple.'

TWENTY SEVEN

It was early evening but not quite dark ten days later when Lisa returned home from a script read-through and she had just put her key into her front door when a cough in the Cheyne Walk shadows made her jump. The sodium street lamp glowed on the top of Judd's bald head. 'Charlie. You're home then. What's the matter? All that paella get too much for you?'

'I just 'ad enough Duchess. Just couldn't take it any more so I've come 'ome.'

Lisa glanced down at his suitcase and up at his round, curiously innocent face, wondering if perhaps he was hoping to move in with her but decided not to say anything, at least for the moment. 'Well, come on in, Charlie. You look as if you could do with a nice cup of tea.'

Once up the stairs she helped him off with his camel-hair overcoat on the landing although he was still suspiciously attached to his suitcase which he even carried into the living room with him where he sat down, took off his shoes and began waggling his stockinged toes around.

''Alf a mo', Duchess. Me plates is fair killing me. Caught a bus from Heathrow din I? Didn't want to attract too much attention like. No one takes much notice of you on a bus. You should try it some time. Everyone leaves you in peace on a bus.'

'Yes, well, look, Charlie. What's going on? Are you on the run or what?'

'Nah. I'm going to take your advice, Duchess. I'm going to turn meself in an' take whatever's coming to me. But I might pull a lot of bird, an awful lot of bird. Me brief says I could pull a ten. So I wanted to see me old Duchess before I see the Old Bill. But I needs just one small favour. This suitcase 'ere is full of money. I mean, there's more than five 'under grand in 'ere an' all I want you to do is look after it 'til I get out of the pokey. *If* I do pull a stretch which is more than likely.'

'Charlie! Ch-a-a-arleee!' She was decidedly unhappy at the prospect of being grabbed by the long arm of the law and being charged with whatever you were charged with when they caught you with so much hot boodle in your house.'

'It's all right, Duchess.' He held up his fat hands as if surrendering. 'I knows what you're finking but this lolly is all right. There's nuffink at all to worry about. Nuffink, all this lolly is straight. Well, *straightish*. It's just that the Old Bill is bound to take everfink when they do get their 'ands on me an' I'd like to 'ave a little somefink when I gets out. Call it me little pension plan.'

'But why me, Charlie? I know we're good friends and I'm honoured you feel you can trust me with your pension but there must be other places to stash it. You must know I'm half mad and not to be trusted. You know that, Charlie. I might have a few drinks one day and go and spend the lot in Harrods. You can spend five hundred grand in there in five minutes. I could buy half a dozen Indian elephants or something.'

'You wouldn't do that to me would you Duchess? Nah. Course you wouldn't. I mean to say what would you want with half a dozen elephants anyway? Where would you garage 'em?'

He laughed at his little quip but she could tell by the uncertainty of his tone the oaf wasn't entirely sure that she wouldn't blow his pension on half a dozen Indian elephants. She was also becoming more and more certain that she didn't want to look after his money. 'No, Charlie. I'll do anything to help you. But not this. It's *you* I'm thinking about here. I really *might* spend it. If you're going to need it when you come out then you are absolutely going to have to find someone else to look after it.'

'But there ain't no one else, Duchess. World's full of tea-leaves. You're the only woman I've ever trusted an' you're too upper class to go around thieving some geezer's hard-earned dough.'

'Oh we're not back on that again are we? My ex-husbands always used to go on about how upper class I am but I'm as working class as you, Charlie. As fucking working class as you.'

'Well, your language is working class, that's for sure. But look 'ere now. You've always done everfink proper for me an' you've never asked for anyfink in return so I trust you. I do. If you ever get a bit brassic, just 'elp yourself. I won't mind as long as you put it back.'

'And what about your wife? How's she going to manage for money when you're in the jug?'

'Mrs Judd will be well sorted,' he said primly. 'Don't you go worrying about Mrs Judd. But if I gave 'er the money she'd spend it wouldn't she? She'd 'ave all the streets of norf London covered in fitted white carpets for a start.'

'She's not *that* stupid. I've spoken to her a few times on the phone since you've been in Spain and she's not stupid at all. She's sweet and supportive and, if you ask me, I think you should go straight home to her and take your pension money too. Charlie, I can't be visiting you every day in the jug either.

Someone's going to have to take you clean shirts and socks and I'm just not any good at that kind of thing.'

'Lemme explain a few things to you. Duchess. When it comes to money Mrs Judd 'as got the brains of a prawn. I'm not saying anyfink about 'er as a woman. All I'm saying is that money does somefink funny to 'er little brain. When she's got it all she wants to do is blow it as fast as she can. That's Mrs Judd's golden rule that is: get it and blow it as fast as you can. But I *am* going back to her. After I leave 'ere I am going over to Totteridge Lane an' I'm going back to her like a good little 'usband should. I've been a very silly boy an' I want it to be right wiv Mrs Judd again. Then I want to 'ave it all sorted with the Old Bill so I can get my life back. All I'm asking is you put the money away somewhere 'til I get out of the nick. Not much to ask is it Duchess? Just this one small favour for old Charlie boy.'

Her mouth was opening and closing when the front door bell rang and Judd began putting his shoes back on as Lisa went to the window and looked down to see a black Daimler with the chauffeur standing to attention inside a bower of yellow roses as Barapov waved his walking sticks up at her.

She waved back before blowing out a long stream of exasperated air. The Russian git had turned up unannounced like this a few times in the past year as if she had nothing better to do than sit around all day waiting for him to hobble back into her life. They still weren't fucking since she had a more or less permanent 'headache' whenever he was around and he almost always stayed at Blakes Hotel but, somewhat mysteriously, her unrelentingly cold treatment of him had, if anything, made his ardour even more passionate. She would never understand men, particularly this one. He had even begun talking of marriage again and how he might buy her a nice mansion in Surrey. She quite fancied a nice mansion in Surrey, as it happened, except she didn't want to share it with him.

He might well, of course, be trying to catch her out with another man since his passionate Russian jealousy was about as big as his foolhardiness, and it was a good job that Daniel wasn't here with her now. She had sworn to Daniel that the Bouncing Codpiece had firmly and finally bounced out of her life. Not that he was bouncing anywhere much these days since not only was he having his usual problems with his tendons and ligaments but he had also now managed to break his big toe doing pointe in *The Tales of Beatrix Potter*.

But the more she considered the situation as he continued to wave his walking sticks at her the more she decided that she wasn't at all cross with him since his arrival might just get her off the hook. 'Charlie, you are about to meet the greatest crippled ballet dancer in the world.'

'Better be orf then, Duchess. Better get on me bike like.'

'No, Charlie. You stay sitting right there. Andrei is very sweet but he's Russian and a bit temperamental. Whatever he says just stay very calm. That's the secret of dealing with Andrei.'

'I'll be on me bike then.'

'No Charlie. You just stay there and be nice. That's all you have to do.'

'Lady, by yonder blessed moon I svear ...' Barapov began as she opened her front door.

'Oh cut the crap, Andrei,' she snapped. 'I've told you time and again to ring before you come over. Come in, if you must, but I'd better warn you now I've got a man in here.'

She was bracing herself to help him up the stairs but he seemed to pull himself erect and float up them without any help from her or his walking sticks. By the time she had accepted the mandatory yellow roses from the chauffeur and got up there herself, she found Barapov sitting opposite Judd and interrogating him with all the quiet menace of a senior office in the KGB.

'Zo. I vant to know for how many years you have known Miss Lisa Moran?'

'Oh blimey, can't 'elp you there. A few years maybe. You used to come down to the dogs in Walthamstow wiv us didn't you Duchess?'

'Dogs? What is dogs?'

'You know. Dogs. Woof, woof. As in dog track.'

'In these years you have been intimate with the Countess here have you? Is that vhat you are saying to me? Yes?'

'Now look, Mr Brezhnev, I don't wanna ...'

'Oh do shut up, Andrei,' Lisa finally intervened. 'All I said was that I had a man up here. I didn't say anything about being intimate with him.'

'I demand questions to my answers. That is all. Give me questions or ve vill have many punches. Zo. Vhat you say? Tell me. For how many years have you been goink fuck vith the Countess?'

'Andrei, just shut up will you?' Lisa shouted.

'You don't understand my answers. Is up to you. For sure because I know you come over here to this country to fuck vith the Countess. You fight me now?'

''Ang on a mo. 'Ang on. I 'aven't come here from anywhere. I'm a bloody Cockney. I was born 'ere to the sound of Bow Bells. *You* are the bleedin' foreigner 'ere mate. You can't come over 'ere telling me what to do.'

Barapov was now standing up and holding out his fists while Judd, having had enough of all this, was also standing up, his fat hands opening and closing. There was going to be an awful lot of blood on her carpets if she wasn't careful. 'Stop all this now,' she screamed. 'Stop all this nonsense now or I'm going to call the police. Here. Does anyone fancy a game of cards?'

The two men were still squaring up to one another when the telephone rang and, not thinking clearly, she picked up the receiver.

'I've been reading in the papers that you've given up smoking,' a posh, slightly slurred voice told her. 'If that's so perhaps I can have back all those ash trays you stole off me?'

Lisa took the receiver away from her ear and frowned at it, unsure, in all the commotion in her living room, who owned the voice. Ash trays? Stolen? She put the receiver back to her ear. 'I'm not at all clear what you're talking about,' she said stiffly. 'Who is speaking please?'

'My ash trays you appalling bag of shit. And I want that ivory one Rex gave me. That was a favourite of mine and you stole it like the common, thieving yard of piss you are.'

John Orlan. Of course. Who else had that elegant turn of phrase? He was probably rolling drunk too: he only ever rang her up for a spot of abuse when he was rolling drunk. She dropped the receiver as if it had become boiling hot and, looking at the quarrelling pair who were now busy looking at her, she decided she was just going to leave them to it. 'I've got to go out now,' she announced picking up her coat which she had left draped over the end of the chaise longue. 'Charlie, you can stay here tonight *in the spare room* if you want and you can leave your suitcase in there too if you want. Andrei you can also stay if you want or you can go but I'm now going out and might not be back tonight. Or tomorrow. Sort out your problems yourselves.'

She walked along the Embankment, squalling traffic on one side and silent river on the other, as if late for an urgent appointment, almost her every joint practically cracking with anger. Her main problem, she knew, was that, although she had never been good at maintaining relationships, she was even worse at leaving them behind. She *was* angry with Charlie for turning up with all that money; she *was* annoyed with Andrei for continually pitching up unannounced, and she positively *hated* John O for abusing her drunkenly whenever the mood took him, but the one she blamed most for this mess was herself. She had never, *ever*, been able to find the words to tell her men to go away; always fudging the issue, possibly because of her pissy middle class politeness or else perhaps hoping they might be of use to her one day. They were all black spots and she wanted them out but when was she going to manage to tell them as much in plain English and look as if she meant it?

She took her bad mood over the river, still angry with herself and everything else, with odd voices breaking through the edges of her consciousness, using words which were trying to build into speeches until she managed to shake them out of her ears, sometimes waving her hands around, as if trying to fend off a swarm of attacking bees, when the night would become silent again.

Warehouses loomed over her when she became aware that she had company, an old woman wearing a poke bonnet and a heavily flounced black silk dress. As fast as Lisa stepped up her pace the old woman kept up with her, not even losing her breath as they both bearded the lumpy cobblestones in this old, dripping area of the city.

The hard faces of prostitutes were briefly illuminated by the sulphurous flare of matches as they both walked on. Drunks lurched out of the darkness and a woman carrying an aspidistra in a pot crossed some wasteland. A police car sped past, its sirens blaring. A pub door was open, showing the bar full of light and drunken laughter.

Lisa began shaking her shoulders irritably, wishing that her black-bonneted companion would get lost. But it was that old pissy politeness thing again. She couldn't just say: 'Hey you, fuck off.' She just had to worm and squirm and hope to somehow shake her off on the next bend, though she expected to find her back at the following one.

Although — as you're here — I do know you don't I? You're Marina from *Uncle Vanya*, the one I took on a tour of the Provinces with the Prospect? The slightly dithery mother of the professor's first wife who, like me, like us all, always yearned for some sense of order. Oh yes, it's all coming back to me now: that recurring and eternal cry of women everywhere. 'Forget all this turbulent nonsense and we can be happy with a sense of routine and order.'

The two of them were still shoulder to shoulder as they went bursting down a small street, no more than a row of derelict shops really, all waiting for the demolition ball. Behind them stood the giant crucifix shapes of several cranes, silhouetted against a light blue sky, all waiting for the morrow and work on the next new stage of the next new development. They came into a square, edged by empty and boarded-up houses with one single street lamp standing in its centre, irradiating the darkness like a lighthouse.

She noticed that the street lamp made an almost perfect spotlight on the bare stage of the cobbled square, harshly brilliant at its centre but breaking down as it tried to shove away the much stronger and more tenacious darkness. Marina took Lisa's hand and led her up to the spotlight, carefully positioning her so that the bulk of her body was largely concealed in the darkness while the light itself shone at a certain angle so that the audience could pick up on the fine features of Lisa's face. 'Don't ever look directly at the light: let the shadows do the work for you here.'

'We'll go back to living the old way, like we did before,' Lisa declaimed to the attentively listening darkness. 'Eight o'clock in the morning, tea: one o'clock dinner and sit down to supper in the evening; everything in its proper place … the same as in other people's lives … like Christmas.'

Lisa had always enjoyed giving this small speech embodying, as it did, a universal call for the conventional and the ordered. Not that there was anything conventional and ordered about her life and she could feel her eyesight breaking up into shiny stripes and wondered how long her gathering migraine was going to last this time.

TWENTY EIGHT

Somehow in the screaming, shiny zigzags of her migraine – and she was not at all sure how – Lisa managed to flag down a taxi and get it to take her to Daniel's flat in Fulham.

Fortunately he was home and not on one of his by now frequent visits to Edgware, responding to her agitated ringing of his door bell quickly and without question, taking her up and lying her down on his bed where she kept whimpering and sometimes groaning, waiting for the migraine to lift. There was no other cure really: pills were just pointless when she got like this and she just had to suffer until it lifted. A few of these bouts had been known to last for days, particularly when she was living with John O in Cadogan Square, but this one, mercifully, only settled in for a few hours before she really did have the physical sensation of a hand loosening its iron grip on her head and gradually detaching itself from her skull.

It was such a relief to see the world properly again and she could sit up and smile at Daniel without her whole brain throbbing with pain. This relief was made the more palpable by the fact that, whenever she did have a migraine, she was always convinced that this one really was going to last forever. They always arrived quickly but never showed any hurry to go away.

Daniel didn't seem to mind that, in spite of all their ground rules, she had invaded his space without warning. Indeed he was as attentive and amiable as the early morning sunshine, making her the Earl Grey she always preferred and fussing around her in the most pleasing way, wondering if she would now like something to eat or if she wanted to go out for a stroll. 'It's not too late. We could have a quiet stroll around the Common and perhaps even work up an appetite for a good meal somewhere.'

'I'll tell you what I'd really like Daniel, darling. What I'd really like is a good bop. We haven't been to a decent dance for years.'

'Ah now. I might even know the right place for that too. El Porto, an Italian wine bar just off the end of Fulham Road which is getting a good reputation for music. It might be all right.'

They walked the long road and the music from the wine bar told them that it was very much open. Two tuxedoed bouncers stood guard on the doorway and one of them said, 'full up, sorry', until he recognised Lisa and waved them both inside. The bar was long and thin with sawdust on the floor and Chianti bottles dangling like bunches of coconuts from the wooden rafters. It was extremely noisy and crowded but, as Daniel was trying to get to the bar, one of the bouncers tapped him on the shoulder and beckoned the two of them to follow him.

They were escorted to a table in a dark corner near the dance floor. The bouncer asked the couple already sitting there to stand up and indicated to Daniel and Lisa that they could now sit down there. They hesitated, wondering if the uprooted couple would show any bad feelings but, on the contrary, they seemed rather pleased. 'The management says the drinks are on the house,' the bouncer said, 'and he'd be very pleased if you'd try a bottle of his favourite Barolo.'

'Barolo would be very nice and please thank the manager very much,' Lisa replied with a queenly nod – she had long taken all such deference without any particular surprise although Daniel had never quite got used to it. 'And thank *you* very much,' she said to the ousted couple who, far from being upset, asked her to autograph a napkin.

The problem with this one autograph was that it attracted the attention of others and, no sooner had she finished the one, than they were all crowding around her table. 'Daniel, darling,' she said, knowing other ways of dealing with such situations. 'Let's have a nice, long kiss and perhaps we'll be left alone. Necking is so rare these days they never seem to want to interrupt that.'

Something wonderful happened right in the middle of this kiss which started with the first bitching riffs of *Brown Sugar* and Mick singing lustily. They began jigging up and down, not breaking off their kiss but opening their eyes wide and looking at one another. Then, along with half of the rest of the people there, they surged on to the floor, especially sprung for dancing. There were now so many bopping up and down on it that the dancers hardly had to make any effort since the sprung floor was doing it for them. She remembered Daniel once saying that anyone who didn't want to dance to *Brown Sugar* must be dead and, if ever he owned a nightclub, he was going to call it *Brown Sugar* since that was the one record that always got everyone on to the floor.

She couldn't remember when she had last felt so happy or so much relished the insistently sexual drive of the beat and it soon became clear that they were in for a dance to end all dances when the next one all but knocked those Chianti bottles off the rafters: *Something Else* with Eddie Cochran.

Nightclub dance *aficionados* know that great dances, somewhat like great sex, often turn up totally unexpectedly. Much depends on the choice of music and the personality of the disc jockey but there's also the atmosphere on the floor, the feelings the other dancers feed into one another and particularly the way your own partner is responding to the music. Lisa felt warmly happy with this crowd, many of whom were passing around drinks which were slopping all over the place, and she was loving the music which was now taking everyone ever higher with the raucous jubilation of the Ramones' *I Wanna be Sedated* and Daniel himself was smiling like a goon on cocaine and acting as if he had stumbled into some new kind of heaven. He always changed when he was dancing; you could tell by his smile he was terminally happy.

And how lovely it was when the tempo slowed and Roy Orbison's falsetto voice began singing about his own endless heartache into the sweating, shifting darkness, with everyone holding one another tight and she was with her man and they had a nice, wet smooch and she felt sixteen all over again. 'I love you,' she mumbled into his ear finally. 'I love you, I love you, I love you.'

She didn't even get upset when, after they got back to his flat, he was unable to fulfil any duties and seemed to pass into a coma on his bed since, despite his allegiance to AA, he had nose-dived into the manager's favourite Barolo too and although he hadn't drunk much it now rather looked as if he couldn't take any at all. But it was just so comfortable and pleasant to have him here next to her, eyes closed and nostrils snoring, that she decided she really had to get a move on and marry him before anyone else got there first.

Her evil moods and migraines could go on for days and even weeks but he seemed to get her out of them by just being around. Orlan, Judd and Barapov — not forgetting the odd ghost or two — all seemed like distant specks in barely remembered nightmares and it was almost impossible to believe the three of them had been actively menacing her mental health only a few hours earlier. She kissed Daniel lightly on his spluttering cheek. Yes, it really was time they stopped messing about; they should get married soon. His youthfulness might be some sort of difficulty, of course, but her old chum Bette had always advised her to go for the young 'uns; they were far more fun, she said, and they weren't so set in their ways. And this one, now she came to look closer at him, had another important asset: a nice, winsome mouth.

Even though he was up against an important deadline with the outline of his book he didn't seem particularly anxious for her to leave and, as she wasn't particularly anxious to get back to Cheyne Walk, she welcomed the opportunity to escape from everything for a few days, lying in his bed and keeping it warm, in case he might feel like being warmed up, or else getting up to buy meals from the local kebab house or Chinese takeaway since cooking was way beyond her range of talents. She even got in help once a week to cook a chicken for the dog.

Daniel was mainly preoccupied with organising and writing up his notes on the Edgware story and working long hours since he had to give Kennington a full briefing late the following week. While she was content to snooze or read while he was working on that, they always had a stroll after their meal for an hour or so and she was amused to discover how often they ended up in a cemetery.

Most people liked to walk around parks but Daniel loved cemeteries – overgrown Highgate was his most favourite anywhere – and often rummaged in the long grass behind the tombs looking for any detritus, examining things like used condoms, whisky bottles or crisp bags, even making a note if he found something new to him. He called these things 'the secret dust in the lining of the city,' one of the clues to the metropolitan DNA.

On such walks he liked to tell her about his progress with the Christopher Reynolds saga. Chris's world had been extremely difficult to penetrate since the lad, as they had suspected from the start, had been a loner with only a few close friends that Daniel could track down. The picture of a persistent fantasist and liar was also beginning to emerge which made it difficult to establish the facts of even the most basic relationships and daily routines of his short life.

Daniel had gone to The London Institute to interview the photography tutor there but, despite his claims to his mother, Chris had never enrolled there. Daniel had also tried to locate the mysterious Brenda who had figured in so many of Chris's letters, when they had allegedly been living in a flat together in the city, but he could find no trace of her either. He had found a book by the Marquis de Sade in one of Chris's drawers and, after getting through several chapters on various sexual perversions, Daniel saw the attraction of this kind of thing to the unformed mind. All normal values were inverted; here were the 'positive' aspects of vice, the primacy of passion, the redundancy of virtue and the 'divine, redeeming' value of violence, all key themes of the eighteenth century romantics and pervasive too in the *Rebellion* series of films.

The boy's school had been predictably unco-operative. The headmaster had only agreed to meet Daniel after he had written him a long letter outlining the kind of book he hoped to write. Daniel had been called in and, in front of two witnesses, the headmaster told him that the school had a proud record and never discussed the past misdeeds – if any – of their pupils, preferring to emphasise their positive sporting and academic achievements. 'You fully understand that do you, Mr Jenkins?'

Ah yes, once a small-minded teacher always a small-minded teacher. Mr Jenkins fully understood that all right.

The one Harley Street psychiatrist who Daniel did get to talk to – on a strictly unattributable basis – opined, on the basis of the little that was known about

Chris, that here was a schizophrenic with strong feelings of hostility and loneliness. 'In such a predicament he could well have adopted fantasy figures who became real. Schizophrenics have little or no sense of personal identity. They are always on the look-out for new heroes and will often attach themselves to a film, a book or a favourite television character. Yes, you can be certain that Christopher knew every action and trick in the *Rebellion* films but there are almost certainly other influences at work. Your problem, as I see it, is to locate and describe those influences and, as you can't talk to your subject, because he's six feet under, I'm not at all sure that this is possible.'

Daniel had also gone though all the *Rebellion* films frame by frame, noting how Chris's imagination had entered almost completely into them. With his Doc Martens, cut-off Levis and close-cropped hair, Chris had come to look like Yuri Pucket's character, Raz. He had loved Raz's favourite food, raw meat lightly grilled with cloves, and his automatic guns had been the same. In his long hours in the forest Chris had almost certainly behaved like Raz and there were even exact parallels between Chris's relationship with his parents and Raz's. The mother was dominant yet loved while the father was distant and indifferent. The films could hardly be blamed for this but it was another element which might explain Chris's preparedness to identify so closely with Raz and ape his actions.

There was more illumination to be found in the films. A policeman at the inquest had not been able to understand why Chris had repeatedly shot up an empty, stationary car, but in *Rebellion 4*, the reason became clear. Raz, cornered by a gang in a Spanish car park, emptied his Kalashnikov into a row of parked cars, turning them into balls of flame. Images of petro-chemical explosions were recurring favourites in all the *Rebellion* films and it was evident to Daniel that Chris had been trying to create similar explosions in Edgware. When Chris ran from his pursuers he always did so at a crouch, US combat style, to avail himself of cover from walls and present a smaller target. Raz had also run like this when had had been chased in *Rebellion 5* and one of the witnesses in the coroner's court had referred to Chris's odd, crouching run.

To all intents and purposes Chris had become Raz. So how many more Christopher Reynolds were out there? How many more bullets were going to be fired into how many more innocent people?

There were still big questions to be answered like where Chris had found his guns in the first place. Another big hole in his story so far was that no one had ever seen Chris watch a *Rebellion* film either on video or anywhere else.

Daniel had located the shop where Chris had rented his video films, even if the manager couldn't – or wouldn't – help him by showing Daniel what sort of films Chris liked to take out. The investigation had led to an arcade where Chris had enjoyed playing computer games glorifying violence and sudden death. In one of the games you could blast through the streets in a car being chased by the cops before picking up a prostitute. After having sex with her in the back of your car you could then shoot her and get your money back.

It was becoming a daunting search through contemporary youth culture and whenever he thought it was hopeless something else turned up to stimulate his interest again.

Yet, in a positive way, what Daniel was hoping would emerge was a defining story of Thatcher's England in the Eighties where the middle classes were breaking apart under the weight of their own self-indulgence and greed while the young were taking off in a search for new identities, often destructive and violent like soccer hooligans.

Christopher would, then, become someone who had been created by this Eighties culture and, if Daniel *could* follow and identify the trail of the boy's influences, he would almost certainly end up with a penetrating analysis of the culture as a whole together with some clear reasons why young people were taking up guns and shooting holes in others. His book would be an inquiry into modern values.

For her part, Lisa knew all about those feelings of bitter alienation which had prompted Chris to fire at those shoppers but, more than anyone would ever understand, she also knew what it was like to be pursued and even controlled by ghosts. The ghost of Raz had taken over Chris's mind just as she was being pursued by sundry others, perhaps not quite as malevolent, but also trying to take her over. Perhaps we are all merely puppets of our own ghosts and perhaps that was Chris Reynolds' real story.

TWENTY NINE

Lisa couldn't even make the simplest connection as she struggled through the King's Road shoppers, loaded down with presents that no one wanted as yet another hateful Christmas came bearing down on her as grim as a policeman holding out a warrant for her arrest.

Another torrent of cold rain poured down out of the leaden sky, nicely augmenting the rigmarole of chirping misery all around her. The shops were bursting with empty incandescence and more street traders than ever were jamming the pavements, offering every known species of junk from horror videos to Coca-Cola towels, from clockwork ducks to 'designer' jeans, designed to fall apart after the first wash.

Somewhere deep in this jamboree was some suggestion that a child had been born in a crib in Nazareth almost two thousand years ago and, when she did finally get back to Cheyne Walk, she paused briefly to look up at the icy drops of rain falling off the bare branches of the trees, fancying the trees alone understood and were weeping in bitter lament for this seasonal madness.

Yet since what cannot be altered has to be endured she had resolved that she was going to weather this annual storm of blood and puke with resolute determination. The food and drink had been bought. The Christmas cards had been ritually sent. A few whizzy parties were in the offing, including what promised to be a nice lunch on Christmas Day hosted by Ava in the Café Royal and Daniel had agreed to stop working for the three days of Christmas and spend it here with her in Cheyne Walk.

He often got moody and stroppy when he wasn't writing but had sworn repeatedly he was going to be relaxed and amiable for the whole duration of this time in hell and, in consequence of such reassurances, she had spent thousands of pounds on a Christmas present for him which, she hoped and prayed, might even tempt him to move in with her for good. It had been a most expensive gambit on her part – perhaps the most expensive gambit she had ever tried with any man – but it might just work. *Might.*

They had been getting on quite well lately but he was starting to shake up her ever-present feelings of insecurity again and she wanted to effect a tighter hold on him. She had called a few times on his flat in Fulham Road during the last week but he hadn't been in. This was no good: she needed to know where he was and with whom at all times and, when he hadn't come up with any truly convincing answers to her troubled questions, claiming he'd been spending a lot of time in Edgware again, she had hired a private detective to take a close look at his movements.

The detective hadn't yet come up with anything, apart from a large bill, but she insisted he keep at it. 'I want to know his every move and acquaintance. Keep going for a week until Christmas Eve and we'll review the situation.'

That extremely plain Helen Grantby girl was still out there somewhere, wasn't she? It would at least be reassuring to know where she was too wouldn't it? Oh yes, it most certainly would.

But one headache, at least, had been solved since Charles Judd, probably in the light of his clear fondness for doing runners to Marbella, had been refused bail and was now a guest of Her Majesty in Wormwood Scrubs where, judging by the list of charges against him, he would be languishing for a long time yet. She hadn't yet got around to visiting him and had even rung up his wife asking her to take his suitcase, with all his pension money, away but, clearly after consulting Charlie, Lisa was firmly told to keep hold of it. 'Charlie says I'm too stupid to look after all that money,' said Mrs Judd with a touching self-knowledge. 'He'll need it for when he gets out so you'd better look after it 'til then, there's a love.'

Christmas Eve turned up on time, as per usual, three days later and Lisa was more relieved than she could say when Daniel turned up at her house on time too. But what pleased her more than anything else was that he was wearing a Hugo Boss suit and a Turnbull and Asser shirt which she'd had run up for him. He was also holding what looked like being a nice present for her 'to be opened in the morning'.

'Daniel, darling, you look wonderful. I've been worrying all day you were going to turn up in jeans.'

'You're looking pretty amazing too,' he replied, twirling her around to admire her new Yves St Laurent party frock with its huge collar of glass and wood beads together with the short ruffed skirt which perfectly displayed her trim legs.

'What do you think?' she asked.

'Terrific. That's what I call absolutely terrific.'

He agreed to one glass of champagne – as it was Christmas – and they toasted one another: 'A very, very happy Christmas to both of us.'

She chatted on gaily about where they should go that night – there were four invitations – saying that she had been prepared to cook the lunch tomorrow, noticing the comic way his head jerked back and eyes widened when she made this claim, but adding that they had both been invited by Ava to a private lunch party in the Café Royal. But he was the boss, it was up to him.

'Is there any chance we can go to bed for half an hour first and get all that out of the way? Just the very sight of those legs of yours is making me as horny as hell.'

'Every chance, sweetness,' she smiled, smoothing her hands down her thighs. 'But I hope that doesn't mean you won't be up to anything when we come back. I mean to say it *is* Christmas.'

'Christmas does last for three days, you know. It doesn't all disappear at the stroke of midnight.'

'Now look here. All I'm saying is I don't want any erections disappearing at the stroke of midnight like that fucking pumpkin. That's all I'm saying.'

The door bell rang and she walked to the window apprehensively only to relax when she saw who her visitor was. 'Oh Daniel, please be a dear and answer the door will you? I've got to pay a bill. Send him up.'

'A funny time to be collecting money isn't it?'

'It's rather a lot actually and it was so much he said he wouldn't be able to enjoy Christmas unless he was paid in full and in cash. Just be a dear and tell him to come up.'

Daniel hung back discreetly when a thick-set man with black caterpillar eyebrows walked in, trailing wafts of body odour, and Lisa began handing over £6,000 in thick bundles of twenties. The man riffled through them like a croupier loosening up a new deck of cards.

'It's all there. No need to count it now.'

'Looks fine to me Miss Moran. You want a receipt?'

'It doesn't matter. Do you want a Christmas drink before you go?'

'No thanks. I'm running late for my son's party. Tell your son here not to bother seeing me out. I can manage myself.' He nodded at Daniel and left, pocketing his money. Lisa shuddered as she reached out to pick up her own champagne.

'What was that all about then?' Daniel asked.

She was too upset to reply. *Your son.* Those two words had brought up the yawning discrepancy between their ages, an issue never so much as mentioned in all the time they had known one another. Those two words had managed to gun down her earlier feelings of optimism and well-being. 'It was just for a little job I've had done in the house,' she said finally in a tremulous tone. 'You'll find out soon enough.'

'So,' he said brightly. 'When are we going to have this half an hour in bed?'

'Oh I'm not in the mood for all that now. What I really need is another glass of fizz.'

For the next hour or so they both had a few glasses and he tried to cheer her up with an upbeat report on the Chris Reynolds book – he was even pretty sure he had tracked down the source of Chris's guns – and she listened to him in a frostily polite way. She usually took a lot of real interest in the subject, but her mind was elsewhere and she had become so upset she could barely speak. She knew she was slipping down into the hole of a really bad mood and he was, at least, still chivvying away at her, trying not to lose her down that hole since he almost certainly knew what had upset her and didn't want to rub salt into the wound by talking about it. There were some issues which were best left not discussed and her age had always been one of them.

She started making noises that she didn't want to go out at all but he did manage to get her into a taxi where she remained quiet and subdued as it took them to The Gardens, on top of the old Derry and Tom's building in Kensington High Street. Maggie was having a do for her old theatrical pals, it said on the invitation card. She wanted them all to come along and cheer her up. You and me both, Maggie, old mate, you and me both.

No sooner had they checked their coats and got into the crowded, mirror-lined lift, where the party-goers preened in front of their own wholly admirable reflections, than Lisa found herself standing next to that toothless old luvvie, Dorothy Pryce-Jones.

'Lisa, darling, how perfectly wonderful to see you.' *Mwah, mwah, mwah.* 'And you're looking not a day over thirty either. Just how do you do it?'

'Lots of sex, Dorothy darling,' Lisa replied cheerfully as Daniel winced. 'A fuck every day and, if you can't do that, wank.'

Dorothy gave one of her long whinnying laughs, which seemed to owe more to aggravated asthma than a spontaneous outburst of mirth, but Lisa could tell she had been shocked rigid and that had brightened her up no end. God how she loathed her own theatrical class, forever prancing about costumed in hypocrisy. Dorothy Pryce-Jones had always hated her about as much as she had always hated Dorothy Pryce-Jones but there they were gushing over one another about how it long it had been since they'd last met and how they had been thinking about one another lately and how they simply must meet up in the New Year.

The lift doors opened. Curtain up.

They were set adrift on a squawking sea of hugs, darlings and *mwah, mwah, mwahs*. Lisa smiled and nodded graciously as she moved through them with Daniel bringing up the rear. She did her best to keep him afloat since she could tell that he had already got as nervous as a lone halibut in a sea of starving sharks and she kept grabbing hold of him and introducing him to lines of faces who she hadn't seen for ages saying how they should meet up in the New Year. 'Lisa, I was thinking of you only this morning …' She hadn't thought there would be so many people here but, ever the gracious star, swam on bravely, clinging to Daniel, squeezing his arm now and then, reassuring him he hadn't been forgotten. But he still managed to get away from her.

This party wasn't up to much, she could tell already: the usual liggers and a lot of crusty buffers who might be rich angels or something to do with theatrical management, along with their tiara'd, wrinkled wives who might have once had a dry sherry with Noël Coward. *Mwah, mwah, mwah*. And Maggie, whose bash this was supposed to be, wasn't anywhere in sight. Sensible woman. So what was Lisa doing here? Why hadn't she just gone to bed with a good book? And where had *her son* Daniel got to? And why was he talking to that boring, old cow? Oh here she was boiling away again … C'mon Lisa. This is a fucking party. This is fucking Christmas. Get on the case.

Lisa had stopped to talk to her old mate Joanie when she spotted Daniel crossing the dance floor and disappearing on to the roof gardens. So he had given up already. So much for his promise to behave himself. She turned and bumped into Harry Bines of Granada with whom they were all still in discussion about the film of *A Series of Surrenders* which hadn't quite yet got off the ground. 'Harry, how lovely it is. Did you ever get that house you were sweating on? In Sittingbourne wasn't it?'

When she did manage to slip the handcuffs of that conversation she went out into the gardens looking for Daniel in this tiny metropolitan oasis of grass, weeping willow and hurrying stream sitting high above Kensington. She had attended the opening of these gardens by Régine back in 1980 and they'd had ducks and flamingos poking about here then but these all seemed to have gone missing now that Richard Branson had taken over the club.

She turned into the dimly-lit Roman courtyard, a place of angled brick marvels where even the shadows struck expensive attitudes. Daniel wasn't there so she re-entered the main garden by a small wooden bridge and there he was, standing on a ledge in front of a high wall and looking out through the railings at the city's glittering nightscape. The disco behind them was barely audible and they were so high up they couldn't even hear the traffic below.

He was such a strange man really who didn't seem to fit in anywhere, least of all this polythene palace. Nothing about him made too much sense and that would always keep him apart from everything. His probably doomed attempt to join the Church might be little more than a need to belong to something. But she was like that too; actresses almost by definition don't belong to anything other than the fleeting definition of their roles; they are always adrift which, in some way, might explain why she loved him so much; because she was like him and he was like her.

'You don't belong to any of this, do you Daniel? It's a world you don't know or care about, isn't it?'

He said nothing for a while, continuing to stare out into the huge night. 'Places like this are all right in small doses but, to be honest, I'd far prefer that small wine bar we found in Fulham the other week.'

'Yes, that was a lot of fun. I'll always remember that place and the fabulous music. And there was that long chat we had in Avignon once when we told one another so much. That's always stayed in my mind. And Paris of course. That time when you saw that vision outside the Sacre Coeur. I thought I had a real nutcase on my hands, I can tell you.'

'I don't suppose there's a lot to choose between us in the mental health stakes, you being an actress and me being a freelance prophet. But I can think of a lot nicer ways of making a living. I've often thought that if we'd both had the same corporation bus — me driving and you taking the fares — we'd have been fine. We could have made it doing that.'

She was motionless and about six feet away from him on his ledge. 'You don't think we're going to make it then?'

'No, I don't.' He looked at her and his words made her heart leap like a startled bird. She could just make out a nervous tic on his cheek in the half light and she knew he was scared that she was going to blow. But she wasn't. He looked so lonely and vulnerable and almost might have been her son, at that. She would have made him a great mother, that was for sure.

'Well tell me one thing,' she said finally, consciously cool and quiet. 'What career prospects does a freelance prophet have?'

'None. There's no money in prophecy, no future. A prophet expects to be misunderstood and have the mickey taken out of him. That goes with the job. He's always got to stay calm in the face of hostility and laughter. He's got to keep plodding on regardless. He's called to it, you see, and has to keep going if only because he's been told to rouse the conscience of the nation, no matter at what cost to himself. Delivering the message is a permanent disability with a prophet. He's stuck with it, like gout.'

'For what it's worth I've always thought you make a pretty good prophet.'
'Thanks.'

'But there's one thing that's always puzzled me. Don't you have to be moral to be a prophet? Don't you have to be *good*?'

'Not in the slightest. One of the Old Testament prophets lived with a prostitute and another was holed up in a cave. Prophets have always had several screws loose. They're just picked and that's it.'

'And what about the Church? You have to be good to get in there don't you?'

'Ah, that's another matter. They do tend to want you to behave yourself in the Church but I'm not too sure I want to go into the Church any longer. Maybe my career as a freelance prophet would be better served by my staying a writer.'

She stepped up on the ledge with him and they both craned their necks to look down on Kensington High Street. 'I shall miss you when you go, Daniel,' she said, amazed at her own calm. *He had just informed her that it was over! She should have tried to rip his throat out but there she was, as calm as a letter box on a Chelsea corner.* 'I've told you before, I've been married to famous writers but none of them are ever going to be half as famous as you. God was very lucky to find you. Don't compromise, Daniel, don't ever take the easy way. They're always going to hate you but you've got to keep ramming it down their throats. And don't go into the Church either. I've never said this before but the place is just stuffed with bureaucratic rules and reverend assholes. Just be yourself and write what you want to say. They'll listen in the end. If what you are saying is true they are bound to listen. The truth will always prevail; we must believe that or there'll never be any point in getting out of bed.'

Two women ran along the bank of the stream behind them, screaming drunkenly at one another and the bass throb of the disco got louder, as if the disc jockey had decided that he finally meant business. 'I've always loved you, Lisa,' he said after the two women had disappeared back into the nightclub. 'I loved you from the first but I've got to go somewhere quiet and get on with my work. I need to settle down somewhere and get on with what I do.'

'And you can't do that with me?'

'I'm not quite sure how to say this but I can't work properly when I'm going out with you. You're always making some kind of noise in my mind and I need a lot of peace to work and think. I'm worried about my friend Helen too. I've been searching for her and can't find her.

'I'm so sorry to tell you this, Lisa, but I can't build any sort of happiness on Helen's pain. I *know* she's in pain but I simply can't find her to help her ease it.'

'What about my pain Daniel? I feel pain too, you know.'

'Sure, but Helen's young and frightened of everything and I'm worried she's gone on the bottle and back on to the streets from where she came. I've got to find her, you see, because I *need* her. It's as simple as that. She's my anchor and I need her and I keep looking for her but I can't find out where she is.' He shook his head and tears flew out of his eyes, a few catching Lisa on her flushed cheek. 'I have just *got* to find out where she is.'

She took the handkerchief out of his top pocket and blew her own nose with it. 'You've got me at it now,' she wailed. 'I've never come across anyone who made me cry so much. Stupid isn't it? Going out with you is like peeling onions. But do one thing for me, Daniel darling. Stay with me over Christmas. I promise to be good. No hysterics, no noise, no threats and then you can walk out of my life forever.'

'That's not a problem now we've cleared the air. You *are* all right are you?'

'Yes, I'm fine and now we're going to become friends. I keep on telling you. If we can't be lovers then at least let's become friends. Chekhov always used to say that people should become lovers before there's a real possibility of them then becoming good friends so let's go back into the party and *enjoy* ourselves.'

They managed to find a seat at the end of a long bench near the dance floor where she put her arm around his shoulders and kissed him on the side of his neck. The pincers of pain were taking hold of her heart again but she was not going to show it. No one, anywhere, least of all in this vacuous dump, was even going to guess at its intensity and, even as her fingers played with the hair on the back of his head, she wondered quite how much pain one old heart could take before it finally exploded. Or gave up.

'You see that man over there,' she said, pointing across the heaving dance floor. 'The one next to the one wearing those stupid antlers. I met him once. He's something to do with dolphins. That's his business. He sends dolphins to zoos all over the world.'

'You can make money out of something like that, can you?'

'Of course. You can make money out of anything at all if you work at it long enough. You're always on about money aren't you? Every writer I've ever met has been obsessed with money and there you are, haven't got a penny.'

She looked back at the dancers, feeling that old familiar ache again. The great pity was she had never got into drugs in a big way. A fair few of her luvvie pals were taking a regular sniff of the old Colombian marching powder these days to ease their pains but they had never done her much good. Drugs made her nuttier than she already was and she'd put a stop to them before they put a stop to her. Not that she would have said no if someone had put something illegal into her hand at that moment. She would have been up to anything to staunch the sorrow that seemed to be leaking from her every pore. How *could* he do this to her and at Christmas too? A bright fucking Christmas present that was.

A fat American waddled over to her and asked her for a dance but she shook her head with a sweet smile. He turned to Daniel and said: 'I would deem it a great, great honour if I could dance with your lady friend.'

'Nothing to do with me. You'd better ask her.'

He repeated his request to her and she shook her head again and again the American turned to Daniel for his blessing.

'Look, if she says no, she means no.'

'If you want to do something for me good sir you can always get me a large brandy,' Lisa said finally, if only to try to break this deadlocked conversation.

'Ma'am, it would be my greatest pleasure.' And to Daniel. 'Can I also offer you a drink sir?'

Daniel shook his head and she looked at him. Pious teetotal sod. How had she ever got mixed up with a teetotaller? All her men had been drunks so why did he always have to be so different? And he was never quite the same when he wasn't drinking. The fun went out of him when he was sober and she always managed to handle him a lot better when he had a glass in his hand. Whenever he had got difficult about anything all she had to do was get him into a pub and he'd do anything for her.

But not any longer he wouldn't; all he wanted to do now was leave her.

Had they been drinking that night they would probably have both been well hammered by now and ended up at the Maple party near King's Cross. That had been a real party that had, full of the drugged and the mad, bopping away like the world was going to come to an end when the song was over. The music had been terrific at the Maple too; not like the drippy suet they were playing here. Culture Club or something.

A large brandy was put in her hand and the fat American again asked her for a dance. 'Miss Moran, I have always worshipped you since your first appearance in *Rebellion*. Just one dance with you would make my Christmas the greatest ever.'

She couldn't believe the evidence of her ears. She hadn't wanted to dance with this big tub of lard and, now that he's bought her a drink, it was as if he was trying to blackmail her on to the dance floor. Why didn't people ever leave you alone? Why did they keep coming back again and again, always wanting something from you, asking for a part of you, again and again, especially when you kept saying no?

But she was going to stay calm. Even though Daniel had chosen this Christmas Eve to dump her she was *not* going to freak out. Oh no. Not doing what was expected of her had always been a key feature of her repertoire. The fat bastard was still standing there, hoping for a dance, so she beckoned him to lower his head for a quiet word in his ear. 'Now listen to me you big bag of shit,' she purred sweetly, pausing so he could catch her sweet smile. 'I've told you once so now I am going to tell you one more time. I do *not* want to dance with you. So fuck off, you stupid American cunt or I'll call the police.'

To her amazement, he went down on one knee and grabbed her, as if hoping for a Papal blessing but what he actually received was an anointment of the large brandy he had just bought for her, poured all over his fat head. 'Oh what an honour,' he moaned ecstatically, slobbering over her hand. 'Let me buy you another one, Miss Moran, so you can do that to me again.'

'We've got a fucking pervert here,' Lisa roared, wrenching her hand free and trying to kick him in his dangly bits before rising to her feet and making her way for the Ladies as fast as she could. Once safely inside one of the cubicles she sat on the pan and wept. She couldn't take any more of this, she thought as she kicked out at the door in anger and frustration. Why didn't they leave you alone?

Why didn't they understand that no always meant no? Not yes or fucking maybe. Fucking no was what fucking no always meant. She stood up and roundly kicked the cubicle door once again.

When she had sat back down again there was a soft knocking on the door and a posh voice which she immediately recognised as Maggie's. 'Lisa, darling, it's me. Just checking you're all right.'

'I'll live Maggie. But that's the trouble isn't it? I'll live and I'll have to live with all the other boring bastards in this world. Why don't they leave me alone? I never bother them so why do they bother me all the time?'

'Perhaps you need a drink?'

'Get me a large brandy would you please? A little bit of oblivion is what I really need.'

'Are you coming out or do you want me to push it under the door?'

'I'm not coming out anywhere. Under the door. Straight under the door.'

Within a minute or so a little silver platter came under the door with a flower, a few chocolates, a card saying Merry Christmas and an enormous goblet of brandy. That was what she called a real Christmas present. Ah yes. Maggie had always done it in style.

'What's the problem Lisa darling? Anything you want to talk about?'

'Oh just some fucking American who won't leave me alone.'

'I know. Americans are dreadful aren't they? I simply don't know *what* was in God's mind when he made Americans. They say that God doesn't make mistakes but he made a very big one indeed when he took the Americans out of his oven. And it's not just the way they act either. I've never yet met an American who knew how to dress either.

'Would you like another brandy Lisa? If you open the door I'll come and sit with you if you want. I'm not enjoying this fucking party either. We could have a nice chat about our old days in rep. I wish I was doing that again don't you?'

'No I don't. Never finding the soap in the shower. Pissing in the sink. Dragon landladies. Wouldn't want to do that again for anything.'

THIRTY

She opened her eyes late the next morning and looked down at the smudged caterpillars of her mascara on the pillow before closing them again with a low moan. A hangover had settled in just above her nose and its sheer ferocity alone enabled her to work out that she had hit the bottle hard the night before. Probably the brandy bottle. Some extremely bad behaviour had certainly accompanied that brandy. She *never* seemed to learn.

At least, on opening her eyes again, she was able to recognise the back of Daniel's head. Well, she'd gone to bed with someone she knew, then, not always the case when she'd drunk that much.

She rolled on to her back and moaned again as her memory began putting a few more fatal pieces of the jigsaw into place. What a nightmare! It had all begun when that sod had described Daniel as 'her son'. They had gone to a party in The Gardens and 'her son' had announced that he was going to leave her. There had been some sort of scuffle with that American colostomy bag on legs. Then she'd locked herself in the toilet and, oh no, she'd had a rather nice party in one of the cubicles with Maggie and various other friends who had come in carrying large goblets of brandy. Oh shit. How many? Small wonder Daniel wanted to leave her. She would have left herself if she'd only known how. Wouldn't it be wonderful to have a holiday somewhere quiet without taking herself along too. Stupid cows didn't come any stupider than her.

She pushed out her legs and sat up on the side of the bed, groaning again as she clamped her forehead with the palm of her quivering hand. Her clothes were scattered over the floor so he must have at least undressed her. She caught a truly appalling glimpse of herself waving her arms around and standing in the middle of the traffic in Kensington High Street, ranting and raving at the passing drivers about something or other. Perhaps fortunately she would never get into The Gardens or have a party in their bogs again; Richard Branson was probably cutting up her membership card at that very moment.

'Her son' was still dead to the world so she put on her dressing gown and went down into the kitchen to find a complete disarray of broken glass in the sink and two whole loaves of bread sliced up as if ready for the feeding of the five thousand in the church picnic. She flung the bread out of the window for the birds and clutched her bursting forehead again. More glimpses of last night came back to haunt her and it was only when she got into the living room, carrying a cup of tea with her teeth crunching loudly on a few paracetamol, that she spotted all the cards along her mantelpiece and remembered this was Christmas morning. The sky was a ravishing blue with a few distant dark rain clouds. Hard sunshine enamelled the brown Thames and a man with arms outstretched was following a child on a new bike as it wobbled along the pavement. Not a single car moved in either direction.

She would take a long walk around the Houses of Parliament to clear her head before wandering over to Ava's lunch at the Café Royal. There would be a lot of larky people there and, with any luck, she would get drunk again. She wasn't going to worry about Daniel; he seemed to have plenty of plans which didn't include her and she wasn't going to spoil her Christmas mooning over him. They weren't remotely suited anyway: he was far too nutty and highly strung for her. The only things he was really good at was dancing and in bed. A woman at her stage in life needed more than that; she needed a tender, consistent lover not some over-sexed Fred Astaire who kept seeing mad visions. A strong mature man with lots of money who was a tiger in bed and would beat her senseless whenever she reached out for the brandy bottle. Yes, that's what she needed. Plenty of understanding and regular beatings whenever she got out of line. There had to be someone like that out there somewhere. She sniffed wistfully wondering where this man might be as she sipped her tea and stared down at the child on the Embankment wobbling along on her new bike.

'Happy Christmas,' Daniel said, kissing her on the back of the head.

She noted he was fully dressed in his suit – doubtless ready to leave – and almost felt relieved it was over. She had even worried that he might have decided it would be a good idea if she *did* cook the Christmas lunch but, despite what she had told him, she had never cooked lunch for a man in her life, let alone Christmas lunch and she didn't want to start any of that nonsense in her old age. Perhaps she'd take a serious look at vibrators in the New Year. They might have solved one of her many problems but she doubted it. 'You don't have to stay, you know,' she told him. 'You made your big speech last night and I'd just be happy if you'd just leave.'

'Are you saying you don't want us to see one another again? What about all that Chekhov stuff about how we're going to be good friends now we've been lovers?'

'Oh I don't know. Look, Daniel, just leave will you? I don't want any more fuss. I'm sorry about what happened last night but let's just draw a line under it shall we? I *was* trying to behave but it was just that brandy all over again. Brandy and Maggie have always been a lethal combination where I've been concerned. Ring me in the New Year.'

'All right, but don't forget to open your present. And remember I love you.'

A memory boomed in her hungover brain like a Chinese gong. 'Oh Daniel, I've got a present for you as well, but you can't take it with you I'm afraid. Well, you could have parts of it if you wanted. It's a bit...'

'What are you talking about?'

'The spare room. I had it converted for you. That's why I had to pay that man last night. I could see you weren't working well and I wanted to help. I wanted to make a base for you here.'

'Let's have a look at it then.'

'It doesn't matter now.'

'Lisa, you've gone to a lot of trouble. At least let me see it.'

She stayed out on the landing while he went into the spare room where he moved around clucking his approval at each item. The walls had been fitted with white panels and were brilliantly lit by concealed internal lights. A state-of-the-art word processor sat on a white desk next to a monitor screen and a 126 dot-matrix printer. On another table was an IBM 72 1V which filed everything on magnetic tape and next to that again a micro-dot machine. On a shelf above the filing cabinet were various standard reference books including *Who's Who*, *The Oxford Dictionary of the Christian Church*, *The Evangelical Dictionary of Theology*, *The Oxford Companion to English Literature* and the *Oxford Dictionary of Quotations*.

A red plastic ladder stood by the window next to a half-size snooker table.

'It's all pretty amazing but I don't understand the snooker table. I don't play snooker.'

'I rang Willis and asked him what every writer should have. He said he's always wanted every issue of *The Times* on micro-dot so that's that machine there. This is the very latest in computers – it really is time you threw out that old typewriter – and you can put all your London book into it. You said you were gathering so much material you weren't able to organise it so that's how. Willis also recommended a snooker table because he always likes to play a frame when he gets stuck. Loosens up the brain, he says. So I got you one. But it's half size because the room's not big enough for full-size.'

'It's lovely, all lovely. And the ladder?'

'Oh I don't know. It's not for climbing on. I thought all this needed some kind of ornament. You can still have it all you know.'

'I couldn't, I really couldn't. Not now.'

'Yes you could. It was all bought for you and if you don't have it no one else will. Leave it here and I'll get it all sent over to you when you're ready. And, as it's Christmas, there's just one more thing. There's no fool like an old fool, they say, but you said you were worried about what had happened to Helen.'

He turned around and looked at her with his eyes narrowing questioningly.

'I've had a few inquiries made and you can find her at 247 Whitechapel Road.'

'247 Whitechapel Road?'

'That's it. She's fine and she's working in a Mission Hall there. She hasn't been drinking, as you feared, and there's no boy friend so you *might* be able to pick up where you left off.'

'Have you had the Special Branch checking her out or what?'

'Daniel, please don't shout. I've got a really bad hangover and can't deal with anything loud. I just got curious to know what had happened to her myself, if you must know. I've always felt ... guilty about taking you from her after you'd been together for so long. *And* I wanted to know she was all right so I got a private detective to check her out. Go over and see her, Daniel. Tell her you love her. You deserve better than me.'

'There's no one better than you.'

'Daniel, it's getting difficult for me now. I've never known how to say goodbye. All I've ever done is walk away and then I usually walk back again because I've got lost. Do the same now will you? But don't come back. I'm going to get very upset very soon so I want you to leave now. Don't do or say anything. Just leave me this very minute or I'll start screaming and breaking things. Go on. Fuck off right now will you?'

Her eyes were red and bubbling with tears but she didn't feel quite as bad as she had expected when she closed the front door after him. She was pleased with herself that she had been so gracious in defeat and given an old love back now that hers had gone cold. Ah, the grand theatrical gesture again, always the fucking grand gesture. Sometimes she really did make herself sick.

Perhaps she had felt motherly towards him after all; maybe he *had* become a son to her and the real reason why she had got so upset when that sod had referred to him as 'her son' was that she would so liked it to have been true. She would have been more than happy to have been a mother to him, giving him all the care and encouragement he needed. At least she would always have had him then, he couldn't have just walked out on her when things got rough. Yet who knows anything at all about things like this? She didn't and she had long given up trying to understand her warring feelings; she'd been faking them for so long, off stage and on, she barely knew what was what in the emotional department any more.

But this was absolutely the last time she was going to get mixed up with a young 'un. They were too self-satisfied, too ready to spurn what you had elaborately planned for them. He had walked out on that writer's study with barely a word of regret and she doubted he would come back for any of it. An older man might have tried to hang on to it or would have valued it more and at least appreciated the effort and expense that had gone into putting it all together. Not him. She took a small bottle of champagne out of the fridge, poured herself a consoling glassful and took it to the living room window where she fished a few more paracetamol out of her dressing gown pocket and stared out over the Thames again, wondering where 'her son' was going to lay his little head down tonight.

One thing was clear. Old Charlie was going to value and appreciate the expense of setting up that writer's study because his pension fund had paid for it. It was a mean thought for a Christmas morning but she hoped he would pick up a long stretch in the jug if only to give her a chance to re-fill his suitcase before he got out. Such ready cash was always tempting and accessible – as opposed to the difficulty of realising any real money from such as property bonds – and she'd nose-dived into that suitcase a couple of times when she'd needed the readies. But it had to be *his* fault when all was said and done. He and Mrs Judd had been warned repeatedly about her financial fecklessness and what could a girl do with a suitcase full of cash except to go out and spend it? But she hadn't spent all of it and he was lucky she hadn't blown the lot in Harrods on those Indian elephants.

Her paracetamol eased her hangover slightly but here, again, was the dull ache of a breaking heart. It got no easier as you got older. No matter how many rehearsals you had you were never ready for the pain of parting when it came back again, as it always did. Oh well, that's what you get when you're daft enough to tangle with a prophet. For Chrissake! Just her luck to go and fall for a freelance fucking prophet.

She finished her small bottle of champagne and picked up the telephone to call her little Russian ballet dancer in New York. At least *he* had never torn up her heart and thrown it away like this. Why ever hadn't she taken her loyal Bouncing Codpiece more seriously?

The Christmas streets echoed with their own emptiness as Daniel walked alone along the Embankment and, just behind the Savoy, he saw a cat attacking a seagull. No ordinary cat either but a big, bruising tom-cat with thick scars criss-crossing his face. He had grabbed the gull and was trying to drag it under a parked car to finish it off. Yet not only was the seagull resisting stoutly but other gulls were joining in the fray, swooping down and strafing the cat with squirting bombs of crap or helicoptering over him in blurs of huge grey wings and white fanned tails as they screamed their displeasure, lunging their long yellow beaks at him. The cat finally gave up trying to murder the seagull and let go of him, rearing on its hind legs to swipe at the other birds with its clawed front paws but the seagulls, having enabled their mate to escape, now flew away calling out to one another in triumph as the skinhead cat, with a last defiant hiss, slunk off into the bushes.

He hiked on up through the litter-blown canyons of the City, keeping to the warmth of the sunshine side of the street as he passed St Paul's Cathedral where the chiming of bells raged over his head. All the churches around Hoxton and Bishopsgate joined in these tremendous carillons proclaiming the birth of the Lord to the empty streets. Jug, jug to dirty ears.

Apart from the jubilant sound of the bells the streets remained full of their own quiet as if they too were joining in this thoughtful time of celebration. The odd car did pass by but Daniel mostly had the commercial heart of the city to himself, walking on with a quiet hope in his heart and barely able to believe it when a few dark clouds came together with the sunshine and fashioned a perfect rainbow over the city, so emblematic of new birth, so colourful and pure, so right for this particular day. A Christmas rainbow.

Lisa had dolled up with elaborate and expensive care for Ava's lunch, trowelling on the lipstick, using lashings of eye-liner and choosing a Versace cream silk blouse with a tight, long but slashed-to-the-thigh black Valentino skirt. Things might be going badly but it never did to show the world your wounds. Glamour was always the best disguise and, when it came down to it, she had a bigger and brighter front than the loathsome Margaret Thatcher.

'I've given up men altogether,' Ava told Lisa over cocktails. 'About every six months, when I feel the urge, I have the window cleaner.'

'I had the window cleaner once,' Lisa gloomed. 'He was terrible, always smelled of cheap soap and had the cheek to start charging me double afterwards. You wouldn't know anything about vibrators would you Ava darling?'

Ava gave one of her full-blown dirty laughs, all gappy teeth and smoker's bronchitis. 'Lisa, honey, not only do I know nothing about vibrators, I don't even know what one looks like. I know it's some sort of sex aid but what do you do with it?'

'Well, it's a sort of plastic dick that vibrates but you've got to remember to put the battery in.'

'Ah, a *vibrator*. One of them! I was married to one once and it was called Frank Sinatra.' They both roared with salacious laughter, acting in much the same way as Lisa had with Maggie. The theatrical golden girls always enjoyed one another when they met like this even if there was the slightly hysterical edge of two elderly women coming close to the end of the line and no longer sure what their place was in the world.

'So what *was* Frank like in bed?'

'I can't remember too much about it to be honest. I was always soused in those days and it was more a drunken fumble in the dark. But it was all right, I guess. He was always sort of enthusiastic, you know *earnest*. He made up for his shortcomings by being really earnest.'

'Frank was one of those was he? Over before he'd begun?'

'Something like that. He was faster than Speedy Gonzales and, particularly when I'd had a drink – which was almost always – I was slower than a milk train. We never got the timing right and, by the time my train had arrived, his station had gone, if you follow me. So it wasn't long before he was crooning over another floozy who kept to a better timetable. Are *you* in love these days Lisa?'

'It's all the usual mess. Why does love always have to be such a mess? That's why I was asking about vibrators. They've always seemed so straightforward.'

'Stick to vibrators, Lisa honey. Yes, siree, if I'd stuck to vibrators I'd be one happy and rich dame by now. Not that it bothers me too much these days. I'd much rather have a large martini. On the other hand ... see that man over there. So distinguished and so filthy – and I mean filthy rotten – rich. Jean-Paul Platini.'

The mournful Victorian façade of the London Hospital towered over Daniel as he made his lonely way along Whitechapel Road. Three times now he had walked past the front door of the Mission Hall and three times he had failed to drum up the courage to ring the bell. There was an AA meeting in there in an hour or so, it said in a note on a bit of paper pinned to the door which he recognised had been written by Helen.

It had just gone half past three and already the light was fading from the drizzly East End streets. Bloated people in paper hats sprawled in front of their television sets in the terraces of the nearby roads and only the odd pigeon or wandering dosser moved on the damp pavements. He stopped outside Aldgate East station and looked around at an area he had come to know well from his London researches. Ten feet away was the alley where Jack the Ripper claimed his first victim. Two shops away was a butcher's, once the site of a Victorian freak show where John Merrick, the Elephant Man, had been discovered. For most of his life Merrick had lived in a room just above the clock of the London Hospital and his remains were still preserved there. Abe Beame, a former mayor of New York, was born along that road and Charlie Chaplin failed miserably when he first appeared in a Jewish theatre on the next corner. The Blind Beggar pub, where the Kray gangsters committed their first murder, was three hundred yards away.

This was the one corner of London to which Daniel had always felt an almost mystical attachment and hoped that he would one day bring to life again in his epic which continued to sprawl through his mind. He wanted all those larger-than-life people to walk again in his pages, to show everyone a glimpse of their greatness and, whenever he was here, he was always sure that he could feel the ghosts of old London slippering all around him. Lisa had her ghosts but he had a whole marching army of them when he got going.

He continued to stand alone in the rapidly failing light of a Christmas afternoon, still too nervous to even cross the road to ring the bell of the Mission House as he spotted a few more people going in whom he recognised from other meetings.

A man and woman ran past hand in hand. A speeding police car jumped a red light and, all at once, the sodium street lamps came on, fuzzy lanterns of light hovering in the rain like an advancing army of giant glow-worms. Huge orange puddles slapped around his shoes as he ran across the road to the Mission Hall. The phosphorescent water broke away from his feet in small dartboarding waves, making the overhanging silhouettes of these old East End buildings dance around him so that, as he ran, he was never entirely sure what was hard reality and what was watery image.

A man in a party hat opened the Mission Hall door when he rang the bell. 'Hi. Have you come for AA?' he asked Daniel with a welcoming and much needed smile.

They walked down a long, brown corridor with spalling plaster and the air stiff with disinfectant. There were about fifty people already in the smoke-filled room but Daniel's eyes immediately fastened on the chairman, alone at the table at the far end, as her eyes fastened back on his. He found a free chair in the corner, sat down, blowing a raindrop off the end of his nose and trying, with his hands, to dry out his sodden hair a bit.

Lisa's eyes followed the direction of Ava's bejewelled forefinger and came to rest on a tall man with silver hair and an exquisite tan. She noted how carefully he used his long hands in his conversation, moving them around with every word, delicately underlining his points in the air.

'Our much-loved Jean-Paul made a fortune out of health clubs, but his wife, who is English and a complete fruitcake, has run off with a polo player.'

'Where did they go?'

'Far, far away. South America, maybe. Jean-Paul is very bruised and lost so I think you two should meet up and perhaps have a little fun. He's got piles of money *and* I hear he's a horny old goat.'

'Hold on a minute, Ava. Hold it right there. His wife has cleared off, he's filthy rich and he's a horny old goat. So why are you introducing him to *me*? Why haven't you bagged him for yourself?'

She brought up her hand to cover another small cloud of bronchitic laughter. 'I told you, Lisa honey. I've given up all that man stuff as a bad job. Anyway I can't be unfaithful to my window cleaner. He's a real sweetie and you wouldn't believe what he can do with that chamois of his. Come and meet Jean-Paul.'

'I am extremely honoured to meet you at last, Miss Moran,' said Monsieur Jean-Paul Platini, his shoes giving a slight military click together as he bowed his head and held out his hand. Ava, smiling magisterially, slipped back to her chattering chums. 'I have seen your Juliet and your Hedda but my favourite is your Regina. Some men would be scared of a woman like that. But not me. I dreamed a lot about you after seeing your Regina. She may have been a complete bitch but she was without doubt a real woman.'

'You think you could handle a woman like Regina, Mr Platini?'

'Most certainly. We would be equals and we would fight and love and love and fight. I've never minded fighting with my women because it always creates more love. Love needs turbulence to survive and grow; without it there is nothing. *Rien de tout*. One might as well be a couple of cabbages.'

Lisa was charmed. He spoke excellent English with only the faintest trace of a French accent and she noticed they were still holding hands and her crotch was poking out slightly as was its wont when she felt the old familiar stirrings down there. He was handsome in an oily, matinee idol way, which wasn't quite to her taste, but she supposed you couldn't expect everything. There *was* an intense smell of money about him but it was those blue eyes, thrown into relief by that tan, that were his most arresting feature. All her true loves had had blue eyes but Jean-Paul Platini's might have been painted by Monet. And, although she wasn't about to admit to anything yet, if he really did enjoy turbulence and fighting in his relationships, he really had come to the right place.

'Mmm. That's the trouble with us English; we always hate any show of passion.'

'But what's the point of anything at all if there's no feeling in it? The English manage to live one chilly day after the next but everyone needs the warmth of passion now and again just to remind them what real life is like.'

And all that old frothy Gallic bullshit too. She was trying hard to maintain a straight, interested expression on her face but it was difficult to control the welling laughter. She had the strangest feeling that the Excalibur of hope had just been lifted out of a cold lake – and on Christmas Day too. A little light warmed her aching belly and Regina Giddens stood next to her nodding approvingly. 'I'm lucky Horace. I've always been lucky and I'll be lucky again.'

'My name is Daniel and I'm an alcoholic. I've always found it difficult to deal with my emotions at Christmas but, there again, I always found it difficult to deal with my emotions at any time of the year when I was drinking. I drank on everything, whether I was happy or sad, whether I was feeling tearful or strong. No matter how I felt, I drank and then drank some more. I stopped drinking for three years with the help of this fellowship. I learned how to deal with my emotions, how to cope with pain and grief, how to celebrate or commiserate without reaching for the bottle. I became a whole man and knew a real happiness.

'But after three years of sobriety I began to drink again. I threw away all I'd gained. I was losing control of my emotions. I didn't drink so much but, even on very small amounts, I found I didn't know who I was. I had lost myself and was back in cloud-cuckoo land. That's where I've been lately – in cloud-cuckoo land.'

He paused, swallowing hard and gazing at Helen. Her hair was short and she wore no makeup or jewellery.

'I really want what I had back again, that's what I'm trying to say. I want a home again, and sobriety. I want to know God again and love, which is impossible for any drinker. I've made the most enormous mistakes and regret them all. But this Christmas I am asking to be granted that one great wish that we all have: to have my time over again knowing what I know now since I now know there is no future in drunken dreams. I simply want to experience the joy of life in the real world again, sober, a day at a time, back with the girl I love. Thanks.'

'Henri, I am ringing you so you will not be alarmed if you see lights around the house,' Jean-Paul said into his car phone as he drove the BMW down the Oxfordshire lane. 'I am only showing a friend around so do not come after us with your shotgun. *Non, non,* we will not be needing you. If you can just open the gate you can get on with your Christmas. We might stay in the lodge tonight. There is fresh bedding there is there not? *Bon.* And Henri, a happy Christmas.'

Lisa's mouth had gone dry with excitement as the car's headlamps sliced up the country darkness with revolving spotlights. Occasionally the lights caught the glittering eyes of an animal in the hedgerows or swept over a small isolated house, its chimney smoking, at the side of the road. Mostly they picked up empty ploughed fields and dark, tangled woods – until the car turned off the road and there, perched at the end of a long drive, on the crest of a hill, was a huge mansion, as lovely as an afternoon nap, sitting there darkly in the middle of the countryside, mysterious and beautiful.

The car's tyres crunched to a stop on the forecourt gravel and Lisa was almost speechless as she got out and looked up at this huge Jacobean pile, as perfect a statement of power and influence as England had yet come up with. But Foxley Hall was derelict and silent: these were the 'bare, ruin'd choirs where late the sweet birds sang'. They walked up to the broken front door like a pair of nervous party goers wondering if they were the first to arrive.

Once inside he switched on a hand lamp and held it high. They looked around the huge, two-storeyed hallway with its wide staircase of cantilevered stone and wandered along a corridor, scanning each of the rooms with their cracked, mullioned windows and saplings growing up out of the rotten floorboards. At the end of the corridor was a chapel, most of its roof gone and the stone altar covered with moss. Wings fluttered in the eaves where the roof had once been.

'My name's Helen and I'm still an alcoholic. It's been a good meeting and you're all invited to take a cup of tea and a mince pie with us afterwards. I'm glad we managed to speak a lot about happiness and recovery today. I've often thought our meetings can get too gloomy, so it's good to be positive, particularly at Christmas, a bad time for a lot of us often as we've lost touch with our friends and family.

'There should always be laughter in recovery; someone once said that he always thought of laughter as the music of God. But we do, of course, have to work for our laughter and happiness. George is right when he says it's not about pleasure-seeking but it might be something to do with giving pleasure to others. You only get the love you give. I've certainly lost a lot in the last five months and I'd give anything to have it back again. *Anything*. All of us make silly mistakes and the mistake I made with the man I love was that I wouldn't let him grow in his own way. I always wanted him to grow in mine. I'm sorry about that. I also wish I could have my time over again, knowing what I know now. There are too many who believe that happiness is unattainable. I've known real happiness and I want to know it again. I want this man to know that I'm really sorry for what I've done and I really love and miss him. He can come back any time he wants.

'Anyway let's, for now, just be thankful that we're all sober today. And let's end with the serenity prayer, not forgetting the seventh tradition.'

Lisa and Jean-Paul paused in one of the bedrooms to listen to the wood pigeons whose every burble was amplified by the ancient emptiness of the place. She walked across the room to look down on the overgrown gardens. 'There are two giant fountains there and a gazebo,' Jean-Paul said softly. 'The stream at the bottom of the slope is a trout stream which I thought of channelling into a lake.'

Scarlett O'Hara smiled graciously as she walked down the steps of Tara to meet Rhett Butler. The sun was high on the white dotted cotton fields and a bundle of little black kids were playing in the trout stream. 'Oh Rhett I've been waiting for you to turn up all my life. I nevah thought you'd come.'

'You knew I'd come Scarlett. There's never been a war that could stop me coming to you.'

She had so coveted that role and there had even been an outside chance she might have got it but they said she was far too young and that bastard Selznick had given it to Vivien. She had known Vivien well — still knew Larry, come to that: they had been neighbours for a while when their highnesses lived in Whistler's old house in Cheyne Walk. The blunt fact of the matter was that poor Vivien had never been able to manage tragic grandeur. The only time she got near tragic grandeur was when she was having a period and there was no sight more tragically grand than seeing Vivien suffering from that. Lisa could have brought the greatest authority and understanding to that role. Damn it! She *was* Scarlett O'Hara and, if there had been any justice in the world, she and Scarlett would have gone to hell hand in hand.

'You must restore this house, Jean-Paul. You can't give up now. Your wife has left you but you should make this place a home again, a tribute to your family name.'

'But it is not very easy, a restoration like this. There might be ten years' work here.'

'What's ten years? Where are you going anyway? You're more English than French now. Jean-Paul, this is where you belong.'

'I cannot do this alone. All this is too much for me.'

'I'll help you. Don't say anything, I always know about these things. With some women it takes time to decide but with me it never takes any time at all. Jean-Paul, why don't we rebuild this place together. I have some money and we can become partners. Jean-Paul this place is more romantic than Elsinore and we'll give something fine to the country.'

'Are you saying you would stay here with me?'

'Jean-Paul, this is the Tara I've been looking for all my life. Just try getting me to leave.'

Daniel took Helen's face in both hands and wept, promising they would never be parted again before they kissed and their hands reached for that which they had missed for so long and unbearably.

For her part, Lisa was almost sure that she was in some sort of dream as Jean-Paul pulled her to him under the bedclothes and their somewhat nervous bodies attempted to say their first 'Hello' of intimacy to one another. She wanted this 'Hello' to be something they would both remember and, most memorably, he first kissed her on the lips and then pushed his head down between her legs and put his mouth there, kissing her lips there too, not moving too much but pressing against her for one long minute after another until she began crying out and knew deep within her that whatever else might happen to her for the rest of her days she would never forget this first 'Hello' here in Tara.

So, as each of these four souls entered into a new communion late this Christmas Day, quite a few tyrannical ghosts packed their bags and fled while other, more cheerful, ones turned up again bringing joy out of terror, replacing fear with happiness. Ghosts didn't always have to be malevolent and this Christmas night not a single one passed through; just joyful ghosts multiplying and merging into one another like so many oaks whispering together in a forest, binding all minds and bodies together on this heavenly night, for all their lives and beyond death, for as long as the stars kept the skies nailed to heaven's vault.

PART THREE

1990

A Lass Unparallel'd

'Now boast thee, death, in thy possession lies,
A lass unparallel'd.'

WILLIAM SHAKESPEARE: ANTONY AND CLEOPATRA

THIRTY ONE

The QE2's foghorn blared repeatedly as the huge arm holding the even huger lamp appeared through drifting grey mists. The pilot boat came alongside, shadowed by blunt-nosed tugs. The arm and the lamp grew clearer, then the tall, beskirted body of the Statue of Liberty on Liberty Island at the entrance of New York harbour. Even on this bitterly cold morning, Lisa felt a surge of warmth, absurdly happy to be back in bad old Manhattan again.

She had played Broadway twice in her career: once as Gertrude in *Hamlet* then as the broken-spirited daughter in a revival of Rattigan's *Separate Tables*, a noisy, melodramatic affair which got rightly butchered by the critics and disappeared almost before it opened. But she'd had some simply wonderful times here. New York was her city: glamorous, exciting, always on the move, although she knew you had to be very careful in those sky-scrapered canyons, that one false move and they'd have your knickers down in no time. After five of the calmest years of her life with Frog One, as she called Jean-Paul after the drug dealer in *The French Connection*, this place could still stoke up her never-very-latent nuttiness.

Yet it had been an enchanting, relaxed five days travelling first class, pigging herself senseless at the Captain's Table every night and then curling up alone in a huge white leather armchair in one of the state lounges, mercifully unmolested as she savoured solitude and champagne. Cunard had done her proud, laying on everything free in return for one Press conference when she disembarked in which she *might* just mention how much she had enjoyed her voyage. Why the American media should be interested in what she enjoyed any longer, particularly after being out of the public eye for so long, she couldn't imagine. Perhaps February was the American media's silly season.

Yet the Press conference might work to her advantage by announcing her presence in America. She and Jean-Paul had suffered badly in the economic recession in England and the real motive for her visit was to dig up a lucrative role in something – *anything* – to bail them out. There was a strong chance they were going to lose Foxley Hall after putting so much work and money into the old place. So here she was again, in the good old US of A, putting up her battered old body for any reasonable offers.

A helicopter clattered through the mist as Lisa stood alone on one wing of the bridge, watching the action unfold across the brackish water and on the thrumming quay. Even wrapped up in her silver fox and partly sheltered by the deck head, she could still feel those ice-cold winds scything down from Cape Cod. New York had the most violent extremes of weather of anywhere she knew – as befitted one of the world's most violent and extreme cities. No half measures in New York: her winter froze your arse off and her summer all but melted you down.

The sun was breaking through now, burnishing the sides of the skyscrapers and making the whole island of Manhattan float, gold on grey, like Xanadu. So would she realise her dreams of discovering gold here?

The gangways were coming into place and she turned to kiss the Captain and Chief Officer. The former had been exceptionally kind to her after she had confided to him one night that she had fallen into grave financial difficulties. He had wiped her bar bill clean and personally explained to her stewards that she could not spare them a tip which, at 15 per cent of the full fare, could have been a significant sum in itself. As it turned out she had given her cabin steward a gold Cartier lighter – a birthday present from John O in one of his rare outbursts of generosity – to sell and divide the proceeds between them.

The Press conference had been convened in the corner of the first class lounge and she *was* surprised to be confronted by four television crews and forty or so reporters and asked so many eager questions. It was as if she had just walked off with an armful of Oscars instead of rotting away peaceably in a rural corner of the Cotswolds. Perhaps predictably most of the questions related to her by now infamous role in *Rebellion* – yet another sequel had opened in the States – but she handled them as sweetly and tactfully as she could, avoiding any public criticism of the wretched series.

But she did become distinctly splenetic when asked about Margaret Thatcher: 'The so-called Iron Lady is a witch made of putty. She's crippled the live theatre, broken the unions and handed over the economy to gangsters and crooks. The property market has gone bust and there's a poll tax which is going to start a civil war.'

'You'd burn her like a witch then would you Miss Moran?' Ah that old tabloid directness again. There was nothing remotely mealy-mouthed about a reporter from New York.

'Yes, I'd light the fire myself and dance around it too.'

It was going well. She was giving these hard-faced hacks plenty to scribble into their notebooks, until: 'Miss Moran, is it true you've come to New York to marry Andrei Barapov?'

'Andrei who?'

'Aw, come on, Miss Moran. *Andrei Barapov*, the Russian ballet dancer. The word's out that you two intend to get hitched.'

'The word is wrong young man. There is no question at all of me getting hitched to him or any other and, if there was, believe me, you lot would be the very last to know it.'

Even as she spoke she did hope that her little Andrei hadn't been shooting his mouth off to the press again and she *was* going to be staying with him in his apartment in the Dakota while she was here after all. But, thankfully, she didn't have to avoid answering any more questions since the Captain actually broke it up and she was plunged into the rigours of customs and immigration. No matter how VI and P you were, you would never escape those bastards in the Big Apple.

'You got any drugs in your baggage or on your person, Miss Moran?'

'None.' She'd made some stupid joke about only the odd ton of cannabis many moons ago and they'd been into every orifice for hours. This was an irony-free zone. 'Nothing at all,' she added to make sure he'd caught her seriousness. 'Nothing, ever.'

She was mildly upset the Bouncing Codpiece hadn't come to meet her with the ritual bower of yellow roses although perhaps it was just as well given their impending 'marriage'. But he *had* sent a stretch limo to pick her up and a tall, black, broadly smiling chauffeur who gloried in the name of Xerxes. As they turned out of the wharf she asked Xerxes if he would be so kind as to drive her around for half an hour, with her window down, so she could savour the Big Apple all over again.

They idled up the Avenue of the Americas and everything was as enchanting as ever in this, the most sculptural of cities, as she tapped the glass behind Xerxes now and then, asking him to brake so she could look those skyscrapers up and down. Each was as unique as a fingerprint, from the pencil-sharp serenity of the Empire State to the scalloped peak of the Chrysler and the absurd Egyptian fantasies of the Pythian. Every building poured pure energy down on to the sidewalks. One side of the canyon was dark and cold, the other ablaze, thousands of windows brilliantly luminous in the rising sun.

Massed crows escalatored back and forth, their warm breath pluming fluffily in the cold air. The din was overwhelming: an enormous, rising babble of policemen's whistles, the electronic whoopings of the cardiac arrest vans, gunshots of backfiring cars, steam jack-hammers, the rapping discos of ghetto-blasters, ships' hooters, angry car horns …

And the speed of everything. Oh my God the speed! Every time Xerxes did pull to a stop all the other cars screamed past him as if they were on the Le Mans racing circuit, hitting the ridges in the roads with their metal underbellies in dancing showers of sparks. Helicopters rocketed from one skyscraper to disappear behind another. Cyclists with whirring sprockets and blurred legs whizzed past the roller skaters and joggers in Central Park. Near the zoo, a police horse, statue-still, its tail raised decorously, was shitting on the road: the huge brown lumps plopping down to create an untidy smoking pyramid in the cold sun.

She blew out a long stream of bemused air and couldn't help but think of the fields around Foxley Hall, so quiet, so serene as she dead-headed the roses with Frog One sitting out on the lawnmower cutting wide shining lines into the formal lawn. You could sit on the patio there and not hear one single alien noise all morning. 'Better get to the Dakota now,' she told Xerxes.

She had never really understood why Andrei insisted on staying in this gloomy Bavarian castle of gabled casements and lintelled windows near Central Park. John Lennon had been gunned down on the doorstep ten years ago and the young still gathered outside to mourn his death. Andrei had said that lightning never struck the same spot twice and it would be too much trouble to move. He also valued the quiet there. All the apartments in the Dakota were virtually soundproof since each of the floors had been packed with soil dug from Central Park.

The Dakota's security was pretty much at Fort Knox level since Lennon's widow, Yoko, had elected to stay there and any aspiring burglar would have to tackle a bolted quadrangle garden, a doorman in a bulletproof glass cubicle, reinforced doors with six tungsten locks each and a whole bank of video cameras and private guards before he even got to the front door of whoever it was he was hoping to rob.

By the time Xerxes had negotiated Lisa and her luggage into the lift she felt as if she was entering a top-security mental home and her paranoia wasn't much eased when Barapov wouldn't open his door. She could hear his stupid voice though: 'Lisa, my angel. My excitement is zo much. *Zo much.* And my heart is beating faster than a drum but I must ask you to stop still vhen I come out. I am goink to open the door. The two dogs here. They must sniffle you first with their noses. Then everything vill be hunky dory.'

When he finally opened the door he was hanging onto the studded collars of the two biggest mutts she had ever seen in her life, a Doberman and a Rottweiler, both with more muscle than Olympic body builders. They growled throatily as Barapov coaxed them both forward to give her a good sniffing.

'You vill come to love these dogs as I do, Lisa. They vill come to love you too. Pat them like zo. Let them sniffle your hands. After ve have a party. I have much champagne. Lots to drink. Yes, now you come inside.'

She turned to thank Xerxes for his trouble but he had already legged it, leaving her luggage behind. 'Chauffeur hates dogs much,' Barapov explained cheerily. 'One of them bite him on the ass and he not forget it. Big bite. Full of teeth, iz not nice. Welcome to New York, my angel.' He closed his eyes and puckered his lips for a kiss which did not arrive.

'Andrei darling put those dogs away will you? *Then* I'll give you a kiss.'

Barapov, dressed in a tight black vest and leggings, which made him look like a whore's black stocking stuffed with footballs, took in her luggage as she walked down the oak-panelled corridor to a living room with windows which looked out over Central Park. Every room had been lavishly furnished to his chaotic taste and in this one the walls had been lined with elaborate tapestries and moody paintings of the Russian steppes against which a discordant Hockney or a Harving stood out. There were lots of mirrors and the ceiling had been tricked out in gold leaf on black, all fashionable no doubt in Czarist, pre-revolutionary Russia. The photographs of many children caught her eye on the closed flap of the grand piano. 'How many bastards have you had since I saw you last?' she asked, carefully putting an indulgent smile on her face to let him know she wasn't having a go.

'Psh! All that finished now,' he replied sadly, picking a champagne bottle out of an ice bucket and beginning to wrestle with the cork. 'Finished for good. I have enough children. Iz no more fucking in Manhattan. All fucking finished. Everyone afraid of Aids. Me too. Ve all vank ourselves blind or get married.'

Yes, that was the real curse of Aids wasn't it? It had put an end to all sexual swagger and manacled the new freedom, dragged everything back into dark Victorian London. She knew the script.

'Talking about marriage, the Press was asking me this morning if I intended marrying you.'

'Iz zo?' The champagne cork remained undefeated. 'Vhat you tell those bastards?'

'*No*, of course. I said I hadn't even met you. So where did all this marriage crap come from anyway?'

'Lisa, angel of my heart. I am zo lonely in this place. Zo lonely.'

She glared at him before snatching the bottle and tackling the cork herself.

'My heart zo lonely. Please marry me. Vhat you say? I have nervous breakdown for breakfast. I cry all the time. My legs do not vork good anymore. I have only my dogs but they do not listen to me. They just piss on the carpets. All I vant is love – your love.'

'It *was* you wasn't it? *You* told them we were getting married.' She gave up on the cork and crunched the bottle back into the ice bucket, snorting at the very idea of marrying this crippled wretch to live with him in this expensive prison with nothing but a pair of savage dogs, the smell of canine piss on everything and a swelling pile of maintenance orders. He should have stayed in Moscow where he was poor but happy.

'Could I lie to you, my angel? Yes, yes, yes. I told those bastards from the Press.' He went down on one knee and, if she'd had something heavy in her hand, she would have hit him on the head with it. 'I told them ve vere made for one another. Lisa, you cannot hold out for ever. Ve fly Las Vegas tonight and marry under special licence. Vhat you say? Lisa, my darling I am so tired of vanking. It put me in such bad mood. Black moods all day vhen I vank and much blacker moods vhen I don't. Vhen I marry you I never vank again. Not once. Everything hunky dory when ve marry.'

'Now look here Andrei,' (very Miss Jean Brodie) 'get this straight in your peasant head will you? I am *not* going to marry you in Las Vegas or anywhere else. *I am in love with another man.* How many more times do I have to tell you? We are the oldest of friends and that's the way it's going to stay. As far as I'm concerned you can *vank* as much as you like and, if you mention the subject of marriage again, I shall go straight out of here and live on the streets and get raped and murdered. You hear? On the streets. *Raped and murdered.'*

'Oh Lisa, you can do this? My heart, Lisa. All these years my heart is goink burst for you and now this.'

'Don't talk such nonsense.' She could feel it all travelling down those familiar tracks which were certainly going to end up in a big, blazing row at any moment now and decided to rein herself in. 'Look, have you got a bottle of champagne in this place which can be opened? I've had a stressful day and I'm thirsty, Andrei darling, *thirsty.'*

'Say you marry me one day, Lisa. Everyone in Manhattan loves me but I am so lonely. And I am no good with condoms. They slip and slide and I lose my hard on. I forget my new HIV certificate and get sent home to my own bed. So I vank much, Lisa, and, when I am vanking, I think only of you.'

'I'll tell you one thing for nothing,' she roared. 'If you don't get some champagne from somewhere soon I'm going to give you a good clip around the ears. Got that? A good clip around the ears.'

'Not deaf just yet, Lisa my love,' he smirked in that boyish way she had always found so winning. 'Not deaf yet.'

She had no plan of action. The general idea was she would sit in this apartment in the Dakota, hit the phone, chat up agents and try to get them to take her to lunch so she could find out what was going on. A fat movie contract was about the only thing that would be of any use but she was even prepared to dredge up some phoney exuberance for a commercial if that's what it had to be.

The reasons for her imminent bankruptcy were still something of a mystery to her. She had never really understood money and three times her accountants had explained it all to her and three times she still couldn't understand how, along with all the other property speculators in Thatcher's once booming London, she had plummeted from paper millionaire to pauper almost overnight.

All she had done, at first, was set out with Frog One to renovate Foxley Hall in the booming Eighties. House prices were soaring by thirty five per cent a year and the banks were all but throwing money at everyone. They had both raised a sizeable mortgage on their stately pile but two lots of builders going bust on them after being paid upfront hadn't helped. Then Jean-Paul's ex-wife had bobbed up from the arms of her polo player in Argentina demanding half his estate. She didn't get it but the legal fees to fight her off were astronomical. It soon became clear that they had spent slightly more than two million on Foxley Hall and the work was still less than half-completed.

Yet it should all have been easily containable since Lisa's property portfolio was still buoyant and they were pressing ahead with the final stages of their work and she was thinking – but only thinking – of encashing her assets when the Stock Market crashed. The SEAQ screens turned into a sea of blood, the city was torn apart and there was carnage in almost every suburban home as interest rates doubled from seven and a half per cent to fifteen per cent. House prices plunged and millions soon found that their homes were worth far less than the mortgages they had raised to buy them.

The banks and building societies began seizing those homes where their borrowers had defaulted and, with their massive borrowings, Lisa and Jean-Paul were pretty much at the top of their hit list. Their debt on Foxley Hall kept ballooning outrageously and they seemed to have no way of reducing it. Her own property portfolio was almost useless. Cheyne Walk was re-mortgaged but that didn't help for more than a month or so and she even threw what was left of Judd's pension down the well of their debt but that barely touched the sides.

Jean-Paul tried everything to raise some capital on his assets but no one had any real money to buy them. The property people in the city were still talking of deals worth millions then complaining of the difficulty in raising a fifty pound cash deposit. Margaret Thatcher's London of fantasy and greed had finally gone bust.

So Lisa and Jean-Paul's great dreams, floated on a tidal wave of funny money, were shipwrecked on the bare rocks of poverty when this tide fully and finally ebbed. After a final council of war in Foxley Hall, Jean-Paul had gone to Europe to try and find someone interested in a few debt-ridden health clubs and she had come here to Manhattan, also in the market for a miracle.

THIRTY TWO

Lisa had always found the Big Apple the most intimate of cities. Everyone knew and mixed with everyone else in the inner circle and, if you had any sort of name, you were not so much invited inside as dragged in by your hair. Albert told her he had nothing on immediately but, if she was free tomorrow night, he'd take her to Elaine's to meet Woody who was in the middle of casting his next film so she might get lucky there. 'But there's a bottom line here, Lisa. Woody doesn't pay the big bucks you seem to be looking for. They're not those kind of films. You work with Woody for the fun of it and the *prestige*. Everyone wants to work for Woody even though his last few films barely turned in a profit at all.'

On another telephone call she learned from Ronnie that they were putting together a big, exciting, new package around Dustin – or it might be Tom – to start shooting in New England in the Fall. He wasn't absolutely certain about his facts but he'd caught some talk they were looking for an elderly lady star for that. The word was Jessica was up for it. Jane was also showing an interest but Jessica had her nose in front. But there were still windows in the package. If she thought an introduction to Robert might help he could probably do that sometime early next week.

Michael told her over lunch at Sardi's that David was bringing in a team from LA next week to tie up the loose ends on Arnie's new one. The line producer had shown him personally the early breakdown figures and they were talking a straight six million dollars so there would be plenty of scope for slicing off a bit of the action there. 'Lemme see now, lemme see. I'll do what I can to find out about that and I'll call you at eight next Friday morning. You just leave everything with your Uncle Michael. Have I ever let you down Lisa? Have I?'

After three days of this she was beginning to conclude that all this excited insider talk meant nothing. Everyone was on first name terms with everyone else but none of them really had the faintest clue what their 'friends' were up to.

They were all either telling hopeful lies or recycling rumours from the gossip columns of *Variety*, trying to wheedle their way into a deal here or else getting cold-shouldered out of a deal there. It was a deep mystery how these barnacles on the good ship entertainment business managed to make a living at all although she guessed the figures around all the deals were so large you only needed to catch a ride on the back of one a year to apply for a billet in hog heaven.

Nothing looked remotely like working out and, when Albert took her to Elaine's to meet Woody, they weren't at first even allowed into the all-important back room because Elaine, the picky proprietor, failed to recognise Lisa. When they did progress to the back room, after a few heated arguments, Woody failed to show because he was off playing his clarinet at Michael's Pub and Lisa had to spend what seemed like hours and hours cornered by Albert who turned out to be a complete name-dropping creep who at one stage, strictly *entre-nous*, claimed that Woody had come in but spotted Albert and run away again because he, Albert, had once spent a torrid weekend in the Hamptons with Mia.

Ronnie rang the following day to report that Jessica had been paired up with Dustin – or it might still be Tom – so there wasn't much point in meeting Robert after all, but Brad was up for something hot with Julia and as soon as he found out exactly what he would get straight back to her.

Her trustworthy Uncle Michael rang her on the dot of eight the following Friday morning to tell her that David had already sorted out the casting of Arnie's new one but, Lisa honey, get this: Avie Glick was in town with Yuri Pucket, pimping their new *Rebellion* film. They were staying at the Loews Drake on Park and – *listen* to this now, Lisa honey – they are in pre-production talks about the next one and the word is out they are looking for some fresh angles and might even be thinking of bringing back Raz's poor mad mother if they could find a suitable actress. 'Lisa, honey, you could even be looking at the thick end of two or three million bucks. I'm sure this isn't what you'd been hoping for but think about it and get back to me if you are interested.'

Lisa thanked him effusively for his time and put down the receiver with a shudder, her mind exploding with questions, answers, more questions. She just could *not* do this film even if it was offered to her – could she? Yet the money would be all right – it would actually *save* her – and it wouldn't really matter if she did appear in it because they were going to make it anyway weren't they? All right, so the work *was* distasteful but two or three million dollars would just about settle their difficulties and save Foxley Hall into the bargain.

But what if the film sparked off yet more copycat shootings? Oh Christ, what if? She was just grateful that the mad Daniel wasn't around. Having that deranged voice of prophecy bellowing into her ear would have been just too much. Come to think of it what had happened to *him*? She hadn't heard a peep from him since that Christmas five years ago when he had walked out on her and disappeared into the East End. No Christmas cards, no calls on her birthday, no nothing.

Yet while she hadn't actually seen him, she had certainly heard about him: his book on Chris Reynolds, *A Suburban Shooting*, had become a minor hit attracting some quite strong reviews and, according to Miranda Haworth, sales, although not exactly storming, were quite decent and ongoing.

The book had been brilliantly done, Lisa thought, meticulously researched and written very coolly, in the spirit of its title, and Daniel had done what he had set out to do which was to get inside Chris Reynolds' mind and find out what had been going on inside it right up to that moment in Edgware when he had pulled the trigger. The *Rebellion* films were undoubtedly a key motive in his actions but Daniel had unearthed plenty of other factors including Chris's reading material, those sordid video and computer games and a fractured relationship with his father.

The real triumph of the book though, she thought, was how he finally presented the story not just as Chris's story but as the story of his generation. Those factors which had made Chris had made others and there was one extraordinary passage towards the end of the book when Daniel had described how he had been taken by a former friend of Chris's to one of their old meeting places in Epping Forest and it had been something like the final scenes of *Apocalypse Now!* with those youngsters in headbands and combat gear lying around a clearing sharpening knives, sniffing glue out of a polythene bag and growling with disaffection.

There was no peace or love in this lot — as there had been in the drop-out hippies of the Sixties or Seventies — but a serious and even murderous aggression as evinced by the hostility of their looks and body language as he approached them. 'I looked around and saw the children of Thatcher's England, the children who torch cars and joy-ride, tear up soccer stadia, burgle and mug helpless pensioners and. occasionally, go on indiscriminate shooting sprees. None of them could be described as intrinsically evil but had been made that way by all levels of a mentally sick media from computer games to films. Even our extensive news services both feed on violence and cruelty only to then feed them back into society a thousand-fold. Chris's story was but a small strand of a much larger story. These kids in Epping were indeed the children of the black rain.'

But in spite of all this, and with her anxious belly right up inside her anxious mouth, she did finally ring back Michael and asked him to tell Avie Glick that, if they were looking for someone like her for the next in the *Rebellion* series she'd at least be happy to lunch with them, if only for old times' sake.

These were dark, difficult moments for Lisa and her unsettled frame of mind wasn't much helped by Barapov who was busy doing his suffering martyr number because she wouldn't sleep with him. Now he stayed out most of the day, claiming he was more or less permanently engaged in a round of therapy sessions, cortisone injections, whirlpool treatments, rehearsals, coaching or actual performances. Despite his complaints about 'vanking' too much he probably had a woman somewhere, she decided. Someone as vain and insecure and, yes, as handsome as him couldn't actually manage to get through a day without some admiring eyes falling on him which made it all the more mysterious that he still seemed to be so interested in her and wanted to marry her. Perhaps he was just a masochist at heart and simply enjoyed the pain of her continual rejection. Not that she much cared any longer. She only wished she had somewhere else to stay in New York and, if she came across another cockroach in the bathroom waving its horrible whiskers at her, she was going to go really spare.

Those fucking dogs managed to leave their stench everywhere too, pissing bright yellow stains on the carpets or sleeping among the piles of his discarded tights and leg-warmers. The refrigerator was full of his ballet shoes and tins of dog food. No wonder he was reduced to wanking so much; she couldn't imagine any normal woman being prepared to put up with those horrible fat fuckers. She absolutely insisted they were locked away when he wasn't around which meant that, instead of barking around her all day long, they were locked in the spare room where they just howled and howled.

Indeed she disliked this Dakota apartment so much she would have moved out altogether if she'd had any money. The Cunard stewards had returned her Cartier lighter: she had been delighted and moved to find it buried in one of her suitcases together with a note saying it had been a pleasure looking after her. So, if the dogs did make her too desperate, she could always pawn that.

What she most needed was to talk to Frog One, if only to learn what he thought about the *Rebellion* development, but she had rung Foxley Hall five times now and was becoming more and more stressed because she couldn't get in touch with him. One of the cleaning ladies had told her that, as far as she knew, Mr Platini was still attending to some business in Europe but she wasn't sure where. This was the longest period they had been apart since they had first met and she didn't like it. There were far too many women around ready to take a fancy to him; he only had to focus his blue eyes and give them a burst of his Gallic bullshit and they were all but throwing their knickers into the air. So *where* was he? And with *whom*?

She had found a half-finished bottle of flattish champagne in the fridge when the ring of the telephone disturbed the silence so explosively she dropped the bottle. It must be Frog One, she thought, but she couldn't have been more wrong: it was Avie Glick.

'Lisa, angel,' the film director purred down the line like some rogue oil spill. 'I was flabbergasted to read about you the other day and even more flabbergasted when Michael told me you were in town looking for some work. Lisa angel, this could be the big break for both of us at this moment in time. We need a new idea and apparently you need the money. How would you fancy being Raz's mother again in the next *Rebellion* film we're putting together just now?'

She closed her eyes, swallowed hard and asked God to have mercy on her poor lost soul. 'I would like that very much Avie,' she chirped with as much phoney exuberance as she could possibly muster. 'As you say I *do* need the money so I would like that very much indeed.'

After spending so much time in virtual purdah in the dripping English countryside Lisa had all but forgotten what real luxury looked like but The Four Seasons restaurant on East Fifty Second Street brought it all back from the angular marvels of the Picasso tapestry in the lobby to the huge, elegant rooms and the clean, uncluttered lines of the walls. Battalions of flunkeys hovered at discreet distances producing endless menus with endless dishes and, for her anyway, without the prices. Indeed the dinner itself, which began with a salmon mousse and a tiny dish of smoked eels quite soon had her insides singing hymns of happiness despite having to eat it in the life-threatening company of Avie, Yuri and their over-dressed, over-painted popsies.

Fame and money couldn't disguise the fact that Yuri had the intelligence of a door knob. But he was affable enough as he and Lisa both told his girlfriend – a sort of blow-up Cindy Doll with a silicon bosom, eyebrows like twin tarantulas and serial killer hairstyle – about their early days in Israel fighting the government and just about everyone else about the script.

Lisa had pheasant casseroled in cognac for her main course, together with a quite superb Volnay, and was at her glamorous and most amusing best, trying hard not to send up Avie or Yuri, which was always a temptation, and be charmingly polite which was particularly difficult with Avie because he kept getting bits of his food trapped in the hair of his nostrils. He had to keep his nostril hair constantly trimmed, she remembered, but he must have neglected to have done it that morning. On another day she might have said something but today she managed to keep her thoughts to herself as she explained: 'The long and short of it is that I pretty much went bust overnight in England and I'm still trying to work out how it happened. You wouldn't believe the problems I've got.'

The actual size of her possible fee hadn't been discussed, of course, but at some point between the sorbet and wild strawberries it began to emerge that yes, they did want her back in the series and, if she would be prepared to spend a few months in Thailand they probably had a deal. 'We'll write the script around you and can quarrel about terms at a later stage but you'll definitely be looking at the thick end of three million bucks, Lisa. You can sort out a lot of problems with three million bucks.'

She even allowed herself a celebratory brandy at the end of the meal, deciding that she very much approved of this kind of life and, if it took a few months' work in Thailand to stem the tides of debt which were threatening to wash away their Tara, that's what she'd do. She didn't even inquire if there might be much violence in the film, didn't even allow the question to crawl through her mind let alone pass through her lips. If they wanted her to go running around Buddhist temples toting a Uzi she'd do it. No question. She was a professional actress who needed to earn a living like everyone else.

At the end of the meal she thanked and kissed them all – even the popsies – and was up and off before the bill arrived, dreading to think what the final damage must have come to as she slipped on her silver fox fur and poured herself into a Yellow Cab outside.

It had begun snowing hard in Manhattan and she sat back in the cab marvelling at the drifting white flakes which were already beginning to lay an astonishing white carpet over everything – the grubby sidewalks, the high wide avenues and even the roofs of the passing cars.

She wasn't even burning up with her routine guilt when she got out of the cab. She paused on the far corner of the Dakota complex as yet more snowflakes came wobbling down between the skyscrapers, glowing like luminous moths in the street lights and settling on everything as if all the angels of heaven had been released to completely whitewash the city's squalor and make everything new again. She took the snow as a symbol of renewal: a promise that life can indeed start again and all for the better, and she would have liked to have walked in it all for a while but she had to try and get in touch with Jean-Paul somehow – or leave a message – telling him that everything had worked out fine. 'My darling, it's all over,' she longed to hear herself say. 'There's no need to worry about anything ever again.'

At least *he* wouldn't be raising any troublesome moral questions about what she had agreed to do. He was a cultured man who enjoyed great drama as much as anyone but he was also a supreme pragmatist who always knew what had to be done and did it.

Even in the thickening snow a small group had gathered outside the Dakota, playing John Lennon tapes on a ghetto-blaster, but she kept her head down and hurried straight past them and through the quadrangle, taking the lift up to the apartment. Yet no sooner had she put the key into the lock than her good humour evaporated. Barapov had forgotten to shut his dogs away before he had gone to the theatre and they were both behind the door, growling and flinging themselves against it. She called out softly to the hateful sods but that seemed to work them up even more. She was *not* going to enter with them on the loose. Right, that was it. *That was it.*

She stormed out of the building without a clue where she was going, then stopped with the dozen or so youngsters on the snowing sidewalk listening to John Lennon singing *Imagine*. They could have been Christmas carollers as they stood there, hands in pockets, shuffling their feet back and forth and looking up and down almost as if they were waiting for their rock'n'roll prince to return.

She turned around wondering what to do when she saw a tall figure bearing down on her which, despite the thick snow, she recognised immediately. The huge nose. The slump in the shoulders. The smiling blue eyes. Her whole body lurched backwards as if she had just been punched hard and she heartily regretted that last brandy. It was that loony from Wales come back to haunt her at precisely the moment she needed to forget about him *and* his wretched work. It was Daniel.

'Hello girl,' he said amiably, towering over her. 'You're still looking terrific and that's a fact. I don't suppose you fancy having my baby do you?'

Her eyebrows soared so much she thought they must have left her forehead as the appalling nature of her predicament sank in. Then her startled mind's eye saw, as if in a hallucination, an aeroplane flying through a clear sky towing a huge streamer which said: THIS MAN IS GOING TO COST YOU THREE MILLION DOLLARS.

THIRTY THREE

'Lisa, it's me, Daniel. You're all right are you?'

'Just what are you doing in this country?' she screamed as if he had no right to be anywhere in the land.

'On an author tour, promoting the American edition of *A Suburban Shooting*. I asked Miranda to send you a copy. Did you read it?'

Oh shit, she'd read it all right. This was all far worse than she could ever have thought. But what could she say? She couldn't even come up with a stray inanity and, without a further word, made a break for it down the sidewalk, head down, elbows pumping, a whole vat of salmon mousse, casseroled pheasant and wild strawberries sloshing around inside her. What she should really have done was risked Andrei's dogs. The fat mutts suddenly appeared almost cuddlesome.

'Lisa, what's the matter?' he asked as he scooted along next to her. 'Are you in some sort of trouble? Don't run away. Let's at least have a drink together or something.'

There was nothing to say. Even her inventive tongue couldn't get her out of this one; she had been caught with her hand in the till by the one man in the world she couldn't bluff.

'Lisa, stop a second ...' Daniel hadn't spotted the fire hydrant and he fell over it, sideways into the gutter. She tore across the road, barely looking from side to side, narrowly missing the bonnets of blaring cars before whizzing down a slope into Central Park which seemed as good a place as any to try and hide.

In its new white overcoat the park looked serene and beautiful with its slopes covered by several inches of snow which was also piling up on the bridges and the branches of the overhanging trees. The snow was coloured brass-yellow in places by the sodium lights and nothing seemed to move except the powerful wings of a startled bird which went crashing through the branches in a storm of disturbed snowflakes.

She stopped hurrying when she reached the lake hoping her churning belly would soon settle. Well at least she had lost Daniel but, in the process, had pretty much lost herself too now that most of the familiar landmarks had disappeared. The snow gathered all available light to itself making an ice-cream wonderland of phosphorescence but there was a vague sense of mental disturbance all around her.

There was a cough and three shadows drifted out of a nearby tunnel. They began to encircle her, black on white, the soft crunchings of their steps made all the more sinister by the all-pervading silence. She was not sure she could outrun them but was very sure she was not going to hand over her shoulder bag which didn't actually have anything valuable in it but that wasn't the point. If they wanted her bag they were going to have to fight her for it. The one question was: were they desperate enough to jump into the lake after her? Another question was how deep, exactly, was that lake? And how cold? 'Don't you take another step towards me,' she warned, pointing at each one of the scraggy men individually and giving her words plenty of frosty Lady Macbeth bite. 'Lay a hand on me and you are going to be very sorry indeed. Do you hear me? Very sorry indeed.'

But they were still bearing down on her when there was a shout behind her: 'Police. Freeze. Raise your hands or we'll fire.'

The men stood still and raised their hands uncertainly, the snow continuing to swirl around them. Lisa moved away cautiously, careful not to giggle since she recognised the voice all right. Not a New York cop but a Welsh nutcase. When she felt at a safe enough distance she set off on a mad gallop again, letting out the excited cry of a kid at play. Never a dull moment with Daniel; she had to give him that; she'd had the best fun of her life when she'd been going out with him. He never seemed to work at it either, just turned up out of nowhere and something completely crazy happened.

'Don't you move an inch,' she heard him bellowing at those poor men again. 'Make one move and we fire.'

She was bounding along in the general direction of Harlem when a sort of abominable snowman, all flailing arms and uncertain feet, came windmilling down a slope towards her. 'Lisa, for heaven's sake slow up a minute will you?'

He managed to get a hand on the collar of her fur coat before she could accelerate away from him again and, still struggling, she managed to unpeel herself from it. A lot of shouting erupted everywhere with a blur of blue and red lights. She was still hanging on to an arm of her coat when she noticed that Daniel was sprawled unconscious in the snow having been whacked with the nightstick of a *real* patrolling policeman. 'You okay, lady?'

'I'm fine,' she cried spreading her fur coat over the comatose frame. 'But just what have you done to my boyfriend?'

'Your boyfriend? I just thought he was trying to boost your fur coat.'

'Oh dear, you haven't killed him have you officer? We were just having a little quarrel, that's all.'

'It's not smart quarrelling in da middle of Central Park in da middle of da
night.'

'I know, I know.' She went down on one knee, pulling her coat up around
Daniel's shoulders. A splash of bright blood stained the snow. 'He's perfectly
harmless, you know officer. Only a writer. Wouldn't know how to mug a baby.
You haven't done anything serious to him have you?'

'Naw. But we better geddim to hospital downtown.'

Daniel had lost consciousness and, when he found it again, he was lying on
a gurney in the corridor of the emergency room next to a black man with blood
seeping though his fingers from a wounded shoulder. A half-naked woman in
sunglasses was singing some awful lullaby and two young Puerto Ricans were
quarrelling loudly. At the reception desk Lisa was berating a white-coated
intern, urging him to attend her boyfriend who might die at any moment.

Daniel touched the side of his head gingerly and found a squealing lump the
size of a duck egg. Lisa took time off from haranguing the intern to tell him she
was going to get it all cleaned up at any minute now. 'Do you realise that nothing – and I do mean nothing at all – has happened to me since I was out with you
last,' he croaked. 'For almost five years my life has been as calm as a village pond
and then wham!'

'Just be quiet now Daniel or you'll be getting hysterical again,' she said
before returning to her attack on the intern who was stoutly claiming there were
more seriously injured people who also happened to have got there first. As if to
dramatise the intern's point the black man with the wounded shoulder let out a
soft sigh and slipped on to the floor in a sprawling, bleeding heap.

'You see, you see,' the intern shouted triumphantly. 'Now that's what I call a
real emergency.'

'Lisa, I think I'm all right,' said Daniel, sitting up on his gurney. 'I think I'd
like to go back to my hotel if you don't mind.'

'Can you walk darling?'

'We'll soon find out.' He stood up. 'Oh blimey.' He reeled and she just about
managed to steady him. 'Everything's in triplicate. What I need are aspirins. A
lot of aspirins.'

'Don't you worry about a thing now. Lisa is here to look after you.'

'Look after me? *You* are going to look after *me?* Do me a favour, don't make
me laugh. My head will explode if I laugh.'

When they finally left the hospital, with a plaster over his bump, dawn was
breaking over the Lower East Side and the city was as they had never seen it
before. Everything was covered with snow. Manhattan, most improbably, had
become a virgin bride who had never had a dirty thought in her life. 'I've never

seen this place look so beautiful,' she said.

'Surprising what a bit of white paint can do. Estate agents are always going on about putting loads of white paint over everything.'

A few cars were slithering slowly down the middle of the road but there was no sign of a Yellow Cab so they decided to walk to the Chelsea hotel where he was staying and, holding hands, they made their way carefully along the piled-up, slippery sidewalks, finding an all-night pharmacy on Delancey where they bought a large bottle of aspirin into which they both dived. Walking was becoming more and more difficult but the subway trains were running so Daniel said: 'Why don't we go to Coney Island?'

They sat side by side on the rattling train chewing the aspirins. The years had fallen away and there was no need to talk. He put his arm around her shoulders and kept it there as the train stopped and started at stations they had never heard of. They might have been any old hypochondriac New York couple sharing a bottle of aspirin on their way to work.

She felt the warmest surges. A lark had always been dear to her, the dingier and grubbier the better. And what could be dingier and grubbier than working your way through a bottle of aspirin on a subway ride to Coney Island? Just sitting there next to him made her realise how much she had missed him. He was always so light to have around and such fun. Jean-Paul always wanted to know exactly what was going to happen next as well as where, when and why. Daniel always accepted whatever the moment had to offer. After a few more stops, overcome by weariness and aspirin, they fell asleep in one another's arms.

At the end of the line the guard turfed them out and they left the station to explore this strange, shuttered resort where the hang-gliding gulls barely made themselves heard above the rolling roars of the Atlantic breakers. They gazed through the railings into the fairground, normally so vibrant and noisy but as quiet as the grave this morning, full of spent screams and vanished laughter, every stall wearing a made-to-measure white cap of snow. Thin dusty streams of snow blew down from girders of the ferris wheel and the high fortress of walls of the tatty roller-coaster.

Tiny snowflakes were still drifting out of the grey sky as they walked on the beach. The winds and tides had cleared it of any settling snow and the sands were miraculous and wild with just a few people walking their dogs in the distance. The further out they walked the stronger the winds, ripping out of their mouths the few words they felt the need to exchange. At the end of the beach the sky was shuffling changes of light and Daniel pointed at a man on a horse, moving in a spotlight of sun and appearing fiery and almost Biblical as it walked knee-deep in the waves.

She enjoyed every moment but the cold winds kept insisting they find some sort of warm shelter so they walked back arm in arm, keeping their bodies low to avoid the full brunt of the wind and, without a word, dived into the secretive half-light below the boardwalk where, with the practised moves of a couple who had only done it a million times before, he took off his overcoat and spread it on the sand and she slipped off her fur and brought it up over both of them and they got straight into one another with a quiet fury of hot kisses and hungry hands, loosening this, pulling that, tugging here and ripping away there until he was right up inside her, as one with her, pushing his hips harder and stronger and harder yet and she was wishing sensations like this could last forever, knowing that he was going to burst at any second now and that ten of this wouldn't be enough. When he did tip up the flooding contents of his wheelbarrow inside her she held him tight and with their noses pressed together she said: 'Don't move an inch. Stay right where you are. I want you back again as soon as possible. It's been a long time.'

'I'll be around again soon enough, don't worry, but there's one hell of a cold wind blowing up my bum. Am I stiffening up yet?'

'I can't tell. But let me know when you're ready to go again. I've got no other engagements.'

'It would help if you stopped talking.'

'A girl's got to do something. She can't lie around all day with her legs open while her man tries to make up his mind whether he's going to get another hard on or not. Tell me something.'

'What?'

'Did you ever go into the Church after all?'

'No. I decided I would be no good at it.'

'I always thought you'd be very good at it and often used to think of you doing your pastoral rounds in your dog collar – climbing into bed with your female parishioners, absolving their sins with your dick.'

'Do we have to talk about this now?'

'I think it's interesting, sexy even. And this latest jump of ours would look marvellous in the newspapers wouldn't it? I WAS ONLY GIVING HER ABSOLUTION, PASTOR INSISTS or PASTOR AND ACTRESS IN FLA-GRANTE UNDER CONEY ISLAND BOARDWALK. They don't write headlines like that any more. So why did you decide against the Church?'

'I decided books would reach more people with what I wanted to say. What did you think of my Chris Reynolds book?'

'Oh let's not talk about that now. I'm beginning to feel something quite nice again. Must be something connected with talking about your books. But do you think you could make this one last a bit longer Daniel dearest? Think slow now. *Very* slow.'

'Well I might manage something if only you would stop talking. Could you stop talking for five minutes?'

'I might if I thought it was going to be worth it.'

'Well if only you'd shut up you might find out.'

'You never did like doing it when you were talking did you?'

'Words just disturb my concentration. So are you going to shut up or what?'

'Come on Daniel. I'll keep quiet quickly enough when I start enjoying myself.'

'And don't start screaming whatever you do or we really will end up on the front page of the *Coney Beach Echo*. Americans venerate their boardwalks.'

'So who's doing all the talking now?'

Her whole body gave a happy gurgle as he went up into her again and she stretched out with both arms locked around his neck looking up at the thin slivers of light between the boards. Then another gurgle of happiness bubbled up as she realised that there were three people under her fur coat; it might be Daniel's hips between her legs but it was Jean-Paul in her mind. This *was* a first. But she had to be very careful not to shout out Frog One's name or she would really put delicate Daniel off his stroke.

Indeed this was the one time she had ever been unfaithful to Jean-Paul but she felt no particular shame or guilt. On the contrary, she was skewered with exquisite, tearful happiness when Daniel had finished since she knew it had taken Daniel's love-making to help her realise that Jean-Paul was every woman's dream. She had finally been given the sceptered orb of a good man's love and with that realisation she had become happier than she had ever dared imagine. 'That was lovely, Daniel,' she whispered. 'Now let's find somewhere warm before I go down with frostbite.'

They found a small Italian restaurant nearby with an old Wurlitzer jukebox and gorged themselves on Del Shannon and spaghetti. It was a happy, doubly well-stuffed, slightly nonplussed actress who finally got on the subway to take them back to Manhattan, still trying to work out how it was that she had to make love with the wrong man in order to discover that she was *in love* with the right one. You'd never work out love if you lived to be a thousand would you? She would have liked to have rung Jean-Paul and ask him what *he* thought but, come to think of it, that was about the very last thing she could talk to him about. The Boardwalk Job was hers and Daniel's alone.

The train clattered above the white suburban seas while the weak winter sun was busy clearing the snow off the roads. She kissed Daniel on the cheek. He was a chaotic fragment from a chaotic past. Nothing had worked for her then, no matter how hard she tried. How lucky she was to have found love and Foxley Hall. She only prayed she would die there, on a warm, summer afternoon, the birds singing in the fields and Jean-Paul holding her hand.

What she absolutely must not do was tell Daniel about her and the new *Rebellion* film. He would almost certainly find out about it in time but, with any

241

luck, she would have hand-bagged the three million dollars by then and he could froth and moralise in his pulpit until next Christmas. But she had established he was only here for a few more days and then he'd be back in London long before her sordid little secret became public.

THIRTY FOUR

For the next three days they used the Chelsea as their base and abandoned themselves to the city that never sleeps in a kaleidoscope of sparkling moments.

He bought cheap, jazzy shirts in Orchard Street and they did a tour of the United Nations building. They went up the Empire State building and took a thrilling helicopter ride around the tips of the skyscrapers. They sat in all-night coffee shops near Wall Street, ate mountains of food in Chinatown and discussed the changing moods of God while leaning on the rail of the Staten Island ferry. When they could carry on no longer they just slept in one another's arms wherever they found themselves.

Their favourite time was just before dawn when the city streets were neither light nor dark and they would walk up somewhere like Madison Avenue, with brown and grey slush piling up in the gutters, revelling in their own loneliness. It was never quiet, though: this city of the purest adrenalin was never quiet — even when she was fast asleep there was always someone prowling somewhere on some mysterious and possibly illegal mission or other.

Barges and dead dogs floated on the Hudson River and scabby seagulls sat on stone parapets facing into the cold winds. Huge, empty warehouses lined the waterfront where they half expected Marlon Brando to appear at any moment with a bailing hook hanging off his shoulder. *I couldda bin a contender Johnnie. I couldda bin someone.*

Come the twilight and the distant sky darkened and the skyscrapers lit up, huge, pencil-shaped cathedrals, every wall alive with stained glass fluorescence. They wandered down these glittering canyons marvelling that man, so small, could create something so rapturously overwhelming, so profoundly beautiful.

And oh how they talked about everything and nothing. She was amazed to learn that he was *still* working on his London book which just seemed to grow and grow with no sign of an end in sight. 'Kennington offered to publish a part of it but I didn't want that. I need to finish it properly but I don't work on it all the time. It was only when you were around that I had the necessary ambition to work at it, if the truth be known. My ambitions tend to be more normal when I'm with Helen and someone has to pay the bills.'

'You made it with Helen after we parted?'

'We did. She's very good for my work and gives me the stability to tackle it every day.'

'Not so noisy as me then?'

'I didn't say that.'

He also explained that it was only when the Christopher Reynolds book was taken up by an American publisher that he finally managed to stop worrying about the bills. 'The book did well enough in the UK but paid very few bills. Books never do.'

'Ah yes, it's always the filthy lucre isn't it? We're all forced to face that one from time to time. There's never been an artist who hasn't been worried stiff about that from time to time.'

'My American publisher doesn't hold out too much hope of it doing too well here either, particularly as it's set in London. They've been talking about me coming over here to write an American one. I don't know. It's not that I'd be short of material – they're shooting one another in the cinema these days – just that I'm afraid the media has so institutionalised violence in people's minds and lives that they no longer care. But it's a real shame it's happening in a country like America, born of a religious dream as it is. Crime and violence are states within a state here and they're busy creating a generation of psychopaths. But who's going to listen to me? Not the media here that's for sure. No one can make any progress here except through the media and, with what I say about them, they're never going to take me to their bosom are they? They're just not going to believe that they are taking everyone straight to hell.'

She went silent and swallowed a lot. She believed everything he said; she accepted that Hollywood in particular had become an instrument for mass destruction but she had her own responsibilities to herself and the man she loved.

So she steered their conversation off such sticky themes and talked about her life after Daniel had taken off into the wilds of the East End, how she and Jean-Paul had become partners and taken on an old country house, all but rebuilding it brick by brick. They had kept Cheyne Walk as a town house but after a series of remortgages it now looked as if that would have to be sold too. 'But Foxley Hall is the most amazing place. I find myself singing from the moment I wake up. Jean-Paul has his moods but I'm more stable these days and can handle them. When people got into a mood in the past I got into a mood too. But we can't keep going into bad moods forever can we?'

Yes, it was working out fine with Daniel as she had always hoped that it would one day. They had managed to become real friends, with the odd conversational fuck thrown in for good luck. She liked to think that they would always meet and talk like this but the real pity was that there was still that one dirty black secret sitting between them, still this oaf with his bandoliers of ammunition hanging over her like Damocles' sword.

What's more he kept bringing the damned subject up, curious to know what she really thought about the Chris Reynolds book but she wasn't prepared to be drawn, saying it was fine and changing the subject. Ah well, a totally guilt-free relationship was too much to hope for, she supposed. Even at their finest there were always the secrets and lies holding all relationships together.

But nemesis was never very far away and she was standing in her knickers in the hotel bathroom getting ready for their final day out on the town when the telephone rang. Daniel shouted out her name and she walked into the bedroom holding out her hand to take the receiver. 'Yers?'

'Lisa, it's Avie Glick.'

She had to use her other hand to steady herself against the wall. Another day and Daniel would have been on that plane. *Another day!* 'Yers?'

'Lisa, honey, I got your number off Michael. I'm sorry, but it's very urgent. Yuri and me are going on David Crosby's show on Channel Seven tonight. As you must know we are talking huge prime-time so we decided it would be a good idea if you came too and we could announce your return in the next *Rebellion* film.'

'That's a good idea is it?' she managed to ask, all but squeaking out her words. *Another day!*

'Lisa, it's a brilliant idea. They're always moaning about the squalor of the *Rebellion* films and you bring it some real respectability. It'll give the new film a good early push and the next one too.'

She felt like crying all night long as she looked at Daniel lying back on the bed, gazing at the ceiling and pretending he wasn't listening. It was such a shame but there was more than a friendship at stake here and she was professional enough to understand that, if you took large piles of money, you always had to take large piles of shit too. This appalling film was clearly going to shadow her right to the grave. 'All right then Avie,' she sighed. 'What time do you want me there?'

She replaced the receiver and sat down at the end of the bed next to Daniel's feet, feeling old and treacherous. 'Daniel, it's not that I told you any lies about what I've been doing here in Manhattan,' she said finally, unable to turn around and look him in the face. 'It's just that I didn't tell you the whole truth and now I only wish I'd managed to escape from you in Central Park. The fact is I've more or less agreed to star in the new *Rebellion* film.'

'You've done *what?*'

245

'You heard.'

'I can't believe I'm hearing this. Say it again will you?'

'For Chrissake Daniel, I've agreed to appear in the new *Rebellion* film. As the mother again. There's a lot of money at stake and I need the money. Just like you do. Daniel, that's all there is to it. I need the fucking money. We all need the fucking money.'

'What about Clare Reynolds? You, of all people, should know her son would still be alive if it weren't for those films.'

'That's controversial. He would have found something else to follow. That's how kids like him are. The reviews of your book said the same thing *and* they said your book was highly controversial. The jury was still out, they said.'

'The only people still out are the psychiatrists – who can't decide on the time of day anyway – and the people who actually make these films. Everyone else is firmly *in*. Do you think Clare Reynolds is out on all this? Or the people that Chris shot?'

'None of this has anything to do with Clare or Chris or anyone else. The next film gets made whether I'm in it or not. Daniel, I'm facing fucking bankruptcy. I'm flat broke and I'm about to lose everything. If I don't do this film me and my man are going to end up in the gutter. Can't you see that? In the fucking gutter.'

He was silent for a while and, still unable to turn around to face him, she heard him crying. 'You belong in the fucking gutter if you do this film,' he announced finally in between snuffles. 'I hope you and your man rot in all the gutters of hell if you do this film. How could you? How could you ever look Clare in the eyes ever again?'

'I haven't seen Clare for three years. Why should I care about her? She never cared about me.'

'She cared for you all right. And that just goes to show what a stupid cow she was doesn't it? Why didn't you tell me before now?'

'I didn't want you to know. I knew you'd get upset and anyway you're leaving tomorrow. I thought you'd find out another time. That was Avie Glick on the phone. He wants me on the David Crosby show tonight. He wants me to talk about the new film.'

'I feel contaminated.'

'I *was* going to tell you but I chickened out. I thought I'd get away with it. When did I ever get away with anything?'

'You fucking whore. That's all you are. One big fucking useless whore.'

The whole of her body was quivering. Never, in all the time she had known him, had he uttered one single obscene word.

'Fucking whore,' he spat again, sniffing a lot and blowing his nose on the bedsheet. 'Fucking old Jezebel. And you were my first mentor. You were the one who made me believe in myself as a writer. What did you always say? Dive deep and then go deeper. What a joke. I became what I am because of you.'

She would normally have wigged out by now, screaming anything that came into her mind but on this occasion she didn't appear to have a single scrap of self-deceit to stand on. He had taken this betrayal far worse than she expected, his eyes red raw with tears, barely able to control his shaking hands. And it *was* a betrayal, she could see that. You could always betray a man but never his ideals. You should never take them away from him. 'Daniel, I'm in such a lot of trouble you wouldn't believe it. I wouldn't be doing this unless I had to. Hold me will you darling, just hold me.'

'I don't hold fucking whores,' screamed the prophet of peace and love, jumping off the bed, grabbing her by the wrist and slinging her up against the door. 'Who, in their right mind, would want to hold someone as pox-ridden as you. Well, fuck off and make your fucking film. I really do pray you rot in hell you fucking Jezebel.'

It all happened so quickly she barely knew what was going on – too astonished to feel any physical pain, too surprised to scream before she hit the door once, got pulled back again and propelled straight out of the doorway to hit the wall on the other side of the corridor with a bone-crunching thump. She had never thought him capable of violence; she still couldn't believe it was Daniel Jenkins – her *friend* – who was flinging her and her clothes out after her. *Wham, wham, wham.*

The odd head appeared along the corridor but they didn't stay gawping for long. This was the Chelsea in Manhattan, after all, and a half-naked woman having her clothes flung at her in a hotel corridor hardly rated a second glance. *Wham, wham, wham.* 'Daniel,' she cried, holding up her arms to protect herself from her own flying possessions. 'Let's not part like this. Let's not do it like this.'

But deaf to her pleas he merely slammed the door and left her sobbing among the debris of opened suitcases and clothes scattered around her feet.

THIRTY FIVE

That evening Lisa had taken more than a few drinks in Channel Seven's hospitality suite but she wished she'd taken a lot more when she sat down in front of the audience under the harsh lights of the studio. She still wasn't totally clear in her mind why she had agreed to appear on this show, she had always loathed anything to do with television, particularly live television.

But there was no need to be coy with herself was there? She needed those three million dollars. Yet, even given that enormous need, she was on the verge of selling out on everything her life had once stood for. Artistic integrity had always meant a lot to her – she had compromised it once before with one of these films – so knowing what she knew about Christopher Reynolds and what he'd done to those poor shoppers in Edgware, her behaviour seemed doubly criminal. Her legs stood up to run her out of the studio; her need sat her down again.

No such qualms for Yuri and Avie, both of them ever-smiling and burnished like boomtown bookies on a winning streak. 'Are you feeling all right, honey?' Avie asked.

'I think I've got a bit of a migraine coming on, Avie. I don't want to say much tonight. Try and tell this Crosby man I'm not up to answering any questions will you? You know everything about the films anyway. I'll just sit here and smile.'

Weep and puke, more like, a small voice corrected her. Weep and puke, you fucking old whore. *You fucking Jezebel.* She still felt the bruises on her side and shoulder after Daniel had flung her out of his room but she harboured no particular bitterness towards him, admiration rather. Perhaps if he'd done that a bit more in the old days they would still be together. She needed the smack of firm authority, as Jean-Paul understood only too well, giving her more than a few sound spankings when she got too silly and boisterous. The real trouble with all those spanking sessions though was that they had both come to rather enjoy them.

'Ladies and gentlemen, please put your hands together for David Crosby.'

'Evening folks,' Crosby read off his autocue. 'We've got a fine show for you tonight and we've brought together, at simply no expense, the people behind the most commercially successful series of films in cinematic history. The *Rebellion* films have made Yuri Pucket the best-paid and best-known actor in the world and he's here to talk to us about them. (Close-up of a beaming Yuri and a round of applause.) The director of the series, Avie Glick, is going to tell us what it's like to be bigger and richer than Francis Ford Coppola. (Close-up of a frowning Glick, who appeared not to approve of such an introduction, and another round of applause.) And last, but far from least, we have that great English actress, Lisa Moran, who, we can reveal here tonight for the first time, has agreed to return as Raz's mother in the upcoming *Rebellion 6* film which begins shooting in the Fall. (Close-up of an even bigger frown than Glick's and a round of suspiciously rapturous applause. *What* was it they were clapping exactly?) So then, Avie, exactly how much money would you say all these films made to date?'

'We never talk figures, David. We leave all that to the accountants; we're just the artists and all I'm ever concerned with cash-wise is that the budget is always large enough to do justice to our original artistic visions of each film. But the money men never leave us short of a dollar or two. Let's just leave it at that.'

'But the merchandising operation around these films is huge isn't it? Far bigger even than the films themselves.'

'David, you are going to have to find someone else to talk with about all that. We just make the films and always get enough to ensure that our artistic integrity is never compromised.'

'But Avie, surely you can give us some idea of the scale of the operation. I mean there's *Rebellion* toys, survival kits, school bags, computer games, diaries, sound tracks, comics. Are we talking two billion dollars here?'

'Maybe not that. Maybe not far short. But look, David ...'

'And doesn't it ever rest uneasily with you that you are making this huge amount of money out of children by using relentless and graphic glorification of violence? I mean let's get right down to it. These films *are* celebrations of violence aren't they?'

Lisa was on red alert and sitting bolt upright. Those words, or words very much like them, had appeared in Daniel's book. Crosby had a well-deserved reputation for chewing up his guests. But hadn't he given all kinds of assurances that his questions were going to be amiable and about *the films*? So what was all this? Avie was starting to sweat and stumble.

With the same lethal quietness of tone Crosby turned to Yuri. 'So, Yuri.' He paused and stared directly at the great man of action, almost as if he was aware of the sheer panic that was building up all around them. 'So, then. What do *you* say to people who claim that the violence in your films is one of the causes of violence in real life?'

Lisa turned to look at Yuri, also curious to know how this blockhead was going to deal with such a question. But this blockhead had dealt with it a thousand times before and wasn't about to rewrite the script now. 'I'm not a psychiatrist, David, but let me tell you this: no one has ever proved a link between my movies and acts of street violence. No one. If a link was ever proven I would pack it all in now, this minute. As far as I'm concerned *this is all just movies*. The *Rebellion* films are just entertainment and that's all there is to it. They are always fingering the film industry but we're not responsible for the violence in the world. The world is violent and has always been violent. Shakespeare did violence and this is, anyway, cartoon violence. You would be mad to believe what we put in our films and you certainly wouldn't want to imitate it. We are holding up a mirror to a violent world. That's all. Nothing more.'

'Lisa Moran? Do you have any worries about appearing in these films?'

'Oh of course. But there again I have worries about getting out of bed in the morning. I have worries every time I look into the mirror and spot another wrinkle. I worry about everything under the sun. What do you worry about Mr Crosby? Do you ever worry perhaps about telling your guests before the show you intend to ask friendly questions when you are planning to ask hostile ones?'

Crosby said nothing and merely shuffled his papers for a while. There was not so much a ripple of laughter or applause. Everyone had twigged they were getting into some serious business here. This was why Crosby had built up one of the largest-ever prime-time audience figures and guests should always know they were taking a real chance when they agreed to appear on his show. You could sometimes get away with it but he did sometimes take out a gun of his own and there might well be blood all over the studio floor.

'Mr Glick,' Crosby announced when he had tidied up his papers, moving ominously to a greater formality. 'I do understand that you are in the entertainment business but so were the Romans when they fed the Christians to the lions. But maybe you can also see that even entertainment can have its tragic consequences. I'd like you all now to meet a young British writer who has made a study of the shooting of some shoppers in England. *He* has no doubt that the *Rebellion* films were responsible. Ladies and gentlemen, give a warm welcome please to Mr Daniel Jenkins.'

The end of Lisa's nose went numb and her heart attempted to break straight out of her chest as the lights went up on the front row of the audience and one of the cameras focused on Daniel, holding a copy of his wretched book in his hands. Daniel, just what are you trying to do to me? And how the fuck had he ended up on this show tonight when he appeared never to have heard about it earlier on this afternoon? Why was he persecuting her like this? Oh Daniel, I'm going to get you for this. I'm going to fix you good and proper for this.

'Mr Jenkins,' Crosby said when the light, uncertain applause had died down.

'Tell us, please, as simply as you can, about the link between the shootings you investigated and the *Rebellion* films.'

'Well the link couldn't be firmer,' Daniel said a little nervously. 'We haven't got the time to go into too much detail but the young man who attacked those shoppers in London was dressed like Raz in the *Rebellion* films, used the same weaponry and mounted the same style of attacks. He owned all the *Rebellion* films on video and watched them over and over again, listened to the soundtracks repeatedly and even had his hair styled in the same way. He *was* Raz. In his mind the *Rebellion* films became myths which sanctioned murder.'

'This is insane,' Yuri shouted. 'It's insane to link my films with every knucklehead who runs loose with a gun. My character never attacked innocent shoppers. Never. He's a good guy who blows away bad guys. That's all he is.'

'Ladies and gentlemen, we are going to take a break. Stay right there and we'll be straight back after these messages.'

As the commercials jangled through the monitors, director and star were on their feet, protesting loudly to Crosby. 'We weren't given any warning about this,' Glick stormed. 'We weren't prepared for any of this.'

'You set us up, you bastard,' Yuri shouted, his thick neck muscles swelling so much it looked as if he was actually going to burst straight out of his shirt collar. 'You never told us you were getting *him* on here.'

'We only found out he was in the country ourselves a few hours ago,' Crosby pointed out calmly. 'His publisher rang us when he saw the trail for our show saying you were on it.'

'Well either this Brit writer goes or we do.' Glick strode across the studio floor towards Daniel. 'Haven't I seen you somewhere before?'

'He was in Israel with us,' Yuri yelled. 'If I remember right he was with *her*.'

'Not so much of the *her* if you don't mind. I've got a name, you know.'

The commercial break had long finished and the cameras were following the arguments. Yuri had identified Daniel but Glick still couldn't quite place him so he rounded on Crosby again. 'We're not going to be set up like this. Either the Limey goes or we do.'

Crosby raised his hands in a form of surrender, clearly about to try to put the whole argument back on a calm, friendly basis. 'Avie – Yuri – listen to me for a few seconds. No one is trying to set anyone up here. Just listen. The streets of America are swamped with violence and here's a rare chance to discuss one of the *alleged* causes. A survey has found that sixty four per cent of Americans believe violent films are one of the main causes of violence in the streets. So, as we're all here, let's at least talk about it. Let's at least see if we can get anywhere on this most important issue.'

'You're not making us the fall guys for all the violence in American streets, Crosby, and I'm certainly not going to stand here and be conned by a cheap jerk like you. Come on Yuri, Lisa, we're out of here.'

Avie marched out followed by Yuri, leaving Lisa with three seats all to herself. 'I'm not going anywhere,' she announced sweetly when she saw the red light telling her the camera was on her. 'I've always liked this chat show and, anyway, Americans do need to learn something about the violence on their screens before America gets destroyed by it.'

This was Crosby's show but even he couldn't quite work out what was going on. 'What is it you are trying to say Miss Moran?' he asked.

'Well, it's very simple isn't it?' She took in a long deep breath and blew out three million dollars. 'There's no mystery about the growing crime and violence of our times since our children are clearly learning it from the screens. Men like Avie and Yuri say it's not their fault but these screens are our teachers and the cinema is where our children go to school. I know Mr Jenkins personally and on this issue he is right. Christopher Reynolds, who shot those people in London, was copying the acts he saw in *Rebellion* films. I've spoken to his mother myself and we know – not believe – *know* that Christopher's world view was shaped by these films. There have been lots of other cases too – ask Mr Jenkins about them. Everyone in the film world tried to cover it up because there's so much money at stake. Two billion dollars can buy an awful lot of bananas.'

Crosby gave his papers another thoughtful shuffle before asking: 'But you were here tonight, weren't you, Miss Moran, to tell us about your role in the next *Rebellion* film?'

'Until this moment I thought I could take the money and run. But I can't. Let me talk to one of your cameras for a few moments.' With the poise of an experienced performer she spoke directly to camera three. 'Mr Jenkins here has written a wonderful book on the subject. It's called *A Suburban Shooting* and everyone in America should read it. It should be made compulsory in all your schools since it tells us clearly what's happening to our youth. Not just one youth but all our youth. The book is an investigation into the life of Christopher Reynolds and asks at what point did a normal suburban child with a strong, supportive family begin growing into a psychopath. Read it and ask if your child could grow up into a Chris Reynolds. Read it and ask if Chris Reynolds was born evil. The short answer is he wasn't.'

She struggled to control her breathing as a few tears trickled slowly down her classically sculpted cheekbones. Three million dollars down the drain! Three mill! Always the grand gesture wasn't it? Always the grand fucking gesture.

'Christopher Reynolds was a good child made rotten and your own children, my dear Americans, are being made rotten too. It's time for this thing to stop and only you can stop it. Thank you.'

A stunned silence followed during which Crosby invited Daniel to sit next to Lisa. 'Tell us about other acts of violence inspired by films Mr Jenkins.'

'There are so many it's difficult to know where to begin. Stanley Kubrick suppressed *A Clockwork Orange* in Britain after learning that young men were putting on bowler hats and going around beating up old people ...

'We're getting reports of random shootings from all parts of the world. Last week there was another attack on a school in California and the week before that a young man went on the rampage in Melbourne, killing three and injuring six. There's no apparent motive until you start examining their dress, their style, the image they have of themselves. If you look hard enough and know what you're looking for you can usually find some kind of film violence hovering around in there.

'A report in the *Journal of the American Medical Association* found that pro-longed exposure to violent television programmes produced ten thousand additional murders a year in America and that the crime rate would be halved if television had not been introduced into this country. Television then has become the prime instigator of modern lawlessness.

'A total of seven hundred reports have established a link between aggressive behaviour in children and their exposure to aggression in the media. How many more reports do they want before they start taking any notice of this clear evidence? When will newspapers stop parroting the lie that no direct link has been established? Avie and Yuri know about this evidence but they choose to ignore it simply because there is too much money at stake.'

He got out of his seat and began walking around in front of the audience. Lisa remembered he liked to do this when he wanted to think and she was so proud of him. His earlier nervousness had gone and he was in control of the situation. Her experience on the stage told her that something special was about to happen. 'Films like *Rebellion* are destroying the moral framework without which your children cannot lead honest, decent lives,' he went on. 'Films like *Rebellion* are turning your children into a generation of psychopaths. These films have become the very templates for gun massacres all over the world. Lisa says that this thing must stop and stop it must. Everything these film people do is a lie. It is not the violence on our streets which is the problem but the film makers' persistent pursuit of that violence. In everything they do they make the violence of the world a million times worse and the real enemy here is the unquenchable appetite for violence which has become the great engine of profit in the American film industry.'

He paused, lifted his hand slowly and cleared his throat twice.

'Unless people fasten on to this truth we are all going to be destroyed by the guns of our children. These films are rivers of evil which infect every young mind they wash over. You have all stood back while your children have been baptised in them and it's only ever going to get worse. It will never go away, it will only ever get worse. The only question, Americans, is are you still capable of resisting? Have you any resistance left in you?'

His speech had been delivered with all the driving passion of a man wedded to the truth. Such words, with their quasi-religious vocabulary, would have a powerful appeal to the American imagination, Lisa knew, and she couldn't ever remember a public moment more powerfully theatrical. Larry had managed it a few times on the stage, but no one else and she stood up and walked towards Daniel with her arms open wide. After a short silence the audience were clapping and cheering.

They stood together holding hands, smiling at the audience as if it was a joint curtain call before Lisa remembered her manners and backed away from him leaving him to take the applause on his own. 'You're going to take me out for dinner after all this, I hope?' she whispered.

'I might.'

'Might? Now listen to me you big shit,' she continued telling the inside of his ear as she escorted him off the stage. 'Your fucking book has just had the plug of its life *and* I've just lost three million dollars. I've also still got a lot of bruises after being attacked by some psychopath in the Chelsea hotel. We don't want this lovely audience to learn about that do we? So there's no *might* about it. I want the best dinner in the best restaurant in town and a good bop in somewhere like Studio 54. And I don't care how early you've got to get up in the morning, either. You owe me a lot, you shit, but I'll settle for a good dinner and a bop. You got that?'

THIRTY SIX

Lisa had always wondered if financial and personal meltdown had a face, a voice or a personality, and now she knew. It looked like her Holborn solicitor Nigel Perris with his well-fed features, neatly trimmed grey hair and half-moon spectacles over which he occasionally peered like some particularly batty High Court Judge.

'I have represented you through three marriages, Miss Moran, not to mention various other difficulties with the law but, almost needless to say, I am extremely sorry to hear you taking this attitude since there is almost nothing I can do for you on this occasion.' His voice was a quiet monotone, honed by the public school, his plump hands resting on either side of her opened, extremely fat file on his desk. 'Really nothing at all.'

'Oh I don't mind, Nigel,' she replied with a breeziness at odds with her feelings. 'I'm only sorry I can't pay your bill.'

'That does not matter in the slightest, Miss Moran. You invariably paid your bills promptly in the past and I must admit we always did rather well out of your divorces even if you didn't. I would be in breach of my duty of care, however, if I didn't again remind you that you have a real claim against Mr Platini. You raised capital *jointly* on Foxley Hall and so, in the eyes of the law, you have a strong claim to any remaining equity in it if – and when – Mr Platini sells it. A very strong claim.'

She shook her head emphatically. 'I could never go into a court of law to fight for money – no matter how much was at stake. Foxley Hall belonged to Jean-Paul in the first place and I'm sure he'll settle his debts with me when things improve.'

Now it was Perris' turn to shake his head. 'You are too credulous Miss Moran. I have never met anyone so ready to trust people of dubious character.'

'I do hope you're not suggesting Jean-Paul is a dubious character.'

'Of course not but you did get tangled up with a few in your time didn't you

255

and you let them all off the hook in the end. They all ran off with far more than they'd brought to the marriage and Mr Orlan got the boat. Now you are about to sacrifice a home in Cheyne Walk, which this man did not even live in, to pay *his* debts on, as you now put it, *his* home.'

'Homes are only bricks and mortar. Anyway I don't mind losing Cheyne Walk. It's always been too big for me and the trees are being felled. Some mornings I wander around it like Banquo's ghost. A one-bedroomed flat for me in the future, always assuming I can scrape together enough money to buy one.'

'It's not good business, Miss Moran. It's not good business at all.'

'But it's the way I am Nigel. If I can't have a man's love then I'm certainly not going to fight him in court for his money. I had love and lost it. I had money and lost it. I'm an old woman now. I don't need love or money any more.'

'Yes, well.' He began closing her file when his mouth made a silent 'Ah!' as he remembered something else. 'We should talk about Mr Charles Judd and the money he claims you owe him. I can send him a letter stalling him for the time being.'

'Well I can't just forget it can I? It *was* his money.'

'You have *no* money, Miss Moran, and all you need to do at the moment is to instruct me to write informing him that you will attempt to reimburse him when your domestic and financial affairs are settled. You will probably not be able to reimburse him, of course, but that is what we should say now, if only to keep him quiet.'

'But now he's out of prison he keeps sending me notes saying that's all the money he's got in the world. What if he sues me?'

'Impossible. The money was almost certainly stolen and no one has title on stolen money. With his record he wouldn't dare sue anyone and I can't think of a solicitor who would take him on.'

'He might have other methods. You should meet some of his chums down Walthamstow Dog Track. Shoulder-pads a yard wide. I promise you they are not nice. All right, send him a letter saying I'm trying to arrange the sale of a few of my paintings. That might keep him quiet for a while.' She sighed and chewed her lower lip for a while. 'I'm right down a deep hole aren't I Nigel?'

'A very deep hole indeed Miss Moran but, as usual, we'll make every effort to dig you out again.'

It was a vibrant, late Spring morning with traffic thronging the streets as she walked back to Chelsea feeling a good deal better than when she had left it. Nothing had been resolved but at least she had done something, if only shown a willingness to see her solicitor who had merely told her what she already knew.

Of all the men who had wandered in and out of her life her solicitor had undoubtedly been the most helpful, forever counselling her wisely over the years, pulling her out of self-inflicted trouble at every turn and defending her interests stubbornly. Twice she had got him out of bed in the middle of the night after the police had flung her into a cell – once for drunk driving and resisting arrest and the other time for assaulting that dyke policewoman who grabbed hold of her breasts. Nigel had fought all her legal actions as if he'd had a personal stake in them, ensuring that, even if she didn't get the house, she at least didn't shoulder all the blame for the marital breakdown when she had almost always been the innocent, injured party. Well, almost.

She occasionally looked around for a taxi as she walked but decided she would probably get home faster on foot. Traffic jams were locking up virtually every city street these days, thousands of engines belching and roaring, making the very sky suppurate yellow, brown and a thick grey which seemed to creep over every square inch of the streets and work its way up the walls of the highest buildings, discolouring the very flowers in the window boxes. The pavements, the park railings, even the white and yellow traffic lines had a grey veneer. 'The earth is broad and beautiful,' she said, recalling a distant line. 'There are many marvellous places in it.'

If only she could have come up with some sort of decent stage role somewhere. The pay wouldn't have come close to settling her outstanding gas bill – let alone all the others – but it would have at least provided some sort of distraction from her present predicament. But there was simply nothing around and the theatre had suffered in the same way as everyone else in Thatcher's boom-and-bust Britain. The Royal Shakespeare Company, some five million pounds in the red, had closed its Barbican and Pit theatres for four months.

The traffic along Piccadilly looked as if it had been stuck there all week and she briefly considered popping into the Royal Academy to cheer herself up. But the crowds were so dense outside Burlington House she couldn't get near the doors so she made her way home, trying to remember if she had put any half-bottles of champagne in the fridge.

The Chesterton's *For Sale* board outside her house gave her a good punch in the solar plexus every time she looked at it. But the loss of the house was hardly the end of the world and she did so look forward to a simpler life in her old age. The real problem with possessions was you were always worried that people were trying to steal them off you.

Yet the reason she really wanted to get away from Cheyne Walk was that, after ten years of solid argument, the local residents had lost and the 'palsied' trees were finally being cut down. It was unbelievable and the mere sight of them being cut up filled her with pain. The job seemed to be taking for ever with the constant savage whines of the chain saws filling up their days. They were killing her very own cherry orchard.

Ranyeuskaya came to stand next to her – Royal Exchange, Manchester, 1971

– also broke but proud, driven mad by infidelities yet still hopeful in a hostile world. They put their arms around one another, bringing a little human comfort. The family had been pinning all their hopes on a new railway running through their land which would save the family name and provide them with a good income from renting out summer cottages. But Ranyeuskaya was unconvinced. 'Without the cherry orchard, I can't make any sense of my life and, if it really has to be sold, sell me along with it.'

'Excuse me, it *is* Lisa Moran, isn't it?' she heard as she put her key in her front door. She turned to see a young man with a bright kipper tie which somehow matched his bright, green eyes and eager, twitching face. His hair had been shaped into a curly mess, in what she believed was called a mullet, and her immediate instinct was to punch him in straight in the mouth to get in her retaliation in advance.

'Yers. And who might you be?'

'Terry Maven is the name, Miss Moran. But do call me Terry.'

She gave him one of her haughtiest, straight-down-the-bridge-of-her-nose stares. 'What can I do for you, Mr Maven?'

'It's very much what I can do for you, Miss Moran. It's very much what I can do for you. I don't suppose you'd like to invite me inside for a few minutes would you? There's a lot for us to talk about.'

'Some sort of journalist are you?'

He forced out a hollow little guffaw which told her she had hit bullseye; she could always smell a hack from a thousand paces.

'Something like that. Yes, you could say it was something like that.'

'I never talk to journalists unless there is something I really want to say to them, Mr Maven, so good day to you.' She opened the door and stepped inside but Maven was half-way inside after her, making it impossible to close the door. 'You are living dangerously, Mr Maven. Very dangerously indeed.'

'Lisa, please. Perh-l-eeese. We *must* talk, if only for a few minutes. I've been assigned to write a series on your life.'

'You've *what*? The door jerked towards his face and he saw he wasn't going to have much of a nose left unless he moved it out of the way.

'Miss Moran, my newspaper has assigned me to write a series about your life. We had this conference and decided that you were one of the most interesting women in Europe. We also know, of course, that you've been having some financial difficulties and we're all thrilled by your stand on the *Rebellion* films.' The threat of the door flattening his nose receded an inch or so. 'But I have to write this series whether you co-operate or not so just give me a few hours of your time, Miss Moran, and I'll be out of your life for ever. The money will be terrific too. But, in any event, I'm afraid we will be digging hard into your life. Awkward stuff could come out, if you know what I mean and it's *your* interests

I want to protect.'

He was almost doing all right until the last bit when he truly blew it. 'Out! Out! Out!' she shrilled kicking him in the shins.

'Lisa, please. Perh-l-eeese.'

'Out! Out! Out! You blackmailing maggot.' She managed to close the door and stood with her shoulder still pressed firmly up against it, shaking angrily. In the old days the hacks at least took 'no' to mean 'no'. They didn't try and black-mail you as well. And why was everyone trying to muscle into her life all the time? Why didn't they leave her alone? Celebrity was a dangerous and bitter pill: that much she knew. You were never on your own when you were cursed with celebrity; people envied you but that envy was built on pure ignorance. Most of the time they weren't even sure why you were famous although she saw that her outburst on the Crosby show had yet again propelled her into the head-lines for no realistic reason. All she'd done was say something everyone knew.

She poured herself some fizz, opened the French windows and sat in an arm-chair looking out over the ever-busy Thames feeling slightly more composed after she'd downed her first glass. She had never had a drink problem but could-n't have imagined how she would have got through life without the support of this lovely stuff. The stress would have been intolerable. Terry Maven indeed! From *The Sun*. Had to be.

How Daniel had managed to give up the drink for so long was a mystery. He had been a raving pisshead when he was living in that grotty flat near the Voodoo Parlour in Hackney and she sniffed a bit of a smile whenever she thought of him, as she often did, particularly when she was taking a drink her-self. She had not heard from him for a while and, for all she knew, he had gone back to America to write there for a while. Writers did better in America. Americans were readier to listen to their writers. They were the new preachers there these days.

So she remembered Daniel with a motherly benevolence although, to be per-fectly candid, she wouldn't have minded if he could have come over to Cheyne Walk for an hour or so to perform a few, ah, pastoral duties. She couldn't recall the last time she had been humming with so much tension and anxiety; she need-ed something – *anything* – to give her some form of relief and Daniel was about the only one who could do that. Her ghosts were massing all around her again, particularly in the dead of night when she could hear their mocking words and laughter. These ghosts were her biggest worry: that, somehow, they would final-ly push her over the edge on which she had been precariously balanced for so long.

Yet it was the tormenting ghost of Frog One who dominated all the others, stalking her every dream clutching a blood-stained sword with which he kept attacking her. She poured herself another drink. How could she, at her age, be sitting here nursing a broken heart for a man who had disappeared from her life and refused to even communicate with her? But there it was. He had already left Foxley Hall by the time she had got back from New York, to live with his brother in Newmarket until matters were sorted out, it said in the curtest of notes, adding that the strain of everything had got too much and he now wished to return to France where he wanted to live alone. Only yesterday she had received a letter from the estate agent informing her she should pick up her possessions from Foxley Hall before the auction in three weeks' time.

It all wouldn't have been quite so bad if, apart from the extremely vague 'strain' angle, she'd been given a proper reason for his defection although she had heard on the Cotswold grapevine that he had gone all but crazy in the pub when he'd learned how she had not only dropped the *Rebellion* films deep in the shit on American television but had also managed to kiss three million dollars goodbye while she was at it. Fortunately for his continuing good health he had not said anything about that directly to her or she really would have let loose the formidable arsenal of Nigel Perris on him. Jean-Paul, of all people, should have known that artistic integrity had always been important to her and that she had always valued that more than anything else in her blighted life.

Oh that film! Having in a sense given birth to the thing she had been haunted by it ever since. She seemed to run into it at every turn and had she so valued her artistic integrity by not doing it in the first place she might not even have ended up in this mess. Nothing could live in the shadow of such evil, according to Daniel, and the Welsh nutcase was probably right about that.

She looked down at the Thames and the tears began again. She blew her nose hard and sighed loudly. It was hopeless, everything was hopeless. At her writing bureau she read a few of her vast collection of love letters, something she often did on blue days, reading again the passionate declarations that had all turned to bitter dross and expensive solicitors. She had treasured every love letter she had ever received and here was a whole life of explosive passion and idiotically optimistic relationships reduced to the rubble of dusty bundles tied up in red ribbons and dotted with mementoes – a pressed flower, a dinner receipt, a beer mat. All the beer mats had been something to do with Daniel: he had been alone among her lovers in being interested in beer.

The front door bell rang and without thinking, because she had become slightly tipsy, she went down to open the door to find the unspeakable Terry Maven standing there. 'Miss Moran, my editor has sent me back to give you one last chance. Please listen to me for two minutes. Perh-le-leeeese.'

She took one step backwards, as if to slam the door on him, but instead lifted her head imperiously to indicate that he was indeed being given two minutes to speak whatever it was that he wanted to say.

'Miss Moran, I know a lot about your life and I don't want to waste any of your valuable time but there are certain key sections of your life which I *must* put to you. I *must* ask you if you have any comment on them, merely for your own protection. We don't need to know anything specific – because we know everything already – but we do need your reaction to certain allegations.'

She moved her weight from one foot to the other and gave another regal inclination of her head.

'It is alleged that Charles Judd left a suitcase of money in your care before he was locked up. Have you anything to say about that?'

'Yes I have. If you ring this door again I'll call the police. Now fuck off!' She slammed the door shut and, sinking to her knees in the silent darkness of the hallway, put her palms together in prayer to the God she truly believed in when the going got rough.

'Please, Lisa, I'm only doing my job,' came through the rattling letter box. 'Perh-le-leeeeese.'

A thousand enemies and barely the strength to fight one of them. She couldn't take much more of this. That much was clear. Chekhov was always calling on us to find the courage to endure but what was the point of enduring all this crap? Just *what* was the point?

THIRTY SEVEN

Hands deep in pockets and with shoulders hunched, Lisa could barely bring herself to look up at the silhouette of Foxley Hall let alone set foot on the drive which would take her to the front door.

She had only just got through the main gate when, with nervous fingers fumbling in her shoulder bag, she wondered if she had the strength for this final confrontation. Perhaps coming here had been one of her madder decisions and she should have stayed home in bed where she clearly belonged. She was wearing no make-up and her face was skeletal, gaunt, her cheeks but bare bones and her eyes sunk into a dark, accusing sorrow.

Here she was again, back in the home which had become the very beat of her heart and which she had fought for so hard for so long before it was lost so quickly. It had been bad enough seeing her cherry orchard in Cheyne Walk being hacked down but the sheer pain of *that* wasn't nearly as bad as the heart-shrivelling agony of *this*. Even in such a short space of time the lawns were overgrown and the box hedges gone wild. Convolvulus was reaching up and choking the very faces of her favourite African lilies and instinctively she went down on one knee to free them from further strangulation. Then she stood up again. Pointless. You really can't say goodbye to an African lily any more than you can say goodbye to a building. You really should have stayed in bed. 'Oh my cherry orchard!' she muttered looking around the garden again with her eyes welling up. 'My sweet and lovely orchard. My life! My youth! My happiness! Forever farewell!'

After standing in the porch for a full five minutes, head bowed and gazing down into the rubble of her shoulder bag, she finally reached down into it and took out a key. A rush of silence all but deafened her as she stepped inside the hallway. One of her Barbour country coats hung from a hook on the wooden coat stand, as on a gibbet. Even on such a warm summer's day the air inside was as cold as frost. She followed a trail of muddy footprints out to the scullery where she ran her fingers along the old Welsh dresser before pausing thoughtfully and rubbing her fingers together to shed the dust. Her lovely Tara had become another Satis House with dust over everything and cobwebs gathering thickly in the corners. But, rather than sitting on her rocker like Miss Havisham, waiting for her man to return, she kept feeling the oddest urges to set to and begin cleaning everything in sight. People often treated her as a famous actress but she was just an old scrubber at heart. Her shadow fell over a cobweb and the spider fled back into a hole in the wall. Lucky spider with a nice, warm home of his own like that.

'Ah've bin running all my life through doah after doah, Stella,' she shouted in a deep Southern accent as she returned to the main hallway. 'It's bin one leaking roof after another.'

Her words disappeared into the distant recesses of the house and she opened the drawing room door whose hinges gave a familiar creak. They had tried everything on that creak, even oil and butter, but still it creaked like an old man trying to get out of bed in the morning. She understood everything about the secret language of this house: knew the ways the ash logs crackled in the inglenook, understood the words of the winds in the chimney, even felt a sudden lift of the spirit when she heard this creaking door since it meant he would be walking in, to be with her.

'But I just cannot believe that a lawn mower could cost so much. Five thousand pounds! That's more than a small car. Can't we just hang on to the old one?'

'Chérie the old one is *foutue*.'

'I've got it. Let's try goats. They've worked well for Damien and they'd be original too.'

'Hardly original if stupid Damien has tried them.'

She walked around the furniture which was crouching and hiding under lots of white sheets. A dozen bottles stood at the bottom of the cocktail cabinet including, unless she was very much mistaken, that bottle of brandy which had moved in with them on the day they had first come here. She bit her lip for a while as she stared at the bottle, knowing there might be some turbulent consequences – and all for her – if she broke that seal but, quite simply, she was past caring. Her hand was shaking so much she could barely get the brandy into her glass and spilt a lot down the front of her dress before she put down two big gulps and then two more.

Much calmer now she refilled her glass and stood at the French windows looking down at the ragged lawns and the mirror-calm lake. A hurrying pitter-pattering sound – a mouse or even a rat? – disturbed her reverie but her darting eyes could pick up nothing in the room except for the sheeted ghosts of the crouching furniture. Oh yes, our lives are full of ghosts, they watch and they wait and, when they are ready, they always torment. She finished her drink and walked back to the cocktail cabinet for a refill.

Not with any jerky movements now Lisa. Calmly. A steady flowing movement towards the firegrate, lifting your glass slightly as you walk and smiling, as if in anticipation of a gift. Now turn to face the audience.

'You should live for those who know you, who judge and absolve you and for whom you have love and indulgence.' *That's very good, Lisa. The right projection, measured, calm.* 'The rest is merely the crowd from whom we can only expect fleeting emotions, good or bad, which leave no grace. One should hate very little because it's extremely fatiguing. One should despise much, forgive often, never forget. Pardon doesn't bring forgetfulness. At least not for me.'

Oh excellent. You'll have got the back row with that. Never forget the back row, best beloved.

'But why didn't you tell me that you'd taken all that money from that Judd crook? We might have been able to have done something about it.'

'Look, I just didn't want to upset you, that's all. And do remember we're flat broke. Skint. Not a bean.'

With one long, unbroken movement she pulled the sheet off the dining table before emptying the contents of her shoulder bag over the beeswaxed surface in a tiny clattering landslide. Lipsticks, spectacles and compacts spun around together along with a large bottle of pills which she unscrewed, pouring a pile into her hand and shovelling into her mouth. She always went everywhere packed these days: you never knew when the mood would fully and finally take you. The long and short of it was that she just couldn't take any more of this pain: just couldn't live with it, didn't actually *want* to live with it. Blue fragments tumbled from her lips as her teeth crunched into the pills and she washed them down with several further hefty slugs of brandy.

Watch your breathing now, Lisa. This is the climax of the play and you won't be able to do it properly if you lose control of your breathing. Just follow the verse as you make your way to your mark. Listen to the beat of the verse.

The sun was dipping down towards the low Cotswold hills sending light slashing through the darkness of the living room as she carefully went looking for her mark. But wherever she stood she only seemed to stare into the dazzle of yet more sunlight. Typical. 'There's something gone badly wrong with the lighting plot, Trevor. There's this ghost standing there on the fucking battlements who's supposed to be all shadowy and it's fucking daylight. Then, when it's *supposed* to be daylight, and the audience should be able to see what's going on, everything goes dark again so there's clearly another fucking lunatic in charge of the lights who should have gone to work in the circus.'

She continued rubbing her lips with her fingertips, occasionally shoving stray dribbles of brandy, saliva and crumbs of pills back into her mouth. But something was going badly wrong here since, instead of feeling sleepy, her whole body was defiantly alive, actually *roaring* with flames of pure life.

'Probably my destiny, since I was born, was not to understand anything and, if you understand anything, I congratulate you. I have darkness in my eyes. I don't see a thing.'

It was all becoming an experience like no other: the old ghosts were trying to flee her body and escape to somewhere safe before it was too late; those old tyrannical ghosts which had haunted the interstices of her being for years, often quiet and dormant, when she was quiet and dormant, but now vicious and brawling in the moments of her greatest stress, even mixing up their lines as they struggled desperately to escape the prison bars of this dying, old actress.

'I'm lucky, Horace!' she cried as she continued to pound herself to death on the anvil of her unrelenting and unquenchable passions. 'I've always been lucky and I'll be lucky again.'

'Now I'm going to stop here for one more minute,' she cried as she finally began feeling all those lovely pills moving in on her various levels of pain. 'It's as if I'd never seen before what the walls of this house were like. And now I look at them avidly with such tender love.'

Oh it was all such a Lisa Moran moment really. Only she could have managed something like this, standing there in the encroaching darkness, watching all her ghosts escaping out of her, waiting and hoping to die – *waiting and hoping* – and fuck all was happening. Nothing. And there she was only feeling slightly sleepy, as fit as a flea and ready to rock.

Women attempt suicide more than men but men are far more successful at it, she had once read. But not today they wouldn't be. She had more balls than any mere man. John O had often put it about that she was the most difficult woman in England and, if difficult is what they wanted, she could do difficult all right. As of this moment she was breezily sailing out of everything.

So she just stood there, her head to one side and the focus of her eyes gone as she washed down yet more pills with yet more brandy. Now, after her earlier roar of life, she could at least feel her legs finally turning to stone and she welcomed that. Finally, she lost her balance and went staggering backwards, pulling the sheets off the chairs, falling hard against the wall, though somehow still managing to stay on her feet as yet another ghost tried to make a run for it. 'Give me my ... my ... give me ...' The words dried up in her mouth. Boos and jeers echoed in her ears. She held up a hand to placate the impatient bastards in the audience. She'd get there. 'Just give me a fucking break will you? Everyone needs a fucking break now and then. I have immortal longings ...' She choked again. 'I have ... immortal longings ...'

No one has ever recited blank verse more blankly than Lisa Moran at the Old Vic last night. Her delivery was so wooden she must once have been apprenticed to a carpenter.

'… immortal longings …'

It has to be conceded that Lisa Moran is the sweetest and most lovable Goneril on record…

'Darling, I don't think we need to go to the market tomorrow. All we're short of is bacon. We can always send Harry on Monday.'

'But I like to go to the market, *chérie*. I like the bustle and the noise.'

She'd gone and lost control of her breathing and needed to stretch back her head to get enough air and relax her neck muscles. And what is more that patch of blue mould had returned on the ceiling. British builders! *Three* times they had been called in to fix the guttering and still the rain was coming in. Fucking unbelievable, that's what it was. No one gave value for money any more. Grab, grab, grab. She on the other hand had always given her very blood. Out on those boards she had even offered up her life.

'I think I'll go to bed soon, darling. I can feel a really nasty migraine settling in so perhaps it'll give me a miss if I can get to sleep first.'

Now gently, Lisa. Softly. Sorrowing. The end is coming and you love this man more than anyone else in the whole world.

It was all coming down now as she prepared her neck for the guillotine. Her voice was blazing fitfully, fluting with passion and pain. She tried to grab hold of the stage curtain but fell to her knees instead.

Lisa, I'm just going to have to give you more notes on this part.

'Oh not more notes, Peter. No more fucking notes. Give them to the critics. I'm all undone now, can't you see? There's nothing left, nothing but the wind and the rain. Nothing but.'

Shadowy spectres flitted through the misty distance. Fires began breaking out in the iceberg's heart. Sounds without echoes, winds without movements, mirrors without reflections. A knock on the door. 'Oh Jean-Paul, please come in, please come in and hold me for a while because I can't seem to cope with all this pain washing around inside me on my own, can't cope at all because it's all got too painful.'

An ominous shape began growing deep inside a black shadow and a thin sliver of light outlined its form. Bulging muscles, bandana-ed head, the narrow oblong of an assault rifle. A hand whacked her head from side to side but her screams were silent, her mind an explosion of concussive stars which kept winking and drifting. 'But it has everything to do with you. Your blood is my blood. I am your mother. I brought you to this country in the first place.'

And I am the evil of your loins, mother darling. I am the evil that you actually brought into the world. Bring me your violence and I will reward you with life eternal.

The rifle butt smashed into her face and kept on smashing into it until she was a mass of bloody cuts and bruises. She couldn't even speak any more, just kept spitting out her broken teeth.

Lisa's body was freezing cold when her eyes snapped open in the moonlight and she saw a mouse sniffing around the edges of one of the sheets draped over the furniture. The mouse picked up something in its tiny paws and began sniffing it with quivering nostrils before dropping it and wandering off out of sight with its shiny tail sliding along behind it.

She tried to turn her head to follow the mouse's path but couldn't move a muscle, not even her hand which was lying in front of her face like a frozen claw. The fingers were heavy with the gold rings of all her men. All her men! What sick jokes they were. She could just about glimpse them dancing around her paralysed body in joy were they to see what had happened to her now. But what *had* happened to her exactly? She considered her position with a surprisingly clear mind and remembered the brandy and the pills and her determination to take the highway to hell.

Well she had clearly failed yet again and was well and truly stuck in this life, probably suffering from extreme hypothermia, judging by the way every part of her body refused to budge so much as an inch.

The mouse sauntered back into view again and she couldn't quite believe how calm she was. She had always hated mice – and spiders, slugs and snails and anything else that might come out from under a stone – everything like that had always put the willies up her so it was very odd that she had even considered going to live in the country let alone actually gone and done it. Poor Jean-Paul was forever being summoned to get rid of this or carry out that and he had always done it very sweetly, never once complaining about her city slicker ways.

The mouse pressed on with its exploration, sniffing its way through a patch of moonlight and disturbing dust motes in the air all around it. It even began moving towards her again and she wanted to waggle her fingers at it, to shoo the thing away but she still couldn't move a single, sodding thing from her big toe up.

Was this death perhaps? Was this the death, the necessary end, that will come when it will come, that Shakespeare was always going on about. There was no pain, no feeling of any kind, just this all-embracing paralysis which was keeping her laid out on the floorboards watching this mouse moving about. Well one thing was for sure. If this was the necessary end she didn't want to end up lying *here* for all eternity. But it couldn't be death could it? You couldn't be dead if you were lying on the floorboards watching a fucking mouse moving about. Shakespeare had never come up with a scene like this and, anyway, death removed you from the physical world and you were surely given a more supernatural role like being a ghost or something.

So this, evidently, wasn't death at all. But she would die soon, she *would*, and, as she waited for the end, the shadow of her favourite role fell over her and she knew that Hedda had come to see her off, that that crazed suburban Lady Macbeth had come to be with her at her end. It was fitting, she supposed; it had a certain healing poetry about it since Hedda had probably shaped her own life and personality more than any other of her ghosts and was here now for her famous final scene. Like her, Hedda had had all kinds of problems, usually to do with love and men, and they were now together sharing a pointless suicidal ending to an absolutely pointless life.

Then something did move inside her, not a limb or even a muscle but a dribble out of the side of her mouth, thick and warm like blood. Without warning, her chest let rip with a small cough, making her dribble even more and scaring both her and the mouse who cleared off fast. She found she could move her lips too, tasting the brandy and fragments of Valium which had got lodged in her teeth.

She wasn't dead at all, she realised with a start, nor even close to it. She hadn't learned her lines properly again, ignored the director and plunged into it, busking it and hoping for the best. Every move and detail had to be orchestrated meticulously to make a success of a scene as big as this. Suicide is a difficult, complex business and she had lost enough friends to know how to do it properly by now. Pills had to be popped singly and not rammed down in fistfuls any old how. They don't stay down unless you put layers of sandwiches on top of them; that was the very first rule of the successful suicide, the very first fucking rule of them all.

The mouse's whiskers returned to the edge of the moonlight, probably trying to work out if it was safe to go walkabout again without being coughed at. Well go on then. The cat's not away exactly but she is far too knackered to get her claws into you.

A long silence followed as a few more bits of pills detached themselves from her teeth like fillings coming loose while a migraine began building up in the front of her forehead, a good reminder that she was still very much clinging to her frail humanity. There was a tinkling in the distance which got louder and then stopped. It had been a bit like beer cans clinking together and she tried to move her body when those beer cans began rattling together again only to stop.

The door creaked open and, with a snap of the light switch, the whole room flooded with light and the mouse fled for good. Footsteps were moving around the room, light footsteps which she didn't recognise. Not Jean-Paul's. A pair of expensive new brogues stood directly in front of her nose. 'Jesus Christ,' a voice shouted as a hand felt down the side of her neck. 'Jesus H Christ.'

She recognised the voice though. Oh bugger me black and blue with a broken bottle. It was that shit from *The Sun*. Oh no. Almost anyone but him. She wanted to protest but could only find a faint wheeze as he hauled her up by both hands around her belly whereupon the bastard began shaking her up and down like a rag doll. I beg your fucking pardon, Terry Maven, but are you trying to kill me or what?

Well he was certainly doing something to her since, after yet another good shaking, she went 'Whaaaaaargh!' as she vomited up brandy, pills and God knows what else all over his shoes. 'Whaaaargh!' she went again as he kept her hanging there, eyes bulging and arms dangling as he shook another gallon of puke out of her. It was going everywhere on the floorboards and she did hope that he was going to clean it all up after he'd finished throttling her like this.

'Come on now Lisa, let's get some more up now. Per-le-heeese, Lisa. Pretty per-le-heeeeese.'

Her defeat was total and all she could think of was that her life was being saved by *The Sun*, if you please. Almost anyone or anything except the fucking *Sun*.

'Lisa, it's me, Terry Maven. Come on and get it all out now. Per-le-heeese.'

'Whaaaargh!,' she went again. 'Whaaaaargh! Whaaaaargh! Whaaaaargh!'

THIRTY EIGHT

Daniel, in a black T-shirt and a pair of navy trousers, sat on the edge of the fountain in Trafalgar Square, watching the rising sun hold the National Gallery in its palely yellow hands and strike the black rumps of the Landseer lions in large, round splashes of luminescence. It was still early and only the occasional car or bus circled the square as the pigeons foraged among the gilded cobbles.

This was a day which promised to be eventful in old London town and he wanted to be a part of it, to run with it, since he was out and about actively looking for an end to his book on London. Having worked on it for so many years he had found that, despite repeated attempts, he was unable to just sit down and *create* an end. He needed to *experience* an end which would then tell him the work was over, that it was done.

He was convinced he would know when this happened but the real trouble was he didn't actually believe he would ever find an end, created or experienced, and maybe he had condemned himself to some endless Sisyphean labour which would stay with him all his life. Perhaps he simply didn't want his work to end anyway: he had known others who had taken on small tasks which had grown into life-long obsessions and maybe that's what had happened here. It had long struck him as a peculiarly strange fate: to be a Welshman obsessed by the hidden interiors of the capital of England.

The sun intensified its bold brilliance, turning the windows of Canada House into oblongs of light, filling the glass bowls of the street lamps with their own radiance and making the spume of the hissing fountains come alive with sparkling reels. A stage had been erected around some scaffolding at the base of Nelson's column and the sound system was being bolted into place.

Sunlight in fountains turn them into constantly moving paintings which talk like babies excitedly putting together their first tumbling sentences, Daniel wrote in his notebook. *But what are these fountains talking about this morning when there is such a great level of threat in the air?*

The Metropolitan Drinking Fountain and Cattle Trough Association built more than fifty fountains like these, based on the city's old medieval system of pumps, conduits and wells. Some in the city had even worshipped these sparkling miracles so much that, in 90AD a London canon ordered that every priest 'industriously advance Christianity and forbid the worship of fountains'.

So there it was: more archaic information which looked as if it was going to keep plodding around his brain for ever, tying up all his little cells in their dusty grip for all time.

A group of men had begun preparing the square's defences, slapping grease on the lamp posts and the sides of the Landseer lions while an optimistic ice cream vendor, given the extreme earliness of the hour, turned up with his van only to be moved on again. Next, the fountains themselves were switched off and drained and there was a swelling sound of increasing traffic leaving a light grey trail of noxiousness in its wake. A man was picking up coins left in the drained pools and an elderly car failed to start at the traffic lights only to splutter into life after another man got out of it and gave it a push. A loud argument broke out between two men who were fixing the loudspeakers about something or other that had been left behind and the policemen with binoculars on the rooftops followed the row with particular care.

Other policemen kept arriving in increasing numbers to take up their allocated positions around the square. Passers-by stopped uncertainly only to move on again after receiving the hardest of stares from the police. Even the Japanese tourists, who photographed everything, were told to move on if they attempted to take photographs. Daniel crossed the square and watched further busloads of police drawing up in Horse Guards Parade on the other side of Admiralty Arch. Horses clip-clopped along The Mall, their huge nostrils snorting. A bearded tramp came shuffling out of St James's Park and began shouting obscenities at the mounted police who ignored him and rode on. Two minutes later a police van arrived and carted off the tramp, still shouting loudly.

The rhythms of this awakening morning became more intense as a helicopter hovered overhead for a full minute before heading off in the direction of Fleet Street. Daniel walked up towards Downing Street, home of the Prime Minister, Mrs Margaret Thatcher, noticing the surveillance everywhere, the men on rooftops watching the every move of every person through binoculars, the rifles kept at the ready, the messages whispered into concealed walkie-talkies. A double line of police stood guard at the entrance to Downing Street while no one at all was being allowed into the street, let alone to knock on the hallowed door of Number 10. A drunk Irishman, with the tail of his shirt hanging out of the back of his trousers, did try to start a bit of a rant but he too was quickly picked up by a police van and carted away. You could have been living in some corrupt banana republic, the way these people were so quickly spirited away in vans.

He walked on for a while until he noticed a New York Yellow Cab going down Horse Guards Parade, stopping briefly to let out three passengers who didn't pause to look at one another — or around — before hurrying off down a side street. They could have just come from an all-night fancy dress party since one was almost completely naked, apart from a loincloth and a bandolier of ammunition criss-crossing his chest, another wore a bulky overcoat and had a Mohican haircut and the other, an awesomely muscular type, wore motor bike leathers with thick sunglasses. They could also have been carrying guns — Daniel couldn't be too sure from this distance — and no sooner had they disappeared than the Yellow Cab drove away at speed.

He strode on briskly, unwilling to even consider the question of the real identities of those three men or what they were about. He was finding himself thinking a lot about Lisa and vaguely decided he might call on her later that morning after all this was over. He hadn't seen her for ages but still thought about her a lot and certainly missed the loopy courage she had often instilled in him. She was always a volatile handful for sure but he now understood why she had always been a writers' moll because she had ways of stiffening their resolve when almost no one gave a damn what they did or wrote. Just by being what she was, she always gave them the courage to be.

Crowds came spooling out of Charing Cross Station at the end of the Strand in disorganised surges dictated by the arrivals of their trains. Many were carrying placards or furled flags and they had none of the wide-eyed awe of provincials coming up to the big city for The Cup. These proclaimed their seriousness in their clothes, in their dark, baggy sweaters, their torn jeans and street-fighting Doc Marten shoes. It was clear that not one of them had spent an hour preening themselves in a mirror before they went out that morning; that they had all just tumbled out of bed and grabbed whatever clothes had been at hand. Some of the girls had made one concession to make-up: thick daubs of black kohl around their eyes which made them look more like professional Victorian mourners than girls moving into the prime of their young lives. The boys wore the odd earring but their heads had been shorn in the skinhead style, giving them an air of violent brutality which the rest of their 'Don't fuck with me' clothes did nothing to diminish.

So these are Thatcher's outcast children, all coming back to haunt mother, uninvited and unruly, and about as welcome as floating turds in a country house swimming pool, Daniel wrote in his notebook. *The politicised hard Left, coming from the slums of Manchester, Birmingham and Liverpool, all in mourning for their lost and frustrated ideals and, when the young lose their ideals, they become dangerous.*

As they began gathering on the Embankment in readiness to begin their march Daniel also note-booked a corresponding build-up of Special Branch. Generally these men were fatter and burlier than the average weedy, black-clad demonstrator, dressed in casual clothes from Marks & Spencer and – that great giveaway – a short back and sides hair-cut, almost *de rigueur* in the New Scotland Yard canteen. These men took an avid and active interest in everything from the odd joint being passed around to the out-of-date tax discs on their rackety vans. Occasionally they cut away from the main groups to report such 'facts' to other men in Marks & Spencer casuals who duly slipped behind a bush to report them back to Head Office on their mobile radios.

The International Marxist Group had a lot of people, many with crash helmets, here this morning as did what was left of Gerry Healey's Workers' Revolutionary Party. Anarchists waving their traditional black flags were in evidence as were the somewhat more moderate members of the All London Anti-Poll Tax Federation along with representatives of the National Union of Teachers, the National Union of Mineworkers and the Transport and General Workers' Union.

Yet what was more interesting and compelling about those convening here on the Embankment were those who had come unannounced and concealed, Daniel thought. He had no doubt that invisible demons were on the loose in these demonstrating streets and that there were far more than the three he had spotted piling out of that Yellow Cab near Horse Guards Parade.

Whistles sounded and stewards shouted orders through loud-hailers when the march finally began. Up went a wonky forest of placards making various demands like BREAK THE TORY POLL TAX or THATCHER OUT or PISS ON THE POLL TAX and off they all went in faltering, ragged lines. Daniel fell in behind a group from Smethwick as they moved off and he knew there was going to be serious trouble when he smelled petrol on the man next to him. The white faces of the patrolling police officers also told they were expecting trouble which, with passions running so high and everyone behaving so twitchily, they were not entirely confident they could contain.

The chanting march could not have been moving for more than ten minutes, with a tremendous build-up of airless heat all around, when the police, clearly acting on pre-arranged signals, tried to arrest one of the demonstrators. Daniel couldn't see who it was exactly but a snatch squad rushed in to take out this miscreant only to fail, leading to a lot of shoving and pushing. Television cameras were quickly focusing on the active centre of the trouble and even seemed to be encouraging it before the snatch squad retired empty-handed and the trouble settled back into an uneasy calm. The increased hostility was now palpable.

For no clear reason the marchers began to surge forward in strange common rushes of energy and he could hear children yelping as mothers attempted to pick them up, to keep them safe in their arms. These yelpings were quite chilling and Daniel decided he didn't want to be part of this any more, that he really had better go home because he was being scared by what he was feeling rather than seeing. Something very bad was going on and he had caught a glimpse of three more Yellow Cabs parked up a side street and wondered how many more of them there were in the city that morning and who, exactly, they were ferrying around.

But, as it happened, he could not escape the march now because he had been caught directly in the middle of an almighty crush of bodies and, in the distance, where he guessed might be the outskirts of Trafalgar Square, three policemen on horseback were laying into the crowds with their truncheons, just clubbing heads indiscriminately. The attacked people were roaring with an anger which seemed to be rolling back behind them in waves, making sporadic bursts of violence break out all around him. He couldn't go back and he couldn't go forward: it was bad enough trying to breathe properly. He spotted the occasional fortunate group which had managed to take shelter in porches and doorways but, when he did try to reach them, he found himself being carried forward again towards those clubbing policemen. He realised that if he did lose his balance, he would almost certainly be trampled to death.

Somewhat ominously, men in black balaclavas had gathered around him carrying weapons, not guns as such but knives and flails. One flung a metal death star towards a policeman and others were rolling ball bearings to upset the horses' footing. Daniel could see that these men in balaclavas were causing most of the trouble, hurling objects at the police, not in some aimless gesture of protest but carefully and accurately, hurting the police horses and making them snort with pain and rear up in terror. Despite what the media were later to report Daniel knew these people in balaclavas weren't who they were pretending to be, that they were a different species altogether, here, now, next to him, and really hurting those police horses.

These masked men were driving the riot and he desperately wanted to see their eyes but couldn't because he wanted to stay alive even more desperately. He found himself running with a group directly into Trafalgar Square where the police were making direct charges into crowds which had by now become so inflamed they were fighting back with whatever was available: scaffolding, placards and even the odd Thermos flask.

One youth hurled a tubular steel chair at the police – where the hell had he got that? – while the rest of the makeshift missiles soared up and clattered down from all directions, so scaring one police horse it reared up and threw its rider. Other youths moved forward wielding scaffolding pipes before they were forced back by another line of police dressed in riot gear and carrying plastic shields and batons. It was all like some sort of aimless African war with intense outbursts of violence followed by short periods of calm when the demonstrators turned away as if they'd just got fed up by it all before they decided to get down to it again and, almost as one, make another charge.

Unable to do anything else, Daniel ran through an opening between the scaffolding-wielding demonstrators and the baton-charging police directly into the square. Suddenly, a petrol bomb flamed up into some workmen's cabins, sending up a bursting explosion which made whirling fire shoot along the roofs. A car was overturned and set alight as screaming mobs ran one way and another only to be driven back by the counter-charging police. Windows were being smashed with a bright musical regularity and, when Daniel did spot what looked like a good place to shelter, the police came after him and he had to run for it again or he would certainly have been clubbed to the ground too.

Nothing made any sense as the drifts of black smoke made this picture of evil chaos all the more vivid. Even the two helicopters swirling around Lord Nelson directly above them seemed frightened and confused as they kept quartering the skies. A youth slipped in a pool of blood banging his head against the side of one of the empty fountains and a steward was calling for order through his loud-hailer when he was almost literally mown down by a marching phalanx of police. Every foot of the square seemed to be full of fighting with huge mobile television cameras on the top of vans moving this way and that – there a rioter hanging off a lamp-post, stripped to the waist and waving a placard saying DON'T COLLECT, DON'T PAY, there a policeman being knocked to the ground and kicked senseless – collecting all these images which were being sprayed up into the implacably indifferent sunshine in dark rainbows of terror.

Every time Daniel did spot an opening – and made for it – it seemed to fill up with fighting, with television cameras locking on the active centres of the trouble, their electronic strings puppeteering every move. When things got to a certain intensity, these seemed to transform into another soaring arc of terror which, in turn, darkened and flamed the blue sky above. He knew things were happening to his mind again, that he shouldn't be here and he kept running around like some terrified ant trying to escape the blaze that was going to engulf him at any second.

Pausing to catch his breath he noticed the three men he had spotted earlier getting out of that Yellow Cab near Downing Street, running past him, the one with the Mohican haircut glaring at him with small, coal-black eyes before running after the others who looked like they were shouldering a medieval battering ram. Then they exploded and disappeared into yet another tottering wall of police who, at that stage, appeared to be taking a terrible beating.

In fact the police were far from beaten and, with every attack, they responded in kind, picking up the stones and placards and whatever, flinging them back at the demonstrators and making them madder than ever. By now Daniel had lost all desire and ability to run anywhere, so he just crouched down on the ground and covered his head with his arms, still gulping on his own astonishment. Then he heard a loud galloping of horses' hooves and felt a sharp blow on his side and a few thumps on his back before the whole of the bloody carnival swirling all around him came to a sudden and dark halt and he awoke in a hospital bed some three hours later covered in bumps and bruises.

'This is the Six O'Clock News from the BBC,' he heard from a distant television. 'A wholesale riot broke out at an anti-Poll Tax Rally in Trafalgar Square this afternoon. Police say this was the worst peace-time riot ever to take place in London. The damage will run into millions of pounds.'

THIRTY NINE

Lisa sat in the armchair in her room in the Chelsea Park Clinic gazing blankly at the television which was carrying the news of the latest disturbances in British prisons. She had never watched much television before but had found that, in her five days here, it was perfectly possible to gaze at the screen for hour after hour with barely anything registering on her consciousness: that she could sit in front of the thing like a rabbit dazzled and immobilised by a car's headlamps.

Yet given that she had recently tried to see herself off in Foxley Hall she was feeling almost alarmingly and distressingly alive. Her eyes had lost their lustre but otherwise she had felt some strange rekindlings of life which, loath as she was to admit it, might have been something to do with all that fucking dreadful television news.

In the absence of anything better to do – and certainly without the necessary concentration to pick up a book and read it – she had not only found it difficult to ignore the television news but had actually become interested in it.

This new fascination had begun the previous weekend with the Poll Tax Riot in Trafalgar Square, followed the next day, Sunday, April 1 – All Fools' Day – when a riot broke out in Strangeways Prison in Manchester. A fight had started during a service in the prison chapel and the inmates had fought their way out of the chapel to take control of the accommodation blocks where fifteen hundred of them set about destroying pipes, breaking basins, dragging their iron bedsteads out of their cells and setting the mattresses alight. One man awaiting trial on charges of buggery and indecent assault, Lisa learned from one bulletin, was attacked so savagely he later died in intensive care.

A few inmates climbed on to the rafters and punched their way through the slate roof from where they began throwing stones, bricks and slates down onto the exercise yard below. Soon there were thirty or so of them on the roof, sitting around a huge hole and throwing down the occasional missile. A stream of prisoners kept appearing on the roof before disappearing again, some returning in donkey jackets to keep warm and black balaclava helmets to disguise their identities. One waved a hastily painted placard saying NO POLL TAX HERE.

The BBC had almost immediately set up mobile television cameras in a warehouse opposite the prison, covering the roof-top events around the clock and, within hours, those prisoners rioting began shouting their demands to their reporters.

Lisa's mild interest in this riot, which had clearly been triggered by the televised violence in Trafalgar Square the day before, intensified when she then learned that dozens of other prisons were quickly amok with violence and riot, including Cardiff, Bristol and Dartmoor. Hostages had been taken and remand centres burned.

Yet what fascinated Lisa about the whole developing story was not the violence itself but how it was being recycled through television. What was all this but living proof that we were living in Daniel's time of the black rain? He had spoken to her about it often enough and here it was.

The usual 'experts' were being ushered onto programmes like *Newsnight* claiming all these riots were to do with bad prison conditions and such-like but, even as they spoke, Lisa sat in her armchair, with her knuckles going white as she gripped its arms, shouting: 'It's television you blind fuckers. Just turn off all the televisions in the prisons and everything would be fine.'

And as she sat there in her expensive room in her expensive clinic hearing reports of men plundering their ghastly prisons, shouting advice at the screen about what to do about them, she kept thinking of Daniel, that other man in her life who was also locked up in the prison of his own visions. Everything he had ever said to her about them was either true or becoming so.

So, even in his absence, Daniel was yet again showing his remarkable ability to stop her thinking about herself and, as she sat there for hour after hour with the television flickering endlessly in front of her, she found her mind and memory roaming over those lovely kissing nights when they would make a little gentle love. She even sometimes wanted it to be over quickly so they could have a good, invigorating chat into the small hours. He was always warm and relaxed after making love and then he would talk about all his visions like the black rain or those mobile television cameras in Brixton with their wheels of fire. His words always painted the world in completely new colours; you saw everything in a new way after you'd spent a few hours chatting with him.

A more literal-minded woman might well have dismissed his words as the ravings of a mad man but she had never, for one second, thought he was mad. He was just different with a remarkably sensitive perception of the way evil worked in the modern world, and she so wished she could be with him now, just to take hold of both his hands, put them together and kiss them and give him a good talking to. She knew he would be watching the news somewhere and be getting frightened *and* he would almost certainly be drinking again. So she wanted to be able to explain to him the absolute burning necessity of staying sober and being brave, how he should continue writing no matter what others said about his work and that, most of all, he should stand up for his visions and tell this banal, unbelieving world, in which they were both so badly floundering, what he believed to be true.

She flicked from channel to channel irritably because she could find no more news, violent or otherwise. Such thoughts were all very fine, of course, but, in reality, she didn't even know where the fuck Daniel was. The one telephone number she'd had of his had been disconnected and he had probably disappeared again into the wilds of the city where, maybe, he belonged. People like Daniel and herself shouldn't be allowed out, she thought. They should be shut away in Strangeways where they belonged although, at this rate, she would almost certainly end up in Broadmoor if she didn't stop shouting at the television.

Her next visitor was her agent, Karen Duffy, who sailed in wearing a big cloak, which had probably been nicked from Stratford-upon-Avon, and carrying a large bunch of lilies She put them down on the bed, as at a funeral, and reached out to take Lisa's shoulders before kissing her on both cheeks.

'Lisa, Lisa, Lisa,' she purred. 'I was so sorry to hear. My own baby, my greatest star. So sorry.'

'And do you know what the worst part of it was? All my life I've done quality work. With the single exception of that *Rebellion* film, everything I've done has been worthwhile and then – when I tried to take my own life – I'm saved by *The Sun*. Can you believe that, Karen? I'm saved by the shitbag *Sun*.'

Ms Duffy remained standing as she looked at Lisa carefully through her lorgnette. This was a rather famous stance which had long been used on West End producers prior to asking them for a lot more money for her stable of thespians. The whole lot were rumoured to be extremely fearful of Karen Duffy and her lorgnette look.

'To make matters worse you're now telling me *The Sun* still wants to run my life story and they're offering a lot of money too.'

'Yes, it is a lot of money, Lisa, and it's money you need to start over.'

'Oh what does it matter if they do run it? I mean to say who *cares*? At least I'll have enough to go and live somewhere quietly. Eastbourne, perhaps. You know, Karen, I've always fancied Eastbourne. Mad isn't it? I've never been there – hardly know where it is but that's where I want to retire.'

'But Eastbourne's lovely. On the sea with beaches and they've probably got a good amateur group there you could work with. Do a bit of directing perhaps?'

'No more fucking drama for this old drama queen, Karen. But I certainly don't want to live in London any more. Have you been following the news? I'm too old for all this rioting nonsense. Too old for London. Too old for every-thing. I was looking in that mirror this morning. It's all gone, my eyes, my looks, everything.'

'Lisa, you've been with me almost all your career. You'll get up there again. You've got yourself into messes before but you're a proper Mr Micawber. You keep falling into shit but you always come up smelling of roses. Look at Dame Peggy. She's eighty odd and she's just gone back to India.'

'No Karen. It's all finished for me. Peggy plays the field too but she's always been luckier in love. All my men were swine. Bar one and he was too young and otherwise engaged.' She lifted her hands and let them drop again. 'All right. Tell *The Sun* I'll tell all. You're right. The money will make a nice little nest egg. But I don't want dear old Charlie Judd getting his hands on it. He's still sniffing around looking for his suitcase you said?'

'Yes he is *and* I've got a funny feeling he might even have put *The Sun* on to you in the first place. But I must warn you they are quite excited about your les-bian activities. They'll be asking you about that. And what's all this about your spanking sessions with Kenneth? I never knew about that.'

'Oh just a bit of drunken horseplay Karen. And what was I supposed to do when Marlene came knocking on my door? Tell her to bugger off? Yes, I won't pull any punches. There has never been anything mealy-mouthed about Lisa Moran. But what was old Charlie Judd after? I mean why would he go to *The Sun?*'

'Revenge I suppose. Simple old revenge.'

'Revenge, revenge. What's the matter with men these days? I shouldn't have botched that suicide.'

'Please don't talk like that Lisa. It really does upset me.'

'I'm not going to try that again. Don't worry. But you should have seen it, Karen. You would have been very proud of me. Six roles all at the same time – Blanche, Regina, Juliet – *and* I can remember every word I said. No, don't worry. It was all far too exhausting and there's nothing worse than having your stomach pumped. Even life is better than that.'

'When are you getting out of here?'

'Well it had better be soon at the rates they charge and I've already got some-one asking about availability in some retirement home in Eastbourne.'

'Do you want me to tell Chesterton's that I'll be handling the sale of the house?'

'Oh would you, Karen darling? That would be a relief. A big relief. Also sort out anything I haven't thought of would you? I don't want to keep anything – *nothing at all* – and, if there's any money left over, send it to me in Eastbourne.'

'I would have thought there'll be a lot left over.'

'Not with *my* debts. I doubt there'll be a single penny. This recession has stuffed everyone. But by God I'll be happy to see the back of that witch in Downing Street. I'd die happy if they got rid of her.'

'Not dying again are we? Stop it will you.'

'Don't worry Karen darling. Everything's going to be just fine from now on. It's all going to be rinky dinky.'

Lisa had resolved that, by the time she got on to the train to Eastbourne, she was going to have just one suitcase, with her most basic undies and clothes and nothing else. All her *haute couture* rags had gone to the overwhelmed manager of the Oxfam shop in King's Road; all her paintings had been shipped to Christie's without a reserve and all her furniture had gone for criminally low prices to a shark who couldn't quite believe his luck. Even all her theatrical photographs with such as Bette – 'my sister across the water' – and Albert were binned ruthlessly. Her one great relief was that Percy her Peke had long gone to the Great Kennel in the Sky so he didn't have to share in all this indignity. From now on everything was going to be as fresh as paint, new as tomorrow.

In the one final act of exorcism she sat down with Terry Maven of *The Sun*, telling him that it would take about six hours to tell her life story and, give or take a quarter of an hour, that's about how long it took. Fortified by the odd Gaulloise and endless cups of coffee, which they both took it in turns to make, she even owned up to her exact age – sixty six! – and where she had been born – in Penang to a Scottish planter father, given to drink and long bouts of silence, and an eccentric English mother who was far more in love with her greyhound.

She described the miseries of her lonely childhood and how – like Bette – she had become a self-made man. Her mother packed her off to boarding school in England so that she could devote more time to her greyhound but Lisa was always in trouble and treated as an outsider by the rest of the girls largely, she suspected, because of the unusual bone structure of her strange face. Everyone taunted her and she was expelled from two schools for 'avid and voracious' lesbian activity. One teacher had actually caught her with her face between the legs of the head girl at Rodean. She was expelled after being there only five weeks – although it hardly mattered because she had been admitted to RADA by then mostly, she was to learn later, because her looks made the interviewing panel laugh. A face as unusual as that would take her far, they thought. 'In a way my face has been my doing and undoing. It's got me a lot of work and lost me a lot more.'

Men quickly came in pursuit of her face and there were women too including Marlene Dietrich who, if anything, was an even bigger bag of nerves than Lisa. They often had a session before a performance which calmed Marlene down sufficiently to face the public. 'She always suffered from serious stage fright unless she had sex in the dressing room and then she was usually fine. I say "usually" because it sometimes made her worse. I think I got a lot of bad habits from her; almost all my old male and female lovers have shaped me in some way or other which might be why I ended up in such a mess.'

But the lesbianism was all put aside when she met Godfrey, an actor-manager old enough to be her father. He was a complete gentleman who looked after her like a father and, after her loveless early family life, she had never felt so completely enfolded, so wonderfully loved. He lived for her – and she for him – and, when he died, she thought she was going to die too. In a sense her whole life became a search for another love like that but she never found it – or even came near.

Then there were three marriages: the first to an unknown artist which barely lasted a few months and she couldn't now remember anything at all about. 'He discovered that I'd had it off with someone else and he just couldn't live with it. He said he still loved me – and I believed him – but he simply couldn't stay with me after what I'd done. He was sorry, he said, but he simply couldn't rustle up the necessary level of forgiveness to carry on.'

She next married Willis, who was a bit star-struck and probably regarded her as some sort of trophy wife, and they got on fine for a while. She suspected she was still suffering from too much insecurity – probably after the splendid security afforded by Godfrey – since she then began rampaging around town remorselessly. 'Coco Chanel liked to rampage around Paris and I'm not sure she ever managed one hour of happiness. Any relationship is over when you begin playing the field like that. Nothing ever works without fidelity. That much I now do know. We always seem to learn the important things in life when it's too late, when too many have been hurt.'

She and Willis drifted apart and she now had her eyes fixed on the great new writing talent in the theatre, John Orlan. 'We never discussed setting up house together. It just sort of happened. It was the Sixties and we always seemed to be leaving one another then. It was all too easy really and having a bit of money helped of course. Poverty has probably kept more marriages together than it's broken up.'

She was married to John O for thirteen years, often taking the lead role in his plays at a time when he was churning them out regularly and had established himself as one of the leading playwrights in the world. But, even though it had a certain longevity about it, things began going wrong almost from the beginning, particularly after a series of miscarriages and two pregnancies which almost went the full term.

It was about here that her fluency deserted her for the first and only time and, without making any sort of comment, Maven just sat back waiting for her to recover her composure. In truth she had never really understood how important all these miscarriages had been in her narrative and how different it all might have been if she'd had a couple of kids of her own who she could have nurtured and worried over and who would have made her less self-obsessed.

'So it was never a restful relationship with John. We were always needling one another, always jealous of one another's successes and later all this stupid jealousy and competition could get quite violent as when I wouldn't do one of his plays and he tried to push me out of a car one night as we were travelling at speed around Sloane Square.

'We were always rushing off to Switzerland with bags of cash, but all our money never did us much good. We bought a large house in the South of France and found we spent most of our evenings discussing the servant problem. John had a bad drink problem and, if we ever checked into a hotel and there weren't a couple of bottles of fizz chilling, he would practically wreck the joint. I once found him rolling around the gutter outside our house. "If only the Press could see the great playwright now," I told him.

'Sexually, I would say it was good for maybe three months and then it was always poor so, particularly after the miscarriages, I was soon playing around again, often looking for cheap thrills like the odd spanking session with Tynan. John O never came close to understanding what rang my bells and would often get so drunk and frustrated he might start knocking me around or even trying to wound me. I didn't mind that too much though – a bit of sexual violence can sometimes be fun – but what it did mean in the end was that we lost our way together. Sexual violence is only ever for the moment: you can never build a stable relationship out of it, don't you think, Terry?'

'I wouldn't really know Miss Moran. I'm from the East End an' we don't do much sexual violence in the East End.'

'Oh come on. I thought they *invented* sexual violence in the East End. What about Jack the Ripper?'

'My family and friends I'm talking about. Jack the Ripper was never family; well, not the last time I looked.'

Lisa had got to like Terry Maven even if she had never developed any real rapport with him: he had clearly been poorly educated but had a quicksilver intelligence unsullied by any complicated ideas or big words. He was a reporter who wrote down what he saw and heard and she could see he was straight and that he thought her an extremely queer cove who probably deserved all she had coming to her.

'I split up with John O over Albert in the end. Albert and I started seeing one another and he even began following us on our holidays. I was pegging out my knickers in the South of France one afternoon and spotted Albert waving at me from the bushes. He came around later, claiming he just happened to be passing by, and then he and John sat on the beach discussing some film deal they were trying to put together.

'Albert even bought me a flat but it didn't work out with him so John and I ended up having this tremendous slanging match which went on in the Press for ages. He said he was going to lean over my coffin when I finally went down into the ground and spit straight in my eye.' Her eyes welled up a little before she took a firm grip on herself again. 'I responded, of course, but it never should have come to that *and* he never stopped loving me no matter what he might have said. He often rang me in the middle of the night long after we'd split up, usually drunk, although he did also call me in a few times when he was desperately ill, wanting to say goodbye.'

She also spoke of Andrei Barapov and how proud she had been of knowing him: how she mothered him a lot and arranged appointments for all his muscle and bone specialists, often wheeling him around there herself. 'He always wanted to marry me but I don't think it was ever love. Andrei had too many problems relating to his deprived Russian background and he was even more insecure than me, always wanting what he hadn't got. But he was so beautiful you forgave him everything. You only had to look at that classical face and into those blue eyes and you were his, no matter what stupid thing he'd done lately.'

She stuck a sharp stiletto into Charles Judd as best she could, insisting that, despite his early generosity to her, there had never been a sexual relationship, largely because what little he had he could never get up. 'Terry, we are talking total chipolata here. *No*, it was even smaller than that *and* shrivelled up all the time.' *So stick that in your pipe Charlie, darling.*

Yuri and Avie also got extremely scathing reviews and she went into the making of the first *Rebellion* film in some detail, relating how the great action hero Yuri was afraid of little things like insects. Avie barely knew what they were doing script-wise, pretty much making it up as he went along. When in doubt with the script, he would let loose a hail of bullets or set up a few petro-chemical explosions.

The one man she didn't talk about was Daniel simply because she didn't really know what to say about him; couldn't even start to describe a relationship which had lasted longer than all the others and yet had come to so little. They had been through pretty much everything but, in a sense, he hadn't really ever been there: he had always been somewhere else. It had often felt as if she was going out with some abstracted ghost who was not really anyone's because he was constantly trying to deal with that civil war inside him.

But he was gone now, along with all the rest of them and she was booked into a retirement home on the seafront in fucking Eastbourne.

The final hour of the interview was devoted to Frog One and, despite his desertion, she was surprised at the devotion of her tone and the esteem in which she still held him. She told of how Ava Gardner had introduced them to one another in the Café Royal one Christmas Day and how he had immediately whisked her off to the Cotswolds and shown her their very own Tara.

She had never had a practical nature – couldn't even put up a shelf, in fact – but, together with workmen and a sympathetic architect, they had contrived to work on Foxley Hall unceasingly and unrelentingly, living in one room at first before fixing the almost non-existent roof and the sagging floors and replacing timbers which had been eaten away by the death watch beetle. Every week presented a new challenge but they gradually managed to put it all together again and, after five years hard work, had restored it to its former glory.

'I had never been so happy or excited. Every day was a new day and on some days we had worked so hard we would lie down on the floor and fall asleep in one another's arms. Happiness, I think, only ever comes from achievement and I'm still so proud of what we achieved with Foxley Hall. That restoration was the only thing I've ever been proud of but the recession came and ruined everything. One minute we were happy and the next it was all taken from us. Jean-Paul announced he couldn't cope and went back to live in France. Meanwhile I, up to my armpits in debt, am now going to live in a retirement home. And that is pretty much that really.'

A few important bits had been edited out but it felt a good interview, possibly the most honest she had ever given. You always gave away parts of yourself in interviews – which was why she had never liked doing them – but it now seemed necessary to give the whole lot away truthfully. Completely wasted on *The Sun*, of course, but essential to her decision to renounce her old life and start anew. *Beauty is truth and truth is beauty – that is all ye know on earth and all ye need to know.* A pity, really, she didn't give the truth more of a run years ago. There had been too many lies which had led to her own undoing. Maybe she should have just stuck to that unknown artist she had first married.

FORTY

Her condition remained fragile when, five days later, she found herself sitting in a much-depleted drawing room in Cheyne Walk for the last time, almost ready and almost willing to call for a cab which would take her to Victoria Station and hence to Eastbourne. But not quite. This was her final London curtain call for sure and she was feeling cold as she sat there next to her one and only suitcase, shivering along with the echoing emptiness of the place and all the oblong blank spaces along the walls where her treasured paintings had once hung.

The front door bell rang and, without taking her usual precautions as to the caller's identity because she was way past caring, she went down the stairs to open the door and was surprised at how high her battered old heart leaped when she found Daniel standing there. 'Daniel, how nice. It seems I haven't seen you for ever. Just stand there and let me look at you.'

But he didn't look good. His face was taut and grey with several newish scars on his cheeks and what looked like the remnants of a black eye. Even his eyeballs looked dull, there was none of the usual sparkly panic in them. 'You *are* all right are you?'

'Yes and no. But I *am* all right.'

'You've been back on the booze haven't you? I can always tell.'

'Well I did have one slip but only one. I got caught in that Poll Tax riot in Trafalgar Square and even had a few days in hospital.'

'I never saw you as a rioter and since when did you worry about the Poll Tax?'

'I was just there you know, taking a look at things and I sort of got run over.'

'I see. Come in, come in. You've just caught me before I leave for good.'

'Leaving for good? Anywhere nice?'

'I don't want to talk about it. Look, don't stand there making the street untidy. Come on in.'

She followed him up the stairs and trailed him around the empty drawing room. 'I've always loved this room,' he said. 'In fact I've always loved this room almost as much as I've loved the woman who lives in it.'

She thought she was going to faint. She really was in an unusually fragile state. 'Oh Daniel, don't start all that again. Let me see if they've left me enough in the kitchen to make you a cup of tea.'

'But I do love you, you know, and I've only just come to understand how much. Marry me, Lisa.'

'Marry? Love? What happened to you in Trafalgar Square? They must have hit you on the head with something very big. You were an unbeliever on matters of love when we first met. Only marry for money, you said.'

'Oh I've changed since then. *You* changed me.'

'Well change back. I liked you the way you were and anyway it's too late for all that nonsense. I'm going into a retirement home in Eastbourne.'

'Eastbourne! Where's Eastbourne?'

'I don't know. How the fuck would I know but that's where I'm going.'

'Is it by the sea? Right, fine. I'll come and live with you there. I'm fed up with writing. We'll retire together.'

'Don't be so silly.'

'I'm not being silly. You and me, we'll sit on the beach in the mornings and I'll read you the whole of Dickens for a start. That should get us through the first six months.'

'Why the fuck would I ever want to listen to Dickens? The only words I ever wanted to hear were ones written by you.'

'Fine. We'll sit on the beach in the mornings and I'll read you the whole of Jenkins. But I'm telling you now that Dickens is a whole lot better.'

'Nonsense! When did Dickens ever see a vision?'

'First chapter of *Our Mutual Friend*, I think.' His tone darkened. 'I've been having a lot of trouble with my own visions lately.

'You wouldn't believe what I've been seeing. There were things running around in the middle of Trafalgar Square that we know nothing about and I've been trying and trying to get hold of you. I kept calling here but there was no one around. Where've you been anyway?'

Now it was her turn to get vague as her mind caught a glimpse of herself choking down all those pills. 'Here and there, darling. Here and there.'

'You're not looking very bright yourself. Have you been ill?'

'Nothing serious. A bout of 'flu that's all.'

'Marry me, Lisa. I know things haven't been too good for you but marry me and we'll work hard to make one another happy. I've got a bit of money; it won't keep you in The Dorchester but I'm not skint.'

'This is all getting very stupid. I can't think.'

'Don't think. Just say yes.'

'No, no, no. And what about Helen?'

'Yes, yes, yes.'

'No, no, no. Stop it Daniel. Stop all this now. We *can't* live together. We've tried it and it just doesn't work and you've got a good woman.'

'Lisa, I sit in a room all day long staring at a blank sheet of paper. Things have been bursting through to me, Lisa, starburst things out of the sky, awful *visions* that scare the crap out of me and I need you around me because you are the only person in the world who can help me with them. You're my only chance and I *will* make you happy.'

'Oh for God's sake don't start crying again. Don't start all that. Look, Daniel, the simple truth is I'm far too old for you. Our ages have come between us.' She took a deep breath and almost managed the truth. 'Daniel, I'm nearly sixty. I've always been slippery on that subject but I'm nearly sixty.'

'That's not old.'

'Yes it is. It's absolutely fucking ancient and it's about twenty years older than you.'

'You're saying you don't love me, then?'

'No. Yes. No. Oh darling, sit down and relax will you? There must be another chair here somewhere.'

'What happened to that nice black leather chair? I used to like sitting in that.'

'It went to auction like everything else. Did you expect me to keep it here just in case you felt like calling? I didn't even know where you were. I'm not psychic you know.'

'Don't start getting your hair off. I was only asking.'

'That's always been your trouble hasn't it? You leave me. You come back. You expect everything to be the same. Then you want to know where your chair is – as if I'm sitting here polishing the thing all fucking day long, waiting for you to deign to sit in it. I've got a fucking life of my own to lead you know. A life of my own. But that's always been your problem hasn't it? So just get out. Go on. Out *now*. I'm going to a fucking retirement home in Eastbourne. I'm going to get a nice room with an *en suite* bathroom and a television and a view of the sea.'

'But you've always hated television.'

'Well I'm going to learn to love it. I'm going to change Daniel. Change in a big way.'

'Do you know what they talk about all the time in retirement homes? Bowel movements. That's all old people care about in retirement homes. Bowel movements. You're going to hate it in there.'

'No I won't. I'm going to love every moment of it *and* I've always adored talking about bowel movements. Now get out, go on.' She began pushing him, none too gently, out on to the landing. 'Go on now ... it's not what we inherit from our mothers and fathers that haunts us. It's all kinds of old defunct theories ...'

'Stop this Lisa will you? Stop this now.'

She began blinking a lot. She had sailed close to the edge again, she knew, but there was nothing to be done about it now. 'It's not that they actually live on in us. They are simply lodged there. I've only to ...'

'Lisa, stop all this now. Please.'

'I've only to pick up a newspaper and I see ghosts sliding between the lines. You understand all that, don't you Daniel? Ghosts between the lines. Lots and lots of ghosties.'

They began wrestling at the top of the stairs and she would have thrown him down them if she'd got a proper purchase on one of his arms. 'Lisa, stop this will you? I can't ... Lisa, *stop!*'

He brought his hand around and slapped her hard on the side of her head. 'Daniel, what's going on with me?' she cried, wrapping her arms around his shoulders to stop herself falling. 'What's going on? I can't cope any more. I've got no one left in my life and we shouldn't be quarrelling like this. Let's try friendship again. What do you say? And there's a few things I *must* tell you about. Let's go out for dinner. We'll go out and have a nice dinner and we'll become great friends and then I'm going to Eastbourne. It's going to be that easy, Daniel. I'm going to make it that easy.'

They walked hand in hand to their favourite Thai restaurant in Kensington, sat down on the vast cushions in the basement and there, in the spice-laden candlelight, she even began feeling quite sexy, leaning into him a lot as they fed slivers of satay and fat prawns to one another. She then explained, as calmly as she could in the circumstances, that she had tried to kill herself in Foxley Hall and that she had been missing from Cheyne Walk because she had been recovering in a private clinic. He looked at her shocked, appetite gone.

'We are now going to become real, good friends and you can come and visit me occasionally in Eastbourne,' she went on, picking up another prawn and squinting into its big, dead eyes before waving it in a small circle in the air and dropping it back on the plate.

Dishes were taken away as other steaming dishes arrived but, by now, they had both lost their appetite. 'Just friendship then,' he said.

'Just friendship. Daniel, you're the beautiful, talented son I ought to have had. But you've got your Helen. She's clearly a good woman so you should just settle down with her and write. That's all there is to it. Sit down and write.'

'If only it were that easy but I've been seeing visions again and I just hate what I've been left with. I'd known that Poll Tax riot had been coming for weeks which is why I was there. We'd had footage of riots in the Soviet Union. Shootings in South Africa. Unrest in Romania. Then Trafalgar Square,

Strangeways and the other prisons. It's all linked. We are locked together in a long season of black rain and it's killing us all. And what is more all this only ever works with the same sort of people by which I mean the black, the poor, the uneducated and the dispossessed. The media is busy bolting a girdle of violence around the world and we are going to die under its weight.'

'So why can't you write about all that?'

He shook his head decisively. 'I don't want to get involved. All this has *nothing* to do with me. This is God's problem and I only just wish he would shut up about it. And if he won't shut up about it I really do need us to get together because you're the only one who can help me to deal with it. I need you Lisa. You are the only one who's ever been prepared to stand up against God.'

'You don't need me. All you need is to sit down and write.'

'I saw things you wouldn't believe in that riot in Trafalgar Square. I saw demons busy driving the riot; demons that no one else knew were there and only the other night I saw London the way I saw Paris the first time we went there. I was walking over Blackfriars Bridge and the whole of the city rose up in fire. A red midnight sun hung over me and it was as if some vast tormented soul was trying to escape the flames. Then there was a shadowy figure rising up on the back of a wheel, exploding into flames and falling back into the river. I've had enough Lisa. I can't stand any of this any more.'

'Daniel, I'm going to beat you up so badly if you're not careful. This is wonderful stuff and you must write about it. You must put all these visions of yours into that book on London which you've been working on for ever. You're so stupid, you know. You talk as if God gives you these visions because he hates you or because he's got it in for you in some way. But even a vision of fire is a vision of love can't you see? Every single one of them has been a vision of love and they've all been yours. You've been given these visions because God is prepared to trust you with them. So stop being afraid of him and start writing about them.'

'So how do you suggest I start going about it?'

'You're being wet now. Start at the beginning you stupid fucker.'

'And where is the beginning?'

'You're the writer; I'm just an old actress. But do you think I've never known what terror means? I know all there is to know about forgotten lines and destructive critics. I've puked up behind proscenium arches time and time again, wishing I was dead. But I've always loved it once I did get on to the stage and into the play. Always. No matter how punishing the role I've always found redemption in giving myself to it.'

She glared at him, picked up a handful of prawns and flung them at the restaurant wall, making the other diners duck for cover.

'All you've got to do is give yourself, body and soul, to your readers. Nothing else matters. You'll enjoy it. The rest of what you do is a mystery but, if you try, *you will win.* So go home and write about your visions and the city in which you find yourself. Tell the world what's going on.'

Three waiters began busily clearing their table in case she decided to fling anything else around.

'There are millions out there dying of worry about violence and crime. It's killed America and it's killing this country. And you understand the reasons because God has explained them to you. I'd die for you myself if I could. Oh Daniel I'd give you all the courage and passion in the world if I could. But I can't and now I'm going to bury myself in fucking Eastbourne.'

A long silence followed as they both stared over one another's shoulders. 'Is there any chance of you sleeping with me tonight?' he asked finally. 'One last time?'

'None. No. We're just friends now. Go home to your Helen and write.'

'You'd die for me, you'd give me all your courage and passion, but you won't sleep with me one last time?'

'Daniel. Sometimes you really do have the brains of a guinea pig. All I want to do is go quietly to Eastbourne and I can't do that with all my sex glands in an uproar because you've given me a good seeing to. *That* is not the way to go into retirement. So Daniel please go home and get on with your life's work. And before you go don't forget to pay this bill because I'm skint. They've even taken all my plastic off me.'

'I'm not too sure I've got any money either.'

'Oh that's absolutely typical isn't it? Absolutely fucking typical. And now, while I think about it – and before I attack you again because I'm really getting worked up now – where the fuck is that book on London you've been going on about forever?'

'I still haven't finished it.'

'Right. I was thinking about that the other day so now I want you to make me one last promise which is that you finally do that journey through the sewers of London that you've always been planning. Will you do that? For me. And you make that journey the end of your book, in which you should also work in your visions, and then give the *completed* manuscript to Miranda. So do you promise?'

She settled down in the back of the taxi at Eastbourne station the next morning and fiddled inside her handbag before taking out a compact to check her face and hair. She didn't know why she was bothering really but she was unbelievably nervous – no, overwhelmingly terrified – about what was about to happen to her. The most difficult thing to accept in this whole nightmare was that she had decided to do this for herself. No one had forced her into it and here she was actually stepping down into her own grave and whistling up the gathered gravediggers to come and fill it up. She wasn't even dead for fuck's sake, even feeling a bit horny, come to think about it, and wondering why she had turned down Daniel so decisively and firmly. What was wrong with having her sex glands in an uproar anyway and surely it was about time she had something on that front? After all it had been almost the only activity which had unfailingly brightened her up in the past.

But no, she had to make the big fucking gesture didn't she? She couldn't merely have moved what was left of her possessions around the corner to some small flat and suggest that Daniel might come and call on her now and then for what he called a bit of oh-be-joyful. Oh no. That would have been far too easy. She either had to sell everything – or give it away like that old fraud Tolstoy – and then take off to eternal celibacy in fucking Eastbourne, if you please, where she was going to die very soon, of terminal boredom, in her boring little room in front of her boring television in this boring town overlooking that bloody boring sea.

And it was precisely the loss of everything she had once cherished which was making her so scratchy, she supposed. Furniture, clothes, paintings – even her house: they had all given her feelings of continuity and security which she had never so much as thought about when she'd had them. She couldn't quite remember the last time she had stood in front of one of her paintings and actually looked at it but she was now missing them quite keenly, particularly the dark savage swirls of her Francis Bacon which she had always loved as much as anything in a museum. It wouldn't have been so bad if her art had produced any money but it had all been thrown down into the well of huge mortgage debts and Karen had subsequently reported that there would almost certainly be nothing left. Her only hope now was for *The Sun* to cough up soon.

Oh yes, cutting the guy ropes was all very well but it wasn't at all pleasant whirling through these streets with just one suitcase sitting behind the taxi driver who was going to get a good clip across the ear if he didn't stop looking at her in his driving mirror. 'Are you her?' he asked after a while.

'Just drive the fucking car,' she said irritably, coming close to tears.

'Sorry I asked I'm sure, but even a cat can look at a queen you know.'

She closed her eyes and blew out some air, her head falling forward hangdog. 'I'm sorry I was so rude,' she said finally. 'I'm just so unhappy. I don't really want to go into this retirement home at all.' She was crying now, dabbing the corners of her eyes with a folded handkerchief. 'I've just lost my man you see – lost everything in fact – and thought I could live here. But now I'm not so sure. Tell me. Taxi drivers know everything. Tell me if this place we're going to is any good.'

'Wallasey's? A right concentration camp, I heard.'

'Concentration camp. What do you mean?'

'Well, you've got your own room and television well enough. They don't

292

bother you in there, I heard, but they do like you to keep your room clean and for you to turn up on time for your meals.'

'On time for meals! What kind of place is this?'

'If you're more than five minutes late for meals you don't get anything. Not even a slice of toast. That's only what I heard, mind you.'

Her eyes began twitching in a flat panic and she even considered opening the taxi door and diving straight out into the road. But she didn't need to do that did she? She wasn't trussed up on a cart being taken to the gallows at Tyburn, even if it felt like it. This was all her own choice. But oh boy she was missing London already: the fragrant Thames, the friendly people, all that lovely traffic. She was too young to die in a concentration camp by the sea, damn it.

The taxi sped along the seafront and she became more alarmed as they passed the pier where two elderly ladies were being pushed along the pavement in their bath-chairs by nurses. Then there were those gardens with anachronistic palms and bright tropical flowers, so beloved of Edwardian resorts like this and, of course, all those bloody waves. Just look at them: in and out, in and out, hour after hour, day after day. They were enough to drive even the sanest mad.

They pulled up outside Wallasey's Retirement Home and she got out to look up at the great imperial sweep of the façade. 'Just stay there a minute would you driver?' she said as she walked ever so slowly up to the front porch. Hands moved curtains slightly. There were lots of eyes on her. Two old gits sat on a bench by the front lawn doubtless discussing their bowel movements. One of them waved at her. Inside two more, stooped over their zimmer frames, were making their slow way along the hallway.

A woman who looked like the camp commandant came out of a side door and strode towards Lisa. The starch in her tiny white nurse's cap seemed to have affected the lines in her scrubbed face and she immediately reminded Lisa of that horrible nurse in *One Flew Over the Cuckoo's Nest* who kept forcing those nasty pills down poor old Jack.

What the hell am I doing here? Lisa thought. Just *what* was I thinking?

'Welcome to Wallasey's, Miss Moran,' said the commandant, holding out her hand.

'I'm sorry but I've got this terrible toothache,' Lisa blustered, not taking the proferred hand. 'I'm so sorry but I've got this terrible toothache you see and I've got to get to a dentist before it drives me mad.'

'We can always book you into a dentist's, Miss Moran.'

'Toothaches play hell with my bowel movements too,' Lisa added inanely. 'Better be going then.'

'Miss Moran?'

Lisa had dived back into the taxi. 'Take me back to the railway station will you? I've changed my mind about all this.'

'Are you sure? You've hardly seen it. At least take a look inside.'

'Not likely. I want to go straight back to London.'

'Well why don't you stay one night while you're here? One night won't do any harm.'

It wouldn't indeed but, there again, she might end up liking the place and she was too young and fit to start trundling around with a zimmer. 'No, no. I know what I'm doing. Take me straight back to London would you driver?'

'It'll be expensive. It'll be whatever's on the clock.'

'That doesn't matter. I've seen enough of Eastbourne. Let's see if they've got a nice room in The Savoy where I can stay for a while. I need to think about this a bit more.'

The taxi sped back along the seafront and she shuddered when she spotted another wheelchaired battalion of old gits being pushed along by their nurses. She had missed death by inches and hadn't even glanced back at the camp commandant who was still standing in front of her retirement home wondering what might be going on with their famous new arrival.

FORTY ONE

On the taxi ride back to London from Eastbourne Lisa learned everything about the taxi driver's life and hard times, of his troubles with his back, his wife and alcoholic son so it was something of relief when they arrived back in central London. But she'd forgotten that it was the beginning of the tourist season so the Savoy was full as was The Connaught. She would have so liked to have stayed in The Connaught in her present mood, having a lot of fond memories of the times she used to drink there with Rachel and Rex. When Rachel died John O had suggested that her ashes be scattered on the floor of the bar there. A typical John O crack that: cruel but quite funny with it. It would be marvellous to be present when they scattered that embittered old bastard's ashes. What a whizzy party that would be.

Fortunately, there was one suite available in The Beverly in Park Lane which she could have for the cost of a single 'as it was Modom'. She only wanted it for a week or so, she explained, until that 'ghastly smell of fresh paint' had left her new flat.

Ah yes, this was where she deserved to be, she thought, as the bellboy carried her suitcase to the lift and showed her up to the Belmont Suite on the third floor where her every need was anticipated and it emphatically did not matter if you arrived late for meals or not at all. You could have a slice of toast any time, night or day, in The Beverly. Ask for a cucumber sandwich and there it was; if you felt like a cup of hot chocolate at four in the morning, hey presto! This was the Park Lane of the fragrant and well-heeled, not smelly old Eastbourne with its boring waves and gangs of old gits droning on about their bowels. The hotel had even settled her taxi fare for her after she had told them she was a bit short of immediate cash. Modom should not worry. Everything would be put on Modom's bill and it was all done so discreetly Modom didn't even get to learn how much the fare had actually come to. But you never needed to ask the cost of anything in The Beverly.

Oh she was never going to leave London again, she vowed, as she relaxed in the plush chintz armchair in her new living room, the last of the afternoon sun warming her cheeks. Her eyes closed for a few smiling minutes, then she lifted her hands to give herself a tiny round of applause for being so brilliant. A little champagne, methinks, to celebrate her return to the city. All those long years in the wilderness and now her exile was over and she was back in the adoring public eye again. She took a bottle of Bollinger out of the well-stocked drinks cabinet and wrestled off the cork before pouring herself a full glass, holding it up into the sunlight, admiring all those bubbles spiralling up in frenzied streams. Bollinger wasn't her favourite fizz but it sure as hell had the best bubbles.

Perhaps she would sit in her whirlpool bath for half an hour later on and then wander down to the Playboy Club for a small flutter on the tables. Victor had long left, of course, but he had kept hold of Stocks, so he might invite her over there for the weekend if she called him up. She had always loved the Hertfordshire countryside and particularly enjoyed sitting in the great Victorian conservatory there, especially that night when she had sat there alone listening to the sounds of distant bacchalania. Victor had a marvellous Jacuzzi at Stocks which was not so much a bath as an underground stream. So who was it that she had once grappled with so memorably in there? She giggled softly and then took another sip of champagne at the thought.

On the other hand she might just go down to the Hilton for a quiet drink before retiring early. She'd had many an interesting chat in there with some whore from Shepherd Market who'd popped in for a break. But why spoil these lovely Bolly moments by going anywhere? She was retired now, she'd hung up her scripts in a manner of speaking so she didn't *have* to do anything at all. Maybe she'd just take it easy for a few days and invite some friends over here next week for a good thrash ... Ava, Maggie, Peggy, Judi, a dozen or so of them with their men when they could all get hog-whimperingly drunk. Lashings of caviar and champagne and a string quartet perhaps. If she could cajole that Russian wanker over from New York so much the better. He could be a real pain when he got going but he was always a joy when drunk enough to start singing those rousing Cossack songs of his.

She finished the champagne and decided it was time to move on to the harder stuff. A pity really Jean-Paul wasn't with her now because he would certainly have loved the moment. They had always enjoyed their sundowners at Foxley Hall, watching the sun settle over the lake with a few lovely gin and tonics. He got better after a few drinks, losing his Gallic seriousness as on that one summer night when he had taken her out and made love to her right in the middle of the croquet lawn. 'It might even improve my game,' he'd said as he was buttoning up his flies afterwards. Improve his game! He was always useless at croquet, always lacked that killer streak which is so necessary in that most vicious of games. He *had* turned out to be a bastard in other ways though. A real bastard he'd turned out to be and all she had ever done was love him desperately. She would have died for him too, and nearly had.

There was nothing left for her now but she no longer cared. The dark would soon look after her. You could always rely on the good old dark.

Long after the sun had taken its leave of the city the remorseless lanes of traffic were still moving past her open windows but, on her knees on the carpet, she neither knew about them nor even cared. Her head was lowered and her hands clasped together as if in prayer and she was sobbing quietly, sobs that rose to long, high-pitched whines of the purest and most intolerable pain.

The Beverly wasn't what it used to be, Modom decided after a week or so as a resident there. The service was distinctly inattentive and they were no longer restocking her drinks cabinet. Also Mr Brioni, the general manager, all brilliantined hair and plump hands, had started asking impertinent questions about the whereabouts of her new flat and when, precisely, might she be checking out. Such questions had become so irritating she had not only stopped going to the dining room for her meals but had also given up asking reception when they were next going to refill her drinks cabinet and began going around to the off-licence in Shepherd Market to buy her own quarter bottles which she smuggled into the hotel in her handbag. It would have been far cheaper to have bought full bottles, of course, but she didn't want any of the *domestiques* getting the idea that she had a drink problem. Discretion was always the key in the discreet world of the bourgeoisie.

That night, a warm Thursday, the bastard with plump hands and oily charm waylaid her again as she was waiting for the lift, hoping that everything was to her complete satisfaction but now wondering if Modom would like to put a small deposit on her suite or let them take an imprint of her credit card which would be of enormous help in their accounting. In that awkward silence between difficult question and awaited answer, Lisa's cheek began twitching, as if it was busy trying to loosen itself from her face, when the lift opened with a depressingly cheerful ding.

'Mr Brioni, my agent will be coming here to sort everything out,' she announced grandly, stepping into the lift and pressing the button for the third floor. 'Do not worry about a thing.'

'And who might your agent be, Miss Moran?' he asked, holding out a fat hand to stop the lift doors closing.

'Duffy. Miss Karen Duffy of Limelight Enterprises. Good night to you, Mr Brioni.'

It was an extremely distraught, if not frightened, actress who finally returned to her room where, with shaking hands, she fixed the security chain on her door and poured herself a fat slug of Scotch. At least room service had replenished the ice, but she kept frowning as she spooned the cubes into a glass which rattled like a deranged castanet as she gulped down a drink which made her feel only slightly better. She couldn't quite understand what was happening; a number of faceless and invisible people seemed to be involved in a huge charade – some evil conspiracy – against her but she couldn't find meaning or motive in any of it, particularly as she had never done any harm to anyone in her whole life. What was the matter with everyone and why had they all got it in for her?

A migraine was threatening and she thought to ring the Bouncing Codpiece in New York and plead with him to come over on the next Concorde but decided to forget it rather than go through the hotel switchboard where they would doubtless demand a cash deposit on the call. The nerve of that manager: the sheer fucking nerve of people.

She poured herself another stiff one and recalled, with a fond smile, the week when they had all sailed into Cannes on Sam's yacht and taken three cavernous suites in the Hôtel du Cap. *And my deah I do mean cavernous.* Simply every room had been awash with chilling champagne and freshly cut flowers. No impertinent questions about the bill there and, come to think of it, she didn't even know if it had ever been paid. Sam wouldn't have bothered and John O had always held on to every pound as if it had been a personal hostage.

The traffic noise in Park Lane seemed louder tonight but it was far too warm to close the windows. She remained sitting in her armchair, only crouching forward, twisted by gut-wrenching spasms of anxiety until she found it more comfortable and even womb-like to wrap herself inside the red, velvet curtains, leaving just a small chink in them so she could look out over Hyde Park.

Was there nobody in all this bustling, noisy city to save her? Ten million enemies and not a single friend? At least she had managed to keep off the brandy and all the madness that came with that. *Little nips of whisky, little nips of gin. Makes a lady wonder where on earth she's bin.* She took another glass of whisky inside her curtained cell and then another, finishing them both in one before blacking out and falling forwards, her splayed legs stretching out from beneath the curtain tassels.

The next morning she was roused by a loud banging on the door and a voice shouting her name. She groaned with hung-over misery, noting it was nearly midday but she did not hurry to answer the door, taking time to put on a dressing gown and splash some cold water over her face. When she did open the door the same fat bastard loomed over her like a dark rain cloud with a dickey bow and she took two unsteady steps backwards, holding up an arm as if about to ward off a blow.

'Miss Moran, I am very sorry, very sorry indeed, but I must ask you to leave this establishment immediately. But please do not worry about payment. There will be no charge but you must leave this room immediately.'

No charge? Leave immediately? 'I don't understand.'

'Please, Miss Moran. I have spoken with your agent and it has been explained to me in no uncertain terms that you are in dire financial difficulty. We have no wish to add to your difficulties but you must leave here this morning, Miss Moran. You must leave now.'

'If I am in financial difficulty, as you say, this is the first I've heard of it. Can I speak with my agent?'

'Of course. Most certainly. Shall I ring her from here now? Let me ring her from here.' He strode into the lounge, picked up the telephone and tapped out a number. 'I have Miss Lisa Moran here to speak with Miss Karen Duffy, please. Thank you.' He waited for a few moments before handing the receiver over to Lisa.

'Lisa, my angel, whatever are you doing there? No wonder I couldn't contact you in Eastbourne. I've been worried out of my mind.'

'Well I didn't like it down there so I came back here. Park Lane's so much nicer than Eastbourne, don't you think. The city always looks particularly beautiful in the summer. Behold this vast city, a city of refuge, a mansion house of liberty, encompassed and surrounded with his protection.'

'Lisa, Mr Brioni called me this morning and I've explained the whole situation to him. Lisa there is no way in the world that you can afford to stay in that hotel. No way.'

'I'll be all right, Karen. I've got a lot of money coming from *The Sun*. Remember?'

'Lisa, even if that were true you still couldn't afford to stay in The Beverly. Your room is three hundred a night – and that's the discounted rate – and last week you took a taxi ride which came to nearly two hundred pounds.'

'Karen, let's go through this very slowly because I'm feeling particularly thick this morning. What do you mean by *even if that were true?* Is there a problem with *The Sun?* They did pay the first instalment didn't they?'

'No, Lisa, that's why I've been trying to contact you. There's been a hitch.'

'A hitch?'

'A big hitch. Terry Maven told Charles Judd what you said about him. Then he went to John Orland and gave him your account of all those rubber fantasies you said you played together on Tuesday nights.'

'They weren't fantasies.'

'Well it's all rather complicated but the long and short of it is that Judd and Orland have joined forces and taken out an injunction against you and *The Sun* won't be running the series until everything's been sorted out. They won't be paying you anything either until it's all settled but they are already saying that it's looking like more trouble than it's worth. I'm terribly sorry, Lisa, but you are flat broke and, with Orland and Judd preparing to sue you for libel, this sort of litigation could run forever. So the sooner you get out of that hotel and stay with me, until we can sort something out, the better.'

Lisa gazed up at the general manager's fat face, then down at the floor, coughing at first as if she was choking but then feeling strangely calm. So the picadors were softening her up ready for the toreadors.

'Don't worry, Karen, I'll sort everything out for myself. I'll speak to you soon.' She put down the receiver and turned, making a sort of confused attempt to tidy her hair and smooth down her crumpled dress. 'I'm sorry I've been so much trouble to you,' she said, her eyes full of tears. 'I thought I had a lot of money coming my way but it isn't. You can also sue me if you wish.'

'That won't be necessary Miss Moran.'

'Look, just send the bill to my agent. I insist. I'll pay it somehow. *I will*. Now give me a few minutes and I'll get my things packed.'

'You do not need to leave immediately, Miss Moran. Please – take your time. Have lunch with us here – as our guest.'

'No thank you. All I need is a few minutes.'

'I'll call a taxi for you then perhaps?'

'No thank you. I don't need anything at all. Nothing. From now on I have no needs. I am cancelled. Little nips of whisky, little nips of gin. Makes a lady wonder where on earth she's bin.' She glared at him hard. 'With love's light wings did I o'er perch these walls. And what love can do that dares love attempt.'

'Pardon me, Miss Moran?'

The tone of her voice became harder and darker. 'Ten o'clock and back he'll come. I can just see him now. With vine leaves in his hair. Flushed and confident.'

'Miss Moran, please rest for a while. Have a little nap and I'll send you up some tea.'

'Flushed and confident, I'm telling you. With vine leaves in his hair.' She flung several hands-full of clothes into her suitcase and without even bothering to fasten it properly, picked it up and walked out of the room, spurning the manager's offer to carry it for her. She took the stairs, pausing on each landing and chewing her lip, as if trying to remember her next line. 'Little nips of whisky, little nips of gin. Makes a lady wonder where on earth she's bin.'

The manager remained with her, continuing to appeal to her to have a lie down. The bellboy actually bowed as she sailed through the front lobby, still in her dressing gown, only to take up a position on the pavement outside and looking around imperiously at the storming traffic as her suitcase fell open disgorging a drift of clothes, undies and cosmetics. The bellboy and the manager dived to pick them up as she shouted at the traffic: 'Night and silence, who is there? Weeds of Athens he doth wear.'

A few drivers turned their heads to look at this half-dressed harridan. 'Night and silence,' she screamed at them again. 'Who is there? Weeds of Athens he doth wear.'

FORTY TWO

The lamp on Daniel's helmet flashed along the slime-sheened sewer walls as he made his way carefully along the underground river of the Tyburn, stooping into the long iron tube which carried the turbid water under Regent's Canal. Yet he was soon walking upright again, making his way down a gently sloping series of levels which looked like a geometric waterfall as it made the water pick up speed and send it skittering down towards Baker Street. After talking and thinking about this exploration for so long he had finally begun it.

Even without his headlamp he would have known that he was continuing to walk downwards by the uneven pressure on his ankles. This sewage system had been first designed to use gravity as the energy to drain away the water: pretty much the whole of central London had been built around a valley which meant that most of the sewers had their own natural fall of several feet a mile.

Yet despite alien smells and deepening gloom he was feeling surprisingly secure and even safe down here. It was probably pointless to speculate why – you either felt safe or you didn't – except that he had studied and mapped out this system so extensively and for so long, he knew all its twists and turns better than those of the streets above. There was also the possibility that there was some deep genetic meaning and experience at work here; several generations of his family had toiled and sometimes perished quarrying coal in the mines of South Wales and he might now well be fulfilling an old tribal function; connecting with his past and what had made him. His forefathers had been happy to work down the pits; proud of the way they had toiled and tunnelled in similarly dangerous conditions to keep the world warm.

But unlike his forefathers with their steel-capped boots and moleskin coats, Daniel had chosen a wet suit and rubber diving shoes for his journey. In his small rucksack he had a spare set of underclothes, a few tins of food, a rolled-up map, a flask of fresh water, an oxygen mask, a methane detector and a metal device for prising iron bars apart.

Now he was some thirty feet below the city, he guessed, walking across level after level of hurrying water. Odd patches of daylight hung in parts of the tunnels: dim clusters of vague silver standing in the darkness like motionless ghosts, indicating the distant presence of a street grille or ventilation shaft. He liked seeing these silvery ghosts since they meant he was near fresh air. The roar of the traffic sometimes infiltrated the silence down here but the predominant sounds were mostly those of pinging drips or hoarse discharges of water sometimes spouting furiously and without warning out of the tunnel walls. Someone, somewhere, was hammering.

He came out on to another level where his lamp shone on the surface of a huge pool which steamed in places as if the water was boiling. Gobbets of brown foam whirled around the wisps of steam. He was beginning to feel at one with the darkness, appearing and disappearing through the odd clusters of light, often barely visible as the light of his own lamp opened up yet more dripping vistas and other sudden discharges of water made him move quickly. His wet suit had been chosen to protect him from the cold although it was the heat that was mostly worrying him now.

This underground labyrinth had been first fashioned in the middle of the nineteenth century by the Metropolitan Sewers Commission after the city had been devastated by three cholera epidemics caused by the citizenry drinking water contaminated by raw sewage. The old cesspools were outlawed and all dwellings were connected to this new network of sewers which were designed to carry millions of gallons of water east of the Thames and hence out of London on the ebbing tide.

Joseph Bazalgette systematised the huge ancient burrow of unconnected sewers by digging out the northern and southern areas of London and joining them up together. Millions of tons of earth were moved and even more millions of bricks laid using Portland cement. Underground aqueducts were put in place and huge beam engines set up to pump the water where gravity wouldn't work for them. Weirs were installed to act as safety valves in the event of flooding and huge embankments built to stop the Thames bursting its banks.

The older medieval system of sewers had remained intact, beginning at the ancient Clerkenwell pauper burial vault and that's where Daniel hoped to get to on his present journey, resting when tired and taking as much time as he needed. He wanted to get right into that distant kingdom beneath the old Palace of Westminster and explore the very heart of this oldest of cities.

But he was nowhere near the end just yet and, the nearer he got to Baker Street, the wider and higher the tunnel became with small elvers wriggling away from his intrusive, rubber feet. Water couldn't be dangerously contaminated with elvers in it, he had learned from his research: they would have died like all other forms of life when exposed to poisons such as the cholera bacillus. At one dark turning the wings of a bird, or perhaps a small bat, fluttered against his cheek and startled him.

Conditions deteriorated when his feet began sinking into several inches of sediment and it became like walking across a beach in a fast-rising tide. Soon he was coming across other smaller sewers joining the main Tyburn artery down which he was still making his way; gaping holes which emerged around shoulder-high, many of them disused and all but blocked by piles of black silt. Strange, dark-leaved plants grew in these black yawns and, if he stared at them long enough, he found that they could change into clown faces with the plants growing out of the whereabouts of their tongues.

He realised he was far from alone on his journey and that he was being smiled at bleakly by many faces as he continued following the river which would eventually take him to the Palace of Westminster. Yet the air was not as gaseous and rancid as he had feared: he had found no pockets of methane or ammonia with his detector and assumed that, as long as the water kept flowing all around him like this, he would be all right. He stooped into yet another egg-shaped entrance and caught his breath when he spotted some worrying patches of red and blue flames flickering in a distant pool. He re-checked his detector but it picked up no dangerous levels of gas as he approached another egg-shaped gap. All the entrances in the system were the shape of eggs since this design had been found to be the strongest for propping up the city above.

A slight worry settled inside him when his ears picked up the distant cannon of thunder. Life might get very difficult indeed if that thunder turned into rain storms since flash floods could build up in seconds down here. He wasn't terribly happy when those motionless clusters of light began moving around either: almost as if they were all coming together for some secret conclave to discuss the past and the future of the city.

But he kept pressing on.

That same thunder awoke Lisa with a jump and she opened her eyes on light brown walls with metal staples running down one corner. The whole inside of the box smelled of biscuits and her grubby hand finally reached out to push open one of the flaps to reveal a small park with dozens of other cardboard boxes dotted along the side of the pathways, many of them lagged with polythene sheets. Thunder rumbled again but they were clearly just idle threats since the sky above the city was surprisingly clear and blue.

Several cardboard box dwellers had already kicked their way out of their homes and were sitting on their doorsteps, legs apart, swigging on bottles of various colours. When they had drunk as much as they could take or needed, they carefully put their bottles back inside their front doors and turned to face the world more amiably, arms folded and loud belches erupting shamelessly from their throats. But Lisa hadn't quite got the knack of such early morning rituals, hadn't yet learned how to settle her raddled body with yet more of the poison that had got her into this state in the first place. So she crawled straight out of her box to throw up over some red geraniums in one of the formal flower beds. The gobbets of gastritis spattered the blooms which quivered and jumped around zanily as if in a storm. Her belly heaved up yet more mouthfuls of acid and she brought her eyes close to the flowers to see what might have been in the puke, to find out, perhaps, what she had been eating lately. But all there was in this acid was yet more acid.

She was in the park near the Embankment station at the end of Villiers Street with a dozen or so others, waiting for their cardboard homes to be cleared away by Corporation workmen lest the sight of them offend the early morning commuters. Mist from the nearby Thames hung on the trees; the grass caparisoned with dew. A squirrel sprang out from behind some shrubs, looked around nervously, dashed back. More were now breaking out of their boxes as she slowly got to her feet and stood there with her eyes fixed down on the pathway.

Even her old friends would not recognise Lisa Moran now; her fall must have broken all records if only for its speed, although in London, it has often been said, you can sink faster and harder than anywhere else in the country. She walked with a deliberately hunched stoop, dragging her left foot. Her voice, when she used it, which was as little as possible, was cracked and expressionless. All her jewels had been pawned and her clothes were threadbare. She wore a pair of granny glasses to disguise her eyes and the distinctive bob of her nose. Her fingers, repeatedly pulling on the skin of her cheeks, had disturbed the old, cosmetic tucks, letting the dewlaps fall.

So she had finally landed her greatest and most demanding role. It required all her intelligence, sensitivity, vulnerability and knowledge of life; an endlessly demanding performance combining instinct with physical danger and unrelenting hardship; a part for which she had been preparing all her life and was now acting out on the perilously huge stage of the streets of London. She had always dreamed of disappearing altogether and had now done so, a *coup de théâtre*, in full view of the British public. Sometimes she even spent the night in Cardboard City under the National Theatre, scene of some of her earlier triumphs and a few later disasters, and such was her present appearance no one there had ever given her so much as a second look. She was just some old bag-lady with no future and no past, shuffling around the pavements in an alcoholic stupor, eagerly awaiting an early and merciful death.

One night she had even found herself outside Langan's in Stratton Street and looked in on the diners. Michael Caine was still there but that drunken oaf Peter Langan had long gone. She wondered what the food was like in there these days – it had never really been up to much – but scarpered back into the darkness when she spotted one of the diners standing up and looking at her with a bit too much curiosity.

So yes, she had found a sort of freedom out on these streets, limping around and picking up whatever she needed. Like Blanche DuBois before her she now relied almost totally on the kindness of strangers but her mental state was often unpredictable, sometimes calm and lucid until her powers of reason broke down again. No one could ever guess at what was going on in her mind, especially her. Some of the things that crawled into her thoughts made her shiver and jump with disgust but she was quiet this morning, enjoying a thundery, sunshine moment by the river before going to the back of The Beverly, perhaps, where the kitchen staff would leave a little something out for her. They knew she would only ever eat the lightest of meals and maybe not even that but, with the head chef's connivance, they often made sure she shuffled away with a bottle of fine wine in her Tesco's carrier bag.

If the weather was particularly inclement or she had been frightened by gang violence they might even allow her to sleep in the vegetable store. She was never any trouble and never threw any of her old tantrums now she was acting out her role as the pained bag-lady with hardly a word so say to anyone. But there again she had always been able to behave herself when necessary; always knew what she could – and could not – get away with. Everything was an act really: even behaving yourself when you needed to was part of the same long play of life.

On the stage the lighting man was your best friend, often more important than the director, but on the streets your real friends were the shadows and she often slipped into their protective darkness if the police ever wanted a word with her, for example, often dribbling copiously as she did so. Not even policemen liked to face an old lady who dribbled copiously, still less go to the trouble of arresting her for vagrancy. But the real beauty of the shadows was that you reversed your role inside them: from deep within the shadows you could see your audience without them seeing you.

This darkness allowed her to watch people moving around fires in the corners of parks or waste ground; she liked to study how they held themselves and their various postures when they were trying to keep warm or begging for money. Thus she could disappear more completely into the street, she could sink into a vast anonymity where she could be safe, particularly when violence broke out – as it often did – and her fellow street dwellers hit one another over their heads or pushed one another into the flames. At the first sign of such trouble she would shrink straight back into the darkness. Violence was the spotlight which always attracted people like moths bent on destruction; the amateurs who knew nothing of the destructive nature of fire and had never understood the safety and strategy of shadows.

It was the timing and pace of her performance that were the hardest to manage — particularly as she was putting away as many bottles as she could get her hands on. There were occasional black-outs and she lost track of the hours and days but that was implicit in the role, wasn't it? A bag-lady has no notion of real time, no anxiety about a change of luck tomorrow since brutal experience insists her luck will never change. Hope dies in the streets and each punishing day is the same as the next. So you have to take everything slowly out here and never hurry or panic even if you're sure the prompt lady has fallen asleep yet again. Think of your physical limitations, your failing energies and take them all into account. Extended and ready improvisation was the key to this particular performance.

So there *were* long moments of appreciative lucidity, such as she was enjoying here now in this park at the end of Villiers Street, and she liked to enjoy them for as long as possible before she went over to her usual bench on the Embankment where she liked to count clouds over the city. But there were no clouds this morning; just a swe6eringly blue sky with that thunder still banging away ominously. Her granny eyes gazed at the debris being pulled along by the brown Thames, hearing the odd bursts of music from the cars sitting in the usual traffic jam behind her, the occasional uplifting chords of Vivaldi or else the odd vulgar burst of rock'n'roll. In her present state she didn't mind any kind of music; it was all just noise anyway.

She continued sitting on that bench studying the old broken hands that rested on her lap, scrutinised the blackened, torn fingernails, and thought that if she could get some work for these hands, she might even be able to take a room somewhere on the other side of the river perhaps, when her present run came to an end. She would give up the drink and organise some proper meals for herself just like everyone else. She would become a normal person again with normal aspirations and normal friends.

But such lucid thoughts about her future survival rarely lasted for more than a minute or two and she would then forget them as she stared again at all the swirling debris on the Thames. Her short-term memory had been an early casualty of life out here on the streets. Nothing could be put in the context of the recent past any more and, when afternoon arrived, the morning had long gone. Everything about her identity had become a blank and she never spoke, never laughed, never smiled. She couldn't even start to understand how she had got into this mess, still less how she might ever get out of it. She had become another bit of the debris sailing on the brown surface of the Thames.

The Tyburn river deepened significantly and Daniel was wading waist-deep in the water, thinking of the Charon and the Styx. More wisps of steam filtered up through the light of his headlamp and there were still hints of fire as the foul water bore away the detritus of a profligate city.

Jonathan Swift had once described similar rivers in *A City Shower*: sweeping away the seepings from butchers' stalls, 'the dung, guts and blood; of drown'd puppies, stinking sprats, all drenched in mud; of dead cats and turnip-tops, tumbling down the flood.'

But here, on his private Styx, Daniel Jenkins, explorer of sewers, would-be city diarist and self-appointed Welsh custodian of London myths, spotted scrunched-up beer cans and bottles, bobbing around the pea-soup-green waters, the odd polythene container, bits of drowned paper carrying lost information, surfing cigarette packets, match boxes, twigs, a shapeless condom or two, nothing that Jonathan Swift might have recognised, all spinning around and around him, an endless, disorganised carousel hurrying to keep an urgent appointment with the great rubbish bin of the sea.

The water deepened yet again and, with his rucksack bumping up against the back of his neck, he held out his arms wide ready, if necessary, to swim for it except that it was now time to get out of the free-flowing Tyburn and lever himself up into another long-abandoned egg-shaped tunnel, no more than three feet in height, which, according to his map, would take him to the whereabouts of the Palace of Westminster. From somewhere in the heart of the city came the tolling of a dark, dead bell. Those with too much sin could not hear such bells, he had read somewhere.

He had to wriggle his way past another mound of solidified silt and, although his progress then became easier, the air became fiendishly hot and he began sweating so much he had to peel off the top of his wet suit and let it lie curled around his waist. Yet he enjoyed the feel of the warm air against his sweating body except for a cold drip which sometimes caught him on the back of the neck, carrying a long, slow shudder down the length of his spine. His beam caught a frog, who sat up and looked at him before letting out a friendly burp and leaping away into the darkness. At least the presence of frogs meant there couldn't be too many rats hereabouts. He was so glad he'd done his research properly for this one: you could tackle almost anything if you were well-prepared, if you knew what you were doing.

He was still, surprisingly in the circumstances, feeling safe and secure, relieved really that, on Lisa's promptings, he had finally taken the plunge. Even down here he thought of her a lot, kept on wondering what she might be up to. He hadn't seen her for ages but would hear from her soon, he knew. All he'd have to do was stay silent for a while and listen out for some sort of uproar, a sudden wigwam of noise and controversy and there she'd be.

After a couple of hundred yards the tunnel got so low he had to get down on his belly and worm his way past yet more mounds of silt until he broke through into a medieval brick vault where he discovered pools of sludge with large white bubbles swelling to the size of footballs and exploding with a soft plop. He took an immediate reading for gas and, on finding no threat, looked around to see he was on a high, wide shelf where, with legs dangling over the edge, he sat for a while to gather his thoughts and resources before lowering himself down into the vault and sinking to his waist in the bubbling sludge. He made his way, slowly and squelchily, along another tunnel where the texture of the brickwork changed completely and some of the cornerstones were so old they actually crumbled under the mere touch of his curious fingers.

Perhaps he had already got back to the reign of Henry II, when the first drainage system had been dug under Westminster. Here were the original sites of the tanneries, suicide cemeteries and debtors' prisons. Bethlehem Hospital would have not been far from here: Bedlam, where all the 'lunatiques' made their 'cryings, screechings, roarings, brawlings, shaking of chains, swearings, frettings, chafings so many, so hideous, so great they were more able to drive a man that hath his wits out of them'.

He walked up a series of steps into another stretch of ancient darkness where he had to wriggle past yet more collapsing holes. Drips echoed as sharply as metal striking glass. The air was so turbid it made breathing seem like chewing on an endless toffee. His headlamp swung one way and another. Had he seen something move? Was someone watching him? Probably just another fleeting shadow created by his light moving across the jagged brickwork. There was barely any cement left in this old brickwork either and, in places, it looked as if a child had merely put them on top of one another haphazardly.

Another ledge presented itself and he went plopping down into a huge pool of water. This time he *did* have to swim, but reached the other side with four decisive over-arm strokes. It was entirely predictable that the city should have been built on so much water, he supposed. Water was the essence of life; the old walls and streams lapping around him had, at one time or another, sustained the city's first inhabitants and given them life although, sometimes, this same water had taken life away. God gives and God takes away. Lisa had always been good on the subject of God, always seemed to have an intuitive understanding of the Big Man's odd and unpredictable ways. But there again even thunder and lightning had always backed off from Lisa and she never seemed to know what a white flag was for. Nothing ever menaced her for long – not even God – and Daniel was now trying to feed off all her vast resources of courage and defiance.

He was finally down in the very bowels of the city or, in another strong sense, the city's heart where she pumped the waters of life into the working brain. By now he was almost enjoying himself, revelling in the dramatic thought that he was way down here trying to burgle the city's soul. This was the original kingdom of Brutus, the legendary founder of the city and he was also brushing up against other city ancestors like Boudicca, Anne Boleyn and Lady Jane

Grey, all still here and speaking their metropolitan testimonies to this dark dripping air.

Daniel's spirit was reaching out, trying to take hold of the historical continuity of it all, but he kept picking up on discords; alien spirits and movements which were nothing to do with Brutus or Lady Jane Grey. He was being *watched* and not by the dark faces of smiling clowns in their tunnels but by something more malevolent.

He turned his head and his headlamp fell on a face and framed it, as if in a spotlight. But this head was like no other he had ever seen: this awesome head was almost completely covered with short, dark nails which stuck out of every part of it. Mazy flames crackled around its coal-black eyes staring intently at Daniel who just stood there rigidly telling himself that this was not real: that this was just the cold heart of another of his visions and he should take no heed of it and certainly not be scared by it; that, as Lisa had told him repeatedly, this was really a vision of love, given to him by God because he loved and trusted him.

Daniel yelped like a smacked puppy and moved off fast in the opposite direction, taking another really small tunnel. This proved a very great mistake since it led him directly to an old plague pit and his headlamp swept over a small field of grey, crumbling bones with many of the skulls and pelvises still curiously intact after all these years. A dreadful sound hung in the air: a dry crepitation, heartbroken, anguished. His problem was that this last tunnel was so small he had to get completely out of it before he could turn around to go back into it and so he was forced to stand on these bones which broke and splintered under his weight as he tried to reach back up to get a handhold on the tunnel's mouth. More bones broke under his weight as the dry crepitation sang out louder. He still couldn't quite get sufficient purchase on the brickwork when he sank up to his waist. Unless he got lucky very soon, he was going to sink into a sea of old bones which had begun chattering like a giant electrification of old piano keys. They all seemed to be crying out for help – *crying out to him for help* – but he'd had enough by now and didn't want to help anyone, just wanted to go home and read a book next to a warm coal fire.

And then, in the middle of all the fright and confusion, he saw another vision of a city in flames – a vision within a vision? – and a flaming figure rose up on the back of a wheel, a fiery figure who was rising out of the river then going back down into it again, a strange meaningless vision which he had seen before but one which seemed to be picking him up out of this sea of bones and enabling him to get back to the small tunnel so he could get the hell out of there.

Lisa's open-air performance had gone right off the boil; her blackouts were becoming more frequent and she was often getting to her marks at the wrong time. What she really needed now was a strong director to give her some clear notes.

'Now then, Lisa, you cross Holland Park and go down to Cromwell Road. Take a short break there, with that really tired look that you do so well, then go over to the Science Museum. But don't hurry in any way and keep remembering the limp. Relax and enjoy the journey. Let your audience take pleasure in your own pleasure.'

Her other big problem was that she had developed mouth ulcers which often bled furiously and could spoil her concentration on her movements. Sometimes her mouth filled up with so much blood she might spit out a huge gobbet, perhaps frightening the life out of some man walking to his office with a splash of blood splattering wetly on the pavement in front of his shiny, commuter shoes. This might be followed by one of her best chilling Lady Macbeth stares and he couldn't get away from her fast enough. Well, at least they knew they'd seen a real performance when they'd seen that; punters were never short-changed when Lisa Moran took to the boards; they always got their money's worth; they even got her blood which was always a winner in any drama and, without fail, woke up the audience.

When she wasn't spitting blood, she might be suffering from dizzy spells and end up falling over in the street. These falls were taking a lot out of her and gave her black eyes, which made her look even more frightful, but the falls *also* provided another tense *momento mori* which could win back the audience's faltering attention.

Sometimes she could approach someone in a crowded street and tell them she was about to fall over so could they please catch her. The shocked look on their faces was a real joy but the fools never did catch her, just stood there, mouths agape, clearly terrified they might catch some terminal disease if they raised so much as a finger to help this dirty and demented creature. Then, as per direction, she would keel over sideways adding another bruise or gash to her already impressive collection.

They did try to get her to a hospital once, but had to give it up as a bad job almost as soon as the ambulance arrived. She had fallen over in Oxford Circus and the man she had asked to catch her called an ambulance. She was regaining consciousness when the ambulance arrived and they just about managed to get her on to a stretcher but that was as far as they did get since, with a loud scream and several manic twitches, she hurdled off the stretcher, pushed her way past her would-be rescuers and fled into the milling shoppers of Oxford Street.

Amid the thickening pain and depression she knew the final curtain must come soon. She could actually smell her own death and prayed that it would come quickly. She was falling apart. No decent food was going into her any longer. They had to stop her coming to The Beverly kitchens after she had stood next to the stove one afternoon and pissed herself.

Her mind was disintegrating along with her body and began playing such tricks on her she had to stop wherever she found herself and try and stay calm as doors opened inside her to let some strange woman in or else closed again to let her escape.

Large moths were fluttering in the sodium lamps of Hyde Park when she came across a whole gang of them – a *tableau vivant* – standing on the path, chatting and looking around at her as if she were some newly arrived, much-loved niece. She couldn't even guess at their names or identities – although they all seemed frighteningly familiar – and what was even more bizarre was their clothes since most of them were wearing heavily embroidered dresses tied tightly around hour-glass figures. They had lots of pearls, furs and aigrettes, with many holding up parasols – even now in the dead of night! One had a high, padded coiffure tied up with beads and lace birds. Another had a live macaw on her shoulder.

Yet there was no real menace in them and Lisa stood quite still as they came towards her and surrounded her, all jabbering away in a most friendly manner about love and loss, the state of the world or man's immortal destiny: high-minded stuff which she neither understood nor cared about. How could she ever get interested in anything like this? How to get hold of a nice, warming bottle of brandy at this time of night. Now *that* would be something to care about and discuss at some length.

Tired of their high-falutin' prattle she moved on but, somewhat to her disappointment and irritation, they moved on alongside her rather like fancy costumed bodyguards, still prattling about things in which she was not the least interested. She even told them to fuck off but they simply took no notice, just stayed with her until, as if by some illusionist's trick, they all disappeared through another door inside her.

There would be no curtain calls for Lisa that night. After the *grandes dames* left her, she had been putting away some really vile wine in the park when she was attacked by spiders and had to keep pulling them off her flesh, squirming handful after squirming handful of the fucking things. But she didn't scream out loud or draw attention to herself in any way; she was still a professional after all, someone who knew how to control her fear *and* deal with mere spiders.

When she managed to get rid of all the spiders she ran to the other side of the park where she paused to catch her breath and take another swig of this absolutely disgusting wine. Cars accelerated past, making her shadow shrink and enlarge in the rolling sweeps of their lights. Even though it was night she was still careful to avert her face. No one recognised averted faces – not even hers. The lobsters knew everything of course; they knew who she was all right as they came out from behind those dustbins, snapping at her ankles with their horrible claws.

But the lobsters were no difficulty, the snap of their claws didn't hurt and she walked away from them in the end, striding along the pavement with her eyes peeled for the boys in blue or those interfering social workers. Those do-gooders were the ones to watch out for. You had to run as fast as you could if one of those bastards got within spitting distance. Keep drifting, that's the first rule of survival on the streets. Keep drifting in front of them like fish fleeing the open mouth of the trawl.

The next thing she knew she was standing in the middle of the traffic, waving her empty wine bottle like a madman menacing a crowd with a meat cleaver. The multitudinous headlights blinded her and the horns deafened her. She cracked the bottle on the car bonnets with pleasing smash following pleasing smash. Lots of demented drivers wound down their windows and shouted at her crazily as she continued walking between the crawling traffic, putting a few more expensive bumps in those shining bonnets with her bottle as a lobster flew out of the air and exploded with one hell of a bang against the side of her head.

Funny that. She knew John O's lobsters weren't much as runners but it had never crossed her mind that they could fly. *Or fucking explode.* But they clearly could and did. Again and again. Flying through the city skies. Exploding against her head. With her just standing. Here. Swatting them. With her wine. Bottle. Oh fuck. The police. Get going. Fast.

Daniel was also having a few problems with his sanity after his encounter with Nail-Head and that terrifying plunge into the plague pit. His frightened heart had gone berserk although he continued on his underground journey because the way he had planned it, it was now quicker to finish it rather than try to retrace his tracks.

He was somewhere near the old Newgate prison now and it was extraordinary to think that many people had once lived and even prospered down here – or so Henry Mayhew had written in his *Journals.* There had been the toshers who had foraged along these selfsame sewers with their poles and lights. Dressed in greasy velveteen coats with huge pockets, canvas trousers and specially enlarged shoes for paddling through the mud, they had operated in gangs of three, looking for nuts, bolts, iron or old rope – 'tosh'. Their great dream was to find a tosheroon: a half crown coin made of copper and silver fired together. At one time there were two hundred toshers working these sewers and many had survived to the age of eighty or more when most people were lucky to manage half that. Perhaps life down here was good for you although there had been reports that toshers had got lost or been drowned or else been bitten by a rat or buried under a fall of bricks.

Then there had been the gong-fermors who once cleared the city's cess-pits or the mudlarks who collected coal or wood and the saltpeter men who extracted nitrogen from excreta to make gunpowder. The city still employed flushers to clear blockages but they would never have got as far as these ancient parts: you'd need the definite talent, if not the sheer fearlessness of a pot-holer, to get all the way down here.

His lamp lit up the fiery red eyes of a startled rat which immediately turned and dashed away from him. So they were still around here, then. The old toshers were forever doing battle with sewer rats, according to Mayhew, although what would they have done if they had met up with Nail-Head? Would they have been quite so keen to have stayed here if they had to share their patch with someone like that?

He had gone a further two hundred yards or so when the tunnel came to a dead end and he had to take a small hole to his left which took him down a steep slope. Always remember that, if it has held up for centuries, it is highly unlikely to move today: the first rule of the pot-holer. The fresh air gusting up against his face told him that he would soon come out into somewhere reasonably open yet the next low passage forced him down on to his belly again, dragging his rucksack behind him with his foot.

Thus far he had been making his way slowly and carefully but he was now unsettled and moved quickly with an eagerness not at all suited to safe progress in such places. This was probably why he lost his balance. As he tried to wriggle out of this next low passage the ground suddenly gave way beneath him and he fell down through what seemed whole acres of darkness until he crash-landed in a passageway. Bricks continued falling all around him, several hitting his safety helmet which almost certainly saved his life and consciousness. His main fear now was that he had broken some bones but, after hauling himself up slowly he found he could stand up, albeit shakily, and his lamp told him he had landed at the end of what looked like a narrow cobbled street with dark buildings towering over him and, in the distance, a huge fiery glow in the sky.

He took in the detail all around and found almost every part of him going cold as his ears picked up some quite terrifying sounds. He spotted animal movements at the far end of the cobbled street and immediately assumed they might be rats, doubtless bred here since the reign of Henry II and about to attack him because they hadn't had a proper meal since then.

They were coming down the street and making their way towards him with great speed when he saw they weren't rats at all but howling dogs – some of the scabbiest, skinniest, meanest dogs he had ever seen – snarling and fighting with one another. Almost as one, they stopped fighting when they got within ten yards of him and he picked up a brick in each hand, waiting for them to leap. He might just be able to lay a few of them out although where this might get him he couldn't even guess.

But they didn't leap. There was a huge, distant bang and right at that moment the pack turned off the cobbles and headed off in the direction of the explosion, all howling even louder in furious pursuit. Another bang, further away this time, and the noise level of the howling told Daniel they had raced off in pursuit of that. Another blast, even fainter now, was followed by the howling receding until the dogs could be barely heard.

Daniel dropped his bricks and stood there panting, trying to recover his composure. Then he heard another appalling sound, almost medieval in its provenance. He had heard that distinctive nightmarish sound once before and he just remained standing there, putting one foot out in front of him defiantly, when a huge van with sweeping searchlights and wheels of fire crossed the cobbled street about a hundred yards away and set off in the direction of the continuing explosions.

Soon the cobbled street was still and quiet again so he made his way along it carefully and stealthily, heading in the direction of that ferocious, red glow. He was sweating so much his safety helmet seemed to be floating on his hair and it was fortunate he had brought that flask of fresh water which he retrieved from his rucksack and downed almost in one. He was fortunate, too, that the light on his safety helmet was still working after his fall, for this street had no formal lighting of its own, although every window held the flickering lights of television sets which, in their turn, suffused the air with a faint, cancerous glow. Daniel could just about make out the dark outlines of heads sitting in front of all those screens, all motionless as dummies.

If he stopped still long enough he could still just about hear the distant creakings of those vans with wheels of fire or the faint howls of those dogs. But he went rigid with fear again when a loud castanet clatter erupted on the cobbles behind him and he was passed by a grey, riderless horse. This surely qualified as a moment when he absolutely had to have a strong drink. Not even the most fervent supporter of AA could have argued him out of that. But of course he didn't have any strong drink with him.

When he got to the end of the street he looked out over an endless red glow sitting on the London skyline with the distinctive dome of St Paul's Cathedral, the National Westminster and Barbican towers and the Tower of London.

The strange beauty and crimson mistiness of the landscape was almost Turneresque and he was about to make his way towards it when the very ground began moving as if in some small earthquake and there were several distinct rat-a-tats of automatic gunfire and the shrill whistle of shells. Hundreds, perhaps thousands, of bandana-ed heads began rising out of slit trenches in quaking fields, all busy firing their weapons in the direction of the glowing city.

More shells whistled overhead, some exploding near the city walls as yet more armed men rose up out of the trenches – wild men with Mohican haircuts and all kinds of guns – men he had seen before getting out of Yellow Cabs in the Poll Tax riot of Trafalgar Square – all now besieging the capital. Others were rising up and joining in the assault too – slithering, hissing alien monsters and psychos with long knives and the distended faces of clowns; men with nails in their heads and hands with fingernails like talons of steel, gangs of youths wearing bowler hats and giant codpieces, all rising up into the sweeping spotlights of those vans with the wheels of fire ...

Daniel had gone beyond fear in this erupting nightmare and, even in the middle of this horrific attack, he found himself recalling some of Lisa's words: *You're such a fool you know Daniel. You think God gives you visions because he wants to punish you in some way. But even the frightening ones are all visions of love and beauty and he gives you these visions because he loves and trusts you.*

Lisa may not have been aware she had gone feral in the city streets but, even in the moments of her greatest madness, when she had been attacked by flying lobsters and pursued by police anxious to lock her up, she seemed to have a wild cat's instinct for survival and, after denting the bonnets of those cars, she disappeared back into the shadows with the lightning speed of a cheetah on the hunt.

She avoided well-lit areas in the parks and was careful not to linger near bus stops where there was always the danger of a bus pulling up, all lit up like the inside of an aquarium. She soon lost the police who were always hopeless when it came to a good chase – and the lobsters – although it was the citizenry themselves she had to keep a firm eye on since, by night and unseen by almost everyone except her, there was a fantastic and growing level of violence everywhere, particularly in the darkness where she liked to hide.

Only three nights ago she had seen an old man sitting on a park bench being set alight by a gang of youths in bowler hats. She had just stood there appalled as the old man rose up, his clothes alive with bright, angry flames, waving his arms around as if trying to semaphore some urgent message to her. What was he saying? Why didn't he just shout for help?

The bowler-hatted youths jumped into a sports car and drove away and this human torch began running towards her till her nose was able to pick up the whiff of petrol which they had poured over him. But she had been in no mood to help – was in no *condition* to help – and disappeared fast herself down a long alleyway.

Yet tonight, still on the run from the police and the lobsters, she came across several of those youths in bowler hats giving another old tramp a savage kicking. Even in her detached haziness she had never got accustomed to such violence, no matter how many times she saw it, but there was something oddly strange about this particular attack since the youths also seemed to be wearing giant cod pieces and combat boots. They sang as they waited to take turns to lay about their victim who was being kicked so badly he could barely manage a low groan of pain. The song – a popular song – had a certain familiarity about it except she couldn't think what it was.

She took a few careful steps back into the darkness when another figure with a certain chilling familiarity about him began materialising on the edge of this assault; a dark spirit of savagery who was muscled, half-naked and carrying a rifle. This brute continued watching the assault with an intense interest for a while before wandering towards Lisa, almost as if he knew where she was hiding until she felt actively menaced by his sheer bulk, his brainless, sneering danger, and decided that she had better make a run for it before he started on her too.

She could hear his bare feet slapping along behind her as she ran – even picked up his heavy breathing and, with another shiny migraine building up, she ran across the road back into the park desperately trying to find some bushes or a patch of darkness in which she could go to ground. But this brute was strong and fast and clever, remaining right on her tail and not letting her get away. What did he want? Why didn't he leave her alone? Finally, in sheer terror and desperation, she flung herself into a lake which appeared before her, wading forward with the cold water lapping around her waist.

Her pursuer clearly didn't like the water since he stopped and just stood there on the bank next to some upturned row boats. But he watched her intently as she floundered on with arms raised outwards, trying to keep her balance which was extremely difficult what with the mud under her feet and all the water weeds which kept softly grabbing parts of her body.

Twice she missed her footing in the mud and fell under the water and twice she bobbed up again, now treading water in the middle of the lake and wondering which way to turn. Her muscular pursuer was still in the same place near the moored boats watching her but, as she turned and turned again, looking for a safe shore she might strike out towards, other muscled apes were coming out of the darkness of the surrounding trees and shrubs, fucking hundreds of them, standing all around the lake as if daring her to try and get out of the water.

That thunder started again and she felt heavy spats of rain on her face. Maybe the rain would make them all go home to wherever, maybe they didn't like anything to do with water, maybe they couldn't even survive contact with the clean rain of heaven. Daniel had often told her that, historically, all street violence in London came to an end when it rained. She would really have liked to have had him here with her now but men were never, *ever* around when you needed them.

Still unsure what had happened to him – if he was at loose in the real world or, more likely, stumbling around inside one of his visions again – Daniel pushed on through the sewers again, hoping to find a way out soon. Something told him they wouldn't be catching him back down here for a long time and he might even go back to Wales and build himself a new life in some quiet mining valley.

There was another reason why he should get out of here fast: the sound of a storm building up over the city and already he could see the water levels rising. It was just as well he had always felt at home in the water. He knew how, if trapped by water in a tunnel like this, you could always find a couple of inches of air to breathe by putting your mouth right at the top of the tunnel. Not *always* but almost always.

He took to another small tunnel but lost his footing and found himself being swept along by a flood, unable to fight it and trying to relax and go with it since he knew that he would soon get thrown out somewhere – most probably in the Thames. All he had to do was keep thinking about his breathing and let the flood waters worry about the rest. But it was hard: even a fish would have come close to drowning in all this.

He ought to rest really, hang onto a couple of those iron rings, say, and recover his composure perhaps, but he didn't. He had to get out: better to die and be done with it than spend another minute down in this hell-hole. His face kept getting spattered by huge grey and brown lumps of scum forcing him to keep his eyes closed as his body was rolled around like clothes inside a washing machine. He was tumbling this way and that with almost no control over anything when his knee was snagged by a sharp object and his head hit against a wall. He knew then, without a shadow of doubt, that he was done for: that the city of dreadful night he had set out to anatomise had fully and finally put an end to his investigation by claiming his life.

The thunder and rain stopped almost as quickly as it had begun, leaving the city streets surprisingly clean with lots of little puddles as dawn began swelling over the skyline with the golden promise of a new sunshiny day.

Lisa was making her way painfully over Blackfriars Bridge, quietly hoping she could make it to Cardboard City before the sun came up; that she could find some vacant cardboard coffin where she could lie down and disappear and wait for the cover of night. She looked dreadful and walked with a limp which was no longer an act. Her eyes were black, her clothes sodden and there were thick purple bruises on just about every part of her body. How long would she have to endure all this? When was she going to be released from all this pain and suffering? Wasn't it about time for the final curtain?

She stopped walking about the middle of the bridge since she could feel another bout of dizziness setting in and knew she was about to fall. She set her feet wide apart and put her hand on the smooth, delicately pillared balustrade to steady herself. All this was so silly. Here she was waiting to fall down in the way normal people wait for a bus. Ah yes, normal people. People like her. If only everything wouldn't spin so much. Why didn't it just stand still?

There was the throaty growl of a sports car which pulled up next to her and the clatter of running feet. Shadows, methinks, when her nose picked up the smell of petrol and she heard the sound of it glugging out of a can. Petrol? Her dizziness was getting worse and she saw that several youths were dancing around her and singing that familiar song again. But what song? Ah well at least they were enjoying themselves, out in their funny bowler hats and wearing those silly, giant codpieces. The youth of today! You just never knew what they were going to wear next. One minute it was safety pins through their lips and the next it's bowler hats and giant cod-pieces.

It was only when the petrol stung her eyes that she realised it was actually being poured over her. Why were they doing this? It didn't make any sense but then, with the dry flare of a match, it made a lot of sense – an awful lot of sense – as the match caught her dress. Her alarmed nostrils registered the smell of burning behind her – no, cancel that – *inside* her. *Right inside her.* They had stopped singing and were laughing as they ran back to their sports car and drove off fast leaving her awake, alive, clear-headed. She clamped both her hands on top of her head as the hot, fierce flames lunged for her eyes.

She was on fire, except that this fire took in the whole city. Huge, dark buildings burst into flames and seemed to revolve around her, moving ever closer to her in a scalding, contracting girdle of violence. There was no escape. The flames were beginning to eat right into her. Searing her face. Shearing off her eyelashes. She glimpsed the rear of the sports car disappearing off the bridge and the deep, brown river flickering below her. The pain was unbearable and she spun this way and that, waving her hands around wildly.

But this interpretation was no good, no good at all. She wasn't remotely in control of anything and the real actress, the great one, always had everything firmly under control. She needed something to surprise the director and astonish the audience and there was going to be no time for a proper rehearsal. She was going to have to fly this one by the seat of her pants and call on her vast experience to conjure up one last bit of pure magic. Fly it all by the seat of her pants. Fly? You never had to tell a theatrical what's theatrical. Yes. Fly!

She climbed on the balustrade, arms wide in a flaming cross, pushed hard with her legs, propelled her burning body straight out into the air. *Fly, Lisa, fly.* Her body seemed to rise up at first, as if on wires, then curved down in a bright, screaming parabola as she cried out in absolute triumph.

As the air rushed past her, with the surrounding city in flames, she knew this was the once-and-for-all scene for which she would always be remembered. Her famous final scene. Yes. The applause was ecstatic, the astonished audience rose to their feet. Not a dry eye in the house. With this one moment she was going to live in the minds and hearts of all her adoring fans forever. The 'lass unparallel'd' was finally being held by death. The most beautiful and loveliest angel of them all was going home.

Her flaming body hit the water with a dull *Whap!* The house lights died. The curtain fell. 'I've been lucky before, Horace,' she told herself before she blacked out. 'I'll be lucky again.'

Her body barely sank into the river at all, maybe going under a foot or so before bobbing up again and whirling around and around on the surface slowly, barely moving in any direction since the tides were on the cusp, not sure which way they wanted to go. She was quietly revolving in the same place with the waking sun cruelly highlighting the wretched condition of her broken body in relentless flashes of swelling light, waiting for the tides to decide precisely where they were going to transport her.

But those tides were in no hurry so neither was she, at first carrying her across the river diagonally, as if she had developed some private momentum of her own, towards the site of Shakespeare's Globe, and then on down by the timbered banks where old iron ladders, once used by Jack Sykes, went down to the edge of the river as gulls wheeled through the growing light and the sound of riverboat klaxons echoed and re-echoed through distant cranes.

Anyone watching her would have enjoyed the unhurried aimlessness of her journey, its complete lack of purpose, the way it deliberately seemed to be going back on itself like some fluttering butterfly undecided whether or not to go home. The silence of it all was compelling too: the city not yet awake with the offices and modern blocks of flats eyeing one another across the river, almost unwilling to look down at the body which was now making its way between them as if by some relentless, driving force, its heart stopped by the shock waves set up by its impact on the water, a bracelet of weed wrapped around its wrist.

The speed of her journey picked up considerably on the ebbing tide and a woman in a white dressing gown on the balcony of her million pound pad in a converted tobacco warehouse spotted it, putting her hand over her mouth before running back in to awake her partner who also came out and stood there with his hand over his mouth. Even in death Lisa Moran had lost none of her capacity to surprise and shock: she still caught the spotlight and held it with an iron fist.

She swept under the church-like spires and steel ropes of Tower Bridge, still not maintaining a straight line but occasionally veering towards a bank as if she had suddenly decided that she'd had enough and wanted to get out, before moving over to the opposite bank where she was spotted by a man in a lighter who rang the river police. But she was too fast for them again, now powering down past the warehouses of Limehouse, all indecision and uncertainty gone, as she raced for that date with the open sea and peace at last.

Daniel's black, wet-suited body came tumbling out of the foaming mouth of the Southern Low Level interceptory sewer near Wapping and there was a burst of riverboat klaxons near the Isle of Dogs as if in ironic welcome at his final arrival in the river. Not that he actually looked human at all, more a stricken seal in his rubber suit, a seal with no sense of direction being carried straight out into the middle of the river by the sheer force of the sewer.

Lisa was heading his way and for one thrilling moment it looked as if their two bodies might actually join up; that they might even somehow contrive a rousing *Mill on the Floss* finale together, locked in one another's arms, the brother and sister, dying in an everlasting embrace, living again, in one supreme moment, the days when they had clasped their hands in love, and roamed the daisied fields together.

But their bodies were caught in different currents. Here in death, they were both replicating the patterns of their relationship in life. All they had ever been were two people who had come to the city to pursue their literary and theatrical dreams, often trying to connect with one another and just as often failing, only to end up a hundred yards away from one another on this hurrying river, a gap which was widening by the minute, almost as if the river itself wanted to point out that they couldn't even get their act together in death, that they could come close but not close enough.

As the two bodies continued moving in haphazard procession towards the open sea, all their ghosts were still there, hovering around their bodies in that place where sunshine meets water, wondering whether to let them go, asking each other if it was time to finally relinquish their tyrannical hold over them and give them up to the communion of this intensely beautiful resurrection morning.

Yet, even when the ghosts finally decided to give up on them, the living didn't and the lovers were pursued by two police launches anxious to take them both into custody.

But they kept moving and, being intermittently pulled under the water and out of view, they gave their pursuers the slip as they continued their triumphant processional path down the aisle of that fantastic cathedral of sunshine built on the fine, big spread of that Thames estuary morning.

END